THE SINS OF THE FLESH

Kate A. Knight

First Published by Khaton Enterprises LLC, United States of

America,

May 2014

The Sins of The Flesh/Kate A. Knight © 2014

ISBN: 9780989646857

Library of Congress Control: 2014909305

ACKNOWLEGEMENTS

Special thanks to the people who made this possible: Jerry, Jeremiah, Laurent, Kristin, Gabriella.

Bob, you are the glue that brought it together.

Katherine H. and Rosmery Q., 'thank you' isn't nearly enough.

For Christian

PROLOGUE

I heard her startle. I felt too the jerk of recognition. My chest ached for her as rough hands trapped the breath she had heaved for a hearty scream. I heard the blows like thunder in my ear as she struck at her assailant with the phone still clutched in her hand. I heard voices – male, Spanish, at least two – and then the slam of a door.

Todd's hands on my arms steadied me. He turned me, led me away along the deserted sidewalk, shielding me from inquisitive eyes. His fingers over mine found the speaker button. There was shuffling, mumbling, quiet voices and the crash of an open palm on skin. The phone clattered to the floor and the call ended.

"Where is she?" Todd asked, all gentleness gone now. The air of command that always surrounded him crackled with new energy. His fingers biting into my arms as he led me further into the dark lacked the consideration he'd shown all evening.

"At the apartment. I have to go." I dug in my heels against his pull. "My car is the other way."

"Mine is right here," he countered, remotely unlocking and starting the engine with the key fob.

I balked. "Todd, don't."

"Don't what?" He turned to face me in the street, the lines of his face rigid, the set of his lips uncompromising. He dropped his hands as if I had burned him. All ten fingers raked through his hair as he stepped away from me. "You don't understand, Amy." His voice was even harder, colder, angrier. "I'm not letting you go alone. This isn't just your problem anymore; it's ours. There is no mine or yours; only ours. Because I have nothing without you… Nothing worth keeping. If we can't fix it together, we will go down together."

I wanted to tell him 'no', but the look in his eyes dared me to deny what was between us. Todd could not possibly know that I had only just begun to understand what it was. It explained everything.

"Get in the car, Amy," he said, opening the door for me. How could I deny him? He had brought me into the light and I had lived it if only for a brief moment. Now, here he was, stepping into the darkness with me.

ONE

I woke up slowly, despite the warmth of a male body surrounding me and the sound of rain falling in heavy curtains outside. This was familiar; this was home now.

A month in the Dominican Republic and I had finally settled into a new routine. It wasn't my house anymore; it was ours. Mine and the man beside me who, hours before had been inside me, who had left a bit of himself there too. It was my little gift to him, one I allowed him everyday in fact, because he needed it. He wanted to make sure I always had him in mind, and it didn't hurt to give him that bit of reassurance.

Aunt Abby said the way to a man's heart was through his stomach. I couldn't cook; but I knew the best MREs – beef stew over rice and mac and cheese – and with GPS, I could always find good takeout. But she had never warned me that the surest way for a man to get inside a woman's head was through her vagina. Todd was definitely inside my head, snooping around quietly as if he didn't want anyone to know what he was up to... that someone was home.

"Where are you going?" came his voice, deep with grog and heavy with sex. He made a half-hearted attempt to kick the sheets off his legs and reach for me. But I was too awake for that. I eased off the bed and out of reach.

"For a run."

"It's dark, it's raining, and it's dangerous." It was four a.m. and he had come inside me for the last time at one-thirty. He was too tired to put much weight behind the complaint.

"Yeah, it gets that way sometimes," I answered, pushing my hair off my face and padding into the bathroom. I shut the door with finality and turned the lights on.

Todd liked light, so much so that there were eight light bulbs framing the bathroom vanity mirror. It looked like a woman lived here, as if she had set down roots... as if Todd knew I wasn't just passing through, waiting for word of my next assignment, hopefully to Paris.

I made the most of Todd's mirror, trying to find whatever it was that had enthralled a man like him. My hair was longer than it had been when we first met. It was halfway down my back now and I would have cut it, except it gave Todd a much longer leash to wrap his fist around. I gathered the dark chestnut mass into a high ponytail then braided it and wrapped it into a tight bun, leaving my face open for a thorough examination.

The skin around my cheeks, and from my neck stretching down to my breasts was splotchy and red. Todd's day-old beard had done that, rubbing away my irritation. I splashed cold water on my face and allowed it to trickle down my neck. That was better. But there was little hope for my kiss-bruised mouth that made me look like a walking billboard for lip-plumper.

My eyes brought balance back to the picture. Sex kittens didn't have eyes that could freeze the dick off a penguin. Mine were chocolate brown, but decidedly lacking in warmth. Smiling only made it worse. Only Todd could make it better. But even the drop of blood that stained the cornea of the left eye was beyond his control. A man's fist had done that to me. Now anyone who got close enough to see the bloodshot that refused to fade with the rest of my bruises knew that that man was dead. The girl who stared back at me from Todd's Times-Square mirror had ripped the man's eye from its socket then shot him in the head, and no amount of cold water would wipe that stain away.

When I left the bathroom, I thought Todd had fallen back to sleep. I tiptoed around the bedroom, getting dressed, keeping my eyes off temptation. I thought I was home free when I tied the final knot on my sneakers without any more protest from his direction. It was just like him to keep me on my toes.

"Why don't you use the treadmill?"

There was one in the bedroom he had converted into a gym long before we met. There were a couple of cardio machines at the Embassy that was now my base. It wasn't a bad idea, so I reminded myself to pack a bag for later.

"Because I need this," I replied, sticking in my waterproof ear buds and strapping the waterproof iPod case to my arm.

"Be careful, baby."

I left the comfort of Todd's arms and our sex-scented room to run into the sheeting rain. We lived in a villa in Altos de Arroyo Hondo II, thirty minutes' drive from the embassy. Our polished wood and wrought iron mechanical gates closeted us away from curious eyes, especially those from the poverty stricken communities we looked down on from our kitchen. We shared the hill with the American School, two Government ministers, two ambassadors, and a handful of Santo Domingo's elite. It should have been the safest place in the city. But every now and then, our world was rocked by news of a break-in or car jacking. Our neighbors were genuinely surprised that the have-nots would one day tire of looking up at the haves and finally do something about their condition.

I was comfortable in this land of contrasts not unlike the one I had left a couple of months ago. I didn't think twice about the dark, deserted and very dangerous streets. Crime was off the charts, fueled by the drug trade. The GDP per capital was under $10,000, but the Gucci and Ferrari stores seemed to be doing good business. But I wasn't afraid, and surprisingly, Todd hadn't protested as much as I had expected. He was aware now of what I had inside me. Besides, I had Bill with me, tucked safely inside the pocket of my running pants.

Bill was my Benchmade Auto-Stryker, and his three-and-a-half inch stainless steel tanto blade had sliced through a man's throat like a hot knife cuts through butter. The blood had spewed as if from a half-corked spigot, soaking me in its sticky warmth. It had taken me days to get it all off. It had sunk into the hard-to-reach places like the creases in my ears, under my nails and behind my cuticles. I would raise my hand to bite a nail and notice a line of dried blood. That disgusted me more than the act of killing.

Bill was much more reliable than water and soap. His aluminum handle had not failed me as I sank the blade deep into another man's belly. He had ripped through skin, muscle, stomach and intestines like paper. The smell was unique: stomach gases and blood, incomparable to anything else... not quite bile-covered egg, with a hint of sulfur and melted nickel. I was certain there were still traces of both men to be found in Bill. He had his own hard-to-reach places, where blood and gore had found a secret home. But I could no more discard him than I could the memory of those men – their cries, their eyes bulging in disbelief that the prey had become the predator.

Did I regret it... stalking and killing three men? Not in the least.

I just wished Todd had never seen me like that. It changed things between us. He was aware of what I was, of the things that lay beneath, the things that kept my eyes cold and dead. And he knew there was more. How could a woman do the things I had done and not cringe or dissolve into tears? He had expected hysterics, not the dead stare of a sociopath measuring him over coffee and eggs.

He was more careful with me now. He would say what he wanted from me and wait for me to fall in line in my own time. There weren't so many questions anymore, and a lot less badgering. I hated to think that he might be afraid. I preferred 'tentative' – the kind of consideration given to the less fortunate so one did not hurt their pride.

Maybe our marriage had something to do with that. Maybe he thought he owned me now. He had won and there was no more need to fight. Maybe I was a curiosity in which interest was waning. But I had seen his books... the ones he ordered while we were still at home in Virginia, like the American Psychiatric Association's *Diagnostic and Statistical Manual of Mental Disorders*. Darlene Pedersen's Third Edition *PsychNotes: Clinical Pocket Guide* was only a month old, so it was new to me. I promised myself to skip through it some time. I could have given him a guided tour of the DSM-IV, if I thought he was harmless. But he hadn't left it at that. He had also bought Bockian and Jongsma's *The Personality Disorder Treatment Planner*, and he tried to hide his little library from me.

Todd's books told me he not only wanted to get inside my head; he wanted to cure me. I would never tell him that better, more competent men had tried and failed, or that I had learned to cope with my demons. Todd could read as much as he liked, as long as he kept guessing. He would have to be satisfied with my heart; my mind and my body were mine to do with as I pleased. And right then, it pleased me to beat the pavement through torrential rain.

It was good for me. Running in the rain, my toes squishing in my wet sneakers as I slapped through the pools of warm water, my lungs straining with the effort of keeping up with the miles, kept things in perspective. I could love Todd Birch forever, but I would never forget how or why I had become this broken. I would find the people who had killed my parents. And I would kill them too.

TWO

I was two hours into scrolling through cables, trying to find something that would help the hours and days to slip by. Competition was high for the cables that promised action, and since it was no secret that I was only 'passing through', I usually got the crumbs after all the meaty assignments had been divvied up.

Santo Domingo was a larger Mission than Kingston, with more people, and a lot more toes to step on. I had barely scraped through sensitivity training, so this was not my ideal situation.

The floor plan also left a lot to be desired.

I had traded the privacy of an enclosed cubicle in an isolated corner for an open floor where sound traveled with the speed and clarity of a flash flood. All my natural inclinations had to be checked at the door. Nothing could grab the attention of the men and woman on this floor like a bid for privacy.

Besides myself, the newest member of this joint intelligence staff was already months into his assignment. I was the only one who was not adapted to the nakedness that was rife at Santo Domingo Mission. Ironic didn't cover the contrast, as residents secreted themselves behind electronic gates and high fences, guarding their privacy with the tenacity of a pitbull. And yet, their eyes and ears were attuned to shadow, furtiveness and hushed voices, eager for news from over the fence. Nevermind the last time I had seen this much thigh and breast was in a KFC bucket. I went to bed with Todd Birch one night and woke up in a living nightmare.

Unlike Kingston, I had the company of another female, Jessica Byles, an investigator with the FBI. From Day One, she had sought me out like a hound to a bitch in heat, perching on the edge of my desk with a mug of welcome coffee, skirt hiked up so high I could see the fingerprints on the inside of her thighs. She never mentioned Todd, not even in passing. In fact, she went out of her way to avoid any reference to him, acted as if he didn't exist and I wasn't married to him. And I just *knew* that at some point, he had left his mark on her too.

As if on cue, she looked up from between two pillars of manila folders rivaling the leaning tower of Pisa, and smiled at me. I looked away before she could mistake my attention for an invitation to make her way over so she could pretend she hadn't fucked my husband.

Everyone – especially the women – talked about Todd Birch.

Ambassador Powell was leaving in two weeks, and although we had an idea of whom his successor would be, that person would not arrive at post until December. As Deputy Chief of Mission, Todd would become the interim head of the embassy. Everyone thought he was right for the job.

He was a natural leader, an entrenched member of the boys' club whom the men regarded as an example – someone to aspire to. He was godfather to four children, gave speeches at birthdays, send-offs and to welcome newcomers. Even my uncle Richard, Director of National Intelligence, approved of him and saw this temporary assignment as the perfect cover.

He had also screwed his way through the pool of Foreign Service Officers and Foreign Service Nationals, leaving behind a trail of orgasming women who would throw their underwear and its contents at him given the right opportunity. His sudden marriage had done nothing to dull his appeal; in fact, it had quite the contrary effect.

The thick, black hair that curled over his collar and swallowed my fingers; those azure eyes that rocked my equilibrium; the firm physique that was more often than not wrapped up in a suit and hinted at the pure masculine perfection underneath, were all tools of a trade. Todd had not yet told me what he was doing here, or whom he really worked for. However, I knew he was not here to run an embassy. I was left to guess, and knowing the things I did for my country, I believed Todd used his looks, his smile, his charm, and soon the title of Chargé *ad interim* to get close to people who, for one reason or another, were important to our Government. Behind the voice that could wet panties faster than a garden hose was a spy, employing everything at his disposal to get the job done.

"It's only you now, Amy," he had told me on our wedding night as he sank so deep inside me our souls touched. "This is all yours... yours alone."

It was a lie. He would do what he had to do to get the job done; and my job would be not to take it personally. Not only was I stuck under the spotlight on an otherwise empty stage; the audience had only come to see the star attraction – my husband. And every single one of them knew the exact number of freckles on his penis.

The days couldn't drift by fast enough while I waited for word of my new assignment. The bullshit cables that landed on my desk couldn't distract a fly, and living with someone was not conducive to my secret habits. Even if he knew, Todd did not approve of self-medication, and so I ran twice a day, and if it got really bad, I would throw in a swim too.

Over the top of my computer monitor, I spotted my Section Chief scanning his domain like a groundhog looking for Spring. Ted O'Brien was working at the CIA twelve years ago when my father was killed. That was one of the first things we had gotten out of the way.

It was my first day and I was perched on the edge of his guest chair, mapping his office, giving him time and freedom to look his fill. The glasses over his moss green eyes failed to hide the quick and dangerous mind behind them. His eyebrows were thin salt and pepper slashes and perfectly matched the thinning locks that curved around his head like the brim of a fedora. The pate was bald and spotted like the back of his hands. He didn't talk much and smiled less, but he was honest. If he didn't like you, you wouldn't have to guess. I knew where I stood with him.

He was nothing like the two men I had left behind in Jamaica – Lowe and Blitzner. One of them was my boss, and the other had fingered me to the locals as the person responsible for the seizure of a marijuana shipment in which a dirty copy had had shares. He'd done it as a test, his personal recruitment exercise, to steal me from my boss who had become quite adept at driving a big-rig over the people he had thrown beneath the wheels. A shank between the ribs was more Ted O'Brien's style. He would want to get close, wanted to look into your eyes as he explained why.

"I knew your father; he was a good man. And I know Admiral Richard McDowell. I don't know you. I've heard about you though. You killed a cop in Jamaica and got yourself kicked out of country," O'Brien had said in greeting.

I focused on the last part, because I didn't know what to do with the rest in such a public forum. John Koehler was more than a hero; he'd been a martyr and no one knew his sacrifice better than his daughter. I kept my eyes moving, logging the location of the filing cabinet, the half-dead cactus plant on top, the view of the parking lot from the window. I could feel the stares boring into my back from the open floor I had just crossed. I had counted seven pairs on the way in and every one of them knew who I was.

I had done a lot in my not-quite decade old career. I had married fucking James Bond. I had taken down a lot of people, some of them worse than others. One of them was a Jamaican cop who had come looking for me with two other guys and a kit that included a sawed-off shotgun but no handcuffs. That was two months ago, during the hunt for Luis Santiago Vargas who had been on the run for a decade.

But who cared about my nabbing a notorious trafficker and fugitive of American justice? I was *that* girl – the one who had killed a host country cop.

"They've sent you here because you've shacked up with Birch and they haven't figured out what to do with you. Don't get comfortable; you're not staying. Kill anything bigger than a cockroach and I will nail your ass to the wall like Jesus on the fucking cross. Got that?" O'Brien had looked ready to jump out of his seat, he was leaning so far forward.

"Yes, sir." I had smiled, my face as stiff as a two-by-four. I had not expected to win any congeniality contest, but this was something else. I wasn't the only one counting the hours until my new marching orders came through from Virginia.

Since then I'd been stuck interrogating databases, following electronic trails, watching and listening to people from afar. I assessed reports, turned them into premises, then relayed them for others to run with.

Now O'Brien had those dirty green eyes trained on me as he debated whether another 'find this asshole' assignment was heavy enough to keep me buried for another couple of days. He took forever to make up his mind, long enough for the steady hum of voices, the tap of fingers across a keyboard, to taper off, and for eight sets of eyes to lock onto him.

This had to be important. The man was nothing if not decisive. Finally, when he had come to terms with the only possible course of action, he crooked his finger at me through his wide open door. He was the first Section Chief I had ever met who wore short-sleeved plaid shirts. The others rolled their sleeves all the way to their elbows if they had to, but they always kept a tie in their desk drawers for emergencies. Ted O'Brien had never had an emergency he felt required long sleeves and a tie. And after a month working with him, I could count on one hand the number of times he had shut his door.

"Koehler, get in here," he shouted through the open door.

He had called me Birch only once.

"Amy Koehler," I had corrected, "my name is Amy Koehler."

He had waved it off as if my name was irrelevant and he would call me whatever he wanted. But I thought he looked at me differently; harder, as if there was something under my skin that intrigued him. Anyway, he never made that mistake again, as he yelled at me from across the room.

That was another thing about Santo Domingo. No one used their desk phones. That would have been too private, possibly secretive, which would have defied the purpose of the open floor plan. There were more backstops here than whores in a brothel. Someone always knew what was going on – the stuff of my night terrors.

There was no point locking my computer or securing my desk before making my way to O'Brien's office. Everything was tagged and numbered, a visible reminder to the user that everything in sight was the property of the United States of America. I was finding it very hard to adjust. I almost closed the door behind me.

"Leave it open and take a seat," O'Brien grumbled as he took his place behind his desk.

The wall facing the open floor was all glass without even the cover of some blinds. Seven pairs of eyes as well as seven pairs of ears were trained our way when really, there was no need. Before my seat could cool, O'Brien would have my backstop's backside – either Jenkins or Scott – warming the cushion as he briefed them on what I would be doing. No need to take it personally; everybody had a backstop.

"It's early Christmas for the locals. We're helping them out with some tactical IT intrusion solutions, and you're going to train them on how we want the technology we've just bought them to be used." He slid a manila folder across the desk. "Here's your brief. Get through it and see me tomorrow at o-nine-hundred. Mitch should be done with installation and testing today. He'll be here tomorrow to answer any questions you might have."

I quickly snatched up the folder while he spoke. There was an instructions sheet with my directives, as well as a manual for the equipment in question. It was over a hundred pages, but everything was originating from the United States. My preliminary assessment was we were either after a local, or wanted something from the police, and planned on using this backdoor to arrive at our ends.

Equipment always came with training directly from the vendor. Even though Mitch was probably the contractor from whom we had sourced the Trojan horse, he was from the private sector, and so did not have the necessary clearance to know our target. Plus he could inadvertently do a thorough job with the training, leaving the locals with an in-depth understanding of the technology, which we didn't necessarily want them to have.

"Who am I training, sir?"

"Their intercept IT SPOC… kid by the name of Hernandez." And by kid, he meant anyone between the age of two and fifty-three – one year younger than him. "He speaks good English. There's no need to stretch yourself on this. You're meeting him at Police Intel HQ on Monday."

I was familiar with the intrusion solution we had provided. Its purpose was to breach HTTPS-based protocols that could leave law enforcement blind. Simply put, criminals could communicate on secure network platforms without fear of real-time interception, unless intelligence agencies had the means to monitor both traffic and content independent of the network providers.

I could already guess that my job would be to train Hernandez, the local Single Point of Contact for Information Technology Interception, on the basics of encryption, including encrypted tunnels, while unbeknownst to him, gaining access to either a locally-hosted or mobile, i.e. roaming, target.

There was a moment of silence, but I kept my eyes on the brief and my ass in my seat, because something told me O'Brien wasn't done yet. I could feel his eyes running over me, coming back time and again to my left eye and its spot of blood. He was moving around an idea from one side of his mouth to the next, like a cow chewing cud.

"Good job pinpointing Morales," he finally spat out grudgingly. "Things went down nice and clean. They nabbed him checking Facebook on the john... never even had the chance to wipe his ass."

Morales was a small-time drug trafficker who used to move cocaine and heroine between the Dominican Republic and Puerto Rico. He made single moms, teenage girls and minor league baseball players swallow pellets for transport to the mainland. I'd had nothing better to do that week, which left me all the time needed to track his smartphone by IP address until I was able to shortlist the ten most frequently used ones. That marvelous modern technology called GPS was used to track every one of his locations until I was able to predict where and what time he took his dump each morning. That was when he liked to update his status and see what friends and family were up to. The rest of the time he was out and about, taking care of business, recruiting couriers, raping the girls and beating up kids who refused to swallow.

This new assignment wasn't much of an improvement over what I'd been doing up to now, unless I was right about the target and he or she happened to be someone important. If not, then this was a babysitting gig, but at least I was allowed to go outside, away from the persistent eyes and whispers. It was only Wednesday and I'd had enough of the women who stopped talking about my husband when I stepped out of a bathroom cubicle. My Spanish was better than they thought – I'd had brief stints in Colombia and Mexico – but even if I didn't understand a word of their native language, there was only one 'Todd' here.

"This is some kindergarten shit, Koehler," O'Brien finally said. "Don't fuck it up, and don't shoot anyone or I will personally rip your fucking face off. Stick to your directives."

His eyes bored into me, his edginess apparent. His concern for this play-date meant one of two things: either he ran a tight ship and was always this high strung; or the target was important and he was afraid of assigning it to his only loose canon. I knew he didn't want responsibility for me – absolutely hated that I was there, regardless of how good I was or how fast I delivered. Of course, it didn't help that wherever I went Uncle Richard was never far behind. And who wanted their boss' boss' boss watching over their shoulder? Behind the steady gaze of a Section Chief was a man who felt cornered. Ted O'Brien didn't like not having a choice, and just for that reason, I believed he *would* rip my face off if I threatened his peace and quiet. I just wasn't sure if he would do it before or after nailing me to the wall.

I headed for the gaping door, already flipping through my new assignment.

"Scott," O'Brien yelled, "come see me."

I didn't make eye contact with my backstop as he went in for his brief. He knew not to take it personally. I didn't make contact with anyone for social purposes, didn't say hi to the people I passed in the halls, never stopped to chat over coffee, and under no circumstance did I do lunch. Todd had done all the explaining long before my flight had landed at Las Americas airport, briefed them on what to expect, and asked them to keep an eye on me.

It was 10:30. In an hour and a half Byles would prop her behind on my desk, flashing me her crotch, and invite me out to lunch – no doubt another favor to Todd. As much as I wanted to dive right into this assignment, I needed to blow off some steam. My lunch hour would be spent doing a steady eight-point-zero on a treadmill. This was my prison, these people were my jailors, and running on a spinning belt was the closest I would come to freedom in a while.

But like everyone and everything else in the Dominican Republic, I was expected not to take it personally.

THREE

From the embassy, I took a taxi as far as Cuesta Hermosa town center, then made the rest of my way home on foot. I swapped out the high heel pumps that went with my Wednesday and Friday outfits for my running shoes, and sprinted up the rough-paved hilly roads. It wasn't just the need to feel the blood pumping through my veins that pushed me forward. Without the cover of trees, I had nowhere to hide if Todd happened along. And he was the last person I wanted to see right then.

Normally in the mornings, we parted ways in the embassy parking lot, then RDVed in the same spot most evenings. But I couldn't bear to look at him after the day I'd had.

I could have taken the taxi all the way home, but I wanted to give his cleaning lady a wide berth as well. I hoped she had let herself out and was long gone, but as I drew closer to my home and the heaviness in the back of my skull persisted, I knew yet another simple wish of mine would be cruelly denied.

Magda was all Todd's. She was well over sixty, but he refused to retire her, and she refused to just go. It seemed Todd was intent on exploring every possible inappropriate relationship while in the Dominican Republic. Her job was to clean, iron and sometimes cook, but the employee/employer line was so blurred, a casual observer might have thought she was his mother. Magda treated Todd as a combination of a treasured only child and the reincarnation of Jesus Christ; and in Todd's eyes, Magda could do no wrong.

Normally I wouldn't have cared long enough to notice. Her presence only became a problem because the woman was convinced I was unworthy of him and had somehow trapped him into marriage.

"Su esposa? Pero yo no la conozco!" *Your wife? But I've never met her,* she exclaimed when Todd first introduced us. As if it was her right to look me over… as if he needed her approval…

"Ella es una buena chica, Magda. Le encantará su." *She's a good woman, Magda. You'll love her too.*

"¿Está embarazada? ¿ Me estás dando un bebé Todd de cuidar de?" *Is she pregnant? Are you giving me a little Todd to care for?* she asked with a mix of hope, joy and trepidation. The latter was born of the fear of my role.

"Todavía no." *Not Yet*

Todd Birch was likely the only person alive who thought of me as a 'good girl'. And to prove everyone else right, I couldn't care less if Magda loved me too. Her opinion of me would have had the significance of a flea's fart if only she could keep it to herself… if only she didn't spy on me.

"Señor Todd," she would say, "the lady came home at exactly five. She did not work today?" or "Señor Todd, the lady brought home three bags today. She take them inside the room." Always in stage whispered English, as if she didn't intend for me to hear, although it was clear she did.

'The room' was my personal space, the second bedroom that I required, which was forbidden to everyone else, including Todd – especially Todd. It fuelled Magda's curiosity and distrust, because she had once been responsible for cleaning it. Now the door was locked to her. I had the only key, which I always had on my person.

Todd would kiss her cheek and thank her for taking such good care of us, for looking out for me especially. Then he would return to me and brush off her concern.

"She doesn't understand why we work together but don't come home together. Frankly, I don't understand it either," he would say, or "She worries about you. I worry about you too." His excuses always came while nuzzling my neck, nibbling at my ear lobe, squeezing a

breast. He thought I was incapable of feeling multiple emotions at once…
that I couldn't be annoyed and turned on at the same time.

Magda's beady eyes would follow me around the house as if I was a
guest in my own home.   And I was expected not to take it personally.
Good help – the competent, security vetted type – was hard to find, and
Magda had served in a dozen US expatriate households in her forty year
career as a housekeeper. Her granddaughter, who was a student at
Universidad Autónoma de Santo Domingo, had interned at the embassy
the last two summers, although internships were usually reserved for the
children of the US expatriate staff. That was how much the embassy
loved Magda.

The front door was unlocked, confirmation that she hadn't left yet. I
schooled my features and tried to ignore the pulsing pressure inside the
back of my skull.

"Señor Todd?" She met me in the entry hall and I had to watch as
the light faded from her black eyes at the sight of me. Her bags were
packed and stood ready against the wall. She should have left hours ago,
but had wanted another glimpse of Todd. He had given her the rest of
the week off so she could visit her daughter in Samaná in the
northeastern part of the country – and so I could get a break.

"Solamente yo, Magda." *It's only me.*

She left shortly thereafter, but stayed long enough to call Todd and
report that 'the lady' had come home and gone to the room.

The heavy drapes were closed, blocking out all daylight, but I would
have been able to tell by feel alone whether my sanctuary had been
violated. All was quiet and still, as it should have been, but the room
failed to cut through the heaviness of the day. It was only Wednesday
and there was nothing to indicate that an improvement should be
expected later in the week.

I hated needing a pill, but there was no denying the desperation that
was setting in. I crawled to the closet and rifled through a suitcase that
was empty except for a small makeup bag. I tried again to exhale the
angst even as I reached for the Tic Tacs. A handful spilled into my palm,
and I sifted through the mints until I found two Xanax. I swallowed them
dry, shed my clothes, stretched out on the bed and waited for blessed
relief.

I was trapped and helpless to change my circumstances. Everything had changed in such a short time that I couldn't pinpoint exactly where I had gone wrong. Two months was nothing, but it was enough to completely alter the course of my life, and not necessarily in the best way either.

For a very brief time I had been filled with hope for the future. I had managed to track down one of my father's assets, and I had begun to understand why he had died. I had collared Luis Santiago Vargas and I had escaped Jamaica with both my life and Todd Birch.

I'd had everything planned, and with Todd Birch at my side, I would finish what my father had started and avenge his death. Todd was the perfect cover, and together we should have taken Paris by storm. That's where Sergei Afanasenko was, and he had been my father's last quarry – the one who had gotten away, the one who would lead me to the American who had been my father's ultimate goal.

I couldn't remember the last time I'd been so wrong.

I had walked into my evaluation interview, certain that the intelligence world was mine for the taking. My latest coup was pulling $6Million of narcotics and a fugitive out of thin air. I'd had a stellar career, which included tours in eight countries; a stellar military record; and I came from excellent intelligence pedigree – a star on the Memorial Wall for my father, and a guardian who reported directly to the President.

If any of the members of the panel doubted my readiness – my emotional maturity – for a prime spot at the embassy in Paris, then Todd Birch would be my trump card. We were engaged, and he wanted nothing more than to close the deal. I was prepared to go all the way with him, because it paved the way for me to be in the last place my father had worked before he was murdered.

Yes, I had just killed a cop and two of his criminal accomplices – who also happened to be wanted men. They had tried to kill me first, and if I had failed, they would have killed Todd too for no other reason than being in the wrong place at the wrong time with the wrong woman. So technically, not only had I defended myself, I had also saved Todd's life.

There were three men on the panel, and they had interchangeable names, like Bill, Dick and Tom. Bill was from National Intelligence, the same agency I worked for, but he reported directly to Uncle

Richard. Dick hailed from the CIA – probably knew Todd or whomever he reported to; and Tom was an on-staff psychologist.

For over an hour they had sat there and picked apart all the cases I had worked over the past eight years; resurrected all the casualties I had directly or indirectly contributed to – well, the ones they knew about; and dragged my father into the brawl that ensued.

It was an ambush. They all but called me fucking crazy. They thought I was unstable, volatile, too hardened by the things I had seen and done... as if they trained us to shit rainbow colored unicorns and marshmallow butterflies.

"NATO and the OSCE require a different set of skills, Koehler," Dick had said, proving with his condescension how he had come by that name. "It's very different from what you've done in places like Yemen."

"I'm very adaptable, sir," I had replied. "That's what I did in Yemen. I adapted."

Shit! New York had nothing on Yemen. If I could make it in Yemen – a Western woman, which should have meant sticking out like a sore thumb – I could make it anywhere. On my exit, I had taken a senior Al Qaeda leader with me, with no casualties on our side. Before judging me for being too hard, they should have thought of where they'd been holding that guy for the past eight years.

"We need diplomats in Europe, Koehler. You don't do well in social settings. Your sensitivity rating is one of the lowest I've ever seen." This came from the shrink who had never before sat across a table from me. He thought he could leaf through my personnel files, my interrogation reports, my past evaluations and pretend he knew me.

"I thrive wherever I'm needed," was my response – and a very diplomatic one too, I thought. "I look forward to new challenges, and opportunities for growth and the development of new skills."

"Let's talk about your father for a bit," he persisted in an unsophisticated attempt to get a reaction from me.

"What about my father? Have we finally found the people responsible for his murder?" I looked from one face to the next, but Tom was the only one who didn't have the decency to look chagrined. The intelligence men shifted in their seats, looking everywhere but at me. That was their shame. All the best minds in the global intelligence community and in twelve years they still couldn't solve my parents' murder.

Three men had come for me, just like a killing squad had gone to my home and killed my family. They blamed me for the cop I had killed, but half my face was fucked up from a fight for my life. It was still too soon to tell if perfect vision would ever be restored to my left eye. What did they expect me to do … lie down and die quietly?

"Specifically, I would like to talk to you about your reaction to your father's death." The shrink was still thumbing through that file.

"I've been seen by four eminent psychiatrists who all concluded that they found me well adjusted in spite of the trauma I had suffered."

"That's exactly what I would like to discuss with you, Agent Koehler."

He stopped flipping pages for a moment, having found something of interest to hold him for a while. I could see him rolling it around in his hands like a succulent fruit, trying to find the best angle to sink his teeth in.

"I've examined your file and I have not been able to identify specific manifestations of trauma. There was a brief period of promiscuity in the months after your parents had died, but Dr. Petersen noted that it might have been related to a possible sexual assault. Can you explain that, Agent Koehler?"

I slowly, silently, exhaled the breath I had been holding. "I'm sorry. I cannot. I have not seen Dr. Petersen's notes."

It was time for Bill to jump in. The direction Tom wanted to take was making him decidedly uncomfortable. He had a sixteen-year-old daughter; he was Uncle Richard's minion, and he would play the fatherly card for Admiral McDowell if he had to. "This right here is why we're concerned about you. You're sitting there like butter wouldn't melt in your mouth while discussing your parents' murder and a possible rape – your rape. You are not a robot, Amy. No one expects you to pretend that these things did not happen, or that you have not been affected by them."

"I have learned to deal with my grief," I said, but I lowered my voice in deference to whatever crisis he was facing with his own daughter. "Those three weeks of grief counseling were very useful."

"Jesus Christ!" This from Dick. "You were seventeen years old. Kids that age don't get over the death of the family dog in three weeks."

"I never said I was over it. I said I've learned to deal with it."

There was a protracted silence as Tom kept skipping through my file, Dick scratched his head, and Bill stared at me with all the concern Uncle Richard had asked him to convey.

"You've barely managed to scrape through your sensitivity tests. You have poor rapport with your peers and you struggle with even basic human emotions. That's not the profile that suits Europe." Really, was he going to be a dick the whole way through?

"I've done Yemen. I've done Iraq. I've done Afghanistan. I want something else. I need a change. You have no cause to doubt my abilities; I've always delivered."

"Why Paris? What's so special about Paris? Why not come home for a while? Or Asia... what do you think about Japan?" Bill was clutching at straws and I was about to start ripping my hair out by the handful.

"You think I'm a cold bitch but you want to send me to Japan?" I asked incredulously. I could just see how that would play out with those little Japanese men with their dark suits and gracious manners. "I deserve a change to go with the other changes in my life. I'm getting married," I told them and melted just a bit, because that was what they expected of me. Drop the armor and become a woman, show vulnerability.

"You're getting married?" I knew I could count on Dick to layer on the derision on top of a harsh bark of laughter.

"We had no idea you were seriously seeing anyone," joined Bill who, we both knew, was playing devil's advocate. Uncle Richard was the one who had told me how perfect Todd Birch was for me. He had urged me to kiss and make up when Todd's intensity – and determination to turn a one-night stand into a long-term thing – had scared the living daylights out of me.

I was pretty certain what Bill meant was, he was surprised that I had actually done it, and in record time too.

"His name is Todd Birch. You may have heard of him. He's based in Santo Domingo presently, but he also intends to bid for Paris." Of course they had heard of him, but I was willing to play along with the bullshit cover about how he worked for the State Department. "He's not a Yemen kind of guy."

Tom narrowed his eyes as if an alien creature had taken my place and he couldn't wait to start dissecting. It was all wishful thinking on his part; no way was this man getting anywhere near my head. Dick kept muttering "Jesus Christ" in what he probably thought was sotto voce. I wasn't the only one who hated the Todd card.

I knew I would have had to marry him to keep him. That wasn't entirely selfish of me; he wanted me for reasons I could not grasp. I also knew having him by my side would increase our chances of getting such a prime posting; that was the reason I had allowed him to catch me. Finding out he was my ticket out of a pigeonhole – the cake as opposed to the icing – was a major disappointment.

I was one of the best in my field, and I felt as if I were being punished for it. I had no choice but to be clinical and unemotional. How many good people had Dick and Bill seen burn out from the job? This was no place for the weak. In this business, allowing anyone to see you sweat was like handing the other team the playbook, which could get you killed. And my father had taught me that the people wearing the same colors and playing on the same team were the best placed to stab you in the back.

"Betrayal never comes from your enemies," he would say.

The interview ended, but I wasn't even out the door when they started arguing about what to do with me.

"I'd like to schedule her for another psych evaluation." Tom was doing a piss-poor job of hiding his hard-on.

"What's the use? You're not getting anything more than what's in her file." I couldn't tell if Bill believed that, or if he was just being Uncle Richard's man. The Admiral was partially responsible for raising me, and any failings that were attributed to my youth could be laid at his feet. And that 'possible sexual assault' had occurred on his watch.

"Do you believe this shit? What the fuck is Birch up to?" Dick had given up on divine intervention and directed this question to Bill.

"I know he was there with her when she killed that cop. Do you think he's in town? He's the one you need to talk to. Maybe he can tell you what's going on in her head."

I got it. They were frustrated. But they were sitting behind desks, being briefed on who, when, and why shit hit the fan. I was usually the one sitting in the room, under the fan, trying to hold the lever down so the grenade wouldn't rip me to pieces.

FOUR

I survived the mobbing, but I left without a clue as to my next posting. I had dinner plans with Uncle Richard that evening, and I had no intention of being left in the dark much longer.

Everyone was home. Aunt Abby met us at the door, shushing Ollie, the housekeeper, out of the way. Her hair and eyes had gone dull, probably from all the powder she stuffed up her nose and rammed down her throat, and I wondered if this would have been my mother's fate had she lived. There was a price to be paid for being married to men whose lifeblood was secrets.

Uncle Richard was manning the BBQ on the back patio that overlooked the pool where his grandchildren played. He was as robust at sixty-five as he had been at forty. His brown hair had a more generous dusting of grey, but it was the only dull thing about the man. He kept in shape and could probably match me toe for toe on a flat six-mile run. This was as relaxed as he ever got, drinking scotch while prodding steaks with the tongs, but the naturalness of his straight back and shoulders reminded me of his prized Dobermans. If I hadn't grown up with him, his eyes would have given me the creeps. One was blue and the other brown; one lulled you into reckless complacency while the other skewered you like an icicle shank. It wasn't just the eyes though. He had given the blue to his three sons, but none of them put me on my guard like Uncle Richard.

Tom was the eldest of his sons, whose sole ambition in life was to be a carbon copy of Richard. Unfortunately, Richard expected more of his children. Tom's wife, Michelle, was an OK starter bride, but Richard had hoped Tom – or Andrew or David – and I would have found our way to each other. I was the daughter he had never had. He grudgingly accepted the role of uncle.

"Of all my children," Richard had once confessed, "you're the most like me. And I have your father to thank for that. With you as the mother of my grandchildren, someday we'll rule the world." He didn't even have the good tact to pretend he was being facetious. I didn't want to rule the world. I wanted to find the people who had shattered mine. Tom, Andrew and David held no appeal for me.

Early in the afternoon, Todd caught me staring at the children who thought nothing of dashing between the legs of the Director of National Intelligence and the Secretary of Defense who was also in attendance. I knew Todd wanted children – longed for them in fact, since he had first received word of Mona's pregnancy. Those dreams had been laid to rest with the fiancée it was rumored he had killed. They would remain so for quite some time to come, because looking at those children, all I could see was another generation of us – hardened, broken people who thrived on secrets, blood and deceit.

The Secretary of Defense parted with his whiskey long enough to scoop me into a fierce embrace.

"My God, you look like your Daddy!" he declared and I had to duck my head to hide my embarrassment from everyone. When would it get easier? After twelve years, the mere mention of him should not have affected me so.

I introduced Todd to the people who were family to me, but only as my boyfriend. Information was weaponry to people like us, the employment of which was based on the principles of need, proportionality and effectiveness. I would share only what was required to effectively achieve my desired outcome, and based on the interview I'd had earlier that morning, I would need the element of surprise.

Besides one whispered, "Why didn't you tell me," Todd never once showed his surprise at the company I kept. I had only ever used first names to refer to my family, so it had to come as a shock to be embraced by these men.

Todd kept his hands mostly to himself, refraining from marking me as his possession as was his habit. He drifted in and out of polite conversation, because that was what he did best. Within a half an hour he had both Aunt Abby and Ollie blushing like teenagers. Fifteen minutes after that, he and my sometimes-cousins were smoking Balmorals by the gazebo.

Still I was never far from mind. Even if his hands were stuffed in his pockets, his eyes were like a physical touch that I could not ignore. Their burning cobalt light branded me no matter where I was or who should have had his full attention. He was not at all subtle in his obsession, and of course Richard noticed. He likely assumed responsibility for it. I already knew he would not rest until he had the rest of my life mapped out for me.

"Amy, what's this I hear about you having your heart set on Paris? I thought you would want to come home for a while."

Sometimes I thought everything would be that much easier if I confided in Richard. He was my father's best friend; he should understand the need for closure. I wanted to tell him about the assets my father had left me, the names he had died for. I wanted to tell him how I had tracked down one of them. I wanted to tell Richard what I planned to do.

My father was murdered because he had tried to unmask an American traitor who had partnered with a Russian arms dealer to offer US support to militias during the 1990's for a price.

If anyone could help it was Richard. Perhaps my father had no idea how far his friend would have climbed or how quickly. Whatever the reason, he had left this task to me, and I had promised him to keep it safe.

"This is my sin," he had said the night he died. "And now I must pass it to you. You have to finish it, Amy. Don't tell anyone; hide it." And so I did.

"Paris is perfect for us," I answered Richard on a sigh, drinking from my scotch and soda so he wouldn't see how badly I wanted it.

"Perfect how?"

Todd found me again, sending a flare of heat through my body. I let it course through me for a moment – long enough for Richard to see – melting my bones and turning me into a pool of wax.

"We're getting married," I said, holding Todd's gaze for a while longer. Even from thirty feet away, he could see the effect he had on me. He turned back to the circle of cousins, one corner of his mouth lifted in a knowing smile as he dragged on his cigar. I turned to Richard and caught him measuring us frankly. "Don't make a big deal about it, because he wants to ask your permission first. He's like that."

Of course Bill had probably relayed that bit of news to him, and Richard had likely dismissed it as a poorly concealed attempt to get my way. Todd Birch couldn't possibly want cold, broken Amy. But there was no denying what was playing out before him. The chemistry between us could have charred those steaks in seconds.

"You wouldn't joke about something like that, would you, Amy?"

"You'll see," I shrugged nonchalantly.

"Tell me about Paris," he said after a short time, and the full force of those eyes pinned me, freezing me like a cold day in hell.

I pulled out my ace. "Todd really wants kids. He thinks he's getting old and he wants to keep me close… thinks children will do the trick. I don't think we'll have much alone time, and I would like to spend what little we have in a place that's conducive to newlyweds." I met his gaze squarely, and this time there was no need to hide my weakness. "Dad always said I should go to Paris before taking on the responsibilities of a family."

"It's a little soon for that, don't you think?" And who did Richard think I was fooling – himself, Todd or myself?

"I love him, and this is what he wants. He won't settle for less."

And neither would Richard. This is what Admiral McDowell wanted for his dead friend's daughter.

I was seventeen years old when my parents died… too old to ever forget my father, and to know what he would have wanted for me. Of course John Koehler wanted his daughter to be happy, but he had invested everything into making me a better version of himself. He was working with the CIA's Counterintelligence Center Analysis Group when he and my mother were assassinated in a home invasion that I had barely escaped from. For him marriage and children were never the end game; they were a means to an end.

But Richard didn't know I knew that. He had raised me like one of his own, and he had certain expectations to which my own father had never given much thought. Richard wanted me on a leash, under control but prepared if loosed.

Both men were pulling me in opposite directions. To the world I had to appear to toe Richard's line, but it was the dead who had guided my every step.

I had met Todd all on my own, but Richard had told me what to do, spelled out how wonderful he would be for me and my career. More than anyone else, Richard knew I never failed at a mission. Things were hardly as smooth as I wanted, and quite a few times I'd had to blow stuff up, kill people, and hightail it out of country. But I always got the job done. The mission that was Todd Birch was no different – my success even came with its requisite fuck-up.

I'd fallen in love with my mark. I hadn't planned on it. I would change it if I could, because it shouldn't have mattered that he had fucked his way through Santo Domingo ... or that he might have murdered his last fiancée... or that the Government liked him better than me.

Under other circumstances, I would have gnawed off my foot to get away from this type of situation. But this time I went with it, because I needed him. I realized just how much influence Todd Birch had while sipping twenty-five year old Scotch in Richard's backyard. This was still a bargain. I wanted inside our embassy in Paris; Richard wanted me shackled; and Todd wanted me for himself. The cost to myself was high, but I would give anything to avenge my real family.

No matter how deeply and desperately I loved Todd, he was first and foremost a means to an end.

Richard drained his glass, but he kept his eyes on me. I felt the pull of Todd's so I broke away from the chill and let the man across the way warm me again.

"I'm going to my office," Richard said, but he sounded far away. Todd was taking a drag from his cigar and I could imagine the tip of his tongue caressing the butt. The August day suddenly felt too warm. "Send him up in five. I'll get to the bottom of this."

That was two months ago. Ten days after the BBQ, I had married Todd in the backyard of my father's house. My tenants – a World Bank executive and his family – hadn't quite moved out yet, but he was an acquaintance of Richard. He was only too happy to oblige when the Director of National Intelligence asked if we could have the ceremony on the property.

The guest list was short: Richard and his clan; a handful of people who had known my father; Todd's elderly parents who were flown in from New York; and a handful of his close friends whose ribaldry was constrained by their high profile dinner companions. I would have settled for a quick trip to City Hall, but Todd wanted to do things 'the right way', and already he had been fielding pregnancy questions.

I recited my vows in good faith, but it seemed my bosses wanted more of an assurance that the marriage was legitimate, which would explain the absence of a decision on our next posting. Did they think I would dump Todd the minute I got what I wanted? Couldn't they see how much of a fool I was – falling in love with a man who did not love me?

Sending me to Santo Domingo with him was a test. All eyes were on me, but no one seemed overly concerned by Todd's motives. Why had he pressed me to marry him?

Of course he played the game well; he was as good at deception as I was. Yes, he'd had to wipe beads of sweat from his brow after his chat with Richard. Yes, his hands were cool and damp, his fingers shaking, his smile tremulous when he asked me, again, to marry him – this time in front of my family. Yes, he had sighed with relief and breathed deeply into the crook of my neck when I accepted. And on our wedding day, he was grinning like the happiest man in the world as I walked down the makeshift aisle on Richard's arm and stood next to him in the shade of my father's garden. When Richard placed my hand in his, Todd had breathed easier, as if he had been afraid I would have changed my mind. Todd Birch played the part of the perfect groom well, but I knew it was all an act.

He admitted freely to having loved Mona – the fiancée he might have killed. But he had never admitted to anything more than raging, helpless desire for me. I had tied myself to a man who did not love me, and I was trapped at his side in a place where everyone knew it too.

It was a long time before I could turn my brain off, but I had no real way of marking the passage of time. It was pitch black behind my eyelids, but it took a very long time – forever it seemed – before the darkness of my soul swallowed me whole.

FIVE

Anne Krieger could hear him out there, shuffling around, pretending his wife hadn't shut him out. The locked door was a permanent 'Do Not Disturb' sign. He knew these brief moments of solitude were sacred. So far, he had stuck to the rules; he was a very understanding man. Amy had given up much for him – independence, dignity, respect; it was the least he could do.

But if he was shut out, Anne was shut in. Staying put, hiding in the shadows wasn't Anne's thing at all. She was the one who excelled at relationships, meeting people. Living in the light. By rights, Todd Birch should have been hers. But Amy was selfish. She took what she wanted without much consideration for how it affected others. She wasn't thoughtless per se. She analyzed everything to death before she acted, but she just didn't care about the lives she destroyed. She would never share Todd Birch, even if it ripped them apart.

"What's mine is mine," she had said. She was angry about that night at the Cove when Anne had fought so hard to claim a piece of the new man in their lives.

"And I guess what's mine is yours too," Anne had replied, trying to shrug off the hurt like a loose shawl.

Amy didn't care. "Todd was never yours. He will never be yours."

"It seems neither was Ed." And this time it was harder to fake it.

Angry, hurt Edwards Cummings, who'd had Matt Boone murdered for hacking US Military intelligence, and compromising an Iranian asset...

"Major Cummings is a tool. You fucked him to get a grip. That is all." It was all so cut and dry for Amy.

"And what exactly is Todd Birch?"

"Mine... all mine." And just like that, a line had been drawn in the sand.

After a while Anne had let go of the anger and tried to release the resentment that was born from knowing she, like Ed, was only a tool. Her instructions were clear: keep Blerim Nesimi on a tight leash. So that is what Anne did.

She had kept Nesimi busy finding Sergei Afanasenko. The Kosovar had tried to push back once, testing the reins to see the stuff of which the handler was made. He should have been putting together a schedule for the Afanasenko household.

Where did Mama, Papa and Baby Bear go?" What did they do and at what time? Who did they meet?

It was tedious work made nearly unbearable by the fact that Anne expected the same for all members of staff – the bodyguards, their wives and girlfriends, the maids, the nanny, the cook, the drivers, the tutors, their friends and acquaintances.

Nesimi should have started in July, shortly after they had met in Miami, and the reports should have been coming in until Anne said when. But after an initial reconnaissance, the reports became sketchy.

Anne wasn't half as unreasonable as Amy. She knew Nesimi had his own business interests as a facilitator for the Camorra. So she had provided the resources needed to build a good team. Her sole requirements were: accurate, thorough and reliable reports; and independent investigators. Each member of the team operated as an island, each pair of eyes fixed on a single target, having not the slightest clue that there were other investigators working other targets.

Nesimi's job was to consolidate the reports and hit forward. Every now and then he should have conducted an audit, that is, hire free agents to test the accuracy and reliability of the reports. It was imperative that eight-year-old Alexei was indeed at his friend's, Constantine's, birthday party at 1400 on August 28, 2011, and that his mom, Natalia kept her 2100 drinks date with Sonia every other Thursday.

But two weeks in and it was apparent that Nesimi was dragging his feet. He was slow on the recruitment even though he had been quick to take up the payments. His excuses bordered on the offensive: "I'll deal with it when I can. The cities empty out in the summer here; everyone goes to the beach. Business, government, work slow down." As if criminals took holidays... as if the mob and the people in the pits ever slept. Anne had had no choice but to show him the precariousness of his position.

Two days later the Carabinieri received an anonymous tip that Vincente Tosti, a Camorra hit-man, would be at the Caserta train station bar in Piazza Garibaldi at noon. Twenty minutes before a cavalcade of wailing sirens descended on the scene where Tosti awaited the 12:15 train, Nesimi received a text message from Anne that simply said "TOSTI".

News of the arrest shocked the clans' leadership. Only two persons had known Tosti's whereabouts that day, and only one of them knew he was heading into Naples for a meeting with a particular member of the Commission. If he had been followed, the blow to the organization would have been crippling. So needless to say, the Camorra had cleaned house. The most notable of the disappearances was Emilio Dessanto, nephew of the Renato Casalesi.

Besides another text sent on the night Dessanto disappeared that read, "I've saved you for now, but you could be next," neither Anne nor Nesimi had ever spoken of the incident. Two days after that, the first report arrived. Nesimi was now well aware the woman he knew as Rose had thorns, and any day, at any time, she could make him bleed. The Camorra did not rely on such precepts as innocence or guilt. The organization thrived on secrecy as much as caution, and regardless of the services or money Nesimi made for its leaders, the Commission would kill him if there was a hint of suspicion around him. And if Rose Gardener could lead the Carabinieri to Tosti, then she could just as easily draw unwanted attention Nesimi's way.

Anne lay in the dark of her room, poring over the reports and memorizing patterns by the glow of her MacBook. Blerim Nesimi had been John Koehler's asset. He had known the man as John Gardener then, and Nesimi had been his Iris. John had traded legitimacy for Kosovo, for information on a Russian arms dealer with an American backer who had promised militias power for cash during the fractious 1990's. After a scheduled apprehension and rendition of Afanasenko fell through in Paris, John had returned home only to be murdered the next day. The American had gone unnamed, the murderers unpunished. Anne knew the key to finding him – the man who was likely responsible for the assassination of a senior CIA official, a man who had apparently been so powerful he could influence US foreign policy in favor of one side or another of any conflict – lay with Sergei Afanasenko.

So Nesimi would watch, Anne would wait, and Rose made sure the snake she held by the tail didn't turn on her. Her confidence in him was high; the man was good at what he did, but she would be a fool to trust him.

It was a lot to keep track of, but John had never said it would be easy.

"Run," he had said. "Don't stop, don't look back; don't forget. Stay off the road as much as you can. Put it in a safe place. Don't let anyone know you have it. Keep it secret until you know what to do."

For years she had thought he was referring to the immediate moment when he had sent her through the window, running for her life. The night they came for him, John had sent her into the rain, pointing her in the direction of safety – Uncle Richard's house. She had fled with his secret, his unfinished work – his sin, he had called it.

His last words to his daughter were not expressions of love or fear for her; they were instructions. Her mission was to finish it, which she could only accomplish if she kept on running, kept to the shadows, and bury regret for the lives she had to take – just as he had taught her. She could not do the things that had to be done by sticking to the rules and norms and moral codes of other – what he had always called 'the road'.

"Are you going to follow the road or cover your ass?" he had asked her so many times – once when she was only fourteen and he had shot her in the head with a paintball gun. She thought she had had him.

"No fair!" she had yelled. "I had you. You yielded."

Then there was the time he took her to the movies – just the two of them, no Mom – and they had watched *Saving Private Ryan*.

At sixteen her father was her only hero, and she had hung on his every word.

"If you were Miller, what would you have done with Steamboat Willie?" she had asked.

"I would have killed him." He said it so simply, yet she wasn't shocked. Instead, she wanted to understand.

"Even if you didn't know he would come back in the end?"

"Yes."

"Even if you knew it wouldn't have made any difference to the outcome? Even if it was your destiny to die defending that bridge?"

"Yes." He had pulled her into his side as they walked back to the car. He kissed the side of her head, mussing her hair that was the exact color of his. "Listen, sweetheart, we're not like regular people. Miller was a regular guy thrown into an extraordinary situation. People like us can't follow their road, because it wasn't made for us."

It made perfect sense. It explained so much about herself ... the detachment from kids her own age, the failure to feel what was expected. She had stayed off the road for as long as she could remember.

As far as "keeping it safe," John had taught his daughter that the safest place was inside her head. God, did she ever learn that lesson! She had kept this thing secret for so long – kept so many secrets – that part was the most natural. And though she wished she could share her burden now that she knew why he had died and what she was going to do about it, he had also told her not to.

They were alone in this, but at least they had each other: Amy, Anne and now Rose.

SIX

Todd Birch was waiting for me when I re-emerged from my space, freshly showered and in control of my universe – well at least it seemed that way from the outside looking in. It was later than he would normally have dinner. I was happy to not have to sit across the table from him.

He was working on his computer in the dining room, dressed in a navy polo shirt and knee length shorts. His hair was wet and had been slicked back from his brow. Every now and then he would use his fingers to rake back the unruly locks that were determined to wreak havoc on my libido.

"Hey," he greeted me, his eyes running greedily over my body, stripping away the grey camisole that matched my lacy panties. "How are you feeling?"

Horny, needy, giddy… Seriously, I had to get over my husband!

"Good." I stuck my wet head in the refrigerator, taking more time than necessary to pull out a Presidente. There was an urban legend that claimed the beer company had quality control inspectors who went around the country, ensuring every bottle of beer was chilled to perfection.

"I didn't know how long you were going to be. Sorry, I already had dinner." He had an appetite for other things. I heard it in his voice; I could feel his eyes burning into my ass. "I made you a plate."

Food Magda had cooked. No thanks. The Snickers I'd had after my lunchtime run would have to hold me until morning when Todd would make pancakes and eggs. I would be running on fumes for my morning run, but there was no question about shirking. I needed it. Until then, I would have to rely on a cocktail of alcohol and the pills I had taken earlier to bring this shitty day to a close.

I straightened and turned to find a question in the way Todd was looking at me. Why wasn't he over here yanking my camisole down and fastening his hot, ravenous mouth to my suddenly aching breasts? Couldn't he see how badly I wanted him? Did he not care that my arousal was fading into frustration? There was no way he could have missed the defensiveness in my posture as I leaned against the kitchen counter and drank from the bottle with one arm across my chest.

"Did you have a good day at work today?" he asked, his eyes boring into me with a different kind of heat now. It didn't make a shred of difference to my body; heat was heat. The slow burn started in the region of my middle again, making me flush from the inside out. I hated the power he had over me, while he remained immune to my near naked form and intentions.

"Nobody died."

He ignored my cynicism, saying instead, "Richard called."

"He called you?"

The beer was cold and crisp and it went down easily, but it wasn't enough to the chill of resentment out of my question.

"He was just checking up... wanted to know how we're doing, and whether we're coming home for Thanksgiving."

My grip on the long neck bottle tightened. That Richard and Todd had a relationship was news to me. The rational part of me said this was normal, that it was a good sign that Richard had welcomed Todd into our fold. But the fact that Richard and I had not spoken to each other since I left Virginia over a month ago appealed to the suspicious part of me.

"What's wrong, Amy?" he asked.

I was stuck in his harem, a thousand miles away from where I needed to be. The highlight to my day was my lying around waiting for him to fuck me. The lowest point was learning of a possible alliance between Todd and Richard that I would have to prepare for. What could possibly be wrong?

I downed the rest of the beer and went in search of another. By the time I had the top off, Todd was there, where I had originally wanted him to be, imprisoning me with those piercing blue eyes, a sinewy arm around my waist, and firm fingers at my chin. He pressed himself so close I could feel the beginning of an erection against my pelvis.

I was so high strung he could have gotten me off with just his breath. But his dick was only mildly amused.

I felt trapped by my desire for him. He could disarm me and make me *want* to be cornered. I was so ashamed of what I had become I couldn't meet his gaze. And if truth be told, I would be completely lost if I did. So I picked a spot on the open collar of his shirt and focused on calming my breath. His scent – sunshine, cigar and man – was just as intoxicating as the rest of him.

"Are you high?" he asked.

"No." I lowered my eyes so he couldn't examine them any more. Todd knew that particular secret. I had never admitted to it, but he knew. He didn't like it, but he didn't judge. His books told him I did it whenever I felt overwhelmed. He wasn't satisfied, but he wasn't going to break in the door when he could pick the lock. He wasn't a complete stranger to me; I knew how his mind worked even if he could only guess at my mental processes.

He was always so full of questions, some voiced and others left hanging, if unspoken between us. I hated it. And that particular question was an extension of the one before. Something had to be wrong if I needed that type of help.

"Are you going to eat? Magda went through a lot of trouble making this for us." Sancocho was a slow cooked stew of meat, plantains, cassava, and corn. Magda cooked it with love and served it over rice. I was the farthest person from her mind as she worked.

"Even if that were true, isn't that what you pay her for?" I bit back, as annoyed with the interrogation as my body's betrayal where he was concerned.

"Do you want me to get someone else?"

I knew better than to answer that question, he had a list of things that could be wrong. He hoped to get to the bottom of my mood by the process of elimination.

"I'm tired. I'm going to bed."

He let me go without protest, and the insult stung. I finished my second beer and welcomed its effects that his absence now intensified. The warmth of arousal dissipated and I grew numb. I was myself again.

It was the middle of the night when I felt him slip between the sheets. I had been asleep for hours, but it wasn't enough to forget the ache of fulfillment denied. My body became instantly aware as he curled his front against my back. His hand on my hip burned me, his breath on the back of my neck reawaken the flames further south, his scent had my mouth watering. When would I ever get enough of him? When would this weakness end?

"Are you awake, baby?" His voice was thick with lust. It vibrated through me, setting off little avalanches as the icy fortress that should have protected me came crumbling down. Todd Birch was the flame that heated my molten core.

His lips touched the sensitive skin between my jaw and shoulder. I couldn't stop the shiver that coursed through me. I didn't want to. I needed more – so much more to wipe my slate clean, to cure the festering wound that was Santo Domingo.

"Don't touch me like that," I whispered, forcing the words past my clogged throat.

He had already slipped off my panties. Now his hand that brushed my hip in feathery strokes stilled, and then the blunt fingers bit hard into my flesh. His breath hitched and then picked up with urgency. His lips at my throat parted for his teeth. He marked me.

"How do you want me to touch you, Amy?"

"Punish me." As if he hadn't been doing just that for months now. As if being in this place and in love with him wasn't torture...

"Why?" his stubbly cheek abraded the skin as he forged a trail to my shoulder. He bit down hard then soothed the ache with a swipe of his tongue.

So it matches.

"Because I need it."

"Aren't I enough?"

The truth was, Todd Birch was too much of what I did not need.

"You knew I was broken. You know what I need."

He stopped everything. I squeezed my eyes shut as he pushed himself up on an elbow and flipped me on my back. He blocked out the light and air, leaving us both gasping in the suffocating darkness.

"I've changed for you, Amy. Why can't you try for me?"

But I knew what he meant was: *I had filled the emptiness Mona had left behind; I had healed him. Why couldn't he be my everything?*

But I *had* changed for him. I had never been this weak for anyone before. But he wouldn't know that. He didn't know what I was like without him. And I could never tell him. He already had so much over me.

"Have you?" I asked instead, because the last thing I wanted was for him to *get* me, so much of me.

"What the fuck is that supposed to mean?" His intensity was like a steady breeze fanning a wild fire. This was what I needed! That fist that was balled against the urge to hurt me was what I needed – only much less restrained. I wanted his hands on me, squeezing the gaping void until it was a speck I could ignore for a while longer.

"Is this about the poker night?"

So it seemed he had not accepted my indifference after all. Maybe that was Todd Birch's power over women. He understood that 'nothing' meant 'something'; that 'do whatever you want' was not permission – it was a challenge; that 'I'm fine' was the earthquake that preceded a volcanic eruption.

Friday night poker was a tradition Todd and his friends used to have before he brought me here. Because I knew Todd and because I knew the men he played with, I knew poker game was only a prelude to a night of hard partying and even harder fucking. I also knew his friends had every intention of turning this poker night into the bachelor party Todd had not had.

"I promised you no strippers, no women, no sex. It'll be just be me and the guys." And because the mask of indifference was still firmly in place, he added, "You're it for me, baby."

What was I expecting … a declaration of love? Todd Birch had the uncanny ability to lift me up and leave me crashing down, both in the blink of an eye. But still, my body burned for him.

"Tell me what you want. I'll show you."

"I want you to punish me."

Anger never felt so good. I hated my weakness for him like he hated enjoying the things I did to me. He turned me away from him, because he couldn't bear to look at me, seeing me luxuriate in his violence and lack of control. He wrapped my hair around one fist and hooked my knee over his arm, then rammed into me from behind. I wasn't nearly as ready as he required and his violent entry burned my core. Each thrust was like a fist pounding into me, feeding the blooming ache into a raging inferno that flooded our bodies and consumed us both.

I cried out my pleasure and frustration: "Please, more!"

He hated me in that moment. There was nothing good or pure about his assault, except it was good for me... it was purely satisfying to me. He pulled harder on my hair, snapping my head back and ripping more than a few strands from the roots. The pain brought tears to my eyes and a shiver to my limbs. I soared higher as his rough breath gusted over my prickling skin. The sound of our bodies slapping against each other, the slick of sweat coating our bodies in each other's scent, his fingers tugging and pinching my aching nipples came together like a beautiful symphony that lifted me higher still.

His grunts, the gravelly rasp of his voice as he cursed and called out my name convinced me I wasn't alone.

"I'm close," he croaked, digging harder and deeper until I felt the heavy beat thudding inside the pits of me.

But it wasn't quite enough. He was holding back, trying to keep that part of him I needed all to himself. I had given so much, and this time I would not be denied. I grabbed the headboard, using it as an anchor to keep me firmly rooted when Todd would have washed me away.

"Come on, Amy," he coaxed, as if the thrust of his hips, the hardness between my thighs wasn't convincing enough.

"No," I gasped, fighting hard to deny the scraps of pleasure he threw my way. "Give me what I need."

"Dammit, Amy, no!"

But he didn't pull away. He didn't stop. He was as hooked as I.

Instead, he wrapped those long, blunt fingers around my throat and squeezed. At first it was just uncomfortable, a tightness that tickled and made me want to cough, the pinch of the wedding band that only heightened his allure. But even though he hated this, he knew what I needed. He pressed his hand higher to the place just below my pulse, and as he slowly cut off my breath, my body succumbed to the flames. Beyond a near painful arch of my back, I lost control over my limbs. I knew what happened by feel alone.

A tremor shook me, pulling the life from his loins, and Todd struggled to keep on hating this. "Yes, fuck, yes," he groaned, grinding into me, seeking the source of that quiver.

I tightened my grip on the headboard at the sound of such a primal sound emanating from such a sophisticated man. I would have gasped, but the air had no place to go beyond my gaping mouth.

Without conscious effort, Todd's hold on my throat had tightened and I felt the edges of the blackness expanding. Over and over, faster and deeper than should have been possible, he plunged into me. His fingers squeezed until the black swallowed me, and all I felt was never-ending pleasure. My hold on the wood slipped. I lost the use of my muscles. My mind was at last silenced. Renewed… that was what I felt.

But Todd never stopped and I fell even deeper in love with him for it.

SEVEN

It takes years of practice evading human contact, and a high degree of I-don't-give-a-fuck to avoid someone who shares your life – someone who was determined to have a we-need-to-talk moment – for a full day and a half. I had both by the bucketful. I went running before Todd work up, then locked myself in the bathroom once he was up and about. I grabbed breakfast on the go and spent the thirty-minute drive on the phone. I was using Jessica Byles, but I figured it was the least she owed me for flashing me every morning. If our sudden camaraderie bothered Todd, he didn't show it. He had more pressing concerns.

Todd hated what he had done to me. He didn't understand why I needed it, and he took it as a personal failing that he could not cure me of it. He had come to accept my love of rough sex, and truth be told, he liked pounding into me, trying to hit bottom and hollow me out. But like a foreign dish he wished to make his own, he had learned to adjust the ingredients to suit his own palate. Usually, the feather-light caresses, the sinuous stroke of his lips and tongue, the painfully slow and deep thrusts followed the violence and always succeeded in heightening my senses. Todd Birch was good at the things he did and I rarely had cause for complaint.

But every once in a while I needed more. Asphyxiation and pain filled a need that had been awakened in me many years ago; it was inextricably linked to my sexual awakening. Nothing could satisfy the need – not even Todd – and ignoring it was not an option for me. Without it, my impulses built until they became uncontrollable, and I would descend into dangerous, self-destructive patterns. Todd didn't need to know why I needed the things I demanded of him; he should have been satisfied that he was the one filling them... the only one I would turn to.

The first time I had shared that part of myself with him, I knew I could love him. On the second occasion, I told him I loved him – a first for me – but it was the truth. He used my need to get me to agree to marry him. And the fourth time, it was my reward for meeting him at the end of the aisle in my father's garden. Last night was only the fifth time, and he had gotten nothing out of it.

That probably irked him more than anything else – realizing I could withhold an orgasm until he gave me what I wanted. Todd took things like that very seriously; no way was he getting off and leaving his woman behind. I just prayed to whatever god was up there that he didn't call my bluff. Sexual frustration would send me in a tailspin, and I was certain I could crash and burn.

I didn't want to rehash Wednesday night. I didn't want to give him a do-over so he could test my limits. And I didn't want to *talk*. In the nearly four months since I had met him, I had done more talking than in the previous year of my life.

Todd was the most effective interrogator I had ever met, which was one of the first clues that he belonged to the intelligence community – not the State Department. As far as I was concerned, his success was a direct result of the seemingly endless reserve of rewards and punishments that he employed. Why give him more ammunition? Home was where I would have liked to drop the mask, but because of who my husband was, I was constantly on guard. It was exhausting.

And very aggravating, I concluded, as I fished a folder from under Byles' generous backside. She was perched on my desk again, but this time in a pair of jeans that had to have been painted on. She made up for covering her crotch by pairing the denim with a tank top with a deep V neckline that showed off an impressive pair of concrete tits. Her blue blazer was wide open and its contrasting suede collar and lapels only called attention to the hickeys and teeth marks that trailed from her neck to the tops of her breasts.

"I have the perfect idea for tonight," she declared, using her whore-red fingertips to comb her hair into a high ponytail. The only person who wasn't riveted was O'Brien.

"I just want to take it easy," I said, and by my bland tone and facial expression she could tell I was already having second thoughts.

It was Friday afternoon and Todd's bachelor party was planned for later that evening. He and I had agreed a week before that I would make myself scarce. Although Byles pretended Todd Birch did not exist and he reciprocated with an uncharacteristic coolness, she knew all the details of the proposed poker night. I wouldn't be surprised if she had slept with each of the attendees, two of whom had their eyes glued to her arched back and jutting chest.

She had offered to be my sidekick for the night, and at the time I had refused. She could be Samantha all she wanted, but not in anyone's wildest dreams was I a Carrie, Miranda or Charlotte. Life had conspired against me though. Since I was avoiding my husband and he was avoiding Byles, I had to reconsider my instinctive decision. Keeping her company was the surest way of keeping Todd away, so I swallowed humble pie and labored through a phone conversation with her while shoveling down Todd's pancake and eggs the morning after our trip to the dark side. I had kept her on the phone throughout the short drive to the embassy and it was with a frustrated sigh that Todd and I parted ways at work.

That was yesterday, and my patience with the woman was wearing thin. This clubbing escapade was looking more like the straw that broke the camel's back.

"That's cool too." Her eyes rolled back in her head, giving seven pairs of eyes an idea of what she looked like mid-orgasm.

I could have happily gone through life without that particular imagery.

"Here's an idea," she tried again. "What do you say to a spa trip then drinks at el Palacio del Son? I'm so sore. I need a massage before I can get into merengue tonight."

I didn't think reputable establishments offered massages for all her sore spots, but I didn't say anything. She would have laughed it off and agreed, and I was determined to avoid the subject of Byles' sex life at work. I just nodded and turned my attention back to the file in my hand, using the steam from my scalding coffee as an excuse for the pinch in my brow. Any comment would only delay her departure.

"A massage would do you some good too... help you to relax."

I mumbled a noncommittal response then burned my tongue with the coffee.

"Pick you up at six?" she offered.

"No, thanks. I'm booked at the Renaissance. They have a nice spa, I've been told."

"Perfect. I have a change of clothes in my car. We can head there directly."

Which thirty-five year old woman kept a change of clothes in her car? I kept that question to myself too, because she was finally leaving.

I spent the rest of the afternoon going over the training module for my sessions next week with Hernandez, the data intercept SPOC for the Departamente Nacional de Investigacion (DNI). Mitch and I had gone over the intrusion suite's capabilities. My directives covered only about forty percent of capacity, which was the extent of the knowledge base to be shared with Hernandez. I had spent most of the morning tweaking the training module, using layman terms as much as possible, spelling out acronyms and translating them into Spanish, on the off-chance that my student needed the extra help. I wasn't still alive because I relied on assumption and left the details to chance.

The more I looked at the material, the more certain I was the technology was compromised – from a local perspective, of course. Though it had not been spelled out for me, I knew there was a portal through which we could access the intrusion on the Dominican side. That would not have surprised me, but the fact that O'Brien seemed to be hiding it from me had my ears perking up. We were going to hack the DNI in order to intercept someone's data communications.

We had a reasonable cooperation relationship with local law enforcement. We had, in the past, requested access to assist in the tracking or apprehension of a criminal target. This new level of underhandedness raised the suspicion that either our target was political or protected by the Dominican Administration.

I was so affected by the potential for another high profile coup that I could have come right there at my desk. This was the perfect opportunity for me to unequivocally prove myself worthy of a Paris post. If only O'Brien would let his hair down and let me in on the secret. I was also relieved that there were indeed secrets within this Mission.

I was waiting all day for a lag in his schedule of conference calls and walk-ins to make my case. It wasn't until an hour before end of day that I spotted an opening. I wasn't the only one with matters to discuss with him however, because from the corner of my bloodshot eye, I spotted Stanley from the US Marshall's Office hefting his semi-truck frame out of his squeaky chair. With the sprightliness of a young gazelle, I sprinted for O'Brien's office, leaving Stanley huffing with effort. I shut the door behind me, and my Section Chief looked up with surprise, followed swiftly by wariness.

"Leave it open, Koehler," he said.

"This is a sensitive matter, sir," I replied, dragging his guest chair closer to his desk.

He hesitated for a moment before leaning back in his chair to compensate for my crowding him. Ted O'Brien pushed up his non-existent sleeves and pinned me with those dirty green eyes, trying to disconcert me.

"What can I do for you?"

"You can start by being straight up with me," I began in a tone that matched his neutral expression. Besides an arched brow, the man seemed entirely unconcerned with my sudden familiarity. "I know you don't want me here. I won't lose any sleep over it, because I don't want to be here either. But if you give me something to sink my teeth into – something of significance to the Priorities Framework – I can start working on my ticket out of here."

The National Intelligence Priorities Framework was uncle Richard's to-do list for the sixteen intelligence agencies under his command. It established the goals and targets for the intelligence community and had a mostly political focus. There was a reason he reported to the President, and nabbing small time blow pushers and the occasional terrorist financer wasn't it. I wanted more. I wanted to matter.

"What makes you think we've been given any such objective?"

"The fact that you're asking me that question."

I waited a few moments for that to sink in. If there was nothing going on, he would have just said so. I'd been raised by the best in the business. Playing devil's advocate was something we practiced at the dinner table. At least O'Brien knew better than to lie to me.

"This intrusion suite," I prompted, because it was never a good idea to leave your opponent too much time to think and try to be creative with their answers, "where's our portal?"

O'Brien sighed, but he didn't lie. "That's above your pay grade."

Well, he would just have to get me a raise, because I wasn't leaving this alone. It was the best thing that had happened since I landed this job a month ago.

"Who are we after?"

"I can't say."

I believed him. I tried not to show my excitement. Assignments above my Top Secret security clearance were rare and politically significant.

"You don't have anyone better for this," I reminded him.

He had set Scott as my backstop, but only because Scott was a robot. We both had military intelligence backgrounds, but he was much better at doing what he was told, never questioning an order, and as far as I knew, he hadn't killed any host country cops. I was nothing like Scott. I asked too many questions, improvised too much, and had killed as many people as Todd had notches on his bedpost.

"What makes you think that, Koehler?"

"You gave this assignment to me. You knew the risks of doing so, but you gave it to me anyway. I'm not psychic but I know you would have rather parted with a kidney than have me work this case, if you had a choice."

O'Brien gave nothing away.

"I'm wasting my time here," I continued, "and the longer you keep me around the more likely it is that things will start to fall apart. Let me be someone else's headache. I need this to get out of here."

I leaned back in the guest chair and allowed him some time to think it over. The chair was stiff and hard – barely suitable for anything more than a precarious perch on the edge. It was not intended for visitors to get comfortable, but I wasn't going anywhere until he made a down payment on my ticket out of here. Thankfully, he really wanted me out of his hair.

"Let me get it cleared," he conceded after a moment. I began to appreciate his decisiveness even more. "In the meantime, I want you to stick to the script. Show Hernandez what he needs to know. Play nice; make him want to work with you. Get some new skirts; Byles can show you where to shop. We're less formal around here."

I didn't blink, but glanced down at my feet where that bit of advice had landed and would likely stay. Jessica Byles acted like a bitch in heat because she knew the moment she returned to the United States she was just an average woman, only two Oreos away from being overweight. Here, she was a true blond and exotic, and she planned on living it up to the max.

"If you get cleared I'm going to be your backstop on this." The man leaned forward and lowered his voice to match our new proximity. His hard stare and kinetic energy sucked the air from the room. "That means you don't breathe, you don't think, you don't even take a shit without my OK, got that, Koehler?"

And just like that, Santo Domingo started looking up. I got up to leave and found the entire team peering over the fence. I wondered if O'Brien would relieve Scott of his duty or keep him chasing my shadow. It didn't matter. O'Brien and I shared a secret and I was the best at keeping those.

EIGHT

I was becoming something of a regular at The Renaissance's spa. An average of forty hours of high intensity physical activity per week had a heavy toll on my body. The longer I waited for word of my next assignment, the more I pushed my limits, and the more I needed every bit of help to ease my aching body.

I allowed Byles to choose her service first then went in the opposite direction. Our post-spa date took us on a tour of the city and nearly every bar in the Colonial Zone. Dominicans came out to party when night fell in San Francisco, so it took us a few hours to find a pulse. The alcohol we consumed had a deleterious effect on the detoxification we'd done only hours before, and as the night wore on, the drinks went down with less thought to our skin or livers.

Todd didn't call, which had everything to do with Byles. He knew we were together, but was consistent in wanting to remain as far away from her as possible. The lack of contact should have helped me not to think about him. I told myself I didn't care what he had done with her, or what he could be doing at that very moment with the evening's entertainment. But there was no bullshitting a bullshitter.

Our last stop before returning to my hotel was Praia. Byles coaxed me in with promises of food and one last drink, but I suspected she wanted to go clubbing. She should have questioned the ease with which she talked me into a spot where there were more nineteen year olds than people our age. It helped that she was too intent on having a good time and showing me how much fun she could be.

Impressed did not cover what I felt as I eased onto a seat by the bar and watched her fill her quota of male attention. Before long, she found herself sandwiched between two Dominicans who already had it in mind that they were getting lucky at the end of the night. They were in for some serious disappointment though, because I had plans for Byles that precluded witnesses.

I ordered her another drink, Tanqueray and tonic. It was a change from the Brugal Añejo and Pepsi she'd been guzzling all night, but it was perfect for cloaking the bitterness of the capsule I mixed in. I didn't have to wait long for her to come find me; she'd spent the whole night checking in, making sure I witnessed how badly and how many men wanted her.

She was a CSI tech's dream. Her red halter-top stuck to her skin, helped along by the sweat from her dance partners. Her lipstick was smeared across one cheek, down her neck and as far as her deltoid – secondary transfer when one of her bump-and-grind partners ran his lips over her mouth, across her shoulders and down her back. Her sweat and breathlessness had alcoholic fumes wafting my way. I smiled and handed her the spiked drink, tamping down the disgust I felt at the thought of Todd diving into her muddy waters.

"What's this?" she asked, already giving the drink an experimental sip.

"Gin and tonic." I raised my glass to the bartender then took a sip. "Seems you made quite the impression with the staff." It was just the thing that would have her downing it in seconds flat.

Her hungry eyes sought out the twenty-something part-time student, one hundred percent Casanova, with the tenacity of a bloodhound. He leered at the promise neither of them realized she would not be keeping. I let her dance for a while longer, but at the fifteen-minute mark, I had to extricate her from a guy with eight arms, one of which was stuck inside her waistband. He snarled at me when I told him to "Back the fuck up."

She wasn't a small girl by anyone's standards, and after supporting the bulk of her weight during our exit, I had to sit her down on the steps until I could bring her car around from the parking lot. Alcohol was contraindicated for the seccies I'd slipped her, because it intensified the effects and could lead to overdose.

For the benefit of the curious onlookers who might want to give an account of our activities, I forced her to sip from a bottle of water while I checked her pupils. They were dilated; her respiration was slower than normal, but not dangerously so. In the event of accidental death, I had to come off as the concerned party left caring for a raving drunk. For someone who worked for the FBI, Byles should have known better than to let her guard down in a foreign country... and especially around me, in light of her history with my husband.

"I'm on Avenida Belice." Why wasn't I surprised she lived five minutes from us? Now there was a very real possibility she had slept in the bed I now shared with him.

"You're spending the night with me. I don't want you alone in your condition," I said as the valet attendant helped me load her into the passenger seat. I didn't bother buckling her in; we were ten minutes from my hotel and if she bashed her face on the dashboard, well, the damage couldn't have left her worse off.

"That's irony for you," she muttered once we were on our way. She was nestling into the headrest, her eyes squeezed tight, probably blaming her bout of dizziness on the alcohol. After tonight, she'd probably swear off Tanqueray, claiming it crept up on her.

"What?"

"Spending the night with you when it's your husband I'm dreaming of."

Just because I was aware didn't make me impervious to the effect of her barbiturate-induced candor. My father used to tell me pain didn't kill, that it was weakness leaving the body, but he'd never had a moment like this.

I wished I could have shed Todd and the feelings he aroused in me with one of the deep, cathartic breaths my father swore could cure everything from shock to a heart attack.

"Were you two serious?" If she weren't high on my unsophisticated truth serum cocktail, she would have heard the edge to my voice.

"I was serious." She laughed harshly, pushing wet tendrils of dirty blond hair off her face. "I should have known better, but you know what he's like. When he turns those eyes on me, I forget my own fucking name."

I pulled up to the valet outside my hotel, stepping too firmly on the brakes. Still it wasn't enough to send her flying through the windshield... more's the pity. A bellboy helped me haul her up to my room, and then I had to suffer through her drunken strip tease.

Once she was done trying to get a reaction out of me, she plopped down on one of two queen beds, ready to bare her soul in nothing but a G-string. I wanted to be as far from her as possible, but instead, pulled the desk chair close. She and I needed to have a heart-to-heart. We were so close our knees almost touched, but it still wasn't close enough for her to feel the chill of my mounting anger.

"Tell me about you and Todd," I began, softening my voice so she could keep the illusion of our having a warm and fuzzy chat. She wouldn't remember any of this come daylight, but it wouldn't hurt for her to feel comfortable confiding in me. Or for me to exercise some control over my wayward emotions.

"Who the hell knows Todd Birch?" Her laugh was gone, but the bitterness was still there. "He was engaged when he got here, but that meant nothing, even though he talked about her all the time. I think that was his way of letting me know it wasn't serious. But Jesus, that man fucked me like I was the last woman on earth – the only woman for him. I forgot all about her!"

I tried not to think about Todd pounding into her. I wanted to close my eyes against the image of his hands and mouth on her titanium tits. But the images were inside my head, behind my eyes, flashing across my brain.

Something broke inside me and I hated it. I had made him special, and yet the things he had done to her, he had also done to me – possibly on the same sheets. It hurt that in his mind we were interchangeable – one warm body was as good as the next; yet he had spoiled me for any other man. I hated that Todd Birch had such power over me.

"How long did it last?" I asked. It was flagellation to which I willingly submitted. I wanted to draw blood and leave scars that could be traced in the dark. I never wanted to forget this feeling, the risk of giving too much to another persosn.

"You assume we're over."

Byles looked at me with a secret smile, but she couldn't have seen me, or she would have been afraid. She went on as unaffected as if discussing the weather. I had the seccies to blame – or thank – for that. In the full throes of the drug, she had no filter, so guile.

"Do you think you have a monopoly on him? You're just new, that's all! Yeah, it shocked the heck out of me that he married you." She shrugged, but I didn't mistake such a casual gesture for contrition. "Well, not just you, so don't take it personally. It just seemed like he wouldn't marry anyone after whatever-the-fuck-her-name-was."

Mona. Her name was Mona, and Todd had claimed to love her. He pretended to have been devastated when she 'accidentally' drowned in the bathtub in her D.C apartment after ingesting a lethal dose of alprazolam. She was pregnant at the time, but the baby wasn't his – a fact Todd claimed not to know until after her death.

Another version of the tale, as told by US Marines Corps Colonel Robert Townsend, the real father of Mona's unborn child – a married man with a family of his own, no less – claimed Todd had killed her when he learned she was having an affair with his archrival.

"When was the last time you two were together?"

"We've been on and off for a year and a half now."

"When was the last time you were off?" I pressed, losing patience with her poor attempt at equivocation. Either she wanted this to be as painful as possible or she genuinely thought she and Todd weren't finished.

"The last time we fucked was in May, but I did suck him off in June." She paused for a second and I was afraid the details would drown me. "I could smell some other woman's snatch on him, but when he looked at me with those eyes, it was like I was hypnotized. I didn't care that he had to schedule us two per afternoon. It was like he was doing me a favor and I would beg, steal and kill to get that close to him. You know what it's like, don't you?"

No, I didn't know what that was like. Two minutes after I had pulled my pants up, I was running away from him. He had been chasing me ever since, oblivious to the fact that I was deeply in love with him. I was good at hiding emotion. If this week had taught me anything, it was that I should keep running. Perhaps that was why he wanted me so. I was far from immune to the effects Byles had described – his hypnotic appeal –

but I was probably the only one who had resisted him. I had fallen for my husband and he didn't even know it. I had told him, but words held little importance to those whose career was deception.

"So what makes you think he's not done with you?" I asked.

"We've been done before," she shrugged. "It was more of a break. And no offence, but I never pictured you as his type." Byles tilted her head sideways as she peered narrow-eyed at me, as if her drunkenness had made her near-sighted. "He likes his women hot and eager, and you... you've got to be the coldest fuck anyone's ever had."

I could see true fatigue setting in. It was a struggle for her to remain upright as she swayed back and forth and to the sides. But I had one more question for her.

"It can't be easy for you, being confronted day in, day out with the fact that I have something you want. Why the pretense?"

"Because Todd asked me to keep quiet."

"And you would do anything for him." It wasn't a question. It wasn't even a statement that required confirmation.

"I love him," she said, sending frissons up my arms and down my spine.

"Why go through all the trouble of pretending he doesn't exist?" That was what had convinced me in the first place that there was something between them. I had thought it was behind them. I was a fool.

"Todd said we had to cool it. He said you have an in with DNI, and he doesn't want to fuck it up." She looked at me assessingly, as if there was something she wanted to ask of me, but she was so intoxicated, she couldn't quite get a hold of it. "It must be big if it's worth the frost bite."

I couldn't help myself and she was so far-gone, she never even saw it coming. I clocked her in the face, not hard enough to break anything, but sound enough for a black eye. I gave myself bonus points for knocking her out cold.

I swallowed two Xanax to help with the throb in the back of my skull. I thought I was playing everyone, but it was Todd who had me in check. I had played right into his hands, given him my heart and Uncle Richard. It was humbling to know that he'd only ever wanted the latter.

It was a long time before the cool fingers of calm began to spread, dulling the edges of my humiliation until it blurred. It was like grains of sand at the edge of the beach being washed away with each pass of the surf.

I let go.

NINE

In spite of a sleepless night Anne was the epitome of serenity. It was a complete one-eighty from where Amy had been hours ago. Anne had a three-hour run to thank for that as she breezed through the front door before dawn. She was happy to report that things were under control once again.

Jessica Byles had made a valid point. Todd Birch was afraid of her... afraid of shaking the volatile cocktail that was Amy Koehler. It explained why he was so careful, walking on eggshells around her issues, going to great lengths to prove his past was behind him. That at least proved he didn't quite have game point. Getting back on track meant looking at Todd and their relationship from a logical perspective. Believing she was the prize simply because Todd had said so was a fantasy she could no longer indulge.

That her husband had married her for ulterior motives should not have come as a surprise. In fact, Amy had pursued him for what she could accomplish with him at her side. Of course, she maintained she hadn't lied about her feelings; she really did love Todd Birch.

Well, he never lied about his feelings either. He's never claimed to love you.

There should have been no expectations. Anne kept that in mind as she made her way into the entry hall.

There was evidence of a party, but not the frat house excess that was expected. Some of the furniture was slightly askew, but effort had gone into setting the house to rights. The cleaning closet door was slightly ajar. The floor was sticky in some spots, so her sneakers squeaked where drinks had been spilled and hastily mopped away. There were two trash bags leaning precariously against the kitchen cupboards, waiting for daylight to be taken out. The counters were spotless with an undertone of lemon multipurpose cleaner, which clashed with the faint strains of cigar smoke. The dishwasher had recently completed a cycle; it was still full and warm to the touch. So was the dryer. Todd could not have been asleep for much more than an hour. Magda wouldn't have to stay a minute after 3p.m. on Monday, unless of course, she wanted to.

Anne made her way to her room. It was dark inside, which was how she liked it. But even with the curtains drawn and the pale light of dawn still hours away, Anne knew something was very wrong. Her sacred place felt different, and its smell was foreign.

Though she remained rooted to the spot, her heart began to pound short, heavy beats. If she didn't start taking deep breaths now, she would begin to feel lightheaded in a second. Her calm dissipated with each drumbeat, and squeezing her key – the only key, Todd had claimed – into her palm until it nearly broke the skin was no help. The sharp bite of the short metal could not conceal the ache of her dying calm.

Call it human weakness. Her eyes wanted to see what her mind already knew though her heart wished to deny. Her space smelled of sex. There beneath the comfort of fresh cotton sheets and the faint aroma of the rosemary she used to cleanse her temple, was the smell of sweat, the false fruitiness of strawberry-flavored alcohol, latex and cum. Anne's nostrils flared under the bite; her clenched fists buzzed as the numbness spread through her body with the silent insidiousness of poison injected into her veins.

Todd Birch had become her problem too, and there was nothing Amy could do to save him.

In the tug of war between logic and rage, there was no distinct winner. There was only a synthetic calm that blanketed thought and emotion like paint on a wall, applied so thick it seeped into the cracks and evened out the bumps. This was not what John Koehler had had in mind when he taught her the finer points of emotional detachment. For now, it would have to do.

Anne flipped the lights so she could see her sheets had been changed. He had never meant for her to learn of this betrayal. That was the reason for the dryer being run. White sheets were white sheets to a man. Todd would not have known the difference between a basic plain weave and percale woven cotton sheets. These were not Anne's workday sheets. During the week, Amy's insecurities arising from her proximity to Todd's harem often left her bathed in cold sweat and the tighter weave helped to wick away the excess moisture.

Todd either hadn't had the time to check the bathroom or didn't realize girls always smoothed their hair after sex. There were loose strands of white blond hair halfway down the drain. The smell of that strawberry body splash was also sharper here. She had freshened up here, and in her effort to cover up what they had done, she had undermined Todd Birch's efforts to do the same.

There were drops of water dotting the sink and vanity, an empty trash bag when there should have been the shavings of an eyebrow pencil left two days ago. The hand towel was crumpled where someone had dried their hands and God knows what else. Todd had done a good job of cleaning up after himself, but even with all his books on human psychology and his excellent interrogation skills, he had no idea how good Anne was at hiding.

"You cannot wipe away your presence if you don't know what was there before," John had said while they played in the woods behind their house. Today, Todd Birch would receive a lesson he would never forget.

Anne's sneakers squeaked on the sticky floor as she made her way back to the kitchen. Not taking out the trash had saved her from having had to crawl through three days of refuse. Amidst bits of used paper towels and napkins, cigarette and cigar butts, ashes, and the general mush of discarded food were three tissue-wrapped condoms and a business card.

There was no name for the establishment that could have been either a strip club or brothel. Against a black, glossy background was the white silhouette of a woman in stilettos bent at the waist, legs spread, knees locked, back arched, and hair in sexy disarray. There was a phone number to request appointments, a name written in pen – Angel – and a client number – 186.

Anne pocketed the card, left the condoms on the floor, and grabbed a bottle of Añejo from Todd's liquor cabinet. It took a moment to douse the bed with its plain weave sheets and the rumpled towel from the bathroom with the alcohol. The sweet aroma of ethanol and sugar blanketed the twang of artificial strawberries. But it couldn't wash away the image of bodies rolling across her bed, smearing her sheets with fluids, tainting the air with their cries, grunts and sighs.

Had she been his gift? A warm farewell to bachelorhood. Had the others watched, or did they join in? Three rounds seemed too much with a prostitute. But with so many spectators, he might have had a lot to prove. They admired him for a reason.

No, not Todd. He led while others followed. He was charming and magnanimous. He would have shared.

Whether he had fucked her or not was Amy's concern. But he had brought them into this place, and he had lied about the only condition that had made cohabitation possible. How many times had he been there before? How many times had he rifled through her belongings, prying into the darkest reaches of her mind, invading her sanctuary with his lies?

Anne quickly stuffed a week's worth of personal effects into the biggest duffel bag she could find. Thursday's skirt was either in Amy's closet or laundry; she would have to improvise. Her MacBook, monitoring gear and makeup kit went on top. Once done, she dragged the bag to Byles' car then returned to the house, ready to see her decision through.

The search for the matches Todd used to light his cigars when his zippo wasn't readily at hand came up empty. The commotion she was certain she had made rifling through drawers barely seeped into Todd's consciousness, making only a small dent in the exhaustion of a night of hard cleaning preceded by harder partying. From the foot of Amy's bed, Anne watched him stir from his too-brief-to-be-truly-restful sleep.

Amy could fight until lions became lambs, Anne would never stop wanting Todd Birch. The sight of him, naked and rumpled; smelling like the ocean and sun; glowing from within as if he had his personal sun inside was a powerful aphrodisiac. He was a beautiful man, even unshaved and so far from the urbane shell he turned out to the world. Even knowing what he had done was not enough to dispel the cloud of attraction that threatened to compromise her judgment.

It was dark in the bedroom. He didn't belong there in the shadows. Anne switched on the ceiling lights, pleased when he flinched, covering his eyes with his forearm. She spotted his zippo sitting on the bedside table before he had blinked away the cobwebs. Then she had it in hand before he could sit up in bed.

She was gone before the sight of his bare chest, narrow hips, and the expanse of hard, ridged flesh in between had its usual effect of flooding her with moist heat. There was no room for anything but the void.

"Amy?" she heard him call, wariness yielding to trepidation, ending in a muttered, "Shit!"

A tense silence followed, broken abruptly by the scrape of the flint wheel and the flicker of a blue flame sucking the air from her room. He liked light; he could have it all Like a magnet, the sound dragged Todd from the temporary paralysis that had prevented him from closing the gap between them. The fire lapped greedily at the rum-soaked bed as Todd's naked feet came slapping across the floor.

Anne would have liked nothing better than to watch it burn. Only fire could cleanse the taint away, and seal the wound of his betrayal. Time would do the rest... cover the ragged edges with a thick, new layer of skin, until there was nothing left to prove he had ever been there. But today it was still fresh, and if she stayed, the fires would consume them all, burning away what was left of reason.

TEN

There was darkness inside me that Todd had filled with light. I had forgotten how cold and stark it could be without him. The colors he had brought into my world were suddenly stripped away, and I was no longer satisfied with what had been there before. There was an ache inside me that was entirely foreign. I survived the following week by smothering that hunger with anger and there was enough of that to go around.

As much as I hated the angst of being with him in this place where I was constantly confronted by the man he was, I also missed the pleasure the mere sight of him could evoke. Todd Birch was my drug and I was withdrawn without him.

I convinced myself that his infidelity was the least of my concerns. I would have been a fool to hold him to such expectations because of who we were. We used our bodies to do our job when needed, and it helped to divorce the heart from the flesh. So how could I reasonably attach my heart to Todd's body? My disappointment in that regard was my own fault. My broken heart was well deserved.

But the violation of my privacy was another matter. Long before we married, we had negotiated the terms of our relationship. Home was our haven from work. It was the only place I had a reasonable expectation of privacy. A space for myself, a refuge into which I could retreat when the pressures of my life became too much, that was my only demand. Todd had agreed to my special needs. He made a place for me in his home, and promised that it would be mine alone.

It was a lie. The betrayal of that trust had effectively dashed the foundation on which we were building our lives together. The other lies – the reason he wanted me, his past being just that, that he was mine alone – were only aftershocks that ripped apart what was left. After that, the decision to wipe him out of my life practically made itself.

The first order of business was to return to the hotel and collect my belongings while Byles slept off the seccies. I ditched Byles' car and dismantled my Government-issued Blackberry, effectively going dark. With no cell signal or GPS to trace, finding me in a city of 2.9 Million people was easier said than done.

The hotel would be the first place Todd would look for me, but Jessica was the last person he would expect to find there. Would he blame her for my defection? He had tasked her with keeping me occupied while he fucked a prostitute in our home. She had failed at that, which would reflect poorly on her performance during our night out. Would he guess what had been disclosed? Would he assume Byles had tired of waiting patiently in the wings for him, and had sent me racing home to him? The thought of Todd discussing me with that woman burned the pit of my stomach like battery acid. But with the belt of my resolve girded, I was able to push even that away.

I took an unlicensed taxi to Avis and got a rental car in Anne's name. My next stop was the nearest realtor's office. The embassy pre-authorized housing for American personnel after lengthy security and background checks. Following procedures, it could have taken me months to find an apartment. In light of my homelessness, not to mention being on the run from my husband, that was not an option for me. And unless Todd announced our split, no one needed to know I had an unauthorized residence.

By noon I had viewed two short-term rentals and signed a three-month rental agreement in Anne's name for a two-bedroom apartment in a high-rise in Naco. It was only fifteen minutes from work, and was run by a management company that specialized in short-term rentals. I paid the full lease term plus the deposit in cash for the convenience of moving in right away and having immediate access to utilities and Internet. I picked up a new phone on the way from the mall where I'd spent an hour outfitting my new place with essentials like food, wine, sheets, and a Thursday skirt.

I compensated for the lack of embassy due diligence by wiring each room with my own monitoring equipment. The result was unsophisticated – IP-routed spy cams wired to motion detectors and re-routed to my work Blackberry. I prayed the Marines in Communications weren't watching as I tested the set up from across town in Los Mameyes. I wasn't so delusional to think I would be able to avoid Todd for more than a week. Even if we were separated by steel-reinforced doors and several buildings, we still worked on the same compound. Once he came to terms with our new situation, I would be able to monitor my residence twenty-four hours from my work phone.

After a marathon Saturday, I holed up in my hideout and prepared for my training session that started on Monday. That was one thing I could look forward to. Working from the Palacio Nacional where the Departamente Nacional de Investigacion was headquartered spared me the ordeal of going into office on Monday morning. I still had to touch bases with O'Brien so he didn't think I had gone AWOL, but work had effectively bought me four more days on the run. Water damage covered my use of an unapproved mobile device, but emails and sensitive material were not authorized for use on my local pre-paid line.

I didn't like that I was going dark from 5p.m. when I left my training site to 9a.m. when I returned for my sessions with Hernandez. But I needed the time to get back into a pre-Todd state of mind, to recall the orderliness and absolute mundaneness of my life half a year ago. That meant focusing on work, while Anne made finding a way to Sergei Afanasenko her priority.

To that end, I was tempted to push O'Brien on securing my clearance for the secret target assignment. It was early days yet, and I knew his excuse would be a curt, "It's Monday." As if he had more pressing matters to attend to… as if intelligence kept regular hours…

"I'll call you as soon as we've agreed on a case study," I told him before heading inside to meet Hernandez.

I only ever called O'Brien from the parking lot adjacent to Avenida Mexico; it was busy with two-way traffic – motorist, pedestrian and cellular – so my communications were secure. After that the device was powered off until end of day when I checked my messages in the same spot. My general location was public knowledge; Byles could easily give Todd that information. But he couldn't come looking for me. Todd would not call attention to himself and risk compromising the true reason for his presence in country by staking out the headquarters of the intelligence police. I was safe here.

I discovered a message from Todd on Tuesday morning. He had to have traced my call to O'Brien. It had to have been an unauthorized trace, because Todd would not have advertised to the entire embassy – especially not my Section Chief – that I had left him.

I deleted the message and got a new phone that afternoon. I didn't want him behind my defenses again. I prided myself on being able to spot a lie from a mile away, but I'd been deceived by the man sleeping in the bed next to me. What could he say to undo that?

In my dreams I heard his voice, halfway between fearful concern and anger, explaining everything away. I wanted him to miss me, which told me I was nowhere near where I needed to be. I threw myself into the training, so I didn't have to feel. I would not be satisfied until he mattered as much to me as any other nameless, faceless creature.

But he would not go away. He found me time and again, leaving messages I never opened.

Because I wasn't with Todd, I found myself with too much free time. Boredom was a terrible thing for someone like me. I actively searched for ways to fill the void.

Hernandez was a forty-year-old devoted father and husband who had joined the police force the day after his eighteenth birthday. He had married his high school sweetheart six months later and had five children with her – all girls. If I had taken O'Brien's advice to slut up my wardrobe, I would have embarrassed both myself and my student.

We worked together well from the outset, and I found him to be a rare, honest man. He did his job almost apologetically, and contradictorily, uncompromisingly. That made him very suitable for the post of Chief Snooper. He trampled all over the public's ill-conceived notions of privacy being a right, but unless the target ran afoul of the law, their secrets were secure. His colleagues called him 'Priest', which was only slightly off the mark. He waded through confessions, but left absolution and retribution to the courts; He focused instead on getting the best leads and preparing evidence-based cases for prosecution.

As was usually the case with men like Hernandez, their quiet honesty made them vulnerable to people like me who had voids to fill. Our work aside, my interest in Hernandez' frankness was purely personal. From the moment I met him, I thought of ways to use him to help realize my private goals.

"Tomorrow we'll go through the different methods of intrusion in depth," I announced. "We'll see how the technology interfaces with the different security protocols and firewalls."

We had spent the day on theory: Why does law enforcement require the ability to access citizens' and corporations virtual networks without agreement from the service providers? What legal framework applies to intrusion, especially when the target is transnational and one country's laws are more prohibitive than another's? How can intrusion-based evidence be developed and presented in a court of law without compromising law enforcement capabilities? How should intrusion-based evidence be presented? How to limit Government's liability while minimizing complaints from the large multilateral corporations that provide secure network services for their clients?

Our discussion did not veer into a debate on the morality. Even if the man was honest, he was also practical. He had a job to do and he was given a tool. He would leave the lawyers and politicians to debate legality and morality.

"I am just a policeman," he said, his English coming easier the longer we talked. "Nobody voted for me."

It was a simplistic but effective approach of shedding responsibility. As I watched him shrug, I found myself craving his naïveté. I was counting on his uncomplicated view of life – not to mention his obsessive protectiveness of his daughters – to see my plans realized.

"Start thinking about case studies," I told him. "Your English is perfect and you're picking up really fast, so if we get through tomorrow's outline early, I see no reason why we can't move on to the practical application." It was the perfect formula of praise and incentive to pique his curiosity.

"There is not one chosen?" he asked, flipping through his copy of the manual.

I could have asked if he was in the habit of letting foreign governments set his priorities. I was also curious whether he often committed to paper, weeks in advance, a target he planned on intercepting. Instead, I settled for the less condescending, less confrontational approach, putting to use the innate sensitivity training required to con a mark.

"Ernesto, you have complete ownership over this technology. You decide where and how to use it. Our stake is in our ongoing law enforcement cooperation." I smiled, marveling at the ease with which the crap rolled off my tongue. I focused my attention on collecting my personal belongings, giving the impression of casual conversation as I continued. No good could come of his awareness of my prevarication. "So no, there are no pre-selected case studies. You identify a target and I'll show you what this baby can do."

All Monday night I thought of ways of getting to Angel. That helped to keep my mind off Todd like a sieve takes the brown out of muddy water. I couldn't stop wondering how he had gotten her, what they had done together, or how many times.

I had dialed the number, but encountered the first roadblock almost immediately. There was an automated system that required credit card information to proceed.

Burning off the frustration wasn't easy either. My old running routes were on the other side of the city and too close to Todd and Byles for comfort. My building had a pool – a rarity in Santo Domingo – but the idea of sharing with the other residents disgusted me.

There were eighteen floors in Torré Gabriella with six apartments each. As was the case with some of the major private construction projects in the city, mine was a front for a money laundering operation. So it was of little consequence to the developers that there was less than forty percent occupancy. In the best-case scenario, I would be sharing bath water with fifty people. If even one of them was under thirty, then they had likely had sex there.

But in the end, I swallowed my distaste, spending an hour and a half on laps until I was chilled to the bone. Dinner was a bag of chips and a bottle of red wine. I thought I missed Todd then, but his absence was more pronounced in the morning when I realized I'd forgotten milk. If he hadn't fucked things up I could have been having pancakes with fresh fruit, whipped cream and syrup. Instead, I had to settle for dry cereal from the box. I double-checked the surveillance system I had rigged as I ate to get my mind off the injustice.

I picked up two steaming cups of coffee from la Dolcerie on my way to work. It was out of the way from Hernandez' office, but the coffee was exceptional. He was partial to cappuccinos and I needed a prop for the coming act. So while he breathed in his milk-laced beverage, I visibly puzzled over Angelika's calling card.

"Ernesto," I started tentatively, flipping the card over my thumb in a feigned nervous gesture. "How old do you have to be to dance here?"

"Dominicans are born dancing," he grinned, already in a caffeine-induced good mood.

I smiled too, but held up the card so he could see the silhouette with its arched back and dangling tits.

"Where did you get that? Don't tell me you're thinking of a change in career?" He tried to joke, but a shadow crossed his features. He did not approve. I knew he wouldn't. A man with five daughters, who had married his high school sweetheart, and whose mother still lived with him wouldn't think of naked women gyrating on a stage as entertainment.

I smirked at him, pretending I didn't see that shadow. "Not quite."

I leaned my hip against his desk and handed him the card. I gave him the time to flip the card over, examining front and back. Average strippers didn't have business cards. That alone told him this operation was larger, more organized and sophisticated than most. The absence of a name for the establishment was another red flag. What reputable business offered cards with no name or address? That was smoke, and I was about to light the fire under him.

"I came across a woman and this kid at the coffee shop this morning. I think the kid was looking for a job or the woman was trying to recruit her. I don't know the whole story. I passed their table and overheard what I thought was a job offer." I checked his level of interest over my coffee cup. He was hooked, so I continued. "I found it strange because the kid didn't look a day over fifteen and she was wearing a uniform – blue skirt, white shirt, like one of those Catholic schools."

I paused again to take another sip and Hernandez nodded, his coffee forgotten for the moment as he silently prompted me to keep the train rolling.

"Well, the woman – she wasn't much older herself, maybe twenty, twenty-two – gave the kid this card and told her to call her if she changed her mind. Anyway, the kid left the card, so I took it and left. What do you think?"

His eyebrows had hiked up then slowly crashed low over his deep-set eyes as my story progressed.

"Oh, I think they're traffickers. They are always looking for young girls. They promise jobs, move them far from home, then their families never hear from them again. They start off dancing then force them into prostitution." He wasn't telling me anything new; I knew the song and dance.

I shrugged, drank more coffee, and retrieved the card. "Well good thing this kid was smart. She practically ran the other way."

He snatched the card from my fingers and held it up to the light. "Did you call the number?" he asked, scratching his beard with the other hand. There was a generous dusting of grey, which made me think he dyed his hair at first. But on closer inspection, I realized that was just the way Hernandez was made – jet hair and silver beard.

My assumption wasn't a far-fetched notion in a country where both genders chemically relaxed their hair and bleached their skin to appear more European. Even blacks claimed Indian heritage on their driver's license, despite the fact that the native Tainos were decimated by the Conquistadors in the earliest genocide in the Western Hemisphere. Anything to differentiate themselves from the more Afro-centric Haitians.

"No. That's not why I'm here," I responded to his question with the American insouciance that was expected of me. Hernandez was already reaching for his cell phone. I watched with a feigned sense of curiosity as he too was stumped by the automated system. "Well?"

"I'll look into this later," he said, his frown deepening as he took another hard look at the card before tucking it and his cell phone out of sight. He rolled his shoulders as he mentally filed away the matter, then reached for his coffee to signal the beginning of a new chapter.

"Maybe it's nothing," I offered, finding our starting page in the manual. "They could really be dancers."

He did not respond and I didn't push further. The kindling had been laid, a spark made. I just had to wait while the breeze picked up and fanned the infant flames. As we delved into the training manual, both Hernandez and I pretended to put Angel from our mind. But every now and then I could hear the wheels inside his head turning. His thoughts were never far from his own daughters, aged twelve, sixteen, eighteen, twenty-one and twenty-three. Any one of them could have been the mythical girl in the coffee shop and Ernesto's simple honesty could not let go of it.

By the time 4 o'clock rolled around, we had already established that Angel was employed at a member's only strip club along the Malecon called The Factory. The phone number listed on the card belonged to a VOIP account, which we traced through its Internet protocol.

"Tomorrow we can look at their traffic," I told Hernandez. Because I could sense his objection, his eagerness to push for more on the spot, I added, "Just in case it's all legitimate, you should think about other possibilities for case studies."

He had nodded his agreement, but he was already invested in The Factory. He had the look of a dog with a bone.

I called O'Brien on his cell phone from the parking lot. He didn't answer at first, so I pressed redial every five minutes until he finally did.

"Jesus Christ, Koehler. Don't you know how to leave a message?" he greeted me.

Voicemail was not meant for secure communication, even if it would leave a trail that I could use to cover my behind when the lid blew off my private campaign. He had to recognize my persistence was the result of the need for discretion, so I didn't take his greeting personally. He could have been annoyed by something else and I was simply in the line of fire. He wasn't malicious.

Somehow I trusted O'Brien not to leave me hanging, claiming ignorance of an impending threat after I had briefed him. My last Section Chief did not inspire such confidence. My job was to make him look good, and if he looked bad – even if he ignored my advice – then I was put on the chopping block.

"I wanted to let you know Hernandez has settled on a case study."

"Anything of significance?"

"It shouldn't be," I lied. I fully intended for it to become significant – at least to Todd and the members of his boys club who were members of The Factory. "It looks like your run of the mill gentlemen's club. Hernandez has daughters and doesn't appreciate their recruitment practices. I'll keep you posted."

"So it's going well?" he asked with only a hint of surprise. "You're not pissing anybody off?"

"No, sir." There was no denying that I often rubbed others the wrong way. I may lie for my job, but I rarely ever lied to myself. Todd was the only exception. I lied to myself everyday where he was concerned. Just that morning, I told myself it was his pancakes I missed... not the warmth of his body as he reached for me in his sleep. Nor his morning hard-on that he would ram into me from behind while folding me over the nearest surface if he caught me between my run and morning shower. "At least not that I can tell."

"Keep it clean, Koehler. You're halfway there."

I wasn't naïve enough to think I had grown on O'Brien. He didn't want me rocking the boat in his waters. I appreciated the effort to tone down the bluster, but I wasn't going to be lulled into complacency. The last time that had happened, I found myself saying yes to Todd Birch. Two months later, I was living out of a duffel bag, making phone calls from high traffic areas, and taking the most circuitous routes home to make sure I wasn't being followed.

It felt like I was in Yemen again. Funny how marriage felt more and more like living in a war zone.

ELEVEN

Hernandez and I spent all Wednesday on the case study. After accessing the administrative accounts for the IP address, we moved on to all the off-shoot accounts, then from the most popular to the least occurring phone and internet contacts. It was the breadth of the network that accounted for much of the time and effort that went into the operation.

The Factory and its affiliates formed a transnational organization in the truest sense of the word. Women were recruited from all over the world and moved around from one location to the next. But the constant relocation was more than a means by which the organization could elude law enforcement; it also ensured a steady stream of fresh girls.

It was bad for business to allow clients to become too attached to the merchandise. Men became protective and got heroic notions about rescuing their 'girlfriends', not wanting them to provide services to other clients. Holding onto a passport, claiming nearly all the girls' money – to repay the cost of transportation, phony work permits, room and board – could only last for so long. Bruising the merchandise was a last resort because it was bad for business, so only the more amenable girls were afforded the freedom to work outside the Factory's locations, in private residences or the nearby cabañas – motels rented on an hourly basis with the explicit purpose of providing a safe and anonymous location where couples could have sex.

In a sense, human trafficking had become the new Peace Corps. The victims were almost guaranteed to experience new things, travel the world, and learn about different cultures.

Because not everyone appreciated being offered a job as a dancer or au pair and then being told she had to prostitute herself to cover her debts, there were also 'the fields'. The fields were where uncooperative recruits were held, drugged and broken in until they fell into step. Walking the beat – sidewalk prostitution – was where girls in the fields made money. There were also mobile brothels, where girls were transported to work sites, like the cabañas, construction sites; or residential apartments out of which sex was sold. On the prostitution ladder, this was scraping from the bottom of the barrel. Girls had very little hope of being promoted to a formal outlet and sometimes died from occupational hazards – diseases, physical abuse or drug overdose.

From a global perspective, the Santo Domingo outlet was low key. The major hubs were located in the United States and Europe, but there were expatriates and sex tourists who still had to be catered to. The Factory Santo Domingo S.r.l. shared a recycling bin with the Dutch ABC and SSS islands, Colombia, Venezuela, Panama and Jamaica. Whether Hernandez wanted to pursue this case across six international jurisdictions was solely his concern. I had my sights set on Angel.

The intrusion solution yielded names, locations and even banking information. Gone were the days of organized crime being a cash only business. And if clients were being prompted to provide credit card information in order for their call to be answered, then business had to be booming.

By Thursday morning, raids were underway at four premises: The Factory in Gascué; an office in the center of the Distrito Naçional from which administration was run; and two torrés, one where sixteen girls were housed in the moderately luxurious conditions, and another at the home of their chief handler.

In total sixteen women were rescued, some of them dragged from the jacuzzi, only to be herded half-naked into a jail cell for safekeeping. Eight arrests were also made. Four women were responsible for ensuring the girls were always accounted for, little luxuries like manicures, bikini waxes and fat-free snacks were available. They monitored BMI, making sure girls with issues worked them out. They scheduled doctor's visits and salon appointments, and organized small shopping excursions.

The remaining suspects were all male – the handler and his muscle, who ensured the girls showed up for work on time and happy. They doled out narcotics according to each girl's need. If a girl seemed to be lagging or had a long night ahead of her, she got some blow or meth to pep up her step. If she was too high, marijuana was used to bring her down. They organized excursions to local parties where new clients could be found. It was members-only and survival required that new clients were constantly being sought. Prospective clients were vetted, the undesirables weeded out, and the operation remained secure from law enforcement infiltration. But the handler's most import function was to ensure that clients checked out and that the merchandise was returned in the same condition she left.

These women were not people in his eyes. They were rentals, and taking care of them was like regular maintenance. Absconding with one was like stealing a car, which carried certain penalties for the thief.

The problem with running an illegal operation like a legitimate business was the existence of paper work that could get a lot of people in trouble. The on call MD, the Government official who had approved three hundred and twenty-four work permits for dancers and masseuses oer a four-year period, the property owners who allowed their premises to be used to operate a prostitution ring were all put under the gun.

Santo Domingo had one shelter for battered women, women at risk and victims of human trafficking. It was privately run with little public assistance, and it showed. Angel spent the first few hours of Thursday night in a jail cell, before being moved to the shelter. There was a marked difference in the lifestyle she led as a sex slave and that of a guest of the State. For the first time in possibly years, she understood what it meant to be poor.

Hernandez got an A+ for practical use of the technology. But before he really started using his initiative, I had to get Angel out of official custody. My plans for her did not include giving statements to the police or participating in the prosecution of her traffickers. If she refused to cooperate, she could expect to be deported as soon as local authorities could locate her passport among the hundreds of boxes of evidence they had seized in the raids. So it was with a congratulatory pat on the back and a bright smile that I bid Ernesto Hernandez farewell on Friday morning.

"Do you only drink coffee, Koehler?" he asked on my way to the front steps of his building, which was a satellite of the colonial style presidential palace.

I pulled up short and took a moment to readjust my purse on my shoulder. I was in a hurry and it showed.

"Why?" I asked, still pleasant, but not trying very hard to hide my impatience.

"I would invite you out for a drink... a real thank you for a most valuable lesson." He shrugged his shoulders. "Plus, you brought the coffee. No real man would allow himself to be held in a woman's debt."

There was nothing remotely nefarious, predatory or lecherous in his honest face. He wasn't interested in me in that way, so I accepted his invitation for a simple get-together at a cigar bar on Avenida Máximo Gomez Saturday evening.

"A young woman like you should be out on a Friday night, so you can meet a nice young man, and let him take you to a merengue club. Old man like me, I'll take a couple hours of your Saturday."

He smiled and I forced myself to smile back. He didn't know I was married. I had never worn my ring, which irked Todd, especially since he never took his off. Work was my excuse. The less people knew about me... the less they noticed and remembered, the better for me. And Todd's two-carat engagement ring was very memorable. Now I didn't need an excuse for not wearing it anymore. It was not as if his wedding band had stopped him from fucking anything that moved.

I sat in the parking lot for ten minutes, trying to understand why I didn't try to get out of Hernandez' invitation. It was still a far cry from trust, but because of Todd, I should have been doubly wary of everyone. My judgment was shot, and I had to be extra cautious where I used to rely on my unerring instinct.

What would my father think about the state of my life now?

Ernesto Hernandez was nothing like my father. He was an honest and simple man who did his job matter-of-factly; and his daughters' happiness was foremost among his priorities. In contrast, my father had lived and died for his job. And he had trained me so well to continue his work that it was hard not to love something you were great at.

I freely admitted that for a heartbeat, I had lost focus. It took me a week to get a handle on my emotions, and I blamed my reaction on the shock of Todd's betrayal. But I was finally in control again, my priorities realigned. Todd could screw his way into the Guinness Book of World Records; it was only his name I needed.

I visualized that control like reins in my hand as I made my way to the shelter for a face-to-face with Angel. I slipped my embassy I.D card around my neck and tucked it inside my shirt. The place was the busiest it had ever been, with the constant coming and going of police officers, social workers, immigration officials, and one news crew. I managed to slip inside the building without being challenged and marched up to the receptionist as if I had official business to conduct.

The receptionist was the image of boredom as she repeated "No lo sé, señor," at regular intervals into the phone she held to her ear. By the look of thing, not only did she not know, she was not in the least concerned either. Without hanging up or even covering the mouthpiece, she turned to me, with an equally lethargic, "Si?"

I gave her a tight smile and fished my ID out of my shirt. I kept my fingers over my name as I tilted the badge in her direction so she got an eyeful of my photo and the *Embassy of the United States of America, Santo Domingo*. That got her attention. There wasn't a mile-long line of visa applicants winding around the consulate everyday just for the fun of it. The Dominican Republic had the highest incidence of immigrant visa fraud in this hemisphere. Being allowed entry to the United States was not unlike winning the lottery. The promise of a visa, or the threat to rescind one, could open more doors than my less than warm nature.

"Un momento, por favor, señor," she said and brusquely put the caller on hold.

"Do you speak English?" I asked in clipped tones to match my tight smile.

Her smile dimmed slightly. "No ingles, lo siento." But she did sit up straight in her seat, pat her perfect hair in place, and gaze up at me as if this was an interview for the last job on earth. She thought better of her answer, because she wrinkled her nose and amended, "Sólo un pocito." *Just a little.*

My Spanish was more than adequate for the impending conversation, but keeping my linguistic capabilities a secret had often proved to be an advantage. People were more honest when they thought you didn't understand what was going on.

"A woman was brought here this morning. Her name is Angel. I am her consular representative and I need to speak with her, please."

The receptionist stared at me blankly for a long moment, picking over the words that stuck, hoping to find something she could understand. After a pregnant pause, 'Angel' and 'Consular' stuck.

"Angel?" she asked.

"Yes," I replied simply. A surname would have been helpful, but I didn't have one. I also hoped she hadn't exchanged her real name for a stripper one. Some men got a kick out of fucking a whore named Angel. "It is important ... and confidential."

Her eyes flicked from me to the buzz of activity behind her. The comers and goers were still out of sight for the moment, and perhaps one of them was a supervisor she contemplated running my request by. She leaned on a buzzer, opening the door to my left, to admit a trio who had already passed the entrance exam. Her lips twisted with the bad taste of her decision.

"No se permiten visitantes," she began hesitantly, as if the standard answer was a personal burden. *No visitors allowed.*

I smiled my understanding of the bureaucracy, but backed up my request by raising my ID badge to her eye level, again concealing my name. "Yo soy su representante consular." I tucked my badge back into my shirt. *I'm her consular representative.*

She stroked her hair again and started chewing on the inside of her cheek.

"Espere un momento, por favor." *Wait a minute, please.*

She backed out of her space and left me to stew. Waiting was risky. She could have gone in search of her supervisor or one of the many cops milling around, lugging plastic bags of possibly personal items for the newest arrivals. My diplomatic immunity meant they couldn't question me, although I had no valid official reason for being there. But they would have my name, which could possibly get back to Hernandez and raise more questions that I would rather avoid. Calling attention to myself was in direct contravention of O'Brien's orders, and could get my ass nailed to a wall and my face ripped off, as he had promised.

But I couldn't run either. That was the surest way to raise suspicion. There was a surveillance camera fixed on the receptionist area that had not been turned on in years. The indicator light was dead, and the ceiling fan that shared electrical wires was stationary and thick with rust. The surrounding area on the ceiling had a large water stain where rain had seeped through the roof. A women's shelter wasn't high on the priority for public funding and NGOs were notorious penny-pinchers, because most of them had no clue where their next grant would come from.

The receptionist didn't seem to have the corner on due diligence either. Her phone was blinking with the call she had put on hold while she left her post unattended. Luckily, the people exiting held the door for those entering once they noticed she was gone. One of them held the door for me too and gestured for me to enter. I had to decline, however, because I had no idea where to find Angel. He shrugged and left.

So much for protecting the victims. Hadn't these people seen *Sleeping with the Enemy*? What if an angry spouse or pimp was intent on eliminating the witnesses to his crime? The receptionist's purse was wide open on the floor between her desk and empty chair. Was protocol more of a priority than security?

When the receptionist finally returned she was smiling nervously and running her palms down the sides of her skirt. My instinct to hang tight was spot on. She looked like someone who was about to do something she knew was at least questionable.

"Voy a tartar de ayudar," *I'll try to help you,* she whispered conspiratorially, to which I maintained an implacable expression. As far as she knew this was official business – not a personal visit – and I wasn't going to fall into the hands of a twenty-something who thought she was slicker than a woman who had survived Todd Birch's interrogation on a nearly daily basis.

She buzzed me in and led me to the end of the corridor, then indicated the third door on the right. The locals were friendly, but she persisted in acting conspiratorially, which was a sign I was about to be hit up for a visa. When the request came, I was able to deflect by quickening my pace and pleading ignorance of Spanish.

There was more water-stained ceiling along the corridor. The floors were clean but done in the utilitarian grey of poured concrete. The walls were a neutral shade of off-white. Straight ahead at the end of the corridor was a more secure door with a wire-reinforced plate for easy viewing. As I slowly made my way to the room the receptionist had indicated, a uniformed police officer exited the secure door. I got a glimpse of a uniformed guard seated just inside what might have been the dormitory. It wasn't enough to keep out a determined intruder or a mutinous mob of victims hell-bent on escape; but it might deter an opportunist. I revised my earlier opinion of this place being a free-for-all.

I slipped inside my destination without appearing to skulk a few moments before the cop got close enough for a good look at my face. There was so much activity going on he might have thought nothing of my presence, but I wanted to avoid any unnecessary risks.

The door I closed behind me was made of plywood – thin enough for voices to carry if we weren't careful. Inside was an empty office space, barely large enough for a desk and two chairs. It seemed more spacious than it actually was however, because there was no desk, and the only other occupant was half my size.

The little snowflake was perched on one of the chairs, blowing cigarette smoke into the air, in contravention of the national law against indoor smoking. She looked up at my entrance, and for a brief time, all I could see was big, round eyes, as clear and hard as chips of ice. They might have been called blue, but seemed colorless, and they took up half her pale face. She looked like a little fairy – Hard Knocks Pixie – because as cute and diminutive as she was, there was nothing enchanting about the arctic freeze that hit me full in the face.

Maybe Todd had a thing for fucked up, frigid girls. Maybe it had something to do with our broken wings. He had screwed Byles too, and though she thought she was hotter than a car-trunk border crossing, her low self-esteem was just as crippling. Todd had a type, and it wasn't just *breathing*.

Byles was blond, but Todd's angel made the other woman's hair look like mud. Her tresses were snow white and cut in a straight line just below her chin. The equally pale eyebrows and lashes spoke of their authenticity. Her nose was as tiny, barely big enough for breathing, and enhanced by a faint smattering of freckles. Her mouth was twisted in a pout that reminded me of ripe raspberries. Even without a drop of makeup, the effect was devastating.

I imagined what she would look like with those dinner plate-sized eyes lined with black eyeliner and a thick coat of mascara, a drop of lip balm, and a smile. Her ethereal beauty, which belonged in a Tolkien book, was unlike anything else I had seen in the Dominican Republic – hence her appeal… if you could get past the child-like body.

Angel couldn't top five feet on her tiptoes, and a good meal would probably round her out to ninety pounds. Her breasts were little mosquito bites underneath her white tank top. Her hips in a pair of denim cutoffs could have been a pre-adolescent boy's.

I remembered the time Todd and I had met at the Viceroy in Miami to hammer out the terms of a relationship. He had wanted to punish me for running away from him.

"It's so good to feel real tits again," he had said, trying in vain to wound me with feelings I did not have.

I wanted to be that girl again, the girl who didn't care who he slept with; the girl before she had fallen in love with him. I didn't want to be the woman comparing herself to the two poles of Todd's bed: the flat-chested snowflake and the iron-breasted, borderline tanorexic.

I watched as snowflake uncurled her limbs and stretched her whole body into a perfect C – backwards – displaying some mad gymnastic skills. Could this girl get any more perfect?

She stubbed out her cigarette on the plastic arm of her chair and exhaled the smoke through her nostrils. She curled around herself, protecting her tender core from whatever bad news I had brought.

I had her full attention, but she didn't say anything. That had probably been her position since being scooped up in the sweep. Something in her eyes – possibly that thing that stared back at me from the mirror – told me she had been raised that way. Angel was not one of the girls who had to be broken in; she knew how to adapt. She paid attention, weighed her options, then made the best decision that would get her what she wanted. So far, the Dominicans had nothing to offer.

I moved the free chair directly in front of hers. I didn't want anyone in authority knowing I was there, and Angel and I had a lot of ground to cover. I held up my I.D. badge for her as I sat, so she could see my name, employee number, my security clearance color strip, an unmade up version of my face.

"How would you like to work for me?" I asked in English, noting how she slowly exhaled a long breath – releasing the tension in a wave she didn't even know she was holding back. That had to be the last thing she expected.

"Who are you?" she finally asked with an unmistakable Eastern European rasp. I was expecting the chime of a bell, but hadn't taken into account years of smoking. Her voice still managed to sound like Christmas in a different sense – cold, austere, but at the same time evoking heat, like swallowing live coals.

"You can call me Anne."

"That says you are Amy." She gestured with a snowy, arched brow to the badge I had tucked into my shirt again.

"You can call me Anne," I said with meaning.

"Whoever you are… what do you want?"

"You to work for me." She scoffed, but I felt it was more self-mocking than disparaging of my offer. "I can make you whomever you want to be… just like me."

"Why?" Why I wasn't accusing her of visa fraud for whatever bogus papers her traffickers had prepared for her trip to the US? Why was I offering her the impossible?

"Because you are useful to me." And just so there was no misunderstanding between us, I added, "And I will use you."

She seemed to consider it for a moment. Obviously she wasn't too attached to the things that made her who she was – her body, her will, her convictions, because not much time passed before she answered. "Can you get me out of here?"

Leaky roofs, stark cold floors, bare furniture, and even barer walls were apparently not her idea of ideal working conditions. I didn't blame her. This place was for real victims; Angel was a survivor.

"How does lunchtime sound?" I asked and she smiled.

"Where do I sign?" she smiled back.

TWELVE

Even with the hectic morning I had had, I still made it in to work before ten. I had things to do and a midday deadline to meet. But first, there were a few things I had to run by O'Brien. He was presently on the phone, but with the clock ticking, I didn't have the luxury of cooling my heels until his schedule cleared.

I made a beeline for his office, ignoring six pairs of eyes between the steel-reinforced door and my goal. The seventh pair belonged to Byles, and even after one week I could still make out the remnants of her shiner beneath the thick coat of liquid foundation and concealer. Regret thudded heavily in the pit of my stomach. I would have liked to witness the full effect of my handiwork while it was fresh.

I pulled up short at her desk, which raised a few eyebrows. She barely moved, was hardly breathing but tried to force down a lump in her throat. By contrast, her eyes were busy, darting every which way, except at me, though there was just about a foot of space between us. I relished her uncertainty for a while then sent her pulse into overdrive by dropping my bag onto her desk.

I didn't allow myself more than those brief moments of payback. I would have liked nothing more than to rip into her – throw her risky Friday night behavior and her conspiracy with Todd back in her face and out in the open. But that would have been an emotional response, which belied the detachment I had worked on all week. I was completely ruined if I could not rise above this.

The next few months were critical, because we were so close to getting Afanasenko and finding his backer. I needed emotional objectivity if I was going to live up to my father's expectations.

It hurt to think of Todd with Byles, giving himself to her, feeding her pieces of me as they discussed my issues and our marriage. I wasn't satisfied with the man he was with me; I wanted the scraps he gave her too. Normally I would never demand such a thing from a man, but I believed Todd when he said I was it for him. To learn that he had lied and I had failed to see it wounded me deeply. There was not much that could soothe that ache. Even so Byles was not the source of our marital discord; she was only a harmless boil that mocked me.

"How are you?" I asked, voice low and neutral, which smacked of concern most of the time.

She could have melted into her swivel chair with the force of the breath she exhaled. Perhaps that was why her short laugh, so different from Friday night's bitter cackle, was now airy with embarrassment. There was an accompanying flush to her cheeks.

"God, don't even ask."

I bent my face into what I hoped was a commiserating smile and hoped it didn't look like the narrowed eyes and flattened mouth that it was in actuality.

"What happened to your face?" I could have made up a story for her, claimed she had done it while drunk, but I didn't feel like doing any work for her.

"Jesus! I don't even know," she whispered, drawing her chair even closer to me. Of course, that had every eye turning our way again. "I woke up on Saturday totally fucked up. I didn't think we'd had that much to drink."

I hummed a noncommittal response then noticed O'Brien standing in his office, phone glued to his ear, eyes fixed on us. There was too much going on that I didn't want him to know. Arousing his suspicion in one area was risky, because the man was thorough and would go digging for more dirt to bury me. I picked up my purse, signaling an end to our chat.

"Hey," Byles whispered urgently, comfortable enough to grab my arm. Those hands had been all over my husband; those red nails scraping across his skin. It took quite an effort to resist the urge to shake her off.

Todd liked marking me, leaving his prints all over my body, preferably in places others could see. He wanted the world to know I belonged to him – a compulsion made stronger by my refusal to wear his rings. I wondered if he had introduced her to marking or if she had been the tutor and Todd the eager student. With that thought came a sharp stab in my middle that made me flinch, stiffening my spine.

"Are you and Todd OK? He was looking for you. He came by the hotel on Saturday."

I could only imagine what had happened, but it was more than I wished to face at that moment. It would explain why she had not slept through to Sunday. Todd had probably gone there Saturday morning, woke her up and grilled her on what had happened Friday night. She wouldn't have remembered any of our conversation, which would have been frustrating for them both. From experience, I knew a frustrated Todd would have been at his primal peak. The ensuing sexual encounter would have been incredible.

He had hammered into me enough times, trying to break down my resistance and empty his roiling emotions into me. I understood what Byles might have faced on Saturday. It was enough to make her think they were on again. It was certainly enough to make her careless. She could barely contain her hopeful expression.

Todd had told her quite a bit about me. Had he confessed to her that I had moved out? The man I had married was a complete stranger to me, but the woman who sat across from me knew more about me than I was comfortable sharing. She was a daily reminder that not only did my husband not love me, there was also nothing sacred between us. I had never had to deal with these issues at work before. It was one more thing to resent about Todd. I had nowhere to hide from the mess we had made. Work was a minefield of little disasters and I had run away from home.

"Just fine," I answered and moved on.

O'Brien was still on the phone, but I wasn't going to wait. I stood just outside his door and stared him dead in the eye, channeling all the awkwardness that one human being could manage. His raised eyebrows and firmly pressed lips would have usually sent me in search of something else to occupy myself. Today, it had the effect of a glass of water tossed on a raging wildfire.

"Can I help you, Koehler?" he asked, one palm covering the mouthpiece of his landline.

"Yes, sir."

With equal parts annoyance and curiosity, he ended his call and hooked a finger, inviting me to take a seat. I closed the door, which got me a dark look but no rebuke.

"Have you lost your fucking mind?" O'Brien started, making me rethink if the closed door really meant that much to him. There were a number of things that could have warranted that kind of greeting, starting with a fire at the house I used to share with Todd and ending with an unsanctioned visit to a women's shelter. Quite frankly, in the grand scheme of things, my insistence on privacy had to rate low, but my priorities often differed from others'.

"I don't know what kind of circus they run where you come from, but you don't just drop off the fucking map in my shop."

That did help to narrow the list of offences, but I couldn't relax just yet. Either Todd had confessed our split and not knowing my whereabouts, or O'Brien had tried to locate me while I had my invisibility cloak on. Personally, the state of my marriage was none of his concern, so I wasn't going to play ball in that arena. My location, however, was his business.

"I'll have my Blackberry replaced today."

Of course that meant Todd would be able to find me too, but since I was back in office, hiding was futile. We worked in separate buildings on the same compound, but my desk was surrounded by his friends and lover. If the gate security hadn't already alerted him to my whereabouts, then one of my colleagues certainly had.

I was different now... ready to face the new challenge he presented. My emotions were under control, my apartment secured, and I had leverage in the works. Cementing the latter was my current priority, and the reason O'Brien was leaning back in his chair, barking, "So what do you want now, Koehler?"

"Remember that gentlemen's club we talked about on Tuesday?"

O'Brien visibly stiffened, his jaw clenching. "The case study that was supposed to be no big deal. What about it?" It was hard to miss the accusation.

"The locals raided it last night and picked up some girls."

"So?" he prompted irritably.

I hadn't tuned in to the local news and didn't know whether the events had received any airtime as yet. The presence of a camera crew outside the shelter meant there was some interest, but there might have been more pressing matters, such as the latest developments in a telenovela series. O'Brien wasn't alone in his apathy for the plight of a few prostitutes. I wanted to flash freeze this moment and send it back to Virginia so they could compare O'Brien's reaction to my lack of sensitivity. What made me a sociopath but my boss levelheaded?

"It turns out one of the girls has made the rounds inside the embassy. She knows names and faces and isn't afraid to talk. I was able to isolate her as soon as I found a couple of our own among her traffic."

"What names, what faces?" he asked, ready to decide whether our liability could be limited by sending them home.

"At last count, there were fourteen expatriates and eight FSNs."

The Foreign Service Nationals were Dominicans who worked for the embassy. The extent of staff involvement gave credence to the conclusion that patronizing prostitutes was deeply entrenched in the embassy culture. The game of leverage took guts, and gambling with the embassy's reputation raised the stakes. I placed my first bet.

"Landon can tell you how she became the main attraction at the Boys Scouts parties."

Greg Landon was one of two Homeland Security representatives under O'Brien's command. He was also one of Todd's closest friends at Mission, and one of the attendees at Friday's bachelor party. The Boys Scouts included most of the law enforcement, defense and intelligence community at Mission, as well as some of the more senior State Department personnel. As much as O'Brien was tempted to brush this under the carpet – even if it meant sacrificing a few careers – the chances of that happening now were slim. He didn't have to stick his foot in the river to know it ran deep.

"Shit!" he hissed, his frustration evident. I felt the barrel of his gun wavering from my direction. "How did this happen, Koehler?"

"How do they fuck prostitutes, sir?" I deadpanned, brows furrowed. O'Brien straightened in his seat, eyes shifting to the closed door, his annoyance shifting to the world outside.

"Why didn't you see this coming?"

"I was unaware that the solicitation of prostitutes was pervasive among embassy personnel. I would have steered Hernandez in another direction, if I had known. The case study was entirely his choice and I did inform you of that decision as per my instructions. We're actually lucky I was there to separate the girl in question."

Because the only thing Section Chiefs loved more than accountability was a successful exit strategy, I aimed for bonus points.

"I am sorry this matter came to light in this manner, but I assure you, sir, it's better we found out now, as opposed to after it hit the press. At least at this stage, I can fix it."

Those pond-water green eyes returned to pin me to my seat. He had a right to be suspicious. He had not yet completely wrapped his mind around the problem, much less come up with a solution. Either I was quick on my feet or up to something.

"I've isolated the threat to a single female." I nodded in acknowledgement of the question he asked with his eyebrows. "The ring works off referrals, and the girls are matched to clients based on their security clearance. Her handlers trusted her not to fly the coop, and in return she brought in a lot of American clients and good money. She had to have been requested by name, and was reserved for clients with good records."

"Jesus Christ!" O'Brien muttered in disgust and surprise. A single girl was much easier to manage than a house full of prostitutes with a story to tell. It was a blessing and a curse, because she was also the single repository of US embassy personnel names and faces.

"I can manage her," I continued, but it was too much to hope that Ted O'Brien would take my word for it. The man was decisive, but this choice wasn't going to be based on my say-so alone. He'd been in the business long enough to know a bullshit merchant when he saw one.

"Why?" he asked. "Why do you give a shit about Landon dipping his quill in the communal well?"

I kept my features impassive, but tilted my chin up and swallowed hard so he could see. "Todd Birch attended some of those parties. For that reason you can count on my discretion."

O'Brien surprised me then. His expression softened. It was there one second and gone the next. Regardless of his professional opinion of me – the fact that he didn't want me in his office – this man empathized with me. I should have felt guilt, remorse… something – anything… that I was manipulating him. But there was nothing.

O'Brien considered the matter for a long moment then sighed. "What do you need to keep her quiet?""

"She likes America and she's for sale." I meant her silence. There had never been any question about her body.

"Let's say we give her an EB visa and ship her out of the country. What's to say she'll keep her mouth shut?"

An employment-based immigrant visa would effectively get Angel out of the Dominican Republic. There was no doubt she qualified. She had exceptional abilities – expertise significantly above that ordinarily encountered. How many seasoned prostitutes had her contortionist skills? There was also a clear benefit to our national interests to get her away from Dominican officials.

With an EB visa, Angel would be able to fulfill her dream of going to America. She was a streets-smart girl; she knew breaking faith meant having her papers rescinded. She would not bite the hand that fed her, and certainly not for the sole purpose of cooperating with law enforcement. She had left Ukraine for a reason and living in a third world country was a means to an end – not the end itself. Deportation to the Ukraine would have been a waste of the past six years of her life. But I wasn't going to share this view with O'Brien for the simple reason that it didn't suit my interests.

Angel was barely eighteen years old when she responded to an advertisement for dancers. It had appeared to be a legitimate job for creative dancers. She used to be an average gymnast before adolescence had wrought a sudden growth spurt and hormonal changes that could not be controlled. But she still had rhythm, discipline and flexibility. She had hoped that would have carried her through. She wouldn't be the first ex-gymnast who had forged a career as a dancer.

But the job was only a front and when it fell through, she fell in line with her traffickers. She spent the next six years being shuffled across the globe. Her travels took her first to Romania and then on to Turkey. She had spent an entire year in Greece, followed by a brief stint in Germany. From there, she was moved to the Netherlands, Spain, back to the Netherlands, and at last to Curacao. Aruba and Bonaire were only a skip away, and St. Maarten a hop. That Todd had stuck his dick inside her disgusted me.

She had hoped her circuitous trail to the US would have taken her to Puerto Rico next, then later to the mainland, but her bogus student visa application was being held up because the shell university in California demanded more money than she had earned thus far. She was stuck for the moment in the Dominican Republic where she faced the very real prospect of deportation if she did not cooperate in the prosecution of her traffickers.

Angel wouldn't hesitate to sign her life over to me if the price was right. Her traffickers had made promises but had delivered much less. Now she had nothing to lose, but at least I was in a position to give her what she wanted. She'd been around the block so many times, she instinctively knew this.

"A visa isn't enough," I answered. "She knows what she has on us. Nothing short of a passport will do."

O'Brien scoffed. "If a visa won't shut her up, a passport won't either," he concluded.

"You're right, sir. She needs a firm hand and proximity. I volunteer to keep an eye on her, but she won't budge from the passport requirement."

O'Brien's eyebrows might have touched his comb-over in his youth when he had more hair. "You're going to handle a hooker who fucked your husband?"

"We don't know that there was any physical contact between them, only that he was in attendance."

"Ordinarily I wouldn't give a flying fuck, Koehler." He cut me off with just his intensity. "I don't want you starting any shit, and I'm not going to give a hooker wings so you can fuck up your husband's piece of side ass."

"Sir, I've spent the past five weeks surrounded by my husband's 'piece of side ass'. Byles sits across a desk from me. I don't need you to help me play stalker."

The effect of my candor had my boss leaning back in his seat. I was offended by his opinion of me as an Intelligence Officer. Being in the know didn't stop when I walked out the doors that kept our work classified. And home was not a place where I could loose the emotions I held so tightly reined from eight to five. My work was my life; I lived and breathed it every hour of every day.

"Don't you have better things to do, Koehler?"

"I don't know, sir. Are there any more dime-bag pushers you need me to trace?" I asked, referring to the small-scale dealers he had assigned me to. It wasn't in O'Brien's nature to back down from my challenge, but he wouldn't have believed me if I didn't protest being fed his crumbs. "Do you have a worthwhile assignment for me, sir?"

"All our assignments are worthwhile, Koehler," he pronounced with true pique, but the roll of his shoulders took some of the sting out of remark. Unfounded accusations aside, the silent release of tension was a positive sign. Either he was confident in my ability to neutralize the impending PR nightmare, or my clearance for the real intrusion target had come through.

I was eager for an assignment I could sink my teeth into… one that could possibly get me out of this country and on a plane to Europe. But it wouldn't help for him to see how badly I wanted this. I refused to trade Angel; she was my leverage over Todd, just as Obrien had assumed.

A deliberate furrow of my brow demonstrated concern. It helped that I practiced these expressions in my off time; imitating honest emotions made my job easier.

"As a matter of fact, your clearance came through."

O'Brien's fingers found and caressed a black binder with Secret classification stamped in red on the front. I hadn't noticed it before, because it was conveniently hidden under a copy of this morning's *Listin Diario*. O'Brien's eyes remained fixed on me though, assessing, waiting for what I wasn't sure.

He had spent the past five weeks keeping me at the end of a tight leash. Anything beyond mild curiosity might have been grounds for curfew, so I raised my eyebrows midway and tilted my head to the left.

100 KATE A. KNIGHT

Still, O'Brien wasn't completely convinced. He handed me the folder and used the time it took for me to apprise myself of the premises to observe me.

My instincts had once again proved true. Nothing in life was free and the United States wasn't giving away advanced interception technology for shits and giggles. The real target for intrusion was Colonel Eduardo Ramirez. He was the third in command of the Dominican Joint Armed Forces Counter-terrorism group. It appeared that under the cover of military cooperation activities with Colombia, Venezuela, and the United States, he was shuttling narcotics between South America and Puerto Rico.

Satisfaction warmed me like a drink of Brugal Añejo. Rifling though a foreign country's military communications was still a big deal. We would never have received authorization from the Dominican government – and certainly not for such a high-ranking official as Colonel Ramirez who undoubtedly had access to defense and national security secrets as a matter of course. Secondly, if the unthinkable had happened and we did make the request, it was guaranteed that the target would have been tipped off. Most importantly, nothing ruined functional cooperation like accusing the other side of corruption.

In summary, a lot was at stake, and putting an end to Colonel Ramirez's extracurricular activities would guarantee me the notice I needed for a Parisian post. As a rule, I tried to avoid politicians; they invited too many cooks to man the broth. And although Ramirez wore a uniform and followed a chain of command, he was political enough for concern. This case required a certain level of sensitivity that would prove I had what was needed to operate effectively in Europe's politically charged climate.

One week away from Todd and my career outlook had significantly improved.

"I don't need to tell you how sensitive this is," queried the man who questioned my obsession with closing doors. The hand raised to his hair smoothed the curve of his comb-over. He was confident but unsure. He knew I had the requisite skills, but he questioned my suitability.

"No, sir. I understand."

"We have the suite installed and we tested our access while you were busy digging up hookers and impressing the locals." He surprised me with that bit of praise. I was also taken aback that Ernesto Hernandez might have cared enough to communicate his approval of me. It made me more amenable to keeping that Saturday evening drinks appointment.

"We just need a way into the Fuerza Armada database to access Ramirez. Our liaison should be here soon, so sit tight for now. After that," his mouth stretched into a humorless smile, "you're going to sift through the data to find what we're looking for."

I was excited, but not enough so to drop the ball on Angel. I only had an hour left to get the passport made and another for it to be delivered.

"Thank you, sir." My smile was appreciative but sedate, as if I'd expected nothing less. It wouldn't help for him to think he had done me a favor. "What are we going to do about the victim?"

It didn't hurt my case to underscore her status as the vulnerable party in the potential debacle, not because I thought it would soften O'Brien's opinion of her, nor because it reflected any sympathy for her on my part. It simply emphasized her appeal to the media, which summed up her importance to us.

"You're sure you can keep a lid on her?"

"I am." If it ever came to choosing between my career and Angel, I would kill her with equal lack of hesitation.

"Then you can have her," he offered, but his disconcerting gaze made me feel as if he was giving me enough rope to hang myself. Both Angel and I were going to have to earn that passport.

THIRTEEN

Todd's little snowflake was really Angelika Prokop, a twenty-five year old Ukrainian former student and gymnast who had dreams of dancing on Broadway. At eighteen years, she responded to an ad in the paper for dancers in Kiev. It took her two days and nearly everything she had accumulated in her short life to travel from her small town outside Kovel to the auditions in the capital. She made the first cut, but was told a part of her salary would go towards room and board. After one week of practice in a studio with eighty other girls, she was dismissed for poor performance, found herself indebted to her host, with no means and no one to return to Kovel.

Her lucky break came when her recruiter offered her a job as a stripper in Romania. Four days later, she stepped off a train in Bucharest and into a minivan with six other girls. Her passport was taken as a guarantee for her mounting debt. It took her only one week to fully understand that she would die a slave if she didn't find a way to earn extra money. She agreed to have sex with the club's clients and pay a fifty percent house tax. One year passed, during which she lived from hand to mouth, before her hosts offered her the opportunity to explore more profitable markets, and possibly, if she played her cards right, a trip to America. She'd been traveling ever since, crossing international borders under student visas or work permits in the hospitality industry as creative dancer, masseuse and once as a translator.

Angelika survived being trafficked for six years because she was adaptable. She distinguished herself as a high-end commodity, commanding premium prices for excellent service. After an early, painful bout of gonorrhea, she learned to keep herself clean. She rarely complained, had an open mind, and picked up languages quickly from clients and other prostitutes alike. She was trustworthy – had never even thought of running off, because she had nothing to return home to – and so was rewarded with little freedoms. She was taken on house calls and site visits.

Angelika was also one of the few girls allowed to keep a boyfriend. He was usually a repeat client whom she was allowed to see off the clock. In turn, he offered gifts and cash, the proceeds of which were always shared with her handler. It was understood that boyfriends never lasted long. Girls were frequently shuttled from one country to the next, especially those who were susceptible to forming attachments. Angelika had also personally witnessed at least a dozen girls who had been demoted. They were moved to obscure outposts, reassigned to cabañas and mobile brothels, where they were forced to work a never-ending line for fifty dollars per day, because their boyfriends became attached and demanding. Physical and sexual abuse was liberally applied as punishment for the least transgression. And Angelika had personally witnessed two girls being killed as a lesson to the others.

Even so, Angelika had no reason to run to the authorities. The Dominican police promised nothing; the shelter provided the bare minimum required by law; she had no current boyfriend who would take her in even if she escaped deportation. There was no Jacuzzi; no manicures, pedicures or body treatments; no gourmet dinners while on dates; and no ticket to America.

I was her last resort.

Two days ago, she was waiting for a student visa. Today, immigration officials were escorting her onto a Jet Blue flight destined for San Juan. Her sole possessions were a US passport, printed itinerary for return travel to Santo Domingo, five hundred dollars in cash, and a small bag containing toiletries and a change of clothes that a consular officer had delivered to her at the airport.

Mid-afternoon found me at my desk, completing preparations for my new asset. The flight from Puerto Rico was scheduled to arrive shortly before 8p.m., giving Angelika barely had enough time to grab a quick meal before boarding was announced. I had every intention of meeting her at the airport.

Would she try to run? Would she try to start a new life in the United States with the seeds I had given her?

I didn't think so. Angelika knew what was so easily given could be taken away with similar ease. I had her passport pinged on the IATA database. The minute she checked in or boarded, I would know. If she missed her flight, I would know. If she tried to buy a ticket to a different destination, I would know that too. It was a very simple matter to flag her passport as a fraud, which would buy her a one-way ticket back to Kiev. O'Brien may have approved her papers, but Angelika was all mine.

My boss had neither the time nor inclination to babysit a prostitute. I had made a case for my involvement, which settled the matter in his eyes. Dealing with Angelika was a simple enough task that should not create a distraction from my primary case however, which was Colonel Ramirez.

It was an exciting day, and not only for me. Greg Landon was called into his first ever closed-door session with Ted O'Brien. It created a tangible buzz in the office, like an electric charge was coursing through the air. When he emerged twenty minutes later, his flushed expression and determination to avoid eye contact with all of his colleagues made that current crackle and hum. All at once the silence that no one had noticed before was broken by the staccato of fingers flying across keyboards and Blackberry Messenger pings shooting off like bullets at an open range.

It was all in vain. Landon had orders not to 'whisper a word of this in prayer to Jesus Christ'. The next obvious source of information was me. I was the unknown quantity, and not only was I not involved in the flurry of instant messages, I was ignoring the incessant buzz of my brand new Blackberry, as well as the peal of my landline. Unless they had Todd included in the rapid-fire message exchange, they could only guess that I was ignoring my husband's calls.

It seemed Byles lost the game of rock, paper, scissors, because she was eventually sent to pump me for information. "Hey, what the hell was that?" she asked, nodding discretely in the direction of O'Brien's office.

"What's what?" I asked, which earned me a disbelieving stare. "Look, I've been out all week. I have a lot on my plate and I don't have the time to keep up with the office intrigue."

"What are you working on?" she asked, as if she really expected me to give her a list.

"A number of things," was my pointed reply as I turned back to my computer where I was drafting a brief justifying our actions regarding foreign national Angelika Prokop.

"Who's your backstop?"

"O'Brien." I didn't glance up to register her reaction, but it wouldn't have been anything shy of shock. "Coffee," I warned, a second before she parked her butt on my desk directly into the spill I had left for her.

I almost sighed when she left to take care of the stain, but my landline went off again. Todd.

I thought that was more than enough excitement for the day, especially since I still had to pick up Angelika that evening. I had never been more wrong.

At precisely one hour and five minutes before end of business day, I came face to face with my past. There were only a handful of people at the embassy who had clearance that would allow them entry into our secure location, and all of them were either present or accounted for. That was why I felt relatively secure from Todd's interference as long as I remained at my desk. That was also why I was completely unprepared for the vision of Colonel Robert Townsend stalking across the open floor in full Marine Corps service uniform. Stalking wasn't an exaggeration, either. If ever there was a man on the prowl, it was Colonel Townsend.

It took quite a bit of effort to keep my jaw from hitting the floor, but there was nothing I could do about the near painful peaking of my nipples.

As a teen I started trolling the steady pool of officers that were never far from home for uncomplicated sex. I was now into my fifth year of retirement from the US Army. I had spent enough time around men in uniform to understand the pull Government-issued apparel had on the female psyche. I should have been immune to the effects of this man. But I was not, and that had everything to do with the man beneath the clothes.

He was the Military Liaison Officer (MLO) based at Mission in Kingston. We used to work together, and had almost followed up on our professional relationship with an intimate one. Right in the nick of time, life got in the way. Townsend missed our clandestine RDV, then I met Todd and hadn't look back, until a moment ago.

My attraction for Townsend transcended the arbitrary boundaries of hierarchy, propriety, honor, and even common sense; but Todd had been there to keep me on the straight and narrow. Even so, the sexual tension between us was further heightened by the acrimony between the two men.

They had traded serious charges. Todd claimed Townsend was the father of Mona's unborn child, which was a punishable offence for a married colonel in the US Marine Corps. Townsend claimed Todd had murdered his fiancée when he found out they had had an affair that may or may not have resulted in a child.

"You know he killed her," Townsend had said. "He's a dangerous man, Amy… He couldn't stand that I had fucked her."

For a second, I had thought I was the bone between two rabid dogs. Then Colonel Townsend poured out his heart and soul to me, admitting to a failed marriage barely held together by two sons, as well as his disappointment in letting me slip away.

As I watched the man dressed to the nines in service charlies move closer, I had to clench my teeth against the quiver of sexual awareness that hit me like a fist in the lower extremities. We hadn't parted on the best terms, but my body forgot all about the wrongs he had done, and focused instead on how extremely right it would feel to have him buried deep inside me.

Then I remembered where I was and why.

After I had killed the cop in Jamaica, Townsend was among the personnel who had assisted with the clean up. He hadn't liked that I was at a secret getaway with Todd, or that my left hand was considerably weighted down with Todd's two-carat stamp. For a time, it was whispered that Todd had brutalized me. The fact that the left side of my face had been all but crushed in my life-or-death struggle with the three assailants – while Todd remained completely unscathed – helped to fan those rumors.

Apparently, victims of domestic abuse were unstable. Tom Pendleton, the psychologist on my evaluation board, hadn't brought up my 'history of possible sexual abuse' during evaluation for shits and giggles. I had Townsend to thank for that.

Townsend's barracks cover was tucked under an arm, so there was nothing to hide the edges of his mouth curving up to meet the crinkles outside his eyes. His eyes were fixed on me, trapping my breath inside my throat. I didn't dare try to exhale, because dissolving into a moan was a certifiable risk. I could feel more than just his eyes on me as he paused for a long moment in the short hallway with a pool of desks on one side and a sterile wall on the other.

Hoping the room-full of people watching wouldn't notice his predatory intent or my doe-in-headlights-begging-to-be-fucked reaction was a waste of a prayer. Determined strides brought him to my side. I was rooted to my chair, almost incapable of breathing, but still had the wherewithal to wipe away the last of my coffee spill with a napkin I had conveniently close by. It was a silent and unconscious invitation for him to assume Byles' usual spot.

But Colonel Robert Townsend was all male – my type of male – with his hard edges, firm grip and animal instincts. I caught his scent as it wafted towards me in intoxicating waves – earth and musk. My body stretched closer for more without a clear command to do so.

His eyes, normally the blue of a hazy sky where the sun broke through, darkened as they roamed over my face and upper body. The dilating of his pupils, the condensation on his skin, the hairs on his forearm that prickled betrayed his arousal. But so did my nipples, worked into stiff peaks that tented my Friday shirt. The man's smile dimmed, but only so he could twist his pink mouth into a knowing smirk, evoking the unsettling image of him pulling the tips of my breasts between those lips.

"Amy," he said, with familiarity that would have gotten us both on someone's watch list back in Jamaica. "Good to see you again."

Dozens of suitable responses flitted around inside my head, but the only thing that stuck was: "Hi."

It was inappropriate, completely unacceptable anywhere except in a bar and perhaps Santo Domingo Mission. It said things I would not have been able to express without revealing too much... things like, 'I still want you... I was wrong about Todd... Can we try again?'.

"You look good," he said lowly. It wasn't quite a whisper, but his voice was so deep it may have sounded like an appreciative rumble to the ears that were perked in our direction. It made my body hum, even though there wasn't a shred of truth behind his words.

My hair was pulled back in a messy ponytail that was more careless than minimalist chic. I wasn't wearing any makeup and my forehead was sure to have that end-of-day shine that was borderline oily. I wished I had known he was coming.

"Thank you," I murmured, barely resisting the urge to tuck a stray wisp of hair behind my ear.

He noticed. His smile stretched as he exhaled a soft breath. I desperately wanted to feel his breath on me. I had dreamt about it many nights, having him thrust deep inside me, over and over, harder and faster than the one before, while panting his need in hot, angry breaths over my sweat-moistened skin.

Why didn't I know he was coming here? I would have prepared; I should not be staring up at him with please-fuck-me eyes.

Or had I been warned hours earlier? Was Colonel Townsend the liaison O'Brien had mentioned earlier? Would fate really throw us together again, especially now that I had removed Todd from my life?

"Let's catch up soon," Townsend said, already easing into a fluid stance. His eyes lingered, swaying between my mouth and my breasts, for an indecent amount of time. Later, I could be embarrassed. Just then, I was trapped staring after him as he made his way into O'Brien's office.

My boss was standing behind his desk, his curiosity aroused by what had caused Colonel Townsend to derogate from his mission. The office door closed between us. Even if the wall separating us was not made of glass, I would not have missed the narrow-eyed gaze O'Brien lobbed between the colonel and myself. They shook hands, finally freeing me from the warmth of both stares.

I nearly collapsed as the pent-up breath left my body. I didn't realize it while I was enthralled, but that breath was the only thing that had held me upright. With it gone, I could feel my knees shaking, as if after an especially long run. I wasn't the only one either.

Byles exhaled loudly, her eyes drifting from O'Brien's closed door to me. A soft smile touched the corners of her red mouth.

"A friend of yours?" she asked from her seat, ensuring all eyes were turned on us.

"Something like that," I answered, defiantly, not because I had proprietary feelings towards Colonel Townsend. I secretly wanted her, or any of the six men staring at us, to tell Todd what they had seen – that I had made a fool of myself with Townsend.

"Introduce me."

"Introduce yourself," I shot back evenly. Did she have to be so blatant?

"I think I just might," she said, running a hand through her hair.

I didn't doubt her, so I shook my head in a mixture of disbelief and disgust and went back to work. It wasn't easy. Colonel Townsend was no better than my husband. He was probably more discrete, because his career and his marriage demanded it, but I had long suspected he would fuck anything Todd had.

My productivity took a nosedive. There were still arrangements for Angelika I had to finish – medical exams, background checks, including arrest records for her and her known associates. But after querying the EUROPOL AFIS database for the third time without a clue as to what I was looking for, I gave up.

It didn't help that Todd kept lighting up my landline, or that Landon kept giving me the shit stare. It was as if he knew I had something to do with busting his prostitution ring, which of course was not the case. For all he knew, I had saved his ass, and the embassy untold embarrassment. Guilt was not a frequently occurring emotion for me, so I returned his glare with a bald one. Regardless of the bravado, I was more on edge than if I had done a line of blow.

Thirty minutes later, the two men in O'Brien's office stood, and every head in my section popped up like a colony of prairie dogs. My heart rate skyrocketed along with my libido when Townsend emerged, a self-satisfied smile deepening the lines around his eyes. I tried not to look at him, but I would have been the only one not staring. Besides, it would have been unnatural, because he made a beeline for me.

Our eyes met while there was still an expanse of hallway and empty desks between us. The shock was like a volt of electricity touched to my skin... my nipples, between my thighs.

"Amy," he said in that gravelly voice that vibrated against my clitoris. "We have work to do. Grab your stuff."

The command – even accompanied by an invasive glance at my breasts, my mouth, the throbbing pulse at my throat – managed to realign my cognitive skills somewhat. It appealed to an elemental part of me that civilian clothing could not completely stifle.

Reflexively, my walls came up and the solar system righted itself. His command reminded me that Colonel Townsend was a superior officer, and that any sexual advances of his part was harassment that I could use against him. It also helped me with Robert, the man. There were certain things I enjoyed while at play that might give the impression that I could be dominated. Only the most discerning partners understood that I was topping from the bottom. And Colonel was one of the least discerning people I knew.

"Mind if I clear something with my boss first?" I asked, already shutting down and gathering my belonging.

"Your boss or your husband?" His smirk was intact, but his eyes had lost their warmth.

I smiled as I brushed by him on my way to O'Brien who was still standing behind his desk, observing. I leaned into his office so I wouldn't be tempted to close the door behind me.

"Is Colonel Townsend the liaison you mentioned earlier?"

"You two used to work together. It should be a walk in the park for you, right?" It was a challenge not to fuck it up. One I accepted with a nod and a smile just as his phone rang. I was halfway out the door by the time he answered. Townsend was there, standing at the ready, as solid as a brick wall.

"Where do you want me, sir?" I asked with a straight face he tried to match.

"My hotel," was his bald reply, although I could almost feel his chest rumbling with suppressed laughter the closer I drew. "Where else?"

He gestured for me to lead the way, but he was so close behind I could feel the warmth of his body. As we passed, I noticed Byles had her Blackberry at the ready, eyes narrowed, trying to hide a devious smile as she furiously tapped out a message on instant message. Landon had the receiver of his landline notched in the crook of his neck while punching in a four-digit extension. In a second, he would greet his party, "Hey, bro."

By the time Colonel Townsend and I reached my rental in the parking lot, my purse was vibrating as furiously as if it could feel Todd's anger.

"Do you want to get that?" Townsend asked, pushing the passenger seat all the way back.

"No, sir."

"Why not, Koehler?" he persisted, stretching one massive arm across the back of my seat.

"Because, Colonel Townsend, we have a lot to cover. I don't need any distractions."

His smile was predatory and pleased as his eyes made the journey from my head to my feet and back again. "You're right. We do have a lot to cover."

If he hadn't called me Koehler, I might have blushed at the insinuation. But he had set the stage for our rapport by pulling rank. He had chosen to dominate me at work at the risk of losing in bed. It was a lesson he should have learned from Jamaica.

Like he shouldn't have reminded me of his wrongs.

FOURTEEN

I made the point of waiting in the lobby of Colonel Townsend's hotel while he changed into civilian clothing. It meant I had to firmly decline his invitation for a drink in his room. He smiled, like a cat in a game with a mouse, pretending I hadn't just turned down an offer for sex.

Upon his return, we assumed a relaxed camaraderie that felt surprisingly confortable given that was never the type of relationship we'd had before. We sat together in the hotel lounge, drinking Brugal Añejo and conversed with surprising ease, navigating the minefield between us like the born diplomats we certainly were not. If not for the electric charge of attraction crackling between us, it would have been as if the intimate weekend Todd and I had shared, leading to our engagement; and Townsend's confession about wanting me, his failed marriage to Tamara, and his affair with Mona had never happened.

I played along well, considering I was plotting my revenge for the damage his rumors had done to my career.

We avoided the topic of Todd Birch by mutual agreement. There was barely enough news from Jamaica Mission to fill a one page brief. My former Section Chief was struggling with my last-minute replacement, whose last tour of Jamaica was five years ago. Understandably, the conditions had changed since then, so he spent more time catching up than actually being productive. Blitzner, the Director of Narcotics Affairs who fingered me for what turned out to be a deadly admissions exam, was in D.C campaigning to have me join his team. Normally, I would not have been concerned, but something Townsend said had the hairs at my nape standing on end.

"Last I saw him, he was getting his ass kicked by Bill Beecher at the Pentagon's squash court," Townsend said conspiratorially, as if sharing an embarrassing secret about everyone's nemesis.

There really wasn't a discerning bone in Townsend's body. If Blitzner lost to Bill at squash, the match was fixed. And if Blitzner cared enough to publicly lose to a man who had retired from active operational duty because of three severe ACL injuries, then he was wooing Bill Beecher, and by extension, Bill's boss, who just happened to be Uncle Richard.

My assignment location was like a bubbling pot of stew, and everyone wanted to add his own seasoning. The high I'd been riding since my sit-down with O'Brien started to wane.

We were wasting my time I could be using to make an impact in idle gossip. I raised my drink to my lips and scooted closer to Townsend.

"So, Ramirez," I whispered. The lounge was slowly filling up with guests in search of a cold drink. Townsend and I had our backs to the wall, our voices lowered, and our mouths covered with either a hand or a drink. "You're the 'in'."

"Not quite, Koehler. I'm the bridge; we still need to find an in." Ever the opportunist, he stretched three feet of arm across my shoulder.

"Any ideas how we want to do this?" I stifled the urge to shrug him off. His touch was disconcerting, because I was painfully aware of my proximity to the massive expanse of chest and tree-trunk thighs, and because he used his no-nonsense business tone. He was dominating me as a superior – not a lover. Sexually, I liked the illusion of helplessness, but this was real. It confused me and angered me. My anxiety built. I inched away, but he pulled me back.

"Hard and fast sounds good to me."

"Colonel Townsend – "

"Yes, Koehler?" His breath fanned my earlobe and sent a shiver up my spine.

"Get your fucking hands off me, sir."

I felt his anger moving through him like magma. He removed his arm from my shoulder and retrieved his drink. I downed mine and scooted away from him under the pretext of laying down my empty glass. There were six good inches between us, but not enough to regain my composure. It wasn't nearly enough, but it would have to do. We had sensitive matters to discuss.

"You know, Koehler," he said with a sigh that did nothing to release any of the tension winding his body into a tight coil. "I'm getting tired of your little game."

"I don't know what you're talking about."

"Like hell you don't. You could have come in your seat this afternoon when you saw me. You want me to fuck you and you're doing a piss-poor job of hiding it." He spanned the inches between us with the slightest angling of his body, crowding me once again, sending my anxiety on a spike. "You've been dancing around this thing between us for months, but I'm telling you now that you better make up your mind soon or I will do it for you. If that's what you need to get over the guilt, I'll be happy to oblige."

I felt like I was slowly waking up from a dream. Did Colonel Townsend just threaten to force me, or was he simply threatening to abandon our doomed flirtation? I turned towards him, hoping to find some clue of his true meaning in his sky blue eyes, hoping I wouldn't drown in them. He was too close. His lips that moments ago almost touched my earlobe were now a heartbeat away from mine. I was afraid to tilt my head to read the threat in those eyes, because any movement on my part would bring out mouths together.

"What did you say?" I asked in a hoarse whisper, my eyes level with his smooth jaw. His scent was a mixture of musk, sweat and mint toothpaste. I was barely breathing so I could keep him out. But he was pulling me in through flared nostrils in deep, greedy gulps.

Finally he eased away, but it was not in surrender. His cellphone was ringing, and from where I sat, I could feel the vibrations. "You heard me," he said, before his dark blond brows crashed into a vicious scowl directed at the screen.

I sighed in relief and put six more inches between us. I still didn't know what he meant by making up my mind for me so I wouldn't feel guilty, but I was inclined to prepare for the worst and act relieved when the best happened.

"It's for you," Townsend said, extending his cellphone to me. Our eyes met across the foot of space, Townsend failing to cover up the fact that he found me amusing. It had to be Todd, and the blond giant's expectation for entertainment was running high. "Hurry up. We have things we need to settle," he added, deliberately vague and suggestive for the benefit of the person at the end of the line.

I held the Blackberry to my ear and could almost feel the gust of warm air that accompanied the harsh breathing on the other end. Either Todd had taken the stairs to his office at a dead run or he was barely holding on to his self-control.

"Koehler."

"What the fuck do you think you're doing?" Todd seethed. The harsh whisper was more than his trying to keep his voice down in deference to his location.

"I'm working," I answered, and by my neutral tone Townsend had to know there was trouble in paradise. He sat a foot away from me, but the intensity of his gaze was like a physical touch.

"I want my fucking life back," Todd continued through clenched teeth. "I want my wife back. I want you to stop acting like a fucking nutcase."

He wasn't the only one. I wanted my life back too, but that required that I excise Todd Birch like the cancer he was. He had turned my own body against me and the weakness had spread like a high-grade malignancy. My response was aggressive, because it had to be. I didn't owe him any explanation after what he'd done, but still I wanted to tell him so in my clinical tone. I wanted no more ambiguity between us.

I couldn't understand why it felt like a betrayal to say those things with Townsend so close, staring at me. I was a fool to feel any loyalty for a man as faithless as Todd.

"Whatever you think I did, you're wrong," he was saying. "If you had taken a minute to listen to me instead of trying to burn the fucking house down you would know I have not fucked another woman since I met you."

"I have to go."

"Listen to me, Amy. You don't want to play this game. I've been patient. I've given you the space and the time you need to calm the fuck down. Now you have to listen to me." He took a deep breath in an attempt to slow his words and breath. He hated losing control. "If you're trying to make me jealous, then you've won. But I'm warning you. Don't take this any further. I will not stand by and let you fuck that man because you want to punish me."

A part of me wanted to stay and hear how he would stop me... how he had stopped Mona. Had she learned about his many indiscretions and kept Townsend's baby so she could punish Todd? Had he really killed her... pumped her full of alprazolam and drowned her in the tub? Did I think Todd was capable of that? I wasn't sure. Did I want to know for certain that he had done it? No.

"Goodbye, Todd."

"Don't you fucking hang up on me," he warned, forgetting in his urgency to keep his voice down. Even Townsend, staring intently at me from a foot away, heard him. What must Todd's secretary, the perfectly composed Helen, think?

"Everything OK?" Townsend asked, using the opportunity to retrieve his phone to stroke the back of my hand with one thick finger.

"Fine," I replied simply, with a neutral smile. I reached for my glass of rum-coated ice before he could misconstrue my shaking hand for a reaction to his touch.

I wanted to hurt Todd. That was the reason I had extracted Angelika, wasn't it? So why didn't I use Mona? That was more powerful than ten Angelikas. Instead of turning him into a social pariah among the peers who meant so much to him that he had sacrificed us to bring a prostitute into our home, I could put an end to his career, and possibly even his freedom. Why did I turn away?

"Listen, Koehler," Townsend said, turning towards me while rubbing the blond fuzz at the back of his head. "I don't want to talk about him."

"Good," I interjected, "neither do I."

"But he's a dangerous man. Obviously things aren't great between you, and that has me concerned. If you're afraid, you can tell me."

Even though I didn't want to, my gaze snapped to his like an over-stretched rubber band. "I'm not afraid of him." I was terrified of the things he did to me, but I was not afraid of Todd.

"Then you don't know who you married."

He was right. I was married to a stranger, but I would never admit that to Colonel Townsend. I refused to continue this discussion, inviting Todd's rival into our marriage felt wrong.

"I need to eat. Can we discuss the case over a meal?" Townsend downed the rest of his drink and scanned the lounge, which had filled up while we were busy playing out our little drama. The steady drone of the growing Friday evening crowd could drown out our conversation, but the number of bodies meant our privacy was compromised.

"Not here," Townsend said, and I had to agree.

"I'll drive," I volunteered before he could suggest convening to his room. Even if his maybe threat wasn't weighing heavily between us, remaining on the premises was still out of the question. Todd was undoubtedly on his way.

Colonel Townsend directed me to el Meson de la Cava on Avenida Mirador Sur. It was an intimate restaurant situated inside an actual cave. It even had the 'authentic' indigenous wall art, featuring a stick man with his balls dangling between his legs. Somehow it suited Townsend: elegant when decked out, but primitive, as the drawings on the wall. It was his rough edges that had first appealed to me... that, and the air of authority that came with being accustomed to command. The latter used to hold so much promise for our sexual adventures, but he had wasted it confusing work with play.

It was a while before we settled at the table the wainscoted maître d' escorted us to. Drinks were brought, and our menu selections made before we were comfortable raising the matter of Ramirez. In the meanwhile, Townsend stared pointedly at me across the small table. My eyes busily took the measure of the place, ignoring his fixation on me.

A steep, spiral staircase had taken us into the belly of the cave, which served as the dining room. The natural light dimmed as the air cooled. A large chandelier and a few wall sconces cast a romantic glow over the bowed heads at the white-dressed tables. The bar had cushioned stools and a small display of dusty wine bottles that probably hadn't been moved since the place opened nearly a half century ago.

The servers were all mixed – a veritable melting pot of European and African ancestry, although every one of them would deny it. The only dark face was that of the sole busboy, and even he would likely self-designate as native Indian.

El Meson de la Cava wasn't the type of restaurant one came to shoot the breeze. It was the Dominican take on elegant dining, a place where men of means took the women they wished to impress. The men were very touchy, and their dates seemed to hang on their every word. A girl with long, plastic nails and a knock-off Louis Vuitton handbag had her date, a man about twenty years her senior with a large Bluetooth headset attached to his ear, take pictures of her with her cellphone – social tagging so her friends would know she had been there.

An older group of well-to-do Dominicans looked at us, the Americans, coldly. They seemed the type to reminisce about the days of Trujillo when they weren't gently swaying to the instrumental of *Imagine*, like tonight. The women had big blown-out hair, perfect nails and airy dresses. Their faces all look familiar; I passed them everyday on the billboards in advertisements and election campaigns.

I was still dressed in my Friday work attire – navy pencil skirt and light blue silk bodysuit – and they could tell. The other diners were more impressed by Townsend in his dark slacks, button down shirt and navy blazer. I had to admit he looked good, but he still lacked the natural urbane sophistication that Todd had. I didn't know why that thought warmed me on the inside, but I was happy to report that it decimated whatever inkling lingered in the back of my mind about acting on my sexual impulses where Townsend was concerned.

"There's a training exercise being held in Baní next week. MARFORSOUTH is helping the locals with combat training techniques. I'll be on hand, along with Colonel Ramirez, for the opening on Monday morning, and then again at closing on Friday when I'm handing over scholarships for short courses at CHDS."

MARFORSOUTH was the US Marines Forces South, which fell under US Southern Command, and CHDS was the Center for Homeland Defense Studies at the Naval Postgraduate School. There was nothing unusual about either the training or the scholarships. It was Townsend's proximity to Ramirez that interested me.

"You're sure he'll be there?"

"Not really, but he's slated for the opening ceremony. He could show up or delegate."

I swallowed a half-chewed portion of squid ink ravioli that burned my throat on its way down. I soothed the burn with a drink of white wine. That gave me some time to recover from my disappointment with his response.

I have an idea, but I need access to Ramirez," I said, which was met by Townsend's hiked eyebrows.

"You have a plan," he mimicked, slightly skeptical, but at the same time not surprised.

"I do, but it won't work without Ramirez. I need his phone." My throat still burned, so I took a gulp of water, making sure to swallow an ice cube in the process.

Townsend leaned back in his chair and sighed, stretching his thick neck muscles by turning his head from side to side. "I'm not even going to ask about this plan of yours just yet. Before we get to that, I want you to explain why Colonel Ramirez would willingly hand over his phone to me."

"He won't," I answered simply. "I have an asset."

"You have an asset," he repeated, and this time the skepticism was there for all to feast on. "You've been here for what – a couple of months?"

"Six weeks, and yes, I have an asset. It won't be any good though if you don't have access to Ramirez."

I mopped up my plate with a piece of bread while staring at Townsend from beneath my eyebrows. His air of expectation slowly melted away, as he realized that I was serious. He scooted his chair closer and leaned across the table so there was only a single stream of pale light between us.

"Tell me about it," he ordered. He was my superior, but he wasn't my boss and I didn't have to tell him about any of my assets. The only person who would be able to link me to any asset was O'Brien, and that was only because I intended to have him sign off on an expense account for her. I had promised Angelika that I would use her, and this was only the beginning.

"Tell me how you plan on getting close to Ramirez," I countered.

We broke off while the waiter removed our dinner plates and laid dessert before us. I hadn't had a decent meal in a week, and so dived right into my coconut pudding. It burned my mouth, but this time, I was out of both wine and water. It was a toss-up between Colonel Townsend's wine glass and his untouched water. The wine was tempting, but he would likely read too much into that, so I reached for his water while shuffling the hot pudding around my mouth.

"You know what's good for a burnt tongue?" he asked me with a lascivious smile.

I blinked past my watering eyes and silently swore as a tear ran down my cheek. "That's sexual harassment, Colonel Townsend."

"Only if you don't want it," he returned. I sighed tiredly, wondering if his strategy for getting me to sleep with him involved wearing down my resistance. "Besides, I was going to offer you some of my ice cream." That would have been just as bad as drinking his wine, which in his book at least, was an invitation for him to come in my mouth. Underneath it all, Colonel Townsend wasn't much different from an adolescent boy.

"Ramirez," I reminded him. "How do you plan on getting close?"

"I don't know. Let me think about it."

"OK, but we don't have much time."

"Tell me about your asset," he tried again.

"No," I replied adamantly, while gesturing the waiter for our check. The maître d' stopped by to offer coffee, a digestive, more wine. I refused without a second glance at Townsend. I had fifty minutes to drop Townsend off at his hotel then get to the airport to pick up Angelika. Since she was traveling on a US passport, it was unlikely the Dominican immigration officials would turn her back.

When I pulled up to the hotel entrance fifteen minutes later, Townsend was still trying to alternately get in my pants and make me tell him about my asset.

"Why don't you come up for a bit?" he asked, turning towards me in the dark confines of my rental car. I turned on the overhead lights to dispel the fake sense of intimacy.

"No, thanks. I have an appointment and I really need to get going."

"At this hour on a Friday night?" he asked, his lips thinning as he pressed them together.

"Crime never sleeps."

"I'll call you tomorrow, Koehler," he said, and unfolded his large frame from the front passenger seat.

I had the car in gear ready to peel off when he tapped on the window so firmly I could not pretend not to notice. He leaned into the tiny space, and although there had to be at least three feet of space between us, he still managed to suck the air out.

"I meant what I said earlier, Koehler. You get tonight, but tomorrow I expect you to fall in line. Don't make me put you in your place."

There was a dark glint in his eyes as Mr. Hyde stared at me. I didn't doubt that the place Colonel Townsend envisioned for me was beneath him, or at least on my knees, my burnt tongue covered in his essence. My anxiety wasn't the only thing that spiked on the lonely drive to the airport.

I was unquestionably and uncomprehendingly aroused.

FIFTEEN

I was right on time picking up Angelika. The minute I made it into the terminal building, she stepped out of the customs and immigration hall. She was dressed in jeans – something from the kids' section – and a black tank top. She was also wearing a brown wig, cut into a bob that swallowed her face, and her eyebrows were darkened to a complementary color with a pencil. I only recognized her at first glance because of her slight frame. She looked like a child, and the casual observer would have expected her to be accompanied by an adult. It would have been an honest mistake if they discounted the stone cold eyes on her.

She stopped for a moment to scan the welcome hall, adjusting a brand new purse on her shoulder. There was no outward reaction when she spotted me. I walked out without acknowledging her, but she followed dutifully. I didn't want to be seen with her, could not afford to be associated with her at all, and she seemed to understand that.

Angelika had to be curious. She could have tried to run. Her willingness to blindly follow my lead smacked of trust, which was uncharacteristic for someone with her past. Yet, it was that jaded history that guaranteed her compliance for now. She knew when she was owned.

Of course, I questioned the safety of bringing this woman into my home – the home I had created without Todd. There was a slight chance her traffickers would learn she had been sprung from the shelter. They could be looking for her. Her wig was good for a cursory glance, but anyone who knew her would recognize her appeal.

In the car, conversation was kept at a minimum. The things that hung between us were too deep for the short drive. The silence between us could have been heavy; it was not, but by no means was it comfortable either. That was a hard bill to fill for someone as accustomed to solitude as me.

We got to my new apartment and I showed her around. There wasn't much in the way of space, just two bedrooms, two bathrooms, living space and kitchen right off the entry hallway. I stood outside her bedroom while she explored the sparsely furnished room and its adjoining bathroom. It established an important precedence about how each other's space should be treated. I also didn't want to be reminded of her hair in my sink or her scent on my sheets.

I told her what she needed to know about my security system. It was a deterrent for her and an early warning system for me. The point was not to catch her in the act of breaking the rules; it was to keep her on the straight and narrow. When used in conjunction with her new smartphone with its eight megapixel camera, I would be able to monitor her whereabouts twenty-four-seven.

"The cameras will tell me when you're here and what you're doing. I'll know when you leave the apartment. When you leave, make sure you take your phone. I'm not your babysitter; I'm your handler, and I would appreciate it if you didn't make my job harder than it needs to be. Don't bring anyone here. This," I made a sweeping gesture with my arm to indicate the apartment, "is so you're safe."

She didn't ask any questions and she didn't say anything. She nodded as we went, one arm wrapped around her middle. The wig dangled from her other hand and she casually slapped it against her jeans. Her uncertainty was seeping through the cracks. It wouldn't hurt to capitalize on her vulnerability, so I gave her some time to stew.

"Are you hungry?"

"I could eat," she murmured, twisting the brown strands of synthetic hair between her fingers.

"Make yourself at home."

I poured myself a glass of red wine and watched as she scoured my refrigerator and cupboards. She kept staring at the contents as if she expected them to change.

"There's nothing to eat," she said. The refrigerator light shining on her pale face made her skin look luminescent. I disagreed with her assessment. I had gone all week on condiments, hot dogs, dry cereal, wine and chips. "Nothing from the earth," she clarified, as if she had read my mind.

"Call the *colmada*. The number's in your phone."

I drank my wine while she ordered eggs, whole milk, whatever vegetables they had, spices, and raw chicken, and asked for it to be delivered. If there was any doubt she was sharp as a tack, she gave out my address without the least hesitation. She may not have had much to say, but she was definitely paying attention.

She declined my offer of wine, but took a seat across from me in the living room while we waited. The wig was in her lap, and she kept plucking at the fibers with her white fingers. Her eyes mapped the bare walls, but redecoration was the farthest thing from her mind just then.

"So..." she started hesitantly, while I looked at her over my wine glass. "What do you want me to do?"

"Nothing you've never done before. I wouldn't want you to be uncomfortable."

"Fuck?"

"Entertain," I clarified.

She arched one perfectly plucked eyebrow. The only other person I knew who could manage that feat as adeptly was Todd. "Is that all?"

"For now." I didn't mean to snap at her, but that thought of Todd caught me by surprise and I hated my failure to compartmentalize him. "There are a couple of ground rules we need to discuss," I said more evenly, emptying my glass.

"Oh?"

"You don't know me; you've never met me. If you get jammed up, I'll come for you when I can, but that only works if no one is expecting me. Do you understand?"

"I do not understand this 'jammed up'." Her pert little nose wrinkled in concentration; her freckles gathered into a tight cluster.

"You're the only one who got out, Angelika. There's a chance they could be looking for you. They might even think you brought the heat... called the cops," I clarified as she concentrated again on my words, her eyes focused on my mouth.

She tried not to show her fear, but the cards were stacking up against her. If she'd felt trapped before, now that she might be hunted, she understood she had to learn to love her chains again.

"I understand," she said, with enough solemnity for me to believe her.

"This apartment is only temporary. It'll take a few weeks to get you better settled. You should know your past is over. If you had friends before you must forget them. The places you used to go, you can't go anymore. Do you understand?"

"Yes."

"Now tell me what you want from this." She'd been positive thus far ... very cooperative. It wouldn't hurt to nurture that attitude with an effective reward system.

"You've given me so much already," she said, the pucker between her eyes betraying her confusion. Even with skin that pale, she didn't have a whisper of a wrinkle.

"There must be something you want," I encouraged. Her worldly possessions consisted of a twenty-dollar wig she had stolen from an airport shop mannequin, and a purse with at most a single change of clothes. Even her passport was on loan.

She thought for a long time, her eyes roaming over the naked walls again. Her fingers picked up the pace plucking at the wig.

"Broadway," she whispered, and it was almost reverently. "I want to see Broadway."

I nodded and got up to refill my wine. "That's good. It's something to work towards. You wanted to dance once... yes?"

Angelika nodded almost hesitantly, afraid to reveal anything that would make her more vulnerable.

"You should go to school then ... study dance." I got up to consider my idea, pacing the empty space between the couch and the barren kitchen table. The apartment might have seemed uninhabited, but it was perfect for me. "That could be your cover. You're a student. How do you feel about Europe ... Paris to be precise?"

Angelika's eyes widened to dinner plates, her breath came in short bursts. "Paris?" it wasn't what she expected. We were so close, why send her back to Europe?

"Yes. Find a school, learn to dance, and if you're good, you could make it to Broadway." It wasn't what she'd had in mind when she admitted to the dream. This was more than she would have ever hoped for, and she was too optimistic despite her history, to turn it down.

The buzzer sounded. The rider from the *colmada* had arrived. She checked the apartment's video intercom before admitting the deliveryman past the electronic gates, and once through, she kept up her surveillance of the front gate to make sure he had come alone. By the time she realized she had no money, I had already placed four thousand pesos on the kitchen counter, taken my glass of wine, and slipped out of the room.

No one knew I lived here – not even my boss – and I wanted to keep it that way. I checked my firearm and waited. I had given her a lot to think about and more to be grateful for. I also wanted to give her some time to come to terms with my offer. I accorded her a few hours while I took a shower and did some work on my MacBook.

It was after midnight when I re-emerged to find Angelika curled up and fast asleep on the living room couch, her empty plate on the nearby coffee table. The television was turned on to the *Law and Order* marathon she had started after having her meal, and grabbing a shower of her own. Her freshly washed hair was almost invisible against the white leather sofa. She was dressed in a fresh tank and shorts, and judging by the palm tree and San Juan sunset print on the front, both had come from an airport shop. She really had nothing and no one.

I didn't think twice about waking her. What recourse did she have?

I thought for the hundredth time she looked like a child. The illusion didn't last long however. The moment she opened her eyes, those bits of clear marble gleamed at me in the semi-dark. Those eyes were too old for a twenty-five year old woman. There was something so heartbreakingly familiar about them that I had to turn the lights on to dispel the mist clouding my head.

For a split second, she almost made me second-guess my decision to use her. The folder in my hand grew heavy as the plastic covering slipped on my sweaty palms.

"I'm sorry. I didn't mean to fall asleep," she said, sitting up and rubbing her eyes. Her body temperature had fallen and now she was cold. Either that, or I had scared her. Her arms were wrapped around her middle, holding in the shivers.

"It's OK." Angelika quickly composed herself, and her hardening shell also strengthened my resolve. I handed her the folder, then took the single seat perpendicular to hers.

"What is this?" she asked, curiosity and wariness warring within her.

The folder was two inches thick, and as she began scanning the contents cursorily, it became quickly apparent that there were only photographs – 8x11 portraits and profile shots – some of which had close-ups of discerning marks like tattoos, birthmarks and scars. It was in essence, a look-book of past and present embassy personnel who might have made use of Angelika's services.

"I want to know if you fucked any of these men." At the shelter, we had already discussed her clientele. She didn't do women, not for personal reasons, but simply because her child-like body did not appeal to the rare females who didn't mind using a prostitute.

She sighed, but I couldn't tell if she was just tired or tired of me talking about her fucking men.

"Is that all?" She asked again. I wasn't accustomed to her inflections as yet, and I couldn't figure out if she thought I wasn't asking enough, or if she thought I was asking too much.

"No. I want to know what you did with them, how often, when, where, whether you used a condom, whether they're cut … everything."

"There are so many," she said, almost to herself, scanning through the pile again, but this time, assessing the scope of work as well as the time and effort required.

I smiled thinly. "Do your best."

"When do I have to get back to you?" Angelika asked, as if she really expected me to leave her the dossier of past and present American personnel, some of whom had Sensitive Compartmented Information (SCI) access on top of their Top Secret clearance.

"Now." I leaned back to give her space, while she continued skipping through the folder.

"I need a cigarette," she said, but she was really asking if it was OK to smoke in the apartment. There was no balcony and it would have been a pain to have to run downstairs every time she needed to smoke.

I nodded and waited for her to return with a carton of duty-free Marlboro Lights. She lit up with a Bic, which should not have – but did – remind me of Todd and his zippo. Angelika pulled the empty dinner plate closer, intending to use it as an ashtray.

As she returned to the first page, I tried to keep my expression impassive, but could not help leaning forward. I didn't need the light to map the laugh lines at the corners of his eyes. The intense cobalt eyes followed me regardless of how I tilted my head. The black of his hair was deepened to pitch. Even freshly shaved, the dark outline of his beard was clearly visible. It was as if the little piece of him captured on paper was warmed to life by my presence. He was beautiful in the dark, but with the flood of the overhead lights, he was downright dangerous. Todd was one of a kind.

How could Angelika overlook him?

"Is this light OK?"

She hummed her approval and pressed on. My confusion bloomed into annoyance that she might not be taking this seriously. She lifted two photos from the folder and placed them flat on the table.

Was she removing the ones she did not know?

That couldn't be. After a few more minutes, Landon's photo joined the growing pile on the coffee table. Todd's by-passed photo nagged me.

"If you're not sure about someone, you should still separate the photo from the others."

"OK," she answered simply, but dragged on her cigarette and kept on sifting through the pile.

Her nonchalance set my blood to boil. I wanted to tell her to go back … to pick him. She had to confirm what I already knew. Todd had taken her into my sacred place. She had been in my bed, her scent forever linked with the musk of sex and sweat and fruity body splash.

As her pile continued to grow, I had to admit that Angelika had come a long way on account of her adaptability. What if she knew about my relationship with Todd? Had she seen my picture somewhere at the house? I didn't keep prints at home, but Todd kept some in his phone. Would he have shared my photo and talked with her about my issues, as he had done with Jessica Byles? Bile roiled in my stomach at that thought, and only a deep drink of wine kept it down.

Did Angelika think I would deny her this escape if I discovered she had fucked my husband? Would she lie to keep what she had now and risk the future I had planned for her? Absolutely. A bird in hand was worth two in the bush, and she would do her best to maintain our accord, even if it meant losing out on the promised Broadway.

It was two hours before Angelika closed the file. She had slept with seventy-four U.S. personnel. Considering there were so many, I was surprised at the level of detail she remembered.

Number eight was potentially a pedophile; he would have to be recalled before he became a problem. Number twenty-six was her most frequent customer. Landon was number fourteen. Number sixty was an exclusively anal customer. Number seventy-three couldn't get it up without a golden shower. It was the kind of information I wanted … just the thing I needed to burn Todd. Because of him, their secrets had been revealed, their weaknesses exposed. So why did I feel a hollow thud echoing in the pit of my stomach? Why hadn't she chosen Todd?

"Is that everything?" I asked in a last ditch effort to have her reconsider the reject pile.

"I believe so."

She looked exhausted, but she would have to endure, because I wasn't done yet. I flipped to a photo at the very back of the no-fucks.

"How this works, Angelika, is you get paid for work completed on my behalf. Once you're on your feet, you'll have to find a job and enroll in school. You won't be able to predict when I need you for an assignment, so you'll have to be self-sufficient. I will choose your location and take care of the formalities, like papers, but the rest is up to you. Keep your cover and don't break any laws."

I gave her a minute to allow that to sink in. She had no questions, but tired as she was, I could tell she was paying attention.

"Now," I pressed on, flipping over the image of Colonel Ramirez, "this man will be your first job. In the coming days I will tell you what I want, and you will do it. For tonight, it's enough to know you've never met him before."

"OK," Angelika mumbled with a suitable level of caution.

"Tomorrow at 10 a.m., I have a medical exam scheduled for you. If you pass, there's something I want you to do for me. You won't be paid. This is so I know you have what it takes to work for me."

"I know how to fuck," she said, but even behind her defiance I heard her hurt.

"I'm sure you do, but an American passport is a heavy price to pay to rent a hole." Her breath hitched from either the dryness of the tone or the threat of retracting her passport and finding someone else. "I will use your body, but it's your brain I need. I chose you because I don't have the time to train someone else."

She was quiet for a moment, but her shoulders began to ease. "You seemed to have made up your mind before you even met me."

"I still haven't made up my mind. You have to prove yourself to me. Do you have any more questions?"

"No."

"Good. Get some sleep."

I was halfway to my bedroom when Angelika cleared her smoke-clogged throat.

"Why me?"

"Excuse me?" I turned slowly, tucking under my arm the folder of discards, as well as Angelika's selections that had my notes written on the backs.

"There were other girls to choose from. How do you know I can do what you want? Why did you pick me?"

"Would you rather I did not?" How could I explain the kinship I felt towards her without opening a window into my soul? I too had buried a part of myself in order to survive. There was only so much bad one could do before it showed in the eyes.

"No … I mean, yes … I mean, I will work for you. But I want to know if I did something … if he is there among the ones I chose."

"You did nothing wrong, Angelika," I replied.

I locked myself in my room and tried not to think. I'd done entirely too much in the past week and I was tired. There was no comfort to be had from her admission. She really didn't know Todd. She hadn't slept with him.

Why should that count? It wasn't the act that mattered; it was the betrayal. Wasn't it? How could I love him if I couldn't trust him?

I swallowed a pill, and hoped the glasses of wine I had consumed earlier would hasten the void. I didn't want to feel the hollow inside me grow.

SIXTEEN

Anne had to admit Amy was the best there was. The lemons that were Todd Birch, his harem and Colonel Townsend, had somehow been made into a giant pitcher of lemonade.

Amy had never before been tested like this. Anne had doubted her ability to extricate herself from the morass that her life had become. Amy was attached to Todd Birch in a way she had thought impossible. She was never that girl, demanding explanations that would help her to excuse a man's behavior. There had never before been cause for excuses. Amy's expectations – beyond occasional sex and complete discretion – were nil. Whether or not a man delivered on either or both, she had always been the one to walk away.

Her emotions were compromised, but at least Amy recognized her limits. As long as she remembered to stay away from Todd, they could still accomplish what they had set out to do.

Amy's decision to manage Angelika was evidence of her superior, strategic mind. Getting the prostitute to roll over on Todd was only a distraction. He deserved it anyway, and no one could accuse Amy of being a saint. Dark angel, maybe… but never a saint. Getting Angelika to fuck Townsend was trickier. If it worked, then Amy could have her leverage and pay him back for the doubts he had raised in Arlington. Or Amy could exchange her silence for his cooperation in relocating Angelika to Europe.

Using Angelika to get to Colonel Ramirez was efficient. If she succeeded in gaining access to his cellphone, Amy could be on her way to winning over O'Brien. That was the type of foresight, adaptability and professional maturity that supported a stellar candidacy for a prime post.

Now, using Angelika to get to Sergei Afanasenko was a stroke of genius. It was also extremely dangerous. If anything went wrong ... if Angelika was caught ... she could not be counted on to keep her silence. Someone with Afanasenko's resources could easily trace her origins back to Amy. Then what they had done to her father would also be done to her.

The key therefore was to get Angelika as close as possible to Afanasenko without the man knowing about it.

Anne went over the heaps of reports that had been condensed into schedules. There was a separate file for every member of the Afanasenko household. She also had projections based on old routines. Sometimes they were spot on, and other times, life got in the way.

Alexei came down with a fever and had to skip violin practice in favor of a doctor's appointment. Natalia cancelled her afternoon drink plans so she could be with her son. And Sergei canceled a weekend in Cannes until his son was recovered. The staff was recalled, huddled inside the mansion in the sixteenth arrondissement, tending to Alexei, making runs to the pharmacy, playing cards with him, changing the channels on the television for him.

After a few days, the household's business and social schedule would return to normal. But try as she might, Anne could not find a nick in the Afanasenko armor. Normally the servants would be the greatest vulnerability, but Afanasenko mitigated against such opportunism by relying on the expatriate East Slavic population in Paris to fill the ranks of nannies, maids, doctors and bodyguards.

There was always the option to crash-and-grab – barge in, guns blazing, and collar the target. It was unsuitable for several reasons. First, it was a suicide mission, and secondly, it would alert the target's criminal network, including his government affiliates that someone was hunting him. Given Amy's limited resources and vulnerable sub-contractors, having a myriad of seasoned mercenaries on her trail was the last thing she wanted.

The only viable option then was to work through the family's associates who had similar recruiting preferences.

Having gone through two hundred pages of data, it wasn't until 4 a.m. that Anne spotted a possible breach. On January 7, 2012, Michel Baranets would celebrate his eighth birthday. In addition to being Alexei's classmate, the boys also shared a soccer coach and a chess master. Their mothers lunched together every second Wednesday.

Michel's father was a second-generation Parisian of Ukrainian descent and heavily invested in the natural gas industry. As far as I could tell, his association with the Afanasenkos was a purely social one; his business interests were heavily scrutinized, and he could not risk financial ties to Sergei. But the men shared a love for capitalism and vodka, and discussed politics and the former while imbibing in the latter at a tea shop in the sixth arrondissement every Friday afternoon – more pressing engagements permitting.

The timing seemed right; the opportunity as good as any years of preparation could offer. With Angelika in Paris in time for a new semester, and in search of a job, she was a natural fit for a place in the Baranets' household.

A plan began to take shape. The sooner Angelika was relocated, the sooner she could begin scanning the classifieds while sipping tea and lugging around pointe shoes. With one of the Baranets' maids conveniently indisposed for several weeks at least, an opportunity could be created for Angelika to move into the household. From a position on staff, she could then create the perfect opportunity for Alexei to be captured and used as a lure for his father.

There were few things Sergei loved more than his wealth, and his son was one of them.

Michel's birthday party was a unique opportunity for Alexei to be separated from his watchers. It was usually Natalia's responsibility to attend birthdays and school functions, but given the close relationship the Afanasenkos had with the Baranets, it seemed a reasonable expectation that Sergei would be in attendance too. If so, it was the perfect opportunity to meet the man in person with minimal alarm.

Separating Sergei from his guards was critical. Doing it quickly was a matter of life and death. It required a different set of skills than what

Blerim Nesimi had thus far contracted for Rose. It was also dangerous to make him aware of the plan. He was as likely to turn on them as help.

But Anne had no other contacts in Europe, and sourcing hired guns remotely was the worst kind of plan. Quite frankly, Anne didn't know what other choice she had. The most she could hope for with such a scheme was to limit her liability to a single target that could be eliminated as required. A bad plan was worse than no plan at all in their book, so that part at least required a more thorough look.

It was 10:30 a.m. in Naples, and by Anne's estimation, Blerim Nesimi would be at the café on Via Chiaia. She reached him on his cellphone.

"You will get your reports this afternoon," he answered without preamble.

"Good."

"You know, Rose, your father was a reasonable man. He spent ten years working to capture Afanasenko. He understood Rome was not built in one day," he chided, and Anne could imagine him leaning back in the wicker chair, sipping his espresso.

"John Gardner is dead, and it only took one day to do it." It took considerable effort to remove the emotion from her voice. She could not talk about him without remembering how he had looked, laid out on the cold steel table, his body broken by cruelty and lead. His left knee was shattered, three fingers broken, and then they put a bullet through his forehead. His wife, Mary-Anne Koehler, the only innocent in all of this, was shot in the back.

It would be a cold day in hell before Anne let Blerim Nesimi know how vulnerable they were, how much their lives relied on his cooperation.

"I have another assignment for you."

"More?" He didn't sound pleased, but he wasn't as resistant as she thought he would be. He was probably hoping for something he could use to burn them.

"I want candidates for a clean up job."

There was a long silence, but it wasn't for lifting his espresso cup. Blerim Nesimi froze. And then, he asked, "What need would you have for such specialized skills?"

"Someone has to watch the watchers," Anne replied, but he would not have been fooled by her nonchalance.

"I've given you good men, trustworthy men," he protested, careful though to stifle his indignation.

"Would you bet your life on it, Iris?"

That's what John Koehler had done. He had bet his life, as well as that of his wife and child, on the trustworthiness of another. The man who had warned her about betrayal was himself betrayed. Of course he knew what was coming. He'd always known it was a race against time, and one he might lose. It was the reason he trained her then set her free.

"I will get you what you need."

"Good. I did not think you were a martyr."

There was a long sigh before his thickly accented voice came across the line again. By then, he had finished his espresso. He would sit there for another twenty minutes, reading the newspaper, watching Claudia serve coffee to the patrons, pretending he wasn't interested in every man who smiled at her and tried to strike up a conversation. Should anyone show too much interest in the girl, her father would relieve her of that particular service and send her to tend the coffee press.

"What do you plan to do about Afanasenko?"

"For now I will watch."

"You Americans don't know how to kill. Any of the men I have given you would gladly do it for half what you have paid me to find them." There was amusement in his voice, and Anne pictured his violet eyes crinkling beneath his pale copper brows.

"Who said anything about killing anybody?" Anne asked, mimicking his flippancy.

"Come on, little Rose. Why else would you need a cleaner?" he chuckled, as if she were the novice and needed to be schooled.

"Keep the reports on time, Iris," she said, ignoring the remark. Now there was no warmth, no feigned conviviality. "And my congratulations on impending fatherhood."

The silence that followed was like an explosion, and Anne derived real pleasure from the exposure of this man's weakness. His attempt to dissemble was feeble.

"What are you talking about?"

Claudia was Blerim Nesimi's twenty-year-old girlfriend and his only attachment. His success in hiding her importance from his Camorra associates for the past four years might have lulled him into a sense of false security. She lived with her father, who at forty-five years old was seven years Nesimi's junior, in a two-bedroom apartment above the café where she worked. Regardless of the parent's personal views regarding their relationship, he had every incentive to keep his opinions to himself and the association a secret. Only last week she had had her first ultrasound and Blerim Nesimi had attended the appointment, claiming the need for a diagnosis for a feigned gastro-intestinal illness.

"I found you and I found Vincente Tosti. Why would I stop there?"

He didn't answer, and didn't try to refute the relationship with a girl thirty-two years younger than him who had had no choice once she caught his attention. But he wasn't breathing either. "I'll send you instructions on the clean up crew."

Anne ended the call on what she thought was a positive note. Keeping tabs on Nesimi's communications was time-consuming, but it was crucial. Keeping him in line meant always being one step ahead of him, but she also had to worry about protecting herself from him.

That probably was not the relationship John Koehler – or the Gardener, as he was known to his assets – had foreseen for his daughter. She was his rose, meant to give shade to the others in his garden. But there would come a time when Nesimi would neither want her protection nor fear its absence. Before that time came, Rose would have to kill Iris.

SEVENTEEN

My anxiety levels were mounting even though I was Todd-free and it was the weekend. I ran as fast and as much as I could even as my body protested the lack of sleep. I was dismayed to find despite all the effort I put into escaping my husband I was not free.

I could move out of our home and change my number hundreds of times; I could run a seven minute mile for nearly two hours; and I could make all the plans I wanted for my future without him. But I could not escape the hollow inside my center that seemed to expand by the hour. It was an angry ball of heat and violent tears that made my chest ache the longer I pushed myself.

Why didn't Angelika pick Todd? If I was wrong about that, what else could I have misjudged? Had my fragile psyche begun to affect my work... or my father's?

He couldn't be guiltier if you found him balls deep inside her.

But what if he didn't do it? What if it was one of the others?

No one should have been there. He lied and you failed to see it. He is even more dangerous than any of us gave him credit for.

I had to get away, but I had nowhere to go. Plus I had responsibilities. Upon my return to the apartment I had to wake Angelika. I knocked on her door for a solid minute. I hoped she was just exhausted from everything that happened in the week and didn't sleep that soundly all the time. I resisted the urge to open her door and call out to her. I didn't want to see her body laid out on my new sheets. The picture my mind had conjured of Todd's bachelor party was already vivid. Why reinforce it with a live feed of Angelika in bed?

I knocked again. I knew she was there. I made sure to check the video feed before entering the building. I could never tell what kind of surprise could be waiting for me, especially now that Todd knew that Townsend was in town. I had run out of excuses for a downed Blackberry; Todd knew how and where to find me.

Angelika opened the door with her white hair mussed and the heel of one hand pressed into her right eye. The other eye was squeezed shut, hoping that if she didn't see me then I wasn't there.

"We leave in thirty minutes."

"What time is it?" she asked on the third try to clear the clog from her throat.

"Thirty minutes for we leave," I said, already across the living room, heading for my personal shower. "Don't keep me waiting."

By the time I returned to the living area, my Sig secured in my waistband holster, covered by a short tunic and blazer and tucked under my purse arm, Angelica was dressed in yesterday's jeans and tank, finishing off a plate of eggs.

"I made you eggs," she said, cleaning away her plate.

"I'm good," I told her, heading for the untouched pot of coffee. I drank standing against the refrigerator, watching as she cleaned up after herself. If she was this fastidious all the time, why had she left so much of herself on my sheets and in my sink? Her movements were stiff and her unease built the longer I stood there assessing her. It was probably just her self-consciousness that had her trying to wipe her presence away... trying to make herself smaller than she already was.

Her flip-flops squeaked on the wood floors when she finally turned to me, drying her hands in a towel.

"I am ready," she said in a voice that was too husky for her tiny frame. She rubbed her neck where the brown wig scratched her skin. Her eyebrows were darkened to brown and her eyes outlined by black eyeliner. It made the glassy irises appear darker – almost blue and her white skin less translucent.

We spent an hour at the doctor's office, ensuring she was as healthy as she looked. If push came to shove, I intended to use Angelika to hurt Colonel Townsend, but he hadn't given me cause to want him dead.

Yet. So Angelika deposited urine and blood for eight major STDs. Then he went about the rest of our day while waiting for her results to come in.

I switched the venue of my drinks date with Hernandez from the cigar bar to Townsend's hotel lobby. A cigar bar would not have been my pick anyway, and I would have suggested a more neutral location – with less risk of running into Todd – if I had not been in a hurry to get to the shelter. Hernandez at least was pleased to hear from me, so pleased in fact that I suspected there was more to the meeting than casual drinks.

At the mall, Angelika picked out a modest wardrobe, stocked up on her makeup and toiletries, then went grocery shopping on O'Brien's tab. I suspected she was still trying to make herself appear small in my presence, so when she labored over the decision to pick out an eighty dollar lace dress, I decided for her. The roles I had planned for her demanded that she dress the part. She was a pleasure toy; I didn't want her looking like a juvenile refugee.

Over an early dinner I told her what I wanted her to do later that evening. Her reaction was measured. I couldn't tell if she thought she had returned to her living nightmare, or if she just wanted to get it over with. But as the day yielded to evening and then night, she became more agitated – well, as agitated as a block of ice could get. And it had nothing to do with her test results. She was given a clean bill of health.

I watched her get dressed in a white dress that at first glance could have been one of my skirts. She rimmed her eyes with thick black liner. But with all that, and even in mile high stilettos, she still looked so young. It didn't help that her head didn't top my chin when I was barefooted. Part of the problem was her progressive slouch – as if she was slowly folding into herself, holding the edges together in her center.

"What is it?" I finally asked, unable to ignore her edginess anymore. Our appointment with Townsend was particularly dangerous because it was personal and barely legal agenda, hidden under the guise of an official briefing on Ramirez.

She shrank even more, if that was even possible, and her enormous eyes widened and darted from one end of the room to the next.

"Angelika." I was short, but we were short on time and I had a feeling she was near hysterical. I had never seen her like this before... Fidgeting to hide the tremor of her hands, chewing on her lip to stop her chin from quivering.

"I need something," she finally said, barely above a whisper.

It took me only a second to understand, perhaps because I had so much experience with the riot, and the many ways to find the void. "Speed up or slow down?"

Everyone had their own way of dealing with the anxiety, but inevitably choice came down to soothing the ache until it was bearable – if not entirely gone; or covering it in a haze of euphoria so the pain didn't matter anymore, even if it never actually went anywhere.

"Speed," she whispered, swallowing hard. Why would I judge? She was only human.

"Let's go to the car. I'll get you something." She nodded although her chin was touching her chest. I grasped her arm when she would have turned away. "When you hide things from me, you risk the job and your life. I need one hundred percent of your focus, and if that means taking care of these urges, then that's what we'll do."

She nodded mechanically and was quiet for the short drive. I gave her fifty dollars and sent her to get what she needed. It was not far from the Factory, where she used to work, but Angelika appeared unfamiliar with the location.

Twice she turned back towards me, seeking guidance as she stood before the closed zinc gates. It wasn't just tottering on four-inch heels on the gravel walkway that had her unstable. She was trembling though her arms were wrapped tight around her middle. She knocked tentatively at first, then, at my nod of approval, tried harder.

Carlito would be wary of her. Given his occupation as a drug dealer he didn't trust easily, not even potential customers, and particularly not those as restless as Angelika. In addition he didn't street deal from that location. It was primarily a stash house from which street-level pushers scored a kilo at a time. He didn't like the heat the fiends brought, and would either deal with her quickly to get her away from his place of business; or turn her away, pointing out where she could find one of the street-level guys. Only the connected went to Carlito, because they were guaranteed the purest coke north of the Caribbean Sea. The more hands that touched his drugs, the more cuts were made.

I was too far away to hear the conversation, but I could tell when she had delivered the message: "Magdalena sent me." Carlito stuck his head out the gate, looked left and right, then took her money and slammed the gate in her face. A very long five minutes later, Angelika extended a single arm through a crack in the zinc portal and rubbed palms to collect her score.

She was smiling as she hurried back. The second her butt hit the seat, she inspected her score, making sure the powder wasn't sticking to the plastic bag. She would probably only get five good lines out of it, but I had deliberately given her enough money for a gram to judge how much she used and how often she needed.

"Go ahead," I told her turning the air conditioning off. We were pressed for time and I didn't know how long she needed to decompress.

She used her house keys to scoop four bumps – two scoops per nostril – then pocketed the rest inside the purse she bought in Puerto Rico.

"Good?" I asked, starting the car and pulling onto the nearly empty side road.

She nodded and hummed, "Very good!" but didn't offer to share.

"Feeling better?"

"Hmm, much better," she murmured, eyes closed and head tilted backwards so she would not keep dragging at the nasal drip.

"Do you need anything else before we get there?" I asked and she hummed 'no' again. "Bathroom? Drink? Cigarette?"

"A cigarette would be nice," she said and this time I felt her eyes on me as I pushed the rental car to beat a red light.

"Go right ahead Angelika. Be comfortable."

"Would you like?" She asked, finally remembering her manners although I could hear the pause. She knew I didn't smoke; the offer was for speed and was born of mistrust, not a general desire to share.

"No, thanks, Angelika."

There was silence for a couple more lights. I passed Townsend's hotel, but I wanted to give her as much time as needed to get her head in the game.

"Why you do this?"

"Because you will earn it." She didn't say anything as we passed through the tunnels on Avenida Independencia. A few more lights and I would double back. "Do you have any questions about tonight?"

She sighed and I could almost feel the evening's earlier edginess seeping out of her. This was the woman Todd and Landon knew – the confident, sexy hooker who could be playful or sexually intense as required.

"I smile, say hello, get him to fuck me when you go," she said matter-of-factly although there was nothing straightforward in what we were about to do. "Make him think it is his idea."

"The bug, Angelika."

"Yes, I know. Keep the pen centered and pointing at us. Not a problem." She retrieved a tube of fruit flavored lip balm from her purse, dabbed some on and pouted in an audible smack. Either she was that good or she wasn't taking this seriously. Good thing I had brought a back up bug for insurance.

In my field paranoia saved lives, so I parked in the darkest corner of the hotel parking lot and sent Angelika to the lobby bathroom to wait for me. I circled the block and parked close to the hotel entrance before heading inside. I was five minutes late and had to wait another ten minutes for Townsend to come down. It was his way of making me pay for keeping him waiting. Even though I had retired from the Army five years ago, the Marine always tried to pull rank.

While Townsend called the elevator, I went to collect Angelika from across the hall. The colonel stopped dead in his tracks when he saw her. I assumed my jeans, Oxford shirt, and tired blazer weren't as remarkable as her tube dress – even if she did have the figure of a pre-pubescent child. Townsend's gaze flickered between us, as if asking both of us if we were for real, but we left the introductions, and indeed all conversation, until we made it safely inside his suite.

"Robert, this is Angelika," I started by way of introduction to Townsend's back as he set about fixing us drinks.

He didn't offer us options, but neither Angelika nor I was picky. Besides, either she was working for an employee of the Quarter award, or she was pleasantly surprised by how physically appealing her mark was. She stared at him unabashedly, smiling as if he were a dream come true. She breathed audibly at times, toyed with her hair and twisted her body as if the sight of him made her edgy… needy.

At first, Townsend kept his cool, staring equally between us. Inevitably though, her silent flattery got to him, and he started showing off in small, but significant ways. He used his height and mass to tower over us as he handed each of us Scotch on the rocks. A flick of a finger showed us where he wanted each of us to sit, while he paced the small space between his desk and the only upholstered chair, dwarfing the physical space and setting the electric charge of sexual awareness on high.

"Look," I said, mentally shrugging off the building tension like a heavy coat, "I can't stay for very long. I have a work thing I need to take care of in about twenty minutes."

"There's something more important you need to take care of, Amy?" It wasn't just the no-last-name rule that had him sounding both familiar and condescending. It wasn't the time to get snarky though. So I had to stroke his ego… It wasn't the worst thing I had ever done.

"I just have to finish something for Ted. I'll be in the lobby, maybe thirty minutes tops."

"I don't wait for you, Amy. That's not how this works." He stood before me, fists on his hips, zipper six inches from my face, assuming a position of unequivocal dominance, relishing the view of me looking up at him. And just like *that* I was reminded of his maybe-promise of sexual assault. Angelika was too intent on the dangerous undercurrents for her own good, so I brushed off Townsend's meaning with a small smile.

"I didn't expect you to. I thought you might like the time to brief Angelika on the plan and your expectations."

The plan was simple: introduce Angelika to Colonel Ramirez so she could introduce an intrusion key into his cell phone. Once we had access to his .do.mil account, we could search at leisure for the narcotics trail. Even compressed, the intrusion key would account for about 1 MB of space. The only way to hide such a large file was in a photo, which meant Angelika would have to send an infected file from her phone to his.

The how and when of her association with Colonel Ramirez were for Townsend to decide. And I was confident Angelika could manage Townsend expectations. In fact, she was almost salivating at the opportunity to test some of those expectations, eye-fucking the blond giant with the tent in his khakis. Either that or cocaine really did it for her, turning the reserved suspicious child/woman into a consummate party animal. I could hardly blame her though. I could hardly deny my reaction to this primal male. It was only my need for control that saved me every time.

Townsend would just have to forgive me for testing her readiness for the major leagues on him. He should understand the dangers of sending an untried, unknown quantity into battle.

By the time I left the room we had the possible 'when' covered. Townsend would formally meet with Colonel Ramirez for breakfast after the opening ceremony for the training program on Monday. There was a possibility of a Tuesday night baseball game, followed by 'other' nightly entertainment. Friday night drinks at the Officers' Club after the closing ceremony was a definite go.

Although it was not yet confirmed, I had concerns about the 'other' nightly entertainment'. I didn't want Angelika resuming old associations where she ran the risk of being recognized.

"Thirty minutes, Amy," Townsend cautioned as I slipped through the door. By the way his fists were jammed into his pants pockets, causing the opposite effect of concealing his erection, it came off as more of a reminder not to show my face before the allotted time had expired.

He didn't have to worry about my walking in on him in flagrante delicto. Angelika had her pen, which she had spent ten minutes stroking playfully with her mouth. And I had left my day planner on his desk, snap side – and camera – facing the bed. If Townsend had paid attention to me over the course of our two-and-a-half year assignment together, he would have known a day planner was not my thing.

Really, what would I have put in it? Wiretap host country officials Monday at 10 a.m.? Recruit prostitute Friday at noon? November 27 was the anniversary of my coordinating drone attacks that killed an Al Qaeda number two in Pakistan.

I would have liked a day planner that came with tips on how to screw over an embassy full of male personnel; hold a colonel by the balls; stay one step ahead of a pissed-off boss and an increasingly impatient husband; all while plotting to apprehend a former Soviet arms dealer and his corrupt US allies. Those would have been some useful tips.

EIGHTEEN

Hernandez was late, which was a problem for me. At the rate Townsend was going, he would not need the full thirty minutes, and I could count on him bitching at me for keeping him waiting. Again.

By the time I was settled at the hotel bar with an ice-cold Presidente, a single ear bud in place, my iPad relaying the feed from room four twenty-five, Townsend was balls-deep in Angelika's mouth. She took it like a trooper, although one hand was angrily fisted in her hair, and the speed of his thrusts caused my feed to buffer. But even if the video required a faster Internet connection, the audio was crystal clear.

"Hands behind your back. Now open wide. Suck, you greedy whore," he commanded, more angry than needful. Now what could Townsend have against little Angelika? Under the bit of polish the uniform afforded, Colonel Robert Townsend was, simply put, a savage – a very angry one too.

But what happened next made me reassess whether I had bet on the wrong pony when I chose Todd and set aside my physical response to his rival.

Freeing the smooth leather of his belt from the loops in his discarded khakis, Townsend created a noose and looped it around Angelika's throat. He obviously knew what he was doing too. He had the noose nestled high around her throat, just below her jaw, and the end of the belt wrapped around his fist like a leash. He had her bent over the end of the bed, her tube dress and panties on the floor along with her pride. His angles were perfect, his movement fluid and angry, as he pounded into her from behind. The rein in one hand pulled her towards him, while the thrust of his hips and the angry slaps laid across her bare ass propelled her in the opposite direction.

The man seemed to get off on pain. The blows fell heavier and more frequently, his grunts and groans and words of encouragement – if you could call 'Take it, you fucking whore' encouragement – increased commensurately with Angelika's moans. Even high on cocaine, she was not enjoying everything about Townsend's play. When her moans became mostly cries, he tightened his hold on the rein, cutting off her protest – if you could call 'Ooh, please, shit, fuucckk' protest.

No, Townsend was definitely no stranger to the game. He read her body expertly, loosening his hold – if not the jackhammer he called hips – as the tension left her body and she began to slump. The uninitiated would have listened to her empty gasps instead of her body. Townsend was not one of those. He knew when to push and for how long.

Yes, I had definitely put my money on the wrong horse... if I could discount his selfishness. The man made no attempt to address Angelika's needs, which was especially selfish given what he had put her through. He could have played with her clitoris, tweaked her nipples, or even run a hand along the curve of her back to reward a job well done. He did not. In fact, the more I watched them, the more apparent it became that Colonel Townsend was in a race and whoever came first would win.

Although I had one ear free so I would not be both blind and deaf to my environment, Hernandez still startled me. I clutched the iPad closer to my chest and pat myself on the back for spending thirty dollars on a privacy screening. The only thing he would have gotten an eyeful of, if he had been so inclined, was my reflection. Hernandez took a seat and ordered two Presidentes.

I safely tucked my surveillance equipment away with more than a slight pang of disappointment for having to miss the rest of the show.

"It's good to see you, Ernesto," I lied smoothly, hoping the cold beer hid my flush.

"Hold that sentiment until you have finished that beer," he chuckled as a bartender laid my second of the night before me.

So it wasn't the pleasure of my company that had brought on this invitation after all. Silly me, for being so unreasonable.

"When I invited you, it was my intention to have a simple social meeting. Now I must apologize that life – and of course the job – has intruded on our friendly encounter. You understand?"

No, I did not understand, but he had given the game away with his enthusiasm this afternoon. Had he found out about Angelika? Had the intrusion solution been compromised? Could any of those two be traced back to me?

My heart beat heavier in my chest, echoing in my ears. Outwardly at least, I kept my cool. I had my father to thank for that. He had taught me the benefit of making the enemy work for it. And if this was more than the friendly drinks that Hernandez had promised, then he was my enemy. It did not matter one iota that he seemed uncomfortable with his next move – hesitant, almost – running his hands nervously over his jet hair, then his salt-and-pepper beard.

After a long drag on his long neck and an even longer sigh, he pulled an envelope from his shirt pocket. He passed it over to me, pushing it across the smooth bar counter with one thick finger. I accepted possession.

Inside was a single sheet of paper, printed in black and white. There was a photo of a male subject, either Caucasian or Latino, with dark, slicked back hair and a neatly trimmed mustache-beard combo. He had a thin line of hair running along his jaw to join his sideburns to his beard, which had to take considerable effort to maintain. Yet he was dressed in a simple, white t-shirt. Definitely Latino. Below the photo was a brief bio for Alex Rivera Ferreiras, twenty-eight years old, resident of Washington Heights, New York.

"Who is this?" I asked, because Emilio Hernandez clearly thought Ferreiras was significant to both of us for a reason I had not yet grasped.

"A drug trafficker," he answered simply before taking another drink from his bottle. I did too, both to give him time to sift through the bullshit he planned on feeding me, and to play catch-up with my beer.

Why he was bringing this to my attention was unclear. Well, I knew he was about to ask me a favor. But I had no idea what he planned on offering in return.

"He is Dominican, but also American, and as you can see, he lives in New York. I thought you might be interested in his activities."

Hernandez was at the core an honest man, and I was even more certain about this because he could not even look me in the eye. Instead, he nervously scanned the bar, the patrons, the large-screen TV airing CNN.

"Ernesto," I started, setting down my bottle with a quiet thunk. "Don't blow smoke up my ass. It tickles, but doesn't really do anything for me. Either you level with me or I'm out of here. What do you want?"

For a moment he looked as though he wanted to protest his innocence. But we both knew it was bullshit. He was a senior intelligence official and this was a basic narcotics case. If Ferreiras wasn't already on state or federal drug enforcement radar back in the US, any José off the street could call the DEA hotline at the embassy to get him some attention.

"Thanks for the beer," I said, signaling an end to our conversation, but I didn't make an attempt to move. The bar was my dugout, and I had another seven minutes before my half an hour was up.

"Wait," Hernandez said with a sigh, meeting my gaze steadily for the first time all evening.

How the hell was he good at his job again?

"Ferreiras is the nephew of César Ruiz Mendez." That meant nothing to me, so I maintained a blank stare. "You may have seen his campaign posters for the presidential elections next year."

"He's running for President?" I asked, confused, because I certainly had not noticed a Mendez running for Office.

"Not openly... not precisely," Hernandez answered hesitantly, ratcheting up my impatience. "He is the man behind El Hombre, a financier of sorts to the Opposition."

And like a wrecking ball crashing through crumbling foundations, my faith in humankind, which apparently had been hinged on Hernandez's honesty, came tumbling down. This was a political mission. He had been sent by politicians to manufacture a scandal that would undermine the legitimacy of their rivals, or at least staunch the flow of cash into the Opposition's campaign.

"Tell me what you want, Ernesto." I wasn't about to give him a break. If he wanted to take a ride to hell he would have to pay the fare just like the rest of us.

"He truly is a drug dealer," he protested, "and I am a policeman. He should be in prison, and his assets seized, not polluting our electoral system."

I finished my beer and gathered my purse. Until I heard a specific request, Hernandez was wasting my time. I could not exactly keep a man in my pocket with intimations and innuendos. And when I thought of all the locals I could have wanted to be in my debt, Hernandez wasn't a half-bad candidate. It blew my mind how many secrets he might be holding.

"I want him arrested," he finally admitted, one thick hand on my arm preventing me from leaving my seat. "I want it to be public. I want his connections exposed. I want the story to be a headline here and in America. I want him to be an example of corruption in this country." His eyes watered from his refusal to blink as he stared me dead in the eye and signed my loan agreement.

For a brief moment, I was struck by the realization that perhaps I had more people in my debt than pockets to keep them in.

"I'll be in touch," I told Hernandez, but with a comforting pat on his wrist. He released me, and I got up to leave, taking stock of the time. I was seven minutes late.

Shit.

I could only hope Angelika had put Townsend in a better mood.

NINETEEN

It was becoming increasingly difficult to decide what to share with my boss and what to keep to myself. Especially when O'Brien stared me down with the full mossy weight of his eyes and asked me about my meeting with Hernandez.

I had to scramble to come up with a story for him. At the eleventh hour, I recalled informing O'Brien of the social call with Hernandez on Friday. Still, the intensity of his gaze had me wondering if someone in Hernandez's camp had gone over both our heads with a request for assistance on the Ferreiras case.

"It was okay, just a beer and friendly conversation." My boss arched one thinning brow at me in a silent expression of disbelief. So I didn't do 'friendly', but I could play the game better than anyone once I knew it *was* a game. Hadn't O'Brien passed on a commendation on the wonderful job I did last week?

"I would like you to authorize an expense account for Angelika."

I could tell by the way his jaw clenched and he leaned forward in his seat that I was at least successful in the art of distraction. For a brief moment I wanted to open the door and let some air into the enclosed space. It was hard to not sweat under the green spotlights that were trained on me.

"Now why would I want to do that, Koehler?" If the electric air wasn't sufficient warning that I was treading in dangerous waters, the ominous tone from my Section Chief would have.

"Because she's working for us now."

"Oh, is she?"

"Yes, sir. Colonel Townsend approved her to work intrusion for us."

"Well, that's a surprise." Somehow he didn't sound surprised at all. He was remarkably calm, like the still before the storm, like air being sucked out of a room right before a grenade blast.

I quickly ran through our plans for Angelika, as far as Colonel Ramirez was concerned. I had her stashed where I could keep an eye on her all day – at home, while IT installed the key on her cell phone. For the second time in as many weeks, I would be running tutorials.

Although I had her phone, I knew Angelika wasn't going anywhere today. She was on a rest-and-ibuprofen regimen to help with the body aches. She was still pretty banged up from Saturday night, and I had seized the rest of her cocaine. There was nothing to be done for the bruising around her neck from Townsend's improvised lease, except a few dabs of concealer and liquid foundation. I would show her how later, so she would not look overused if she were called in for work tomorrow.

"How much does she know?" O'Brien asked, the tension in his jaw only marginally relieved.

"No more than required."

"You think you have this all figured out, don't you, Koehler?"

"No, sir. I'm just trying to do a good job."

He sighed in a long, slow breath, rolling his head around on his shoulders. Although he leaned back in his chair, I could not afford to relax just yet. He looked like Uncle Richard right before he put someone in their place, which was invariably beneath him.

"Let Townsend pay her."

"I don't think that Colonel Townsend wants his money crossing hands with Angelika." Both O'Brien's brows skyrocketed. "Just in case the purpose is misconstrued." For the first time in my life, I witnessed Ted O'Brien going bug eyed.

"Did he fuck her too?"

"At this point, that would only be speculation."

"Speculate, my ass! You are an intelligence officer." Even with the office door closed, I wasn't certain our conversation was private anymore.

Time for another about-face.

"I can confirm that she has slept with this man though." I quickly maneuvered a one-eighty, handing O'Brien the personal file for Angelika's number eight.

"He has pedophilic tendencies. I could confirm illicit conduct with a search of his personal computer, but I'm not sure that would be in the best interest of the Embassy. I recommend repatriation before he becomes an embarrassment. The State Department should also be informed, so they can conduct an investigation and decide whether a quick and quiet separation would be more appropriate than public prosecution."

O'Brien reached for the file with one hand and fished a tab of antacids out of his desk drawer with the other.

"How many were there?"

"Seventy-four, Sir."

"Seventy-four times?" O'Brien asked, fishing his glasses from beneath a pile of paperwork and setting them on the bridge of his nose.

"No, sir, she has slept with seventy-four unique personnel... Some of them two and three at the time."

"Colonel Townsend?" he asked, as if I had not just evaded that question.

"Seventy-four past and present members of staff at Santo Domingo mission." I did not want to lie if I did not have to, especially because this might come back in a formal interview.

"I want this off my plate, Koehler. I have neither the time nor inclination to deal with this shit, so you make sure this and the girl disappear," he said around a mouthful of chalk.

It seemed O'Brien wanted me gone too, because he shooed me out with a flick of his fingers. But at least he was poring over the file I had given him. My business mostly done, I complied... well, mostly. I stopped at the door.

"About that expense accounts, sir..."

"Do whatever the fuck you want, Koehler, but get her out of here."

He wasn't even looking at me when he issued that order. He had both thumbs and index fingers massaging his temples, while staring down at the personal file between his elbows. I left, but O'Brien clearly re-thought giving me carte blanche, because my office line rang the moment my butt hit my wheeled chair.

"No more than twenty thousand, Koehler. Pace her."

I could do one better than pace her. As soon as I tied up a few official loose ends, I was booking her ticket to Paris. O'Brien would never see or hear from Angelika again.

Mondays were becoming increasingly hectic, but I didn't mind at all. I was making strides, building O'Brien's confidence in me, and hopefully finessing the powers that be with my sensitivity and political acumen.

I spent the rest of the morning managing my active cases and following up on a couple that had been delegated to the operational or prosecutorial teams. Then I got to work on Hernandez's request, checking whether Ferreiras had already popped up on anyone's radar. It was just my luck that the NYPD had an active surveillance on him. However, unless I got a federal team on the case, I could not call in Hernandez's marker.

Our in-house DEA agent was Michael Martinez, another Boy Scout – one of Todd's good friends and poker partners. He was present at the bachelor party, but had not slept with Angelika there or on any other occasion. I had to figure out a way to get him on the Ferreiras case, but lying and claiming this was on the official docket was out of the question. There was no dodging O'Brien when it finally came to light. By then, there wouldn't be much he would not do to get me out of his office.

Just because Martinez hadn't done anything wrong yet didn't mean I could not bend his arm a little.

I waited for him to leave for lunch, then ran him down in the public courtyard. It probably blew his mind to find me on his tail, calling his name, intent on a conversation that others could witness.

"Hey," I called, meeting him in the shade of the Economic Affairs wing. The midday sun beating on the concrete walkway and off-white buildings cast a blinding glow from which I had to shade my eyes.

"Koehler," he said in greeting, but it was also a question. I had never sought him out before, never shared more than a handful of words with him, not even the day I had met him in Todd's living room.

"I have a person of interest for you."

His brown eyes were narrowed in a mix of suspicion, confusion, and protection against the searing light, but he was slow to respond. He was not an unattractive man. His black hair was longer than I liked, scraping his shoulders, and his olive skin looked warm to the touch. The bottom row of his teeth behind his too full-for-a-man's lips was crooked, which somehow added a layer of charm when he smiled. But I did not see any of that just then. I saw a mark I had to make.

"Yeah?" he finally asked, running one hand between his hair and collar and coming away with a sweaty palm.

"Yes. I got a tip while working another case."

"Why would they come to you?" He looked me up and down as if to see whether anything had changed. No, I was still a cold, hard bitch, and he had no idea what Todd saw in me.

"Like I said, I was working another case." I shifted from one foot to the next in a show of impatience, hiding behind what he would consider normal behavior. "Look," I continued, pressing beyond his wariness and obvious dislike for me as a woman, "it's political. The NYPD is sniffing up the guy's ass and I don't want them to fuck it up. So send your guys in, build a case, and wrap it in a nice pretty bow for me by the New Year. I'll send you what you need. Cool?"

"No, we are not cool. We have never been cool, even if my boy is sticking it in you."

I tried to find a shit to give because Martinez didn't like me. I came up empty, and the shrug of my shoulders said as much. The only thing his crudeness had earned him was a higher spot on my shit list. "Whatever. Just do your job."

"Does O'Brien even know about this?"

"What kind of question is that?"

"A straightforward one. Who is the backstop on this?"

"It's my case; O'Brien's my backstop. I got a tip, and I'm passing it on to the *competent* agency." I enunciated my words and counted off tasks on one hand as if this was the simplest thing in the world and he was too stupid to follow otherwise. It pissed him off; there was a definite tint of pink beneath his cheeks, and his respiration began to spike. He would have been suspicious if I had played nice all the way.

"Listen up, *bruja* –" he snarled at me, when what he really wanted to call me was *puta*. This time I didn't give him the time to dig his own hole.

"No, you listen up, Martinez," I whispered since we were now so close I could spot the tiny beads of sweat on the bridge of his nose and across his upper lip. He had inched forward, expecting me to compensate with a full step back. His jaw clenched in a failed bid to put a lid on his annoyance when I held my ground. "We are on the same team. If you don't want to scratch my back, then I sure as hell will not cover your ass."

"What the fuck are you talking about?" He looked at me like I had lost my mind. I knew what he was thinking…since when did I do anyone any favors?

"Right," I said with a dramatic roll off my eyes, "like you weren't at my house two Fridays ago, fucking that hooker."

He opened his mouth to protest immediately, then shut it abruptly. His entire face flushed as he grappled with what to say, to deny his participation without outing his homies.

"I don't know what you're talking about," he concluded, but stood there ready to lob whatever else I had back in my court. Even if I didn't know what I knew, even if I was only grasping in the dark, he would not have convinced me. All the fight had gone out of him; he had resorted to duck and cover.

"Save it, Martinez. I know about Angel, and if you want to be an asshole, then I can arrange for Mrs. Martinez to meet her too."

Our eyes clashed and I felt the anger radiating from him in waves. I held my ground. I knew the moment he spotted the bloodshot in my eye and remembered how I had come by it. He remembered I did not back down.

"You don't want to piss her off, do you?" I asked, but what I meant was, 'you don't want to piss *me* off'. I continued, "I mean, you are a stable man. You've got a nice house, beautiful kids that look up to you. Trust me, you don't want Angel showing up at a divorce hearing, or God forbid, the DHS investigation. "

"I did not fuck that whore," he seethed at me, so out of control now that he jammed his finger in my face. I didn't flinch, but a couple of staffers on their way to the cafeteria did. Martinez stood erect, jaw clenched and temples throbbing under the strong surge of blood and rage.

"Save it for the judge, Martinez." Because I did not want to come off as a complete bitch, I patted his arm comfortingly, but he only tensed under my touch. "Look, it doesn't have to come to that. All I'm asking is for you to do your job. In a timely manner."

"And not tell O'Brien." I never said he was stupid.

"Tell him; don't tell him. I don't care. Just make sure your people get on top of it asap. I want an arrest by the New Year and I want to read about it in the *Listin Diario*. But, you should know that if you want to start playing he-said-she-said, I have a lot more to say than you do."

His hands raked over his hair in a show of annoyance, but also capitulation. "I don't know why I'm doing this. I didn't do anything wrong."

He seemed calmer though. At least he was taking stock of the environment and not so focused on being angry with me. It made perfect sense for him to want to limit his liability.

"And if there's nothing? If this guy's clean?"

"Then that's it." Martinez let out a sigh of relief, as if he truly expected it to be that easy. "But I doubt it. NYPD has had him under surveillance for months now."

"Then let them handle it."

I shook my head. "It has to be federal. There is a local hook and I have the narco file to prove it. Plus the deadline is non-negotiable."

"Why?"

"Because," I said on a sigh of impatience, "it links back to my case, and I don't like loose ends."

"I still don't understand why you had to come hit me with your bitch card." I couldn't blame Martinez for trying to find my weak spot. The problem was he had found it, but let it go when I returned fire.

"What are you talking about? Can't you tell I'm working on my teambuilding and social skills?"

Martinez erupted in laughter, showing off his crooked teeth and the deep laugh lines at the corners of his eyes and mouth. He really wasn't a bad looking guy, and at least he had found the humor in all of this.

"You should let your husband teach you how to play nice, Koehler," he said to my back. I still had a lot of work to do, and now that the Ferreiras case was being handled, I could turn my attention elsewhere.

"I play to win, Martinez," I replied over my shoulder.

He stood there as I walked away, and I was pretty sure I heard him mutter, "What a fucking bitch."

TWENTY

I had just stuck the end of a chocolate bar between my teeth when O'Brien exited his office.

At first I was not concerned because he could have been on a staggered lunch break. But when he deviated from the main corridor and came to rest right before my desk, the gunk of chewed up milk chocolate, caramel and nuts landed like a heavy ball in the pit of my stomach. I had to squeeze my legs together against the sudden urge to pee. I took my time lifting my chin to meet his gaze. His eyes were as green as I felt looking into them. The whites were shot through with red, and the outer edge of the right one ticked... much like the edges of his firmly compressed lips.

Before I had the chance to drive myself crazy, wondering which of my schemes he had discovered, he gently laid a folded Post-It before me. I couldn't do anything about his glare, so I focused on the note. I had to pry the sticky ends apart to find 'Room 325' scribbled in black ink. It was Todd Birch's office. The chocolaty-caramel ball in my stomach began to churn, waking all the butterflies.

"Get over there now, Koehler. Fix whatever you have to fix, but I don't want to get another phone call from *anyone*." He didn't say what it was about and I wasn't about to ask. O'Brien was red-in-the-face angry. That wasn't good for me. I needed him convincing and sincere when he told the evaluation panel I was an excellent, well-adjusted, politically sensitive officer.

"Consider it settled, sir," I told him, but I did not move. I couldn't. My insides were so tied up in knots that any movement on my part risked tugging on them and physical pain.

"What are you waiting for, Koehler?"

I looked down at my desk in a futile bid to clutch at straws. I would see Todd again, and much sooner than later. Why would that thrill me as much as it scared me? I had spent the entire week building my resolve against him. Nothing he said would make a difference.

Maybe he won't even have to say anything. You already have your doubts. You want him back.

It's not the infidelity that mattered. It's the fact that I cannot trust him.

Keep telling yourself that. Maybe one day you'll actually believe it.

Shut up!

"What the fuck did you just say, Koehler?"

I mumbled an excuse about making sure IT had everything squared away for our case before they shut down for the day as a cover for having told my boss to shut up.

"Don't go anywhere, don't do anything until you've dealt with this," he said, jabbing his index finger into the Post-It. How was it I felt that poke in the middle of my chest when he hadn't even touched me?

O'Brien was right behind me as I slung my purse over my shoulder and crossed the hallway. I was afraid he would follow me all the way, and I couldn't shake the image of being kicked out of class and sent to the principal's office. I shredded the Post-It as I walked, because it gave me something to occupy my eyes while passing those fixed on me. I cut them off as well as O'Brien's advance when the steel reinforced doors closed behind me.

And then I was alone, meandering through a maze of hallways, exterior courtyards, and atrium, followed by more corridors. I found Todd's corner office before the fluttering in my stomach settled, but at least I had the outward trappings of calm firmly intact.

Everything was different in Todd's world. There were carpeted floors, woven in vivid colors, like red or blue. It was still a government installation, so the hairs were short and rough, dimming down the luxury. His secretary sat behind a desk made of natural materials, like wood. Her chair was dark leather on mixed media legs and wheels, and the walls were done up in muted tones to match her voice. The wainscoting was of real wood, which created texture that kept the eye stimulated. Helen's workspace was at least four times the size of mine. It was hidden from public view by both its ideal location out of everyone's way on the second floor, as well as a door and functional key.

Todd's office was three times the size of hers, and even had an en suite bathroom, real, honest-to-God drapes and even thriving plants. There were ceiling moldings instead of tiles, and floor-length windows that opened to let in sunshine and fresh air. Just as the starkness of my office suited me, Todd's environs were a reflection of the man.

Helen was months away from fifty-two years old, but clung well to her forties. She was American and had followed Todd from one deployment to the next. She hadn't attended our wedding, but she did present us with china during my first week in Santo Domingo. Besides that encounter, our meetings were rare. I did not mix work with Todd, so there was little or no reason for Helen and I to become better acquainted. I had no opinion of her, and if she had one of me, she did an excellent job of keeping it to herself.

"Ah, Mrs. Birch –"

"Koehler," I reminded her automatically.

"Of course." Helen did not miss a beat. There was no opinion, no judgment. "My apologies, Ms. Koehler." She gestured to one of the two upholstered chairs placed against the wall opposite her desk. "Please have a seat. Mr. Birch will be with you in a few minutes."

Helen was as accustomed to command – couched as polite requests, but commands nonetheless – and immediate compliance, so did not expect a reply. Her telephone was lit up and she was already lifting the receiver to warmly murmur to the other person on the line. I was standing over her and I still could hardly make out what was being said. It did not matter though. I was not sticking around. I had done as my boss had asked; it was an unfortunate case of poor timing, but Todd was busy. I turned to leave.

"Ms. Koehler," Helen called after my retreating back. "Mrs. Bir – excuse me – Amy, please wait." But I was already out of sight to match Todd's out of mind.

I had only made thirty paces when a firm hand closed around my arm. My body knew his touch and welcomed it even though my mind rebelled at the contact. I allowed myself to be led without understanding why. It would have been a simple matter to break his hold, but my skin craved him. My lungs took him in with greedy breaths. One week of building up my walls and Todd Birch had decimated them like an angry wave.

Closing my eyes against the visual assault was only delaying the inevitable, but there was still a small part of me that was reviled by my weakness.

He had his cell phone against his ear, listening so intently I knew to be quiet. I kept my eyes down as he tugged me along. His dark suit was as deep as his eyes mid-climax. I knew without looking that he was wearing a lighter shade of blue shirt and a striped tie with it. I had spent a significant period of my life in uniform so I recognized the neurosis in him too. Mondays were his blue-on-blue days. In my Monday skirt and high heels, three of my paces made one of his and I found myself scrambling to keep up.

Finally his call ended and the cell phone disappeared inside his jacket. I felt his eyes on me for just a moment. It was all he ever needed to have me gasping for breath.

"Don't you think I've been chasing after you long enough?" He asked for my ears only. It was ironic he cared what Helen thought, but had brought my boss into this.

"Helen, hold everything and come back in an hour," he said in passing to his secretary.

"Yes, Mr. Birch," was her brisk reply without any sign of resentment for the dark cloud I brought to her little piece of government paradise.

The carpet muffled my steps, but the edges of my narrow skirt were stretched to the limit of my patience. It was the first opportunity for resistance and I seized it with both hands. I tugged against his hold as we crossed the reception area, but Todd tightened his grip, which had me bouncing into his side like a rag doll. Unbalanced by my attire, as well as the purse slung over my free shoulder, I would have fallen if not for him. Judging by the forbidding look he threw me, I would be lucky to leave this encounter with only a sprained ankle.

"Lockup, Helen," he said, right before he tossed me inside his own office.

While I situated myself and caught my balance, I heard the door slam and the lock engaged with some finality. It ratcheted my annoyance to new levels, finally overriding the longing the sight of him had ignited, and stiffening my spine with the stirrings of anger. It was the much-needed shot of immunity that allowed me to look into his eyes and not fall at his feet. Todd Birch was still the most beautiful man I had ever met, and he used to be mine... even though I didn't know nearly enough about him, like why he unconsciously organized his wardrobe like someone accustomed to wearing uniform... Then there was his history with Colonel Townsend, which predated even Mona.

"Did you fuck him?"

Todd had his hands on his hips, staring at me from against the door, blocking my escape. Outwardly he seemed calm, but I knew better than to believe the illusion. Col. Townsend was a hard limit for him, and knowing what I did about Mona, I was aware he could become physical... irrational... violent.

"You brought my boss into this because you're jealous?"

"Answer my question, Amy," he pushed through his teeth. As the seconds ticked by without a reasonable response, he became more restless. He shrugged out of his jacket and moved past me to stand behind his desk – classic alpha move. But I didn't want to play with Todd anymore. So far we were both lousy at this marriage thing, but he had the power to tie me into knots with those eyes, that mouth, his hands. I was destined to lose to him... get lost in him. I turned to face him, pushing past my anger to find a reason.

"Listen, Todd," I said on a deep exhale, "I don't want to do this anymore. We're obviously no good for each other."

"No, you listen to me," he cut me off, fighting now to hold the leash on his anger. One hand raked through his hair, revealing a wide expanse of chest, dwarfing me and minimizing my objection. "You are my wife. Nothing will change that."

"You changed that." The last thing I wanted to do was let him know that he had hurt me. I wasn't convinced I had just done a great job of that.

He paused, as if recognizing my weakness and taking a moment to decide whether to respond to it or take advantage. He sighed and his hands went into his pockets. "I did not have sex with a prostitute. I have not had sex with anyone since we've been together, Amy."

"It doesn't matter," I said and frowned because it came out hoarsely, as if my voice had cracked. But there was no reason for that. I was fine and even if I believed him, even if the doubt Angelika had raised was not now a fact, it made no difference.

"Like hell it doesn't. You thought the worst of me and you're using Townsend to get back at me. I've answered the question you should have asked before you ran off and started acting crazy. Now answer my question, Amy. Did you fuck him?"

"You'll just have to understand if I don't give you the benefit of the doubt, Todd. You lied to me. You betrayed what trust I had in you. I won't give you more, and right now, I just want to move on with my life."

Todd shot from behind that desk like a bullet from a gun. Before I could prepare myself for physical contact, he was before me, blunt fingers gripping my shoulders, pulling me closer and shaking me when my hands against his chest offered resistance. He was as hard of body as he was earnest and angry. I cringed at the way my body responded to him, melting from the heat he exuded. Desire seeped deep into my bones, sending an electric current coursing over my nerve endings, making me feel both alive and languorous at the same time.

"You are my wife, dammit! You are my life and I am your future. There is no moving on without each other, Amy. There is no 'end' to us, especially not over this bullshit. Do you understand?"

I shook my head because I was afraid to speak. He could not know how deeply affected I was by his closeness. I kept my eyes fixed on the knot of his tie, because I could feel the blaze of his depthless blues boring into me, trying to raze my willpower.

"Think for a moment," he said, almost in a whisper, as if what he had to share was just between us. "You're an Intelligence Officer. You are not this illogical, emotional woman. Look at the bigger picture, Amy." And then, as if I was blind, he drew it for me, taking for granted that I trusted the hand behind the brush strokes.

"Do you think I would have brought a prostitute into our home? Do you think I could plan something like that with the intent to deceive you? For God's sake, Amy. You arrange the canned food according to size and color. I know I don't have a chance in hell of hiding something like this from you. I was going to explain what happened."

I opened my mouth to remind him that he had tried to cover up what he had done. He shook me so hard my teeth clicked together.

"It was a bachelor party, Amy. The guys bought me a stripper, but I swear to God I did not touch her. Others did, and there was nothing I could do about that. My choices were to give them our room, our bed, or the spare. I know I promised it to you, but it was the lesser of two evils."

I didn't want to hear him. I didn't want to look into his eyes. I didn't want to be weak anymore. I kept my eyes on that tie as if my life depended on it.

"I didn't want them in our space, and I could not explain to these people who have known me for years, and who have spent as much time in that house as theirs, that my wife of two months keeps a separate bedroom. How would I explain that without hurting you or us?"

My lack of response irritated him. I felt it in the tension and his body. I breathed it in on his frustrated sigh. But I wouldn't give in, not again.

"The truth is worse than anything they could have imagined. My wife is crazy. It's bad enough she needs her space so she can run off and pretend her parents never died and there's nothing in the world that can hurt her. Imagine if they knew she pretended to be someone else, so she won't feel at all?"

He could not have hurt me more of he had slapped me across the face. I didn't want him inside me at the same time as *that*. Todd Birch didn't know half as much as he thought he did. But he still knew enough to hurt me. And even if I couldn't be angry with him, there was nothing to stop me from hating myself... despising my own weakness. I had given him that power over me.

"Don't fucking touch me," I shouted at him. "You don't get to touch me, and you certainly don't get to talk about them."

"The hell I don't," he yelled right back and reached for me again. I fought him, even though I wasn't prepared for it and I couldn't imagine hurting him like that.

My purse ended up on the floor, my blazer covering the flap. Four-inch heels and a pencil skirt were not made for combat, and as I had recently suspected, Todd Birch was at least as well trained as I was. We clashed in a barrage of interlocking wrists and elbows, and he met me beat for beat, block for block. My speed was checked by his superior strength and my compromised equilibrium.

He pushed and pulled on my limbs, using the momentum of my own body to keep me off-center. While I focused on not falling, I could not get a firm enough foothold to do likewise. Todd was able to press me further back, step-by-step. The one time I could have gotten a solid blow to the chest or throat that would have at least cheated him of breath and focus, he broke the force behind the blow with his fist in the V of my elbow. I lost the extension of my arm, a shoe, and whatever feeble advantage his determination not to hurt me might have afforded. In the next instant, he pushed me off center with a shove to my shoulder.

I stumbled, trying to catch my footing and kick off the other shoe, but Todd pressed ahead until my back was flattened against the wall. The side of his powerful body kept me in check; one arm locked my elbows, while his chest and core kept the rest of my body immobile. The final stroke of defeat fell as his massive palm forced my right cheek against the wall. Todd wrapped my ponytail around his fist to keep me in place. I could not move, could barely breathe with his weight and closeness bearing so heavily against me.

"We belong together, Amy. I could no more stop touching you than you could stop wanting me."

I was angry and frustrated enough not to be afraid of meeting his gaze. What was the point of avoiding him anyway? He knew! And he didn't have to look into my eyes to be certain. He had invaded my soul a long time ago, but now he was declaring his conquest, beating his chest and roaring at the sky. The fire behind those ocean-blue eyes burned a trail from my exposed neck down to my heaving breasts, then back again before resting on my lips.

"Did you let him touch you here? Did he take what is mine?"

"Fuck you."

When our gazes met his were black. It turned my insides in a not-in-the-least unpleasant way.

"Gladly," he said softly, and his breath was a physical caress that raised the goosebumps on my flesh.

Todd jerked my head back by my hair and pushed my face harder into the wall so his mouth could take possession of the exposed column at my throat. I wanted to cry out, but I was afraid the sound would be a moan as his tongue stroked the sensitive flesh below my ear all the way down to my clavicle. His teeth grazed me. It ignited an inferno inside me. The touch of his warm breath only fanned the flames. I was burning.

His teeth sank into my skin on the second pass and the ache was so debilitating that I did not at first hear the buttons popping off the only Monday shirt I had taken from our home. With one hand he yanked the edges apart. It was the cool air and then his warm hand against my skin that told me I was bare to him. Again.

"Not here," he said before his tongue made the journey in reverse.

I didn't know I was breathing heavily until the tip of his tongue stroked under my chin and I felt his breath gusting on my dampened skin. We were in sync. I wanted to stop it, but felt I would die if he didn't kiss me soon. My lips parted in invitation, but my eyes were squeezed shut in denial. And when I tried to hold my breath, it was a gasp that betrayed my need for him. Todd's lips brushed mine in a faint caress that I might have doubted ever occurred had it not been for the burn.

"Did you give this to him, Amy?"

I opened my eyes, and for a split second, I thought I saw... hurt. But then my eyes adjusted to his closeness – there wasn't even a breath between us – and all I could see was his anger and desire. Of course Todd wanted me. He liked women; they loved him; and I was no exception. I was better than most at denying the undeniable, but he still saw through my walls.

"I hate you."

It was a long shot that ricocheted off his steely armor and pierced my broken heart. Todd was so unaffected by the blow that I had only succeeded in wounding myself.

"No, Amy," he said with a slow shake of his head.

He released the hold on my hair so I could face him – not that I wanted to after that epic failure. He could feel the fight and pour out of me in slow degrees, but he did not release the hold on my hands or the press of his body against mine. Instead, his hand trickled down the side of my thigh and lifted the edge of my skirt in painful increments.

"You love me," he said.

Long before he found my weeping core, ages before one finger and then another slipped beyond the edge of my panties and stroked me, I could not deny him. In fact, I shifted, more to give him room than in protest. He followed, lodging one knee between mine so I was open to him. Again.

"You're so wet for me," he moaned.

Heat warmed my cheeks, but not in anger. It was embarrassing how wet I was, but with Todd, like this, I had no shame. His fingers slicked across my quivering flesh in a caress that weakened my knees. I sagged, and this time, he did let me go for a moment.

It was my only chance to prevent this, to push him away in no uncertain terms.

My arm snaked up his shoulders, testing the muscles that bunched under his cotton and silk blend shirt. I smoothed the fabric as I went, my fingers stroking the sliver of skin exposed between his collar and hair. And then we sank into him. I could drown in this man, lost in the depths like my fingers in his hair. My nails scraped against his scalp, eliciting a guttural moan and sending my thirst for him to fever pitch.

His response vibrated through his body from head to toe and back again. I felt it too, because Todd had hooked his free arm under my bottom and had hoisted me up so I could wrap my legs around his hips. Those fingers that had decimated my resistance ripped through my underwear with similar ease. That pathetic barrier against him fell to the floor in scraps next to the puddle of my self-respect.

In that moment I didn't care, because his fingers were inside me, stroking me carefully once, twice... so he was soaked in my essence. The air between us was heavy with the scent of my arousal.

"Tell me you want this, Amy. Tell me you love me."

I closed my eyes against him and shook my head 'no'. But Todd sank knuckle-deep into me, and the cry was ripped from my soul. "Yes."

"Beg for it."

"Todd, please," I cried, even as I hated myself for meaning it. His scent mixed with mine – sunshine, indigo, and happiness – and I wanted it... craved it like the next breath stuck inside my chest. It hurt. I cried tears, but Todd kissed them away.

I could feel the cool of the metal buckle of his belt biting into the softest part of my leg. But in a moment, his naked arousal stroked my soaked flesh and I forgot any discomfort. There was no space between our bodies, which I grieved. I wanted to see him, to wrap my fingers around him, and taste the bead of moisture that I knew would be there. Still, there was no time to feel the loss acutely, because Todd was inside me in a heartbeat.

It was so hard and rough and angry that my head cracked against the wall. I would feel the effects later. For now though, there was only pleasure. Just then he barreled into me as hard and fast as his hips could manage and my needy body would allow. Bodies clashed as I tried to meet his strokes. We slipped and slid, my body sucking at him greedily, while Todd pushed deeper and harder than he had ever felt comfortable doing before. He would break me and I welcomed it.

"You're so fucking hot for me. No way he could have fucked you and left you so needy. You like the bite and he likes to give pain."

I couldn't come to grips with what was happening fast enough. Todd had never raised Townsend between us like this before. Todd had accused me once of leading Townsend on because I thought the colonel could hurt me like I wanted.

"Who are you kidding, Amy? You like being brutalized. It turns you on harder and faster than my tongue on your cunt... We know why you're keeping Townsend in your back pocket... You think you can push him to beat you, that he'll really give you what you want..."

Of course, I had denied it at the time. Now that I knew what the colonel was into, I wondered how Todd had come by that knowledge too.

Then Todd tilted my hips at an angle and plunged even harder and deeper than before. The sensation rocked to me. I knew he was using my body to get the answer to the question I refused to acknowledge, but at that precise moment, I didn't have the will to care.

My body hunted release; my mind was an evil co-conspirator. I could only focus on the feel and scent of the man inside me, the incredible things he did to my body, and those eyes, to the exclusion of everything else. Each thrust and breath took me farther away from the place where I should have been: behind my walls.

"He would have loved bruising you. He would've wanted me to know... in the way you walk, the way you hold me." He sank deep and stilled. And like a puppet on the end of the master's string, my core contracted around him, proving that he knew me better than I could control myself. "Just like that, Amy."

"Please, make me come, Todd."

There was no pride left, no anger or shame; nothing but the crippling desire for more and more of this man.

Todd pushed the edges of my torn shirt away, exposing my torso. A quick tug and my bra was torn too, right down the center, just like the rest of me. When one hand closed around my breast, squeezing and plumping it for his mouth, I didn't mind at all. When that hot, wet mouth closed around the tip, I cried out. The shock had me spasming and grinding against him – his mouth, his hips, trying to put out the flames; my fingers scraped against his scalp and pulled at his hair, trying to get him so deep inside me that we would remain one forever. It was a long time, but it wasn't nearly enough.

"Todd," I cried, my need so urgent, it was painful.

He ignored me. He went from one breast to the next, sucking as much of the mounds into his mouth as he could hold, clamping down with his teeth, then laving the ache away with his tongue.

"Look, Amy," he said our bent heads touching as we both gasped and stared at what he had done to me. I was bruised and would remain so for upwards of a week. "He would have put his mark on you just like this."

And even then I was too aroused, hanging by my nails off a cliff, to be horrified. My nipples were so hard, begging for more, that Todd would have to be heartless to deny me. I cupped them for him while he devoured the sensitive flesh, squeezing as he pulled deeper, increasing the suction of his mouth until I whimpered helplessly.

This time, when he moved his hips, sliding out of me and then in again, it was sweet torture. His long, slow and deep strokes hollowed me out, until I begged for release. In and out he moved, not stopping until he was buried to the hilt and our pubic bones kissed. And all the while his mouth worked my breasts, tugging on the nipples with his teeth, softening the hurt with his tongue, sucking so hard the blood settled beneath the surface.

His mouth was hot and wet, but his breath coming in quick bursts cooled me. A shiver coursed down my spine, chasing the vibrations as pleasure seeped into my bones and melted them.

"Make me come, please, Todd." I needed it so badly.

But Todd was angrier than I had ever seen him. He held onto his control, maintaining the deep steady strokes when he knew I needed him fast and hard to find release like this. We would have stood there for an hour while he slowly built the pressure, until finally my body broke under the strain.

Our needs were different and Todd proved it too, when he came, spilling hot, wet and heavy inside me. He groaned so hard against my breasts that his wordless cry echoed through me. His fingers bit into my thighs, steadying me while his entire body shook with the intensity of his climax. I could feel him shooting inside me, the furious jets of his release bathing me in his essence. I tried to ride the waves of his climax, but it was too little and definitely too late. Todd was quick to set me down and slip away. His spent flesh hung between us, glistening with our combined desire, hard enough to tip me over if he had wanted.

I stumbled and almost fell over. Todd held me by the arm until I found my balance, but he was so far away, his arm was fully extended, his eyes vacant once the waves of ecstasy had receded. There could not have been more distance between us.

I was wearing only one shoe, but that could not account for how shaken I was. It was what he had done. Todd had never punished me like that before, leaving me unfulfilled and humiliated. But leave me he did, and I had never felt as low with anyone before.

Todd disappeared inside his en suite bathroom while I stood there, back against the wall, too shocked to move. The toilet flushed. I heard water running, splashing in the sink. Then after a few moments that felt like forever, his hand slapped against the light fixture and he reappeared.

He was the image of urbane beauty, as if nothing had just happened between us, as if he hadn't just run over the speed bump that was my heart on his way to proving a point. Todd seemed surprised that I was still standing there. But then he tucked that away too with the ease of zipping his fly.

Something else bloomed inside my chest, in the spot where my heart had been, drowning out the ache in my core. It was like swallowing a ball of air that could not be dislodged. I wanted to thump against the pain, but my arms hung at my sides like soft noodles, refusing to heed the command from my brain. And as the pressure inside me built, I lost control and cried. The heavy tears spilled over in hot streams, and my only consolation was that they were silent.

"Get dressed, Amy. Helen will be back any minute now and I do have other things to do today."

Get dressed.

I focused on doing as he ordered. My panties were torn beyond repair, as was my shirt. But at least I could hold the edges of the latter together and button my blazer to hide the worst of the damage. My bra was shredded too, making a mockery of its job, but I couldn't take it off without exposing more of myself to him. I smoothed my skirt down over my hips, and woke up my pride from the floor where it slept. I left the panties on the floor and went for my shoe.

I could still feel him inside me. Soon his cum would stream down my thighs like the tears on my cheeks. I had to get out of there. I needed to be away from him. But judging by the way he slipped into his jacket and sat at his desk, tapping the keyboard until his computer came to life, I might not have been there at all.

Shoe on the right foot, equilibrium back in place, I tucked the edges of my shirt into my skirt and smoothed my hair with my sweaty palms.

Breathe, Amy, breathe.

There were beads of sweat on my brow, so I wiped those away along with the tears, and brushed my hands over my hair again.

All better, now. Everything in its place.

I slung my purse over my shoulder and turned to leave. I didn't want his bathroom. I didn't want any part of him anymore.

"Go home, Amy," I heard him say just as I reached for the lock on the door. "I'll square things off with O'Brien for the rest of the day, but I want you home when I get there tonight."

I should not have turned to face him. The only reason I did was to see if there was any of the remorse he should have felt but which his voice failed to convey. There was none, no softening; only careless, cruel disregard. He didn't even look at me: he glanced between his keyboard and monitor, tapping away while my heart bled all over his fancy carpet. I shouldn't have looked back, because once I did and I saw what he was, I wanted to hurt him as much as he had hurt me.

"Do you want to know why I like the pain?"

There. I had his attention. I pulled my blazer closer around me – a physical barrier to his eyes that sought the brand he had left on my skin.

Finally our eyes met, and I could only hope mine were as hollow and uncaring as his.

"My parents died when I was seventeen and I didn't want to go on without them. I couldn't understand why my father had saved me when he chose to die. Then a couple months later, in November, uncle Richard insisted I attended the Marine Corps Ball with Adam Rutherford III. He wanted me to be normal again."

Even twelve years later, I couldn't help laughing at the irony that Richard would think a seventeen-year-old attending the commemoration of the Marine Corps birthday with the Secretary of State's son who was five years older was normal.

"Anyway, I went. Then we went to his house where he raped me. I was a virgin when he tore my clothes off, wrapped his fingers around my throat, and rammed into me forever. I passed out; he almost killed me. I thought he was going to kill me. And I realized I didn't want to die."

Even from across the room I could see the change in Todd. He was hard again, jaw clenching as he ground his teeth together; hands curled into tight fists that could have cracked wood. His spine was rigid, his shoulders tense. And though he tried to breathe calmly, his nostrils flared. And his eyes... God, those eyes made me believe he had murdered Mona. It was inside him, the type of rage one needed to kill another person, even someone he had loved once.

"Adam revived me, cleaned me up, told me how much I liked it, and asked if I wanted to go see a movie with him the following weekend." My hold on the blazer slipped, but this time Todd's eyes remained with mine. I held the edges tighter, and in the face of his rage remained composed.

"Of course, I went with him. I was so grateful. He made me feel and I was so glad to be alive. I've craved it ever since – the pain, his hands around my neck, marking me, the strength of his body holding me down, reminding me that I had things to live for. So thank you, Todd Birch, for reminding me of the man who raped me."

He shot out of his chair, sending it rolling into his fancy French doors. His heavy carpets slowed the trajectory, so it bounced harmlessly into the white frame, then disappeared behind his heavy drapes. Todd's hands curled around the edge of his desk, as if he wanted to toss two hundred pounds of government issued furniture across the room. But he just stood there, staring after me, breathing out the rage he didn't know how else to control.

I left him staring after me, those empty eyes no longer casual in their indifference. His gaze reached out to me, pleading now, although he never said a word.

Finally, we were even. He had used my need for him against me, to strip away my layers until I stood raw and quivering before him. And I had used his need to master me to hurt him right back.

I went home – my home – but wondered along the way why my victory felt so hollow.

TWENTY-ONE

Just when I wanted nothing more than to hide away from the world, everyone and his grandmother came knocking at my door. Townsend wanted to meet to discuss his breakfast RDV with Ramirez. Martinez was blowing up my phone with questions about the Ferreiras case. Angelika complained about not feeling well, without the benefit of a specific ailment. Byles, ever a glutton for punishment, invited me out for a *bachata* party at Jet Set. And to top it all off, Uncle Richard called.

After informing Townsend to put his recap on ice, I ignored all his phone calls and messages with threats of dire consequences. There was no urgency besides his desire to see me, fuck me, bruise me. And I had had my daily fill of territorial males.

A more polite response to Martinez had him holding all his questions until I returned to office Tuesday morning. I knew he was worried about his wife, but for God's sake, we had a deal. I wasn't going to screw him over without giving him the time to fulfill his side of the bargain.

I handed Angelika the rest of her cocaine, which ended all complaints. She remained in her room, bending her body into pretzels in the name of exercise. Byles, I ignored altogether.

But Richard I could not avoid, even if I wanted to.

I knew some form of contact with Todd had precipitated this phone call. Richard rarely phoned me, and the frequency of our interactions had further declined since he and Todd had bonded. I got that he was concerned for me. He wanted me 'settled', and apparently Todd fit that bill for him. I had avoided relying on his influence to advance my career, because if I didn't ask for any favors, then he couldn't try to ground me with conditions. Indeed, the last time I asked him for a favor – going over Townsend's head to secure SOUTHCOM's support for one of my operations – I ended up married to Todd.

"Amy," Richard greeted me, sounding every one of his sixty years, "what's going on? Are you okay?"

"Of course, Richard. I'm fine. Why do you ask?" Feigning the direct opposite of how I actually felt was like scraping the bottom of the barrel that had already been overturned. My nerves were shot, my hands shaking, and my throat clogged from fighting back tears.

"Todd called," he said, and waited for me to hang myself with the rope he had laid out.

"Oh?"

"Yes."

"Well, what did he say?"

"Where are you, Amy?"

I sighed tiredly and at least that was the truth. "I'm working on an important case and haven't seen as much of him as I would like. Is that why he called?"

"Amy, he's very worried about you. He's been asking questions."

I unleashed my impressive reserves of wariness. Todd asking questions was always cause for concern. Add Richard to the equation and the scenarios were downright dangerous.

"What do you mean? What kind of questions?"

I should have walked away from him this afternoon. Of course he wouldn't take what I had said and skulk away with his tail between his legs. My only excuse was I was angry and ashamed, and I wanted to hurt him back. It was no excuse, of course, but shoot me for being human.

"He asked about John and Mary-Anne. I told him what I know. I saw no harm in telling him; it's all a matter of public record anyway."

Except for the 'who' and 'why' of their murders. Of course I hoped Richard felt ashamed. A senior counterintelligence official of the CIA was executed in a home invasion, and even after twelve years, the government, including the DNI, claimed no knowledge of the reasons or perpetrators.

Everyone had a breaking point. Even terrorists got to a point when they had killed one too many people, witnessed one too many scenes of devastation, and lost it ... their will to continue, their rationale for doing what they did, their minds. I hoped John Koehler was Richard's breaking point. The President may be the ruler of the Free World, but Richard was the most powerful man in the world, and he claimed to not know who had murdered his best friend.

"He also wanted to know about after."

"After?" I asked, pulling the bubbling cauldron that was my anger off the flames before it boiled over and burned me. "What about after?"

"He asked about Adam Rutherford."

I remained silent, in disbelief that Todd would discuss my sexual history with the DNI. It said a lot about their relationship, how comfortable Todd was with the man I walked on eggshells around, even though I grew up as part of his household.

"He was very angry, Amy," Richard continued, and I could hear the steel behind the words, as if it reinforced his spine. His voice vibrated with the rigidness, like a taut line that had been pulled. "He thinks I didn't do enough to protect you."

As if I wasn't dealing with enough already, Todd had gone and blown my mind. He had accused Richard?

"You've spoken to him about this." It wasn't a question.

How else would Todd have known about Adam Rutherford? He was killed in a motor vehicle accident the day after his father left office – a fatal combination of alcohol, cocaine, speed, and possibly Richard, who at the time was the head of Naval Intelligence. We had never spoken about it, but only the naïve would dismiss that possibility. By then, I was a West Point cadet with an extensive pool of angry young men to choose from.

"You know how tenacious Todd can be."

"And I know how vague you choose to be." He sighed, as if our polar opposite dispositions accounted for this misunderstanding that threatened their relationship. "You should discuss this thoroughly with him, Amy. Make sure he understands what really happened."

I would have laughed, but the urge to cry was stronger. Uncle Richard actually cared what Todd thought of him. He was equally guilty of courting this relationship with Todd, which led me to the question of why.

Who really was Todd Birch and what did Richard want with him?

This new state of affairs made me suspect that perhaps Todd was not the only one guilty of using me for my affiliations. Richard had had his eyes on Todd, but I had been too blinded by my own agenda and self-importance to see it. I needed answers. I had to find out Todd's purpose in Kingston the week of the Fourth of July when we had met. Was it orchestrated? Had I played directly into Richard's hands?

Was this really how Richard went about succession planning? And if so, wasn't Todd jeopardizing his relationship with Richard with these accusations.

Suspicion revved my flagging energy.

The only reason Todd would have accused Richard was on my behalf. For him to be angry about something that had happened over a decade ago, he had to care about me. And to direct that anger towards Richard meant he cared more for me than what the DNI could do for him.

That was the problem with hope. It knew no fear; it was stubborn enough to bloom in the dark.

"Don't worry, Richard. I'll talk to him."

I just didn't know when. I had already given all I had and then some.

TWENTY-TWO

The Tuesday night baseball game was a 'go'.

I was terrified, and without the luxury of a pill to soothe my frayed nerves, I could not completely hide my state of mind from my boss.

"Licey is hosting Estrellas Orientales," I responded to O'Brien's close scrutiny. I didn't have to dig far to find a nervous grin.

"I didn't know you were into baseball, Koehler," he said with a narrowed glare over the rim of his glasses.

"I wasn't always into it, but Todd's a fan. Los Tigres is his team, and I got sucked in. It'll be pretty exciting to see them play at home."

"You're not there for the fun, Koehler," he reminded me pointedly, because he couldn't fault my excuse. He was still pissed off for being dragged into the middle of the disagreement between Todd and me. My response and the convenience with which I brought up my husband had the dual effect of reassuring my boss that we had reconciled and there would be no further need for him to be dragged into our affairs.

"Everything is under control," I added. His slow nod and the ease with which he dismissed me – a flick of his fingers that sent me scurrying from his office – were as much indication of his renewed faith in me as I could expect after yesterdays debacle.

I did not want to disappoint O'Brien. Failure would not endear me to him, and I had a niggling feeling he was tallying my misdeeds. Normally, we would have all gone into this operation with a moderate expectation of success. That was why we had plans B, C and D lined up.

But over the last few days, I felt everyone was gunning for me – O'Brien; Townsend, who was royally pissed because I blew him off Monday afternoon; and even Martinez who, if he was smart, was biding his time for my fall from grace.

At this stage, confessing my reservations about Angelika to Townsend or O'Brien was a definite no-go. She was high, and I was sending her into an operation blind. I had no remote or electronic surveillance to monitor her progress. She had only a cell phone; and I had old-fashioned binoculars to keep her in my sights.

My stomach hurt as the anxiety rolled through my middle. I broke out in buckets of sweat and had to blame it on too much coffee. Eating was impossible and the by the end of the day, I was an emotionally unstable, hungry, smelly wreck. As much as I would have liked the synthetic calm of a pill, that wasn't going to happen. I needed to focus. I could not risk missing a single detail. Finally, when I felt as though I was about to crawl out of my skin, I went for a run.

That helped for a while. Then Angelika disappeared, or as she claimed, made a slight detour. I had watched her board a taxi, which should have only taken a few minutes to get to Estadio Quisqueya. But half an hour later, Angelika was nowhere to be found.

With only a spotty wireless Internet connection to work with, tapping into her phone's GPS from the stadium parking lot proved to be a pain. I had no choice and very little time. By the time I had access, she was already on her way to me, having wasted thirty minutes on her little shopping trip.

Angelika saw nothing wrong with going into a public venue where she risked being spotted by narcotics dogs with at least fifty dollars of cocaine on her person. When I had given her the money for refreshment, I expected she would have used it on a cold drink and an empanada. Silly me for not thinking like a drug addict.

At least her seat was safe. I had bought her a Palcos A grandstand ticket just behind the right-handed batter's box. It was one of the best seats in the house, and a gamble, since I could only assume Colonel Ramirez had great seats too. The plan was for Angelika to innocently run into Colonel Townsend, whom she had met and become acquainted with on one of his earlier trips to Santo Domingo Mission. Townsend would make introductions, and hopefully Ramirez would take to Angelika like a fish to water.

Thankfully, Angelika wasn't a sloppy high. Yet. She was just horny. Her role was not overly complicated either. She had to somehow get the intrusion key into his mobile phone, which I was certain had a portal to the *.mil.do* Enterprise account. She could either send him her contact information in an infected VCF file that had been installed for exactly that purpose; or a photo as an attachment, which was the preferred method given the size of the key file

I dialed her number when the GPS showed she had reached the intersection of Avenidos Tiradentes and San Martin.

"Call me back when you pull up out front. Do not enter the stadium without my say-so."

Traffic was heavy and slowly streaming into the stadium parking lot, so it was another fifteen minutes before she unfolded from the taxi. I thought she would have been really flying by then, but she looked sober enough as I directed her to my location by phone. The fact that she had remembered to stay in the cab, as opposed to walking in from the street in the interest of time, seemed to confirm her sobriety. Angelika was restless when high and would not have supported sitting in a car as it crept towards its destination at twenty minutes per mile.

"Where is it?" I asked as soon as she closeted herself inside my rental.

She looked at me with wide, blank eyes, but kept her pouty, raspberry lips pressed together. Those eyes were rimmed with thick, black kohl, and the lips darkened to a deep, berry. The effect made her skin glow, although the childlike appearance was toned down. Wedges gave her height a boost, and a slouchy shouldered top revealed an intriguing amount of skin at her neck and shoulder. It also left the question of her breast open for investigation. Her white blonde hair was slicked back, and under the right light, seemed to give her a halo. I understood why her parents had given her that name.

"I know you went to Carlito's. Where are the drugs?"

She sighed, but reached into the waistband of her denim skirt and pulled out the bag of cocaine. I was comforted to see that she hadn't taken a hit yet; she still had some control over her urges. It would have been reckless, stupid, but at the same time, expected, if she had done a bump in the back of the taxi. I could only hope she was as discrete, concealing the nature of her activities from the driver when she pulled outside Carlito's warehouse.

"I didn't think you would mind," she said plaintively, but handed the bag over to me.

"I don't care that you're using my money to buy blow," I said with enough to sarcasm to disconcert even the unflappable Angel. "But I do mind when you don't follow instructions." I balled the bag into my fist to break the visual link she was so desperate to maintain.

"I'm sorry," she said, still remarkably composed, except for the nervous licking of her lips.

"Angelika, I need you to focus."

"I am," she responded, then again, "I am," when I allowed the silence to stretch uncomfortably between us. "I swear. I just need a pick up if I have to fuck him again."

She didn't know anything about our target except that he would be with Colonel Townsend. She knew it was a distinct possibility that she might have to sleep with the 'other'. But if Ramirez expected Townsend to break the ice, or if he was suspicious of being set up and wanted the other man to set the pace, then Townsend was in it for our country. And so would Angelika.

I might have empathized with her if the circumstances of our meeting had been different. And if I wasn't running an operation and needed her services. She had been in my home, her fruity scent on my sheets, and her hair in my sink. She had chosen the life of a prostitute, and in a week, she would be sent to Paris, all expenses paid, to pursue her dream. Yes, she would be working for me, but she would be adequately compensated from the money my father had given his life to save.

"Take what you need now and leave the rest here."

Time wasn't on our side. The game would start in about thirty minutes, and we were in for a three-four hour match-up. If she was lucky, she would still have some fumes to run on.

To her credit, Angelika didn't argue. She gave a 'cross-that-bridge-when-I-get-there' shrug and did two lines. Her attitude explained a lot about her circumstances. Angelika could not plan for two minutes beyond the present, and so, had become accustomed to making do with whatever she had before her.

I cut her loose and waited a few minutes before finding my own seat next to the visitors' bullpen. With my binoculars, my placement afforded me a ninety-degree view of Angelika's seat. I also expected Townsend and Ramirez to be somewhere between the forty-five and one thirty-five degree angles. So far, Angelika was in place, playing with her phone so she wouldn't look awkward and out of place while waiting for me to text her Townsend's location.

Not that he was an easy one to miss. Townsend was large, blond and beautiful in a barely-tamed way. I was attracted to him on a physical level, and from this distance, the deleterious effect of his lack of charm was MIA. He wore jeans well with the help of the belt he had wrapped around Angelika's neck. I knew the pale, blue button-down shirt matched his eyes even if distance spared me the spectacle. His sun-kissed skin glowed, and the spikes on his flat-top begged to be smoothed by a feminine hand.

The man at his side was another matter entirely. I tried to be objective in my appraisal and concluded that on his own, Colonel Ramirez would have been a solid, average-looking, middle-aged man with a full head of dark hair that was generously sprinkled with grey. He was lucky if he topped 5'8". He was also casually dressed, but had a square frame that was both boxy and lumpy. Fifteen years and fifty pounds ago his dimples would have added a certain charm, but now they were hidden in the creases of his jowls. He wore wire-rimmed glasses, but didn't look bookish. He didn't look anything, in fact, and if not for the blond next to him, I would have overlooked him completely. Stable... that was what Colonel Ramirez personified, while Townsend was an animal on the prowl. Angelika was not going to be as impressed with him as she had been with the other colonel.

My gamble paid off. The colonels took their seats one row and three places to the left of Angelika. She did a good job of making up to me her earlier faux pas, and for the first time all day, I felt the knot in my belly begin to slip. She didn't dive into the task ahead. Instead, she became engrossed in the game, cheering on the three successive strikeouts of the visitors. She waited until the server traipsed down the aisle, delivering drinks to other spectators before placing an order for a bottle of water. While turned in her seat to complete the cash transaction, she made eye contact with Townsend whose surprised reaction to seeing her there was straight from the textbooks. A hug, a kiss, and a handshake later, seating was adjusted so she could be placed between both men.

An hour into the ballgame, things were going smoothly. Colonel Ramirez's shoulders eased commensurate with the broadening of his chest under the full impact of Angelika's flirtation. I began to relax.

Angelika was subtle in her interest in him, but encouraging at the same time. When he pulled back, she turned to Townsend to pick up the slack. When Ramirez moved in and exerted his dominance, she yielded. She allowed him to touch her – a one-finger caress of her thigh, an arm extended behind her seat, and finally a palm flattened against her back. Angelika leaned into his touch, accommodated his maneuvers, and tilted and twisted her body in his direction whenever she laughed or cheered. Those subtle mannerisms were favorably received, and by the end of the fourth inning, the almost dour Colonel Ramirez was glowing.

I ordered a Presidente, which came in a plastic cup. I wasn't going to sweat the small stuff. Even though she was high and apparently enjoying herself, Angelika never lost sight of her purpose. At the seventh inning stretch, the cheerleaders began their routine, which presented an opportunity for Angelika to snap several photos with her phone. As she discussed her photos with Colonel Ramirez, for a moment I thought she might have found our in. However Colonel Ramirez had only a mild interest in their sexually suggestive moves. I ended up squeezing my cup too hard, spilling my beer, when he shrugged and his smile faded into a mild scowl of disapproval.

I personally found his condescension hypocritical. He was in the act of picking up a woman at the ballgame with little regard to his wife, and yet he objected to young Dominicans shaking their pom-poms, tits and ass in swimsuits and knee-high boots. Granted, their version of cheering was less technical and more hair-tossing-meets-booty-shake. I understood it wasn't the norm in Major League Baseball, but I wouldn't have been as intrigued if not for Colonel Townsend's text.

Colonel R. Townsend: 2:30

He couldn't have spotted me from my position, so I assumed he wanted me to use him as a reference point for something to his right, in the vicinity of the home team dugout. I scanned with the naked eye to survey the forest of bodies in various degrees of relaxation, then took a closer look with my binoculars.

There was Todd. His face flashed momentarily across the screen of the jumbotron that had zoomed in on the cheerleader's routine. Featured for a split second between a pair of mile-long legs, I thought I might be delusional. The binoculars eventually confirmed what Townsend already knew. Todd Birch had an up-close and personal view of the spectacle – courtside seats, in fact. He couldn't have had a better spot if he was one of the cheerleaders. And if I wasn't mistaken, he was actually sitting in the middle of five empty seats that coincidentally corresponded to the five young ladies bouncing along the raised platform three inches from his face.

Contrary to what I had told O'Brien that morning, Todd and I had never watched baseball together. He was big into the sport, which I had assumed had something to do with his New York upbringing. It hadn't occurred to me that his interest in the sport in the Dominican Republic was more rooted in the sideline entertainment. But it was just like Colonel Townsend to toss a stun grenade on top of the combustible situation that was our relationship.

Colonel Townsend was an expert at destabilizing us … egging Todd towards violence and making me doubt. Mona came to mind. It was too much to hope he would pass up the chance to play on my insecurities and Todd's reputation. Distracting me from our purpose in that stadium to focus instead on the scantily clad women shaking a cocktail of bleached hair, tits and ass in my husband's face was childish. That Todd seemed to be enjoying himself immensely wasn't going to change anything between us.

I kept my focus. My only concern was ensuring Angelika got that key into Ramirez's phone. Several times the binoculars would have strayed to the right, but it was by pure dint of will that I kept my gaze centered.

The beer was a bad idea. The alcohol reawakened the warmth in the pit of my stomach that made my insides feel as though there was a real fire raging there. The ball of dread rolling around my middle all day suddenly felt heavier. My chest felt as if flakes of rust were being sucked into my lungs. Breathing was harder, and it was as if I was suffocating on dead air. My fingers, shaking and wet with sweat, slipped over the rubber armor coating of the binoculars. I had to squeeze my hands between my knees to keep them dry and steady.

I focused on Angelika. She was doing so well. I concentrated on slowing my breathing, emptying my lungs of the poisonous air before filling them with the aroma of fried dough and malted barley beer the vendors peddled, going row by row.

The matchup between the two teams resumed, but I couldn't say definitively whether the blue or green team was up to bat. The binoculars swayed to the right. The cheerleaders had changed out of their uniforms and returned to their seats. It wasn't hard to spot them once you knew they were there. They were as much on show as the men on the field.

One of them was laughing so hard as she relayed what had to be the funniest joke in human existence, that she "lost" her footing and tumbled into Todd's lap. Perhaps she thought it was in her best interest to stay put. Todd had one arm loosely wrapped around her waist, stabilizing her while she conversed animatedly with her colleagues. Apparently high-waisted skinny jeans and four-inch stilettos had never been more dangerous.

She was young, bright and beautiful; her skin, hair and teeth were well maintained. She was both blessed and took care of herself; her body being the product of hard work, good genes and a healthy diet. I wasn't sure where to put her on the scale of Todd's female interests. Her vivaciousness put Byles to shame. She had a sultriness about her that was very different from Angelika's, but by no means less captivating. On the curve index, I fell *way* behind, and even if she had been enhanced, she was still bouncy with youth and happiness.

It didn't hurt that she had a sense of humor either. Her teammates and my husband were having a rollicking good time as her story progressed with flourish and an expressive face that would have gotten her killed in my field.

I knew that laugh. It rumbled inside his chest so deep, she would have felt the vibrations to the very tips of her breasts. It was deep and warm and made his skin glow against his very white teeth. Such joy was more dazzling than infectious, so it was no surprise that she stilled and her smile slipped as she gazed at him. She placed her palm against his cheek just like I had done so many times before. She wanted to feel his warmth deep inside. I also knew from experience that his fast growing beard would tickle and scratch at her palm.

Please don't let her kiss him. Please don't let her kiss him. Please...

It was what I would have done. It was silly of me to think a specific moment belonged to me, but it didn't change the fact that I wanted him to protect that ... to save something that was entirely our own.

She swayed – leaned in actually – as the smile faded from both their faces.

Please don't kiss her. Please, Todd, don't.

My phone pinged with an incoming message. I reached for it with considerable desperation. I didn't want to see what would happen next. I couldn't breathe and there was moisture on my face.

Colonel R. Townsend: *How cozy*

I couldn't look at him either. Seeing the pleasure he took in my humiliation would have crushed me. I set the binoculars down and wiped my face with trembling hands.

"Él es bueno, ¿no?" a man two seats away asked with a grin. Licey was out on a foul and lost the inning. Alvarez who had a batting average of .500 was up next.

"Si," I smiled. *Yes, he was very good.*

There were only a handful of us on the visitors' side of the stadium. There were few others with which to share his excitement, and I had been so enthralled he probably thought I had money on the game. The underdogs were going home with the win, and some Licey supporters were leaving their seats.

My phone pinged again. This time it was Angelika.

Angelika: *Goodnight. Don't wait for me.*

I put her in my sights as Alvarez hit a double. Her fingers were entwined with Colonel Ramirez's while he and Townsend had a brief discussion over her head. A few moments later, another text.

Colonel R. Townsend: *Dollhouse.*

The fact that they were going to a strip club set off alarm bells. Angelika knew she had to stay away from former associations. There was a distinct possibility she might be recognized, whether by a former client or a handler. This operation wasn't worth the risk. I needed her alive and in Paris in a couple of weeks.

Me: *Rain check.*

Angelika: *Don't worry, MOTHER! I am a big girl. Will be OK*

Somehow I wasn't reassured. I tried Townsend.

Me: *That's a no go. Birdie can't fly that far. Too much baggage.*

Colonel R. Townsend: *Always knew you were a tease.*

Dammit he didn't know Angelika's history; he wouldn't understand. And Angelika's false sense of security was because she had a colonel on each arm, and as usual, she couldn't see the consequences waiting for her after tonight.

It was possible I was being paranoid. Dollhouse and Factory were unrelated. The odds were in our favor that a former handler would not resurface so soon after the raid. And even if she was spotted, making checks required time, and if I could create a false trail by stashing her at Townsend's hotel, then I still had a few days to get her safely out of the country. It was not as if anyone would try to grab her in mixed company. If they had half a brain they would track her for extraction later.

Plus a former client might approach her if she was alone – not if she had two guys hanging off her and one of those happened to be a built, blond giant and the other a local somebody.

Me: *Take her home when she's done. RDV at 6 a.m.?*

Colonel R. Townsend: *I am a married man. How would that look?*

He had to be kidding me!

Colonel R. Townsend: *Looks like tango has a cabaña in mind. I'm flying solo tonight, unless you want to even things out.*

The cabañas were rented on an hourly basis. It wasn't nearly enough time to lose any tails Angelika may pick up. And Townsend was being a jerk, refusing to house her for me, but also rubbing my nose into Todd's latest indiscretion. Was that how he handled his own marriage… tit for tat?

Me: *It's a dirty job and someone has to do it.*

That may have covered Townsend's 'concerns' about appearances, and with a stretch, it could pass for an excuse for Todd's present company. Did I believe it? Absolutely not. And apparently, neither did Townsend.

Colonel R. Townsend: *If it makes you feel better.*

I knew where Todd was concerned my will was weak. Before I could stop myself I had the binoculars in hand again. Her seat was still vacant and Todd had his hands full. One rested casually at her hip and the other on her denim-clad knee. She was still talking, but her fingers absentmindedly combed through the hair at Todd's nape. They looked comfortable together … relaxed. A small smile touched the corners of his mouth, but his eyes were on the game. There was nothing amusing there for Licey fans. Pie hit a home run and the home team lost any hope of a comeback. There was no going back for us.

I needed air. I left as fast as my insensible shoes could carry me. I hadn't expected any trouble tonight; I hadn't anticipated anything more strenuous than a moderate walk.

Why did he still surprise me? How could I let him hurt me like that over and over? I'd always known what he was like. And after yesterday in his office, there was no doubt we were broken beyond repair. Forget the stubborn hope Richard's call had incited. Like weeds breaking through concrete, I was being ground back into the dust under Todd's boot.

He would never forgive what I had made him do, or forget the cruel words I had flung at him. It was only natural that he move on with his life, lose himself in someone as different from me as right was from wrong, light from dark. I was too damaged … unsalvageable. Not even Todd could save me, and he no longer had use for me. For God's sake, Richard was worried about what Todd thought of him! The tables had turned there just as completely as they had with us.

The game wasn't quite over yet, but the score didn't matter anymore. Everyone knew how it would end. I pushed through the ever-growing stream of spectators until the cool night air fanned my sweat-slicked body. I chose my path carefully; I wasn't blinded by tears or any illusions of where Todd and I were headed. I willingly lost focus to take care of business. Angelika and Colonels Ramirez and Townsend were tucked neatly inside a drawer and put away as I went on the hunt.

I was very good at certain things, including finding people who didn't want to be seen. Of course it helped that Todd didn't care about that; he lived in the light and loved every minute of it. He had never given a single thought to how his actions reflected on me. His car was parked in the middle of the parking lot, diplomatic plates clear for anyone who cared to notice.

I waited at the end of the row, in the shadows where I belonged. It seemed as though I waited forever. The lot was emptying and the river of cars flooded onto Avenido Tirandentes had begun to flow, easing the congestion. There was no need for him to hurry; he'd been having a good time and there was nowhere to go until traffic had cleared.

When finally Todd appeared, he had his arm around her shoulder. I backed further into the darkness, welcoming the emptiness that filled my soul. I liked the pain. I needed it. It made me remember. It would replace all the longing in the days and weeks to come.

The company branched off. Four women in a Jeep and Todd plus one in his SUV. They waved to each other, made plans to meet at the gym in the morning. Todd opened the door for her while she chatted excitedly with her friends, trying to jam in all the things she hadn't been able to say over the past three hours. He took her bag with the blue uniform peeking out in a silent plea for her to get in. So patient, and yet not patient enough. He sighed with a tender smile as she finally blew kisses and hopped into my place. No, it wasn't my place anymore... hadn't been for a long time.

Todd closed the door behind her and walked with his hands in his pockets around the front of the vehicle. His head was down, his back turned to me as he moved purposefully away. And then he stopped. My heart stuttered. I inched away again until my back caressed a chain-link fence, adding four more feet to the thirty between us. The fence rattled imperceptibly, completely drowned out by the beat of my heart and the rush of my blood through my veins. Tires scraped over gravel; the occupants of the vehicles waxed on excitedly and angrily about the game; Todd stood there, unmoving, staring into the darkness.

There was no way he could have known I was there. I couldn't see my own hands stretched in front of my body. He turned fully to face me, his back erect, his hands hanging at his sides, fists clenched... on guard. His eyes, illuminated by the light cast by the slow-moving cars, were wide – not the least narrowed as one trying to discern. He didn't look away, didn't glance around. He stared dead at the spot where I stood.

He *knew* I was there. The slight breeze ruffled his hair and mine, but it was his gaze that made the down on my skin stand on end. His lips moved. I couldn't hear him, but I felt that whisper to the marrow of my bones.

"Amy."

I didn't move, was barely breathing, but the inferno inside me raged. I was sweating though it was nearly midnight and the air was balmy.

"Vamos, mi corazón. Sé que te gusta de tomar toda la noche, pero a veces es bueno darse prisa..." She laughed, settling back in her seat and closing the door. *Come on, my love. I know you like to take all night, but sometimes it's good to hurry.*

No, Todd never had any problem staying all night. Unless he didn't want to, like yesterday in his office. She knew him so well.

Her voice was tinny, but she hadn't lost the playfulness that made her the life of the party. I was grateful to her for breaking our trance. I heaved in a particularly painful breath as he turned towards her.

Todd didn't smile at her again. A slight crease marred his brow, but I didn't think for a second it was meant for her. He *knew* I was there, an intruder. He threw one final glare my way, and when he turned away for the last time, his countenance was still grim. He climbed in and started the ignition.

Wonderful. I hoped I had ruined his evening. It was only fair. He had ruined my life.

Suddenly I didn't feel like hiding anymore. So as he pulled away and the glow of his taillights cast a red hue over my corner, I stood my ground and let them wash over me.

There could be no more doubt between us. We both knew what had to be done. I would walk away and he wouldn't try to stop me again.

Just as I had let him go.

TWENTY-THREE

I slept well for the first time in about three weeks. Or I would have if I hadn't been cruelly wrenched awake. My work – and if I were truly honest with myself, my nature – didn't allow me the luxury of eliminating technology from my bedside. I had as many alerts programmed as I had fingers and toes. There were at least a dozen targets and physical installations under surveillance that I had to keep on top of twenty-four seven. My phone was a lifeline that kept me abreast of changes requiring an immediate response. A fully juiced portable charger and reliable Internet connection were as necessary as a loaded gun, and I never went anywhere without either.

Then there were the people who needed to reach me at any hour of any day. Todd hadn't been one of those in a long time, it seemed, and I expected he would never be again.

The problem with technology was it wasn't human and it couldn't reliably anticipate my demands. Todd Birch was no longer a concern or consideration, but I hadn't told that to my phone. So it peeled incessantly, the alert of an incoming call bouncing around the four walls of my barren bedroom. I should have blocked him, but after tonight I didn't think I would have had to. There was no need to hide anymore; he certainly wasn't. It didn't help that I was so exhausted after the game that I'd only had the mental capacity to strip and burrow under the sheets.

"Koehler," I answered, pushing away the fog of too brief rest. I didn't want him to think I was crying, because I hadn't shed a single tear.

"Amy." He sounded relieved and surprised, as if he hadn't expected to reach me at all, much less on the first try. Should I not have answered? There was an awkward silence. I tried not to feel uncomfortable. *He* had called *me*. *He* had made a public spectacle of himself.

"I need to see you."

Not a chance. I doused that stubborn weed of hope with a generous dose of Roundup – the memory of last night.

"There's no need." Something was stuck in my throat. I found myself sitting up in bed to clear it away, before the truth of those words struck me. I sank back against the pillow, determined to close this chapter.

"Yes, there is, dammit." He was angry? Why? "I'm outside."

"Todd, it's 2a.m." I pushed my hair off my face with a sigh of frustration. It had only been two hours after all. It felt like much more, but at the same time, not enough. "I was asleep." He knew I didn't do that very well. He used to complain about it all the time.

"You can let me in, or I can do a door-to-door search."

Compromising my anonymity was the only threat that would have gotten me out of bed. It wasn't like I was going back to sleep after this anyway. Plus I had no reason to be afraid of him – or more specifically, my reaction to him.

I did a quick search for messages from Townsend and Angelika. There was none. It was early hours for them anyway, so I was not concerned.

"I'll buzz you in. Apartment 612."

I debated getting dressed in the jeans and Henley strewn on the floor. That would have seemed contrived. Todd knew what I slept in. But I still pulled on last night's khaki shorts and pulled down my camisole to cover the waistband. Out of habit I grabbed my Sig Sauer to answer the door. I checked Angelika's room on the way. Empty.

Todd was still dressed in last night's clothes. He looked tired walking through my front door. Dealing with me did that to people. His entertainment might also have been responsible. Someone had done a thorough job running fingers through his hair.

I closed the door behind him then headed for the kitchen. I didn't want him in my bedroom; I didn't want trouble sleeping there when he was gone. My couch was a no-go as well. I didn't want him getting comfortable in my space. He wasn't staying long, which was why I didn't offer him anything from the refrigerator. Plus, if he got a glimpse of the contents, he would know I wasn't living alone. I filled a glass at the tap and drank standing up, my firearm on the island that separated us.

Todd took his time looking around the open space, but he didn't comment. My place was a little bare, but I didn't need much and was accustomed to doing without. I wanted him gone. My glass hitting the fake marble counter brought his attention back to me.

He cleared his throat, but still sounded hoarse. Maybe he was coming down with something. Funny. He seemed to have been having a great time a couple hours ago. But I did that to people too – ran them down, made them sick of me.

"I need to explain what you think you saw tonight."

I couldn't believe he was going to distort this into one more thing I did wrong. My perception might have been off recently, but there was nothing wrong with my vision. I thought we had come to an agreement tonight: he wouldn't have to hide and I wouldn't be the crazy, emotional wreck he had accused me of being; we would go our separate ways.

I was frankly tired of the seesaw, so I held up a hand to stave off whatever explanation Todd felt he owed me. "Please, don't." So that wasn't the best attempt at not being angry, but at least it was better than crying.

"Let. Me. Explain," Todd forced through clenched teeth, as if I was the one being obtuse.

"There. Is. No. Need." I could give as good as I took. "Really, I'm fine." And I was. I wasn't sure for how much longer, but I expected him to be long gone by the time I ran out of OK.

"It… she was for work."

Now he sounded like me, trying to hide my attraction for Colonel Townsend behind a long-standing accord. We made sacrifices for our country and they shouldn't be held against each other. Except, Todd had never really accepted that rule where I was concerned, and I had no idea whom he worked for, much less what he did. I had to hear this, even if a part of me knew it was a mistake to encourage him in any way.

I sighed and shifted my weight from one foot to the next, head tilted to the left in rapt attention. But my arms were crossed over my chest. I would listen. There was nothing that said I had to believe though.

"Her name is Lily Barroso." So she was named after a flower; that I believed. "She has three brothers. One of them is a short stop for Licey, and another is a boxer."

Here Todd paused and my skepticism redoubled. Was he going to claim he was using the sister to play groupie to the brother? I knew he liked the team, but this was ridiculous. This man had the DNI scurrying for damage control! My incredulity was harder to hide than I cared to try.

Todd moved closer until his hands lay flat on the kitchen island. His eyes were somber, the set of his mouth grim. I mastered the urge to retreat. It was more important to appear strong than to maintain the distance between us. It made looking at him that much harder, but I tapped into the bleakness he had dumped me in last night.

"Amy, look at me." Our eyes met. I couldn't let him in. His eyes had an uncanny power over me. I looked away. "Her brother is Felix Barroso, the boxer. Yesterday, he returned from a six-week training camp in Cuba. He is mine, Amy... my asset, and Lily is a means to see him without Havana learning about it."

I don't believe him. I don't believe him. I don't.

But I couldn't lie to myself. I hated hope. It was the source of all my weakness, and one day, it was going to get me killed.

I couldn't look into his eyes and not believe. So I closed my eyes – squeezed them shut in fact – and turned my head away for good measure. I felt him reaching for me. The apartment was dark, lit only by the light of the moon and stars peeking through my naked window. I couldn't see him reaching for me, but I knew it with the same accuracy with which he had pinned me in the shadows of the parking lot. I moved away, retreating until my back hit the refrigerator. How many times would I allow him to break me?

"Amy," he whispered.

I shook my head. No. No more. Not again. I opened my eyes, but kept them focused on my bare toes that had started going numb. I had them curled under my foot, squeezed together like the vice closed around my heart.

Todd straightened, circling, ready to pounce now that he smelled blood in the water. "You asked me once if I would tell you what it is I do."

That was a long time ago ... in Jamaica. I'd still had my illusions back then, thought I was in control of my life and where we were going. It was before he gave me that ring ... before the stain in my eye.

I had no control now and no direction. I was lost, left adrift in the barren wasteland that was my life without Todd. And here he was again, reaching for me, trying to anchor me to him. He was moving towards me, skirting the barriers. Again.

I bolted. I ran in the opposite direction, trying to reach my room where more than just air stood between us. He didn't catch me. I had spent my whole life running; it was what I did best... what my father had trained me to do.

But Todd and I and doors were a weak combination. He had ripped through my steel walls time and again with just a look, the faintest touch. What use was a wooden wall against him? He kicked it in, splintering the frame and sending the knob slamming into the wall. There was the master bathroom, but he stood between me and its door, which once I considered it, wouldn't have stopped him either. He had me. There was nowhere else to run, nowhere to hide... no shadows here at all.

There was nothing stopping him from holding me. I could have fought, but that was not an option just then. He had beaten me on Monday, which I had blamed on my not being prepared. A tight skirt and stilettos were the least suitable armor for a physical confrontation, regardless of what Hollywood claimed. I didn't want Todd topping me when I had no such excuse, so I didn't give him the chance.

"Townsend and I first met twenty years ago. We used to be very good friends, but we used to bet on everything ... who could piss farthest, who could do more, screw more, fuck harder... and it eventually ruined us. We've been fighting ever since."

Once upon a time I would have wanted this. But I knew why he was telling me now. He wanted to suck me back in to that time. I shouldn't have listened. I should have fought him with everything. But I was weak... much too weak where Todd was concerned.

Todd held me by my arms. It took everything I had to struggle against the combination of his firm hands on my skin; his indigo eyes beaming into me, stripping away the layers I tried to hide behind; and his voice that warmed me from the inside out. I stilled, but my fists were clenched against his chest. Still, I couldn't bring myself to take the final step and open completely to him … touch him.

"There was a girl."

Wasn't that always the case with Todd? If it wasn't Mona, it was someone else … someone he met in a café; someone he worked with; Byles; Lily. There had always been and would always be a girl.

"I told myself I didn't know he really cared for her. He claimed she was just another lay and I didn't look further than that. I should have known, though. He was different with her, but I was too wrapped up in myself and our pettiness to care. I pursued her for weeks and when I fucked her, I told him all about it. Just like we used to do."

I was married to this man and I had never seen that look on his face before. Todd did what he did. Sometimes he was apologetic, but I had never seen him so torn by regret, turned inside out like a latex glove with the powdery side exposed. He had certainly never exhibited such remorse for any of the humiliation he had piled on top of me. "My past is my past" is what he would say and I had to be satisfied with that. This thing with Townsend was so much more. I felt tears stinging the back of my eyes, and I wasn't sure who they were for – Todd, faced with such emotional conflict; Townsend for the betrayal he had suffered; or myself for loving him regardless of the things he had done.

"Townsend was really into her, but his pride wouldn't let him take her back after what I'd done. It broke all of us. We used to do our thing, but he had never been cruel about it before. He wasn't into hurting women before, but that changed too. He married her sister out of spite and he's been a sadistic son of a bitch ever since."

My eyes rounded in my head. Tamara? Townsend's wife was a rebound from the sister?

Don't judge me because I want you. It's been a long time since Tammy and I have been OK," Townsend had told me in Jamaica. Now I knew it was more like never.

And though he had wanted me before Todd ever appeared on the scene, I realized the truth behind Todd's warning months ago. *"He wants you, and now, because of me, he won't stop."*

"Yes," Todd said with a nod. He had been watching my face for the realization to sink home. "Tamara's sister. He was so bitter about the whole thing. You understand why he couldn't pass up the opportunity with Mona ... and now you."

Not only had he had an affair with Mona, in all likelihood he had impregnated her too ... and it was all to hurt Todd. It was a cruel, childish game between two grown men and the toll was measured in lives.

"Don't look at me like that," Todd said harshly, shaking me. "I've beat up myself enough over what happened between us. I don't need you to judge me too." He swallowed hard and I watched the movement at his throat. I still couldn't bring myself to look him in the eye. "I've wasted a lot of time and energy wishing I could go back and fix what I did... or somehow make amends. There isn't much I wouldn't give. I've sacrificed enough so we could wipe the slate clean."

"Mona?" I asked in a hoarse whisper. Had he given her up to Townsend?

He shook his head, still refusing to give voice to the darkest recesses of his soul. But I saw it. For the first time, Todd's eyes were good for more than just laying me bare. "I won't give you up to him, Amy. Never you."

Such need. I had to break the contact. It was too much. My heart needed him, said it wouldn't beat again with him so close but still so far away. My knees failed me, but Todd only tightened his hold on my arms and held me up. My breath escaped me in a sob.

"I won't give you up, Amy... not to him, not to the past – neither yours nor mine... not to anyone or anything."

"Why?" I asked and it was broken. That was the first clue that I was either crying or on the verge.

"You know why." His mouth was set in a grim line again. I could see myself in his eyes – not my reflection, but my sorrow.

It wasn't enough. I shook my head. "No. I don't."

"Amy, you know. I just told you." I shook my head so hard tears spilled over and my sleep-tousled hair stuck to their tracks. "Why do you need me to say it?"

"It's not fair," I sobbed. It wasn't fair that he ripped through my defenses like a wrecking ball, only to fortify himself against me from my rubble.

"Let me tell you what's not fair," Todd whispered. "It is unfair of you to run from me, to use the feeblest excuse to tear us apart. You are my wife! I have never given anyone else as much of me as I have given you. And you throw it back at me at every turn."

I took his anger and matched it. Of that I had a surplus... enough to level him and cover myself for years to come. I pulled away, but his fingers held on tight, digging between the muscle and bones. I wasn't free, but it hurt and that was good enough to ground me.

"You brought a prostitute into our home. You put your friends and your reputation above us. And last night, I saw you; I was there the whole time. You let her touch you. You gave her a part of you that should have only been mine. It was out there in the open for all to see. And do you know who else was there to witness my humiliation? Everyone! Anyone who knows me and you."

He looked away from me, impatience making his clenched jaw tick, as if he wanted to minimize the importance of appearances.

Who cared what others thought when he and I knew the truth? Todd did, especially when Townsend was among the *others*. Plus, I had never had a clue about the truth – the truth about what he did or felt for me. Physically, we were good together, but if Todd didn't love me, then it was *all* about appearances ... what I could do for him.

"You should have known better, Amy. I've told you over and over. I've shown you a million different ways. You're *it* for me! Lily is nothing to me. There isn't enough room inside me for anyone else."

His eyes blazed at me, and I realized I could never fight fire with fire where Todd was concerned. His weakness was being faced with mine. Nevermind how much or how deeply he could hurt me, he hated it when he did.

"Did you fuck her?" I asked after a deep breath. I held it in, waiting for the answer I knew would rip me apart.

"No," he said, but he wasn't looking at me. Todd stared right through me.

It was a lie, which was worse than telling me the truth. I wanted to rail at him. I wanted to hurt him back. Instead, I let go... released the anger with a deep breath.

Pain won't kill you, Amy. Pain never killed anyone.

"Please leave," I told him without any feeling at all. Sometimes, feeling too much could do that... cancel everything out so only the vast nothing remained.

Todd looked at me and finally saw me. He saw the eerily calm woman he had requested. Then he decided he didn't like her at all.

"That was before us," he whispered, but it echoed inside the nothingness.

"Go."

I finally succeeded in loosening his hold on my arms. My victory was short-lived though. I should have known Todd would not have given up so easily. His hands cupped my chin and dug into the hair at the back of my head. This close, I could smell her perfume on him. My stomach rolled and I was hit by a wave of nausea. It burned my throat like his words burned inside my empty chest.

I didn't try to block him out by closing my eyes. I wanted him to see what he did to me. I wanted the tears to scald him too. They boiled on my inside before bubbling to the surface in humiliating waves. I wanted to hurt him too, but every time I tried, it seemed I ended up hurting myself more.

"You listen to me, Amy."

Our faces were less than an inch apart as he pulled me into him. My fists were trapped between us and I used them to push, trying to keep him away from me. They were useless.

"I left the Marines nine years ago to join the Defense Intelligence Agency. I've done what I had to do in order to get the job done. I've never been ashamed of that before. Not until I met you. You make me want to be a better person, and the things I used to do, I don't anymore.

"Lily is one of those things. She knew not to give it more importance than what it was, and she knows it's over now. I'm telling you there was nothing between us tonight, and there hasn't been for five months."

He took a deep breath and pulled me even closer. Our noses touched, and then he pressed his forehead against mine and closed his eyes.

"The girl has her pride. She likes putting on a show for her friends. And playing her rich, American boyfriend is a small price to pay so I can meet her brother away from the public eye. There. Is. Nothing. Else.

"Felix spent six weeks in Cuba, training at the Rafael Trejo Gym, and collecting intelligence from a relative of a contact inside the Ministry of Revolutionary Armed Forces. I pay for Cuban military secrets and Felix is my courier. Because of Lily I know the Cubans are selling their old Cold War era military equipment to North Korea. Tonight I learned when and how they plan to move it."

As far as work went, Todd's trumped mine for importance to the National Intelligence Priorities Framework. I would have been jealous if that part of me hadn't already been used up. If I were Richard, and I had to choose between us, I would have chosen Todd too.

"But it's not worth it if I lose you, Amy." His breath fanned against my face, drowning out the scent of the other woman. "If I could go back and undo all the things I've done to undermine your faith in me... if I could erase all the women I've fucked and used for what they could do for me, I would. But I already know from experience that I can't undo the past. I can only promise you the present and the future, Amy. I can swear that there hasn't been anyone else since you."

"Why?" I asked again, because if he was willing to give me an inch, then I wouldn't be satisfied without the full mile. I had never seen him this open... so vulnerable... and I wanted everything.

"Because I love you," he whispered so softly, I thought I might have imagined it. "Since the moment I laid eyes on you, I knew you were going to be a big deal for me. I saw you standing by the bar with that fool—" Rodgers, from the ATF and his local girlfriend "—and I fell for you. I love you, Amy."

Cruel hope didn't just have the power to harm me. It could free me too, and until Todd had said those words, I was only a shadow of the woman I was always meant to be. That someone like him could love me was empowering. I could do anything.

I kissed him. It was so easy. Our lips were only a breath apart and I suddenly felt so light. It took no effort at all for us to meet. And God, he was sweet! He was every dream I had ever had, every happy moment in my life. And he was hungry for me, almost as ravenous as I was for him.

His tongue inside my mouth swept me away. His fingers dug into my skull, begging me to open, to touch him too. And because he asked so eloquently, I did not resist.

We came together in a blinding heat and frenzy of limbs, tongue and teeth. Todd groaned deeply when my fingers tunneled into his hair, holding him hard against me. He pulled away for a breath, but my teeth closed onto his bottom lip, plumping it, pulling him back where he belonged. I shouldn't have worried that he would leave me again. He only wanted to lift me by the back of my thighs so I could wrap my legs around his waist. That was good, because I was melting like a brick of chocolate over his heat.

My world shifted on its axis. Or there was the sensation of movement as Todd took us to the bed. He would have risked life and limb if he had tossed me down, but he craved the contact as much as me. He wouldn't let me go. He laid me down gently, and followed close behind, hovering over me, hooking my knee over his elbow so I remained open to him. His jeans and belt were abrasive as he ground his arousal into me. I was a quivering, molten, gasping mass of nerves and greed and need.

Todd found a breast just when it needed him most. He squeezed, priming it for his mouth and making me crave that contact so much I begged with an agonized cry.

"God, please!"

He shifted away, his fingers at my breast stilled. I felt the lack profoundly. "I'm sorry, Amy," he gasped, his lips bruised red and slick from our kisses. "About the other day...I wanted to punish you, so you would feel the emptiness I felt when you walked out on me. I wanted you to know that you would always need me... that you could never leave me. It got out of hand. I was angry, and I'm sorry. I never meant to hurt you like that. I was no different –"

I cut him off with a hand pressed against his mouth, sealing the words in. "Don't say anymore." I shook my head, both to keep the past from standing between us again, but also in disbelief. Unless I had lost my mind from that kiss, those were tears shimmering in Todd's eyes. "Don't say his name. Don't say what he did. I don't want him here between us. This is different. It was never the same – not even close. I'm sorry I tried to hurt you by saying those things."

He pulled my hand away. He kissed the palm, the wrist, caressing the spot where my pulse throbbed with his tongue. "I can't hurt you again. I can't do that to you again, no matter how much you think you need it."

"I need you more. All of you, though. I have to have everything."

Todd feathered light kisses all along the inside of my arm. I used to think nothing could undo me like violent need and anger, but Todd's tenderness - that look in his eyes – filled me to overflowing. I shivered.

"You always had me, Amy. I was just afraid to say the words. I was afraid you would take it and walk away. The last few weeks have taught me that nothing is worth losing your trust."

He kissed me again, sealing our mouths and hearts together. Our skin craved each other, coming together like two candles burning in the same pot. My hands delved under his shirt to feel his warmth. He was burning up, feverish with want for me. His heat coiled inside me like a shot of radiation, consuming me from the inside out.

Our clothes were shed in a flurry of impatient hands. My tongue stroked the skin above his left nipple, up his neck, and traced the shell of his ear. "I love you," I whispered.

"Fuck, Amy," he gasped, ripping the straps of my camisole in his haste to get at his pound of flesh. He sucked one breast into his mouth, nearly devouring me whole. His mouth, pulling hard, tugged at my core in the most delicious, throbbing pain I had ever experienced.

I had to hold on tight and my fingers found purchase in the back pockets of his jeans. I squeezed on the hard muscle beneath, pressing him harder, grinding him deeper into my pulsing center.

Todd was never satisfied with half of me. He switched breasts, which gave me only the slightest moment of reprieve to undo his belt and the fastenings that conspired against me, keeping us apart.

I cried out in both sweet agony and frustration when Todd laved an overly sensitive nipple with his burning tongue, while a brass button defeated me. Thankfully, he also came to my rescue, freeing himself so my trembling fingers could wrap around his erection. I squeezed and stroked him from sack to tip, twisting my grasp at the knob. The man shook.

"Jesus Christ!" he groaned, right before crushing my mouth with his.

One thick hand grasped my wrist and squeezed until I let go. My own moan was one of protest, cut short when he kicked off his pants and briefs. He pulled away long enough and far enough to shrug out of his shirt and pull my shorts and panties down my legs.

"Let me taste you," I pleaded, gazing with longing at the proof of his desire for me.

"Not a chance." He brushed aside my greatest wish with the same ease as he pushed my hair back off my face. "I need to be inside you right now."

Well, it wasn't exactly right that instant. Todd took the time to grasp my legs at the knees and spread me wide. He wasn't gentle, and I guessed old habits were hard to die, because I looked forward to his roughness. I was up on my elbows, ready for him, panting with need.

But Todd hated losing control, and could not resist the chance to realign the balance of power. He killed me with his tongue. My stomach clenched and my mind went blank at the sight of his thick head of glossy hair and the broad shoulders nestled between my legs. Our eyes met and my mouth went dry. He licked along my slit in two leisurely laps then sucked my clit into his mouth and sent me spiraling into a violent climax.

"You should see yourself right now," he whispered. I could imagine the sight I made – head tossed back in abandon, eyes squeezed shut as the tremors shook me; legs spread wide open. "You're so fucking beautiful. And you taste so good. I've missed you so much."

Too much, perhaps, because by the next breath, he was deep inside me. His groan vibrated through his core, and it was Todd's turn to throw his head back and arch his body in exquisite joy. God, it was better than I remembered.

"I love you," I cried, hips pressing against his, begging for more, while my nails sank deep into the muscles of the shoulder said it was too much.

"Yes, Amy," he cried, pulling away inch by excruciating inch. And then he rammed into me, sinking hard and fast. "You are my home now. I can never have too much. I can never get enough."

And then he really moved, plowing into me like our lives depended on it. And in a sense, it did. I was building again, and I would have died if he had left me hanging.

Scooting up on his knees, Todd pulled me closer, hoisting my hips so my bottom laid in his lap. He had an enviable view of where we were joined, of his slick length sliding into me until I took all of him. My view was of his naked body, his taut chest, shoulders and arms, flexing with each thrust. He pressed a thumb against my clit, which sent me shooting for the stars again.

Todd grunted as my body tightened around him. He cupped my bottom, lifting me higher so he could really power into me. I tried to hold onto my own cry, because I wanted him to feed my senses. The sound of our bodies slapping moistly together; the scent we created together – sunshine, sex, woodsy musk; the sight of the work of erotic art that was Todd's body in motion; the sound of his grunts as the primal part of him was unchained. I wanted to feel the jagged edges of his control slipping away as he pumped harder and deeper, lifting me higher and higher. I couldn't get enough of knowing how affected he was by me.

Our bodies were coated in a sheen of sweat. Todd's jaw was clenched tight, trying to hold off the waves until I succumbed again. His thumb flicked almost frantically over that tight ball of nerves at the apex of my thighs. But he never relented for a moment on his sweet assault.

I managed to pull myself up so I straddled him. It was deeper like this, gazing into each other's eyes as our bodies bowed to our need. There was no room to hide as I rode him, breasts flattened against his chest, our mounds and caves fitting perfectly together. There was no escape as his rhythm guided my hips, the thrust of his hips bouncing me in his lap, his rough hands pulling me back where I belonged over and over again.

"I'm going to come again, Todd," I called out, before he wrapped his tongue around mine.

"I know," he said against my mouth. "I can feel you."

"Come with me," I asked, alternating between moving up and down, having him slide in and out of me; and rocking back and forth, pressing over and over against that wall of need deep inside that made me break out in shivers.

"Yes," he groaned and pumped deeper and harder and faster. I felt him pulsing, pushing his scorching release deep inside me. And it set off an avalanche of a climax that rocked me. This time there was no doubt; my world spun off its axis.

Our bodies clutched at each other, our tongues chasing the sweat that coursed over us both, our mouths catching each other's cries. At last we had soared so high, we were burned by the sun and fell back to earth and to the tangled sheets in a mass of liquid bones and desperate cries.

We breathed each other in greedy pants, but it wasn't nearly enough. Todd stretched out and pulled me into the crook of his arm so I could make him my bed. I liked it. His heart thudded heavily beneath my cheek and at last I felt at home.

I was on the brink of sleep when I found my voice. There was still a question that weighed heavily between us.

"Did you kill Mona?"

It seemed forever before he answered, and I struggled to keep my eyes open and my brain functioning. I felt him take a deep breath then release it in a slow sigh. I had no control over my body, but there was Todd showing off his restraint.

"No," he said quietly, tiredly. "But I didn't save her either." And then from so far away that I thought it was a dream, Todd whispered, "But I will save you, Amy, from everything and everyone. Even Anne."

TWENTY-FOUR

It had to be a dream. I couldn't remember having ever been this happy before. Not even with my father. Yes, I loved him more than life, but I had taken our time together for granted. I'd thought we would always be together, and so I had never stopped to appreciate how much I loved him and how happy he made me.

It was different with Todd. I thought I had lost him so many times, and there were still so many challenges that threatened to tear us apart again, that I was able to appreciate our time together even more. I loved him. He loved me. And I was happy.

I didn't want to leave that time in the past. I didn't want the realities of our lives to intrude, but they inevitably did. It was 4 a.m. when the next alert came. In the best-case scenario, it was only Angelika. But the facts were: I had no lock on my door; Todd was in my bed; and Angelika was about to walk through the front door.

I got up and got dressed in jeans and the henley I had ruled out earlier. Todd sent my heart shooting into my throat when he stirred. I froze, hoping he would settle back to sleep. He rubbed his eyes with the heel of his hands in that way of his that gave me a glimpse of what the man had looked like as a child. His blues met my browns and I lost my breath.

"What are you doing?"

"Go back to sleep. I'll be right back."

Of course, Todd sat up in bed. The sheets were bunched loosely around his hips, distracting me, making me think there was a chance he would do as I said.

"You're not going running." It sounded more like an accusation that a question, especially since he eyed my jeans in a narrowed gaze. "Come back to bed." His voice was firm, all trace of sleep gone in an instant.

"No," I rushed to reassure him, although I couldn't help the sideways glance towards my wide-open bedroom door, or the clear view of and from the living room. "I'm not going anywhere."

"Then come back to bed." He didn't sound as though he believed me. It was a challenge. The honeymoon was over.

"I have to get my firearm. I left it in the kitchen."

Todd stared at me for a long moment and I held my breath to stop myself from glancing at the gaping doorway again.

"What's going on, Amy?"

From the look in his eyes, the hardening of the edges of his mouth, I knew Todd wasn't going to back down. Two hours ago I hadn't known he had been in the Marines, and I hadn't known for whom he worked. I had guessed a lot and I'd been wrong. But I *knew* Todd would not let me go.

"Do you trust me?"

It was a lot to ask the man I kept running from at the earliest opportunity. But he still answered without hesitation. "Yes, Amy. I trust you." He was that good. I might have believed him if I wasn't me.

"If I asked you to stay here and not come out, no matter what happens, no matter what you hear, would you do that for me?"

I didn't like my pleading tone, but if I had any hope of saving us, I knew I had to shed the layers for him.

"No." Todd got out of bed.

I bolted, even though I didn't have any hope of keeping this from him. I got the firearm and checked the security feed that Angelika had come alone. Todd hopped into the living room, still closing the fastenings on his jeans. He had foregone underwear, and the denim hung low on his hips, showing off an impressive expanse of bronze skin dusted with dark hair, wrapped around hard ridges and taut muscles. I didn't want

Angelika seeing him like that. I was tired of sharing him with other women.

"There is this work thing," I said, trying to look casual as I guarded the security monitor and tucked the firearm in the back of my waistband. This was so far from an ideal situation.

Todd crossed his arms over his chest and cocked a brow at me, plumping *everything* for my viewing pleasure. And Angelika's too if I didn't get him to retreat. Todd wasn't as built as Colonel Townsend, but he was hard in all the right places. I wanted to run my tongue over his hills and valleys just to test the density. Angelika wouldn't mind the view at all, even if she were the type to compare.

"Someone is coming up and I would rather you not be here for this."

"Is it Townsend?"

I should have known he would go there. He knew we had worked together in the past. He knew Townsend wasn't in Santo Domingo for the pleasure of my company alone. But Todd also knew the colonel would not pass up the opportunity to hurt him through me.

"No. He is involved, but it's not him. I could never bring him here."

"Amy, you wouldn't have been able to stop him," Todd said, propping one hip against my couch. He had more to say, but held back. It didn't matter. I knew what was left unspoken. I hadn't been able to stop Todd either.

Just then I heard the elevator ping in the hall.

"Go put a shirt on. I don't want her seeing you like this."

It was a last ditch effort, but after a brief face-off, he complied. I knew I had a handful of seconds, tops, so I yanked open the front door before Angelika could stick her key into the lock.

She was surprised to see me there, and even more shocked when I closed the door behind me, leaving both of us standing outside. She was a mess. Her hair had suffered, standing up in some places. Her eye makeup was smeared, making her look more like Beetlejuice than a raccoon. And her slouchy top hadn't seemed quite so loose when she had left the apartment last night.

But she was definitely high. Her pupils were huge, leaving the clear irises space for only a slight ring. She had dosed again, and recently too.

"You can't be here right now," I told her, one hand clutching the doorknob and the other turning her by the shoulder.

A wedge formed between her eyes that hinted at a frown. The corners of her mouth turned down. "Where do I go? I have nowhere."

The doorknob rattled and I held on for dear life.

"Go to the pool. Stay there until I come for you –"

The decision was literally wrenched from my hands. Todd stood in the gaping doorway, eyes shifting between Angelika and me. I didn't think he could have been any angrier, but recognition struck as he peered closer at the waif. He came back to me, but only stared with his jaw ticking and the pulse at his temples throbbing.

I was caught and I knew my face said it all. Stuck under the halogen lights of the common hallway, Angelika said it all clearly. I clamped my mouth shut and fixed my countenance into something my father would have been proud of. Todd was going to have to work for it. I wasn't admitting anything.

Angelika however, was another matter entirely. She devoured Todd, came back to me, and went back to him as if following a ping-pong match. Her white eyebrows hit the roof before she turned that poor excuse of a frown upside down. She remembered him for sure now.

Todd stepped back into the apartment, but kept the door wide-open in an obvious command for us to follow. Angelika looked to me for guidance, which Todd didn't miss at all. They both knew I owned her.

"Go to your room," I told her. "I'll come to you." And Todd didn't miss that either – that Angelika had a room inside my apartment.

We moved the tense silence inside and Todd closed the door – barred it in fact – with the lock then his body.

"Hi," Angelika offered, then took her time leaving when he acknowledged her greeting with a nod.

Todd stared at me as she went. I wasn't going to act guilty, I told myself. I kept my eyes on my asset, waiting for her to disappear, waiting for the click of her door before facing off with Todd.

"What the fuck are you up to, Amy?" I had expected thunder and lightning when he ripped into me, but what I got was deadly calm. I knew enough not to take it for granted. Our new basis for trust was at risk here.

"I'm not up to anything," I answered evenly. "She's an asset – an official one – bought and paid for."

Todd wasn't buying it. He grabbed me by the arm and dragged me back to my bedroom. I was steered inside and the door kicked behind him. The frame was splintered though, so it bounced right back. Todd didn't care. He backed me into the bathroom and slammed that door behind us. He hit the light, which flickered on to the beat of my heart stuttering. I steadied myself with a series of deep breaths as Todd advanced, backing me up until my butt hit the vanity and I had nowhere else to retreat... nowhere to hide. Even then he crowded me more, looming over me, until his arms stretched around me, bracing against the sink, imprisoning me.

"What are you doing, Amy?"

I wasn't anymore fooled by his calm now than I was thirty seconds ago in the living room. His pulse throbbed, and it obviously took some effort to keep his breath calm.

"I'm telling the truth. She's working a case for us." I was proud of myself. My voice didn't waver. I looked him directly in the eye. Might have clenched against my roiling stomach, but outwardly I kept my cool.

"How did you come by her?"

I wasn't used to being held accountable like this. Todd demanded things from me I hid from my own boss. He wanted the whole truth, didn't think twice about asking me to defy my compulsions. For now though, it pissed me off. Forget not taking his calm for granted. He needed to be more careful with me too.

Okay, he was a bigger deal, but I wasn't nothing.

"I tracked her from our garbage the night you brought her into her home."

Pushing back made him take stock of our positions. Todd had the mirror behind me to evaluate his reactions. I had only him. And he seemed to realize I would mirror him. Finally, some give. It wasn't surrender; it wasn't retreat; but I welcomed this platform for negotiations.

"Why did you go after her, Amy?"

"I wanted to hurt you."

"Did you? Did you hurt me?"

Todd understood the type of damage we were capable of didn't always have immediate consequences. We were silent nuclear disasters, our effects enduring long after the initial blast.

"Yes."

He sighed, and his breath fanned the hair tumbling over my shoulders and down my back. He closed his eyes, but there was no need. I felt his disappointment. I wasn't sorry, but I still had to wrap my arms around my middle against the cold. When he opened his eyes again, when next he stared into my soul, he had pulled the edges of his composure together. I didn't like the bleakness.

"What did you do?"

"I created a database of everyone who used her."

"Everyone?"

"Every one of us," I clarified.

"Who knows about this?"

"O'Brien knows."

My gaze had slipped to the lump that bobbed at his throat when he swallowed my revelation. A finger tilted my chin up, so our eyes met again.

"And you," Todd added.

I nodded.

"Landon?" he asked, adding two and two together and coming up with four.

I nodded again. So there had been fallout there that my boss had not shared with me. Todd's friend had confided in him, perhaps asked for his intercession. Knowing what I know now, I wasn't surprised.

"Martinez?"

"Yes." I had no reason to be ashamed, but bearing that in mind took effort. So, his friends had complained to him about me. They were the ones asking him to choose. Not me.

"So you knew I hadn't slept with her." My husband still had the ability to surprise me. Was the choice that simple for him... our union taking precedence over their careers? When had I become his primary concern?

"I doubted her recollection."

Todd moved closer. His cotton clad chest pressed firmly against my crossed arms.

"And now?"

My eyes rose and got stuck on his mouth. Mine went dry. I swallowed, trying to generate some moisture. Todd licked his lips and my breath got stuck in my throat. I couldn't talk around it, so I shook my head 'no'.

"Do *you* trust me, Amy?"

That brought me back to him. My heart rate spiked, pushing blood too fast through my body. My respiration kicked in too, going too fast to take in all the air I needed. There wasn't enough going to my brain. I risked fainting as a panic attack gained momentum. Todd wasn't asking *if* I trusted him; he was demanding that I do.

Todd pressed his mouth against mine. His were warm and soft; mine cold and hard, but he swooped in and breathed calm into me. Todd pulled me back from the brink, warming me one stroke of his lips and tongue at a time. My body welcomed him. My fingers found his biceps, then his shoulders, his neck, his hair…. My lungs took him in with steady gulps. Long before I had had nearly enough, he pulled away.

"Yes," I breathed, as he stared down at me. *I will trust you.*

"Good," he whispered and kissed me again, briefly this time. And then he was gone, only inches away, but it might as well have been an ocean. "Now tell me what you're doing with her."

"She's an intrusion key."

"Sanctioned?" I nodded. "Then why is she here?"

"I took her before. I planned on using her against you." I swallowed and tried to brazen it out. I couldn't bring myself to look him in the eye though. I felt, more than saw, him nod, prompting me to continue. "I didn't have anywhere else to hide her. The sanction came after and she hasn't been paid yet."

"You worked her in." It wasn't a question, but I nodded anyway. "Where does Townsend come in to play?"

"The target is local military. Townsend is the liaison." I bit my lip, feeling around in the dark for the edges of this trust.

"Amy…" Todd prompted, and I had to rush in before he put words to the question that would prove my deception.

"I also used her for leverage against him." I didn't know how to read Todd's narrow-eyed gaze. He might have approved and that was grudging admiration, or maybe he didn't recognize the woman he had married and was suspicious. "Townsend doesn't know yet."

He chewed that over for a moment, but kept me pinned with those eyes. Finally, he sighed.

"You don't want to play those games with Townsend. I've known him for a long time. He's nothing like Martinez."

"His marriage may not be worth anything, but his command does."

"The say-so of a prostitute isn't going to change that."

I didn't respond, but I didn't flinch from his stare either.

"You have more than that?" I shrugged. Todd's eyebrows went up. "Photo?" I didn't so much as blink. "Video?" If Todd knew me as well as he claimed, he wouldn't have been so surprised. "Did money change hands?"

"No, but my database establishes conspiracy. His position puts him at the top of it. And the crackdown on the Factory makes her a victim of international traffickers."

"Fuuuck, Amy," Todd hissed.

"It won't come to that."

"You don't know who you're fucking with, Amy," he said, one hand raking through his hair.

I wasn't arrogant. I knew the value of warnings, especially from a reliable source. Plus, Todd seemed to be thinking. The least I could do was give him time and listen.

I'll save you, Amy, he had said in my dream, *from everything and everyone. Including Anne.* I believed him.

"You said he doesn't know yet." I nodded. "Well, what were you waiting for?"

"For this job to be over."

"Why?" He must have thought it was like pulling teeth with me.

"I wanted a clean break."

"From me?" His brows crashed down and he moved in closer. His unconscious response to the mere thought of separation from me flooded me with warmth.

I shook my head, still mystified by the fact that someone like him could love someone like me.

"From him?" There was both hope and anger in those two words. I looked Todd straight in the eye, which was the worst thing I could have done if I wanted to forget my promise of trust. I nodded. "What did he do to you?"

"Nothing," I said on a deep exhale, trying to replace the air Todd had sucked from our close quarters.

"Has he threatened you?"

I wanted to deny it. I didn't want to add a spark to the tinderbox that surrounded these two men. But Todd wouldn't allow me to look away.

"Nothing that had me really worried. He's just intense."

"Not enough to worry you, but serious enough for you to blackmail him," Todd rebuffed with heavy skepticism. He did a damn good job of making me feel like an amateur. And that I certainly was not.

"I wasn't going to be antagonistic," I said in my own defense, at which Todd scoffed. Now I was insulted. "It would have been in his best interest to help me."

"Help you?" Todd asked, pushing away from me to slouch against the bathroom door. Why did I miss him already?

"Yes. I would have asked him to help me move Angelika and explain why it would benefit him to do so. I would have also asked him to lay off with the... the advances." I reinforced the last through gritted teeth, brushing off Todd's narrowed gaze. "The video was only a break-in-case-of-emergency measure."

Todd relaxed by small degrees, but his hands were braced against his hips as he looked me up and down. Hopefully he was convinced I wasn't a complete moron. "Well, you can just forget about that. I'll take care of Townsend."

I didn't know how I felt about his take-charge-and-rescue attitude. I had relied on myself for so long, it was hard for me to relinquish control. But clearly Todd knew what he was talking about. He knew Colonel Robert Townsend.

Todd came back to me, standing so close our lower bodies fused, denim-to-denim. I gripped the vanity behind me, bracing myself because I knew he was about to rock my world again.

"In the meantime, I want you to stay away from him," he said, running his hands up and down my arms.

"I still have to work with him," I panted.

"I don't want you to be alone with him," he said, as if he hadn't heard what I had said. "Call me if you have to."

I was halfway through rolling my eyes at the impossibility of that when Todd took hold of my face. He held me still so he could brand himself on my soul.

"Wherever I am, whatever I'm doing, I will come to you, Amy. You don't have to worry about what anyone has to say about this. Richard knows how I feel about your safety."

"Todd –" I said, not liking this new role he had crafted for me.

I wasn't helpless. And he couldn't protect me if he didn't know about all the pots I was stirring. I didn't want to lie to him, but there were things I could not share. He thought he knew me. He thought he knew about Anne. But he didn't know enough, and I was more afraid than ever that one day he would learn the truth and he wouldn't want me – couldn't love me – anymore. What would become of me then, after I had learned to rely on him?

He kissed me, with the full knowledge of what it would do to me. When I was reduced to playdough in his hands, Todd pulled away.

"Now," he said, running his thumb across my lower lip, sealing himself into my flesh, "why do you need Townsend to help you move her?"

It bothered me that he might have had Angelika floating in the back of his head while kissing me. "I have to move her to Europe and I don't know anyone there. I thought maybe he could help. O'Brien wouldn't be sympathetic."

"Why Europe?"

Todd didn't miss a thing. I'd known this about him before. The only thing at stake then was my sense of security. This was something else entirely. But could I lie to him now? And if I broke trust and he found out about it, would we ever recover from it? My palms became slick with sweat just thinking about it.

"Hide it," my father had said.

"I can't tell you."

He was going to push. I felt it deep in my bones and it made me sick. I swallowed repeatedly, pushing back the urge to retch. Todd's hands found my arms again and caressed me, trying to soothe me.

"One day you will," he said. I doubted it, but I was so relieved, my breath escaped me in an audible gasp.

"Do you need to manage your asset now?" I nodded. Todd stepped back and tilted his head in the direction of the door. "Go ahead. I'm going back to the house. I have to get ready for work. I expect you to come home soon."

I nodded again. The moment his gaze released me I bolted for the door. There was no denying he had let me off easy.

"Amy," he called before I could make good my escape. "I'll help you move her. You don't need Townsend for anything."

I nodded and turned to go up again, knowing I had escaped by the skin of my teeth and only because Todd allowed it.

"One more thing Amy," he said.

This time I was halfway through the door. I turned hesitantly, afraid to meet his eyes, but aware I had no choice. The considerate lover was gone and in his place stood the agent.

"When I said I would save you from everything and everyone..." I nodded, swallowing and tasting the burn of bile this time. "I'm saving you for myself... not *from* me."

As if I needed him to tell me that...

I pulled the door closed behind me, and this time, perhaps the only time, Todd left me with the illusion of getting away.

TWENTY-FIVE

"Are we in?" I asked for the third time in five minutes. I was operating on three hours of sleep and it had been a hellish morning, preceded by an even more gruesome three weeks. Coffee didn't help. I had no time for a run. My more illicit activities had to be checked now that Todd had resurfaced and was paying closer attention than ever before.

I needed to eat something today. Coffee and candy weren't going to cut it any longer. Stomach acid was slowly burning a hole through my digestive tract, and if I didn't neutralize it soon, an ulcer was definitely in my future. Then I would never get Todd or Uncle Richard off my ass.

I was reduced to pacing six feet of scuffed tiles behind Sergeant Garrick Moss, the communications tech dedicated to my intrusion program. He sighed for the third time in under a minute and rolled his eyes. Even though I was standing directly behind him, I had a plain view of his contempt for me. His privacy screen reflected his image back to me like a mirror.

"I don't have time for you to fuck around with this," I snapped, because if it were Colonel Townsend pacing behind him for ten minutes, he would have damn well given him a blow-by-blow account of his activities.

I had Angelika cooling her heels in the lounge. After the stunt she had pulled last night, I didn't trust her to be on her own. Her phone was plugged into a router via USB adapter. The router was plugged into Sergeant Moss' laptop so he could find the glitch in the intrusion key on Angelika's Nokia. I wouldn't know whether Plan Alpha was a success until Moss confirmed we had remote access to Colonel Ramirez's communications. The problem was Moss was taking his own sweet time.

If Alpha hadn't worked, I had Colonel Townsend to contend with. So far I had dodged all his calls and it was only 8a.m. I didn't put it past him to just show you at my desk, which was why I was hiding out in Comms, aggravating the living daylights out of Garrick Moss.

Not that Moss didn't deserve it. He was being a prick and I suspected he was deliberately on go-slow because he didn't like me. Fucking Jarhead. It was time to get in his face.

I bent at the waist, one arm resting on the back of his swivel chair, the other on his desk, blocking him into his tiny cubbyhole. I moved in close, so close our noses almost touched when he turned to stare me down with narrowed eyes.

"I'm going for a walk. I'll be back here in exactly 5 minutes. And if you still haven't gotten your shit together by then, they are going to need a scalpel and forceps to get my foot out of your ass."

He tried not to blink, determined not to lose a face-off with a girl. But I wasn't like the girls he was used to, hence his dislike for me. Blood surged up his neck until the tips of his ears glowed. The blush clashed with his cammies. He looked away in the direction of a snicker of suppressed laughter. I could guess who the guilty party was; he was the only one not staring at us. I left them to it, heading in the direction of the ladies room.

I was going out of my mind. My stress levels were off the chart, and the coke fiend waiting for me in the lobby wasn't helping my state of mind. Her unexpected arrival last night had precipitated a conversation I had never imagined having with Todd.

It wasn't entirely her fault though. Townsend had refused to shelter her. But she should have known better than to allow Colonel Ramirez to deliver her to my gate after leaving a cabaña, and after having spent a considerable amount of time at a strip club. She had shown zero regard for her safety. That was the story of her life. Angelika was incapable of anticipation and hadn't the slightest clue about risk assessment. It was the reason she was in her present predicament.

It was imperative therefore that I bring this operation to a close and get her the hell out of this country so I could offload the compromised apartment. Leaving her alone there was no longer an option.

*And if you're so good at what you do, why are **you** here?*

Here meaning wrapped around Todd Birch like a desperate scarf.

"I can't do it all on my own. Todd can help."

You were never alone... just lonely... and horny. Now look what you've done.

"Shut up," I snapped. The girl in the mirror glared back at me. I looked away, hardly washing my hands, because I knew she was right. I got out of there as fast as I could. Imagine how it would look if anyone walked in and saw me talking to myself. With my luck, it would probably be someone my husband had screwed.

I stayed away from my Section even though O'Brien might have been looking for me. I briefly considered going to see Todd, but quickly dismissed that idea.   Anne was right. Todd's ego didn't need more stroking. Plus time was up for Garrick Moss.

I walked as casually as my Wednesday skirt and brown pumps could manage, slowing down the click-clack of my heels echoing through the cavernous room. Everyone looked up, tracking my progress over coffee cups, printouts and three ring binders. Everyone except Moss. He was still scrutinizing Angelika's Nokia when his focus should have been on his laptop by now.

I casually perched my behind on the edge of his desk in a good imitation of one of Byles' trademarked moves. I smoothed down the hem of my skirt and reached for his desk line, tapping out the number I knew by heart and letting it ring on speaker. I smiled down at Moss in a grimace of bared teeth, positive the light didn't reach my eyes. Moss glared back.

"Townsend."

"Colonel Robert Townsend, how are you? This is Amy Koehler and I have you on speaker."

Moss started moving his fingers across the keypad with a level of efficiency I was witnessing for the first time. There was a rustle of paper around the room that went pretty well with the roll of chairs over the tiles and cleared throats. The Joker smirked again.

"Now why would you want to do that, Amy?" came the lazy reply across the line. The smile behind it was dirty. "What if I want to talk about what happened last night?"

"I'm not shy." Todd was going to be pissed when he heard about this, but desperate times called for desperate measures. I didn't have any more time to waste with Moss. And Todd's only demand was that I not be alone with the colonel. I was well within my bounds.

"You could have fooled me. You've been avoiding me. And I thought you and I were well beyond the awkward morning after phase."

Okay. He got a smile out of me although he was probably hoping for a giggle. I had to uncross and re-cross my legs. I wasn't going to lie. I was still attracted to the man, especially when he was being playful – okay, juvenile. But I wasn't going to do anything about it.

"No, not running. Just busy. I'm in Comms, and you know the rules... no comms when in comms." All wireless communications were barred in this secure location, a mandate that was reinforced with signal jammers.

"About last night," Townsend said smoothly, indicating his unwillingness to abandon his play on words. "I don't usually have to ask, but..." he chuckled during that brief pause that had my skin tingling with both anticipation and trepidation. "Was it as good for you?"

Moss flushed again. No, pink definitely wasn't his color. Townsend and I weren't the only ones enjoying this conversation either. There was a low whistle somewhere behind me, and what sounded like hands clapping in a high five.

"Hmm," I mumbled, "the jury's still out on that." I tapped my finger on Moss' computer to get his attention. It would have been more dramatic if my nails weren't so short, but who was Moss trying to kid? Of course I had his attention. "Are we in?"

He shook his head 'no' and my heart sank to my toes in real disappointment that matched Townsend's groan when I relayed the negative response.

"I want another shot," Townsend said. "Let me redeem myself." But the game had gotten old really fast.

"What went wrong?" I asked Moss.

He passed on the obligatory greeting and introduction to Townsend.

I did the tap-tap again so he would get on with the explanation, so

Moss at least knew the fun and games were over even if Townsend wanted to keep on acting like he was sixteen.

"I can't say for certain. There are a couple of possibilities, but in either case it's a failure, sir. Tango might not have opened the VCF file; his anti-spyware software or System Administrator may have blocked it; or he might not have received the file in the first place."

There was a sigh on Townsend's end. I bit my lip on the frustration ready to slip out and thought about our options. There was an inherent risk of discovery in all our backup plans – the risk increasing the farther into the alphabet we ventured. But it wasn't like I could return to my Section without a salvageable plan for O'Brien.

"Could your girl have sent it to the wrong number?" Townsend asked.

Unlikely. I also noted how quickly he distanced himself from the potential shit storm. She was as much his girl as mine, especially given how well he had tested her mettle. And he was the one to have provided Colonel Ramirez's mobile number. That made Angelika 'our' girl.

"That's a negative, Colonel Townsend." I turned to Moss again. "Is there any way of finding out if it was a system block? And if so, can we override it?"

But he was already shaking his head. "Not without internal access." Which was like saying we couldn't get to the cash inside the bank safe without first being inside said safe.

"Well, at least we have the next three days to get it right."

Of course Townsend was quick to move on to the backup plans. He was just the liaison. Responsibility for success rested squarely on my shoulders. The risk was all mine to manage. Plus he hadn't had to fuck a man old enough to be his grandfather.

"Koehler," he called, only willing to return to formality when it suited him. "I'll pick you up at 1100 for lunch. We'll discuss then." And apparently it suited him for us to meet privately.

I picked up the receiver from its cradle and hopped off Moss' desk. Turning my back was a failed bid for privacy. The rest of the floor was wide open and the room was hollow with high ceilings and wide walls. Just as my heels echoed off the floor, so was my hushed mumble replayed in an intimate whisper.

"Can I confirm that in a few minutes?"

There was a brief pause as Townsend's brain switched gears again. He came back to me sounding much less friendly. "I think you've forgotten how this works, Koehler. You seem to do that a lot."

"There are conflicting considerations, sir." That was a new term for Todd Birch, and I thought it suited him perfectly. I couldn't *not* meet with Townsend. We had work to do and the clock working against us. I knew how to protect myself. Todd would have to be satisfied with our meeting in a public environment. But knowing Townsend, I suspected he would simply take me back to his hotel without giving me a choice of locations. I already knew what he would say... the nature of our work required privacy for secure communication.

"Resolve them, Koehler. I'll be there at 1100." He hung up on me.

I was beat but not defeated. I wasn't as helpless as the colonel thought, and I didn't need Todd to save me either. I pocketed Angelika's phone while flicking through the internal directory. I never had a reason to dial the cafeteria before, and unless Todd had fucked one of the staff, they would not have a clue who I was.

"Good morning," I said in my most charming tone when a clearly distracted voice picked up the line. "This is Mrs. Birch. I would like to make an order for pickup at 11:00 for Colonel Robert Townsend."

Between the name I had never used and the title no one could ignore, the staffer came to attention. I knew they had to be good for something.

"What's on the menu?"

TWENTY-SIX

I had a plan. It was a good one, but I wasn't sure Townsend was going to go for it. O'Brien was my backstop, and I planned on keeping him in the back of my mind, not at the forefront of my operation. If I could fix this within the next hour, there was no need for him to ever know that Plan Alpha had failed.

Townsend could be a problem. He could try to tie up this operation with his personal agenda. And now that I understood the lengths he would go to hurt Todd, I wasn't going to entertain him in the least. Todd didn't think I could play in the big leagues. Well, he had never seen me play.

11:00 a.m. found me seated across from Angelika in conference room 2B, three boxes of cafeteria food ready and waiting for Colonel Townsend to arrive. It would probably come as a surprise to him to find Angelika inside to the embassy. He couldn't possibly be more shocked than the other members of staff who knew her from her Factory days though.

Santo Domingo was the largest Caribbean Mission, but it might as well have been a wading pool judging by how quickly word spread. Angelika wasn't wearing her brown wig today and dressed in cutoffs and a tank top that didn't offer much of a disguise. She was shivering by the time I collected her from the lobby, and I considered giving her my blazer. But when Client #14 did a double take, then came to an abrupt, slack-jawed halt on his way to the Fraud Unit, I decided against the act of generosity.

It wouldn't hurt for all the concerned parties to know I'd had access to her. When Martinez called a couple of minutes later to ask if we were 'cool' I knew the news had spread like wildfire. Good. Fear was a good motivator.

Angelika was nervous, and I knew the reasons why. She was coming off a cocaine high, and was dying for a cigarette. She knew I was aware she hadn't mentioned her acquaintance with Todd the night she helped me with my database. In addition, I didn't bother hiding my annoyance at her advertisement of our location or the risk she had taken with her visit to a strip club. She knew her performance thus far was under review.

All things considered, she had done a good job, which was the only reason I hadn't ripped her a new asshole. Not that she wouldn't see that as a good thing. Knowing Angelika she would likely turn it into a sexual advantage.

Based on her account, Angelika and Colonels Townsend and Ramirez had left the ballgame to visit Dollhouse. After half an hour, Townsend had left. Alone, she specified, because smart as she was Angelika had not missed the sexual tension between us and did not want to make the same mistake she had with Todd.

An hour later, she and Colonel Ramirez retired to a cabaña on Santo Domingo's Vegas-like strip off the Malecón. They had spent the next three hours soaking in a jacuzzi, snorting cocaine, and testing the sturdiness of the king-sized bed and stripper pole. Angelika even had the cell phone video of herself trying out some of her gymnastics moves. Colonel Ramirez could be seen holding the camera in the mirrored walls and ceiling in the background while she worked the pole. If Angelika didn't like her job, I couldn't tell.

She had sent Colonel Ramirez her contact information early in the evening. She never had to sleep with him, but I think his offer of cocaine had something to do with her sacrifice. As much as her habit was beginning to annoy me – not in principle, but because she was being sloppy – this time, I was glad she had stayed to party. Her video would come in handy as Plan Alpha version 2.1.

Townsend finally arrived with what I had come to term as his don't-fuck-with-me face. His striped green shirt, fastened all the way up except for the very first button, made his eyes look aquamarine. He had probably spent some time at the hotel pool this morning, because he was more tanned than I remembered from last night. He looked as crisp as a golden shortbread cookie, and judging by the expression he wore, he was about ready to snap.

"I bought lunch," I preempted, shifting one of the takeaway boxes in the direction of the seat I had reserved for him at the head of the table. "And I have good news."

"What's she doing here?" he asked, nodding in Angelika's direction. I wanted to ask if that was the standard greeting he reserved for the women he had fucked, and remind him it didn't bolster his campaign to get me in the sack. But that would have added fuel to an already volatile situation, even if I no longer needed Colonel Townsend to act as liaison. Well, that depended on the success of Plan Alpha version 2.1.

"Have a seat," I added warmly. "I'll explain."

Colonel Townsend didn't like taking direction from a retired female Army Captain, whether it was direction to the meeting venue I had texted to him, or the seating arrangements I had made.

Like the predictable jerk I knew he would be, he decided to put me back in my place right then and there. My penchant for preparation came in handy though. Just as Townsend had me backed against the wall and pinned in my seat, his body caging me, my self-appointed knight in shining armor appeared. His question about my motives for carting Angelika around to the embassy died on his lips.

Based on the things Todd had confessed last night, I knew I ran the risk of provoking a physical confrontation between him and Townsend. However, there were several factors that I hoped would play in my favor when it came to avoiding such an occurrence. Firstly, they had behaved cordially in the past when it was just the three of us around a table at Rituals in Kingston. Secondly, we were all at work where violence would not be ignored, regardless, or perhaps, because of who they both were. And thirdly, there were ladies present. As primitive as they were sometimes, they were both officers, not cavemen.

Judging by Todd's expression as the door swung closed behind him with a tad too much force, I may have over-estimated the importance of those factors, particularly the third one.

To say that Todd was angry would have been tantamount to calling the Pacific deep. Just then, the color of his eyes was a good match for the

Mariana trench. I had never seen them go that dark outside of sex. The tension in his jaw and the rigidity of his spine certainly mimicked his posture at the apex of his climax, right before he slammed violently into me for the last time.

It probably didn't help Todd's state of mind that Colonel Townsend decided to match him glare for glare, scowl for scowl. The blond warrior straightened too, as if he had forgotten that survival, evasion and escape were also critical components of SERE training. As he stood toe-to-toe with Todd, albeit separated by eight feet of conference room furniture, he was all about resistance.

"What the fuck do you think you're doing with my wife?"

With my peripheral vision, I spotted Angelika's look of surprise. She was in the process of making herself invisible in the corner, so the movement was quite conspicuous.

The men were ticking time bombs. The creases around Townsend's eyes and jaw jerked involuntarily, probably to the same tempo as the fists Todd had clenched at his sides. It was time to diffuse. I moved double-time in the direction of the only contender over whom I could claim some influence.

"Hey," I said, pressing a hand to his core when he kept a visual on the behemoth over my shoulder. God, he was hard. It was like pressing against a living, breathing wall.

Townsend was a couple inches taller than Todd's 6'2" and probably topped my husband by thirty pounds of mass. But I had sparred with Todd only a couple of days before, and as much as I wanted to claim a wardrobe handicap, the ease with which he had topped me, reduced my eighteen years of martial arts training to child's play, spoke for itself.

Townsend wasn't a complete daisy either. In comparison, he was built like a semi, and those took quite a bit of time to hit top speed. Todd wasn't going to give him the grace period to warm up. A fight was an all around bad situation that I had to avoid at all cost.

Amy Koehler, the pacifist. Who would have ever thought it would come to this?

"What are you doing here?" I whispered to Todd in an aside. That got his attention, just like I knew it would. Of course I knew exactly what he was doing there. I had sent for him – indirectly, but I had done it anyway. Now some of that anger was directed at me. It wasn't anything I could not handle, and it was successful in getting his mind off Townsend for a crucial moment. It was a lesson in survival that Colonel Townsend should have noted.

"What am I doing here?" Todd asked in disbelief as if it was completely natural for us to meet like this. His eyes had not cleared yet, but I still counted his divided attention as a boon. I tried to lead him to the farthest corner of the room. Todd didn't budge, and neither did Townsend.

"We are working here. That's what is going on."

Todd pounced, gripping my arm with authority. "Are you fucking kidding me?" he exploded.

It blew my mind that Colonel Townsend thought he had the right to intervene on my behalf. But that was what he tried to do, pulling up short only as I turned on him. I had to use my body as a physical obstacle to halt any forward momentum from either side.

"Have you lost your mind?" I asked the colonel, and by this time the hysteria in my voice was real. He was about to ruin my plan. "This is none of your business," I said with a finger pointed in his direction. I felt pressure against the hand I had resting on Todd's middle. "And you," I charged, panic getting the better of me now, "we are at work. I am working. There is no need for this."

Todd held onto my arm again, and this time, we both kept our eyes on Townsend to make sure he wasn't going to make the same mistake twice.

"We talked about this –" Todd started, but I had to cut him off.

"Yes, we did, and so far you are the only one not sticking to the terms."

"He was in your fucking face," Todd charged over my head, forcing me to press harder against him. Every time he looked in that direction I felt like I lost a bit of ground. "He was going to put his hands on you."

Thankfully Townsend remained silent, stewing in a decade-worth of rancor. He could have escalated the confrontation, claiming something to the effect of once having had both hands on me. He would have been correct too... But that was all he had had, before I had met Todd, when we had both been at work, with all our clothes on. I had already confessed the encounter to Todd, but I doubted he would choose to remember in the heat of the moment.

"Nothing was going to happen," I emphasized through gritted teeth, grateful Townsend didn't scoff.

My protestation resounded with the optimistic side of Todd, because he seemed to calm down a bit. The changes were minute, but significant, because the blue was returning to his eyes. He flexed the hand that gripped my arm like a vice, crinkling my silk shirt.

"Say what you need to say to him quickly. I'm not leaving you alone with him." It was a concession that was not a fair assessment of our situation. Angelika was doing a great job of making herself small, but she wasn't completely insignificant.

Still, I had averted a disaster and I wasn't about to start looking this gift horse in the mouth.

Townsend chose that moment to pipe up. "This is unacceptable, Amy." The problem was, he couldn't have his cake and eat it too. He couldn't exert his authority while infusing the degree of familiarity that 'Amy' incited.

"There isn't much to discuss," I told him over my shoulder, keeping my hands firmly on Todd. "I would've told you over the phone that Plan Alpha is still a go for now, but you insisted on… on eating," I finished in a scramble. 'Eating' sounded much less intimate that 'meeting' or 'seeing me'.

It turned out Townsend was mimicking Todd, because he too had started backing down from the physical confrontation in favor of the verbal clash. When that opportunity fizzled as well, they resorted to throwing death stares at each other.

"Angelika has another 'in' with our target. There is a video she could share, along with an invitation for another encounter." All eyes shifted to the shivering waif in the corner, who flushed now that her efforts at channeling a chameleon had been shot down in flames. "Not that you're going to keep any resulting appointments."

I had a flight reservation on hold for her, and I planned on confirming the moment Colonel Ramirez opened the infected file.

"Okay," she agreed, always amenable when the possibility of access to cocaine existed. "What do you want me to do?"

"Call him. Tell him what a wonderful time you had. Ask if you can see him again. Ask if he wants to see the video of you dancing. Get his email." She nodded, her eyes wide as she took her instructions to heart. But the phone remained on the table, a good foot from her hands. "Now," I prompted.

She gazed at me with surprise and her eyes opened wider, if that was even possible. "But I saw him last night. It's too soon to call him, no?"

"It's not a date and you're not looking for a boyfriend." She looked crushed, as if I had hurt her feelings. Then her eyes flickered between Todd and Townsend briefly, before falling to her lap.

Was this girl for real? Was that how she coped with her job... by thinking of the men she had slept with as her boyfriends?

Whatever method was behind her madness, it worked, because she sounded convincing as she flattered and giggled and flirted with a man who could have been her grandfather. Despite the eye rolls and quirked lips from the witnesses, Angelika mined the universal male flaw – ego.

She got the job done. The video was sent to his *.mil.do* email, in deference to his wife's potential access to private communication on the home computer.

Ten minutes later, confirmation came in from Sergeant Moss.

We were in.

TWENTY-SEVEN

I wasn't the only one with plans.

Ted O'Brien was one of those guys whose idea of the perfect retirement included a boat, a rod, and still waters. He had been slowly working his way towards that dream when I arrived on the scene.

Dying of a heart attack and having any member of his team detained by a foreign power were threats to his peace of mind and retirement plan. Apparently, every time he laid eyes on me, he saw one of those nightmares coming true. Something had to be done to prevent that, so O'Brien was busy with his plans to have the secret wife of the Deputy Chief of Mission removed out of his office.

He caught my attention as I made my way back to my desk after lunch. Colonel Townsend had stormed out of conference room 2B and disappeared in the direction of Comms. Todd had left to track the other man's progress, making sure he wasn't lurking behind any columns, lying in wait. I had escorted Angelika back to the lounge where she would sit in air-conditioned discomfort for the rest of the day.

"She doesn't leave here," I informed the private security guards stationed at the lobby doors. It was a precaution I did not regret in the least, because Angelika had not seemed content with the arrangement. She complained about the cold and the fact that everyone was looking at her. I wasn't completely unfeeling. I loaned her my Blazer, brought her some coffee, and left her to reflect on the poor judgment she demonstrated last night.

As for her other concern – about the scrutiny she faced – I was unmoved. I wanted her to be seen.

The problem was, O'Brien had eyes in the back of his head, especially when he was looking for any reason to get rid of me. He clearly thought I was up to no good, hence the impromptu invitation to sit down with him. Behind closed doors.

"I brought you some lunch." I announced, depositing the take-away bag with the lunch Townsend had declined on O'Brien's desk. Such consideration on my part warranted a double-take.

Besides a midday candy bar, O'Brien had never seen me chew anything before and thoughtful wasn't the word that came to mind when anyone thought of me. That I had gone out of my way for lunch for anyone was a matter of grave concern.

"Cafeteria had ribs. I know how much you like ribs," I added with a straight face.

No, I didn't know much about O'Brien's dietary likes or dislikes. I had seen him eat a BLT sandwich one afternoon, and I had never known a single non-vegetarian who had a disparaging word to say about ribs. The probability was in my favor that I had pinned him correctly.

That disconcerted him in no small amount, and a distracted man could not be on the offensive.

"Great news." I started as he flipped open the lid on the Styrofoam box nestled inside a plastic bag. "We have access to the .mil.do enterprise. I plan on spending the afternoon sifting through his data to find out what he's been up to."

Which was also a polite way of letting O'Brien know that I had important things to do.

"So why the hell is there a prostitute sitting in the lobby? I thought I told you I never wanted to hear from her again."

News did travel fast. I didn't see Landon on my way into O'Brien's office, but that might not mean anything. It was lunchtime. Martinez was at his desk, his landline nestled in the crook of his neck as was often the case. He didn't look like he was in damage control mode. He looked like he was taking or following up on tips on Dominican traffickers and dealers.

"Sergeant Garrick Moss encountered some technical difficulties with the intrusion key and needed her equipment for diagnosis." Names, dates and locations gave a much-needed boost to my credibility where my boss was concerned.

"Her equipment?" he deadpanned, his tone thick with skepticism. I focused on his eyes to keep from laughing. There was nothing funny about the lichen color of those eyes.

"Yes, sir, her mobile device. Once we ascertained the first attempt was a failure, we had her make contact again. The second attempt was successful, giving us direct access to the enterprise. Sergeant Moss is doing the download as we speak, and I'll be doing the analysis as soon as I'm out of here."

"So why is she still here?"

"She's on standby, sir… just in case."

"Do you expect any more problems, Koehler? "

The longer we kept our portal open, the greater the chance of discovery. We tried to minimize our exposure by running in, grabbing as much as we could as quickly as we could, then closing the door until the next time. Where there were tracks left in the sand, we tried to brush them away, or cover them with harmless information and dead-end trails.

Providing technology solutions to partner countries gave us the opportunity to assess their existing capabilities. That wasn't foolproof though; we were not their only international partners. So in spite of all the counter-security measures, any number of things could go wrong. O'Brien knew this too. So his question made me pause.

Was it a trap? Was he trying to get me to issue a guarantee that he could later use to discredit me? I broke our deadlocked stares then came back again. Had I missed something in his lack of expression?

"One can never be sure, sir." I resisted the urge to fidget with my empty hands. O'Brien stared back at me over the rim of his glasses. The box of food, my peace offering, remained mostly untouched between us. A strange game of chicken was underway.

"What about the hooker? Does she fancy herself a writer? Some people think hush money is free money."

"First of all, I guaranteed that would not happen. Secondly, she was paid for services rendered, not her silence."

"Are you sure about that, Koehler?"

"Absolutely."

And yet my reassurance did nothing to alleviate the tension between his shoulders, or redirect the hard as nails stare he stabbed at me. I was on the verge of adding that Angelika was on her way out of the country as soon as I got to a computer, but something about him made me hold onto that piece of information. O'Brien was thorough, and coupled with his mistrust of me, I knew one clue would likely lead to questions, like where and why.

"Martinez has been busy lately," he casually tossed out, fingering a pen, rolling it between his fingers as he leaned back in his chair, waiting for fish to bite.

I did not respond beyond the shrug of my shoulders. O'Brien would have to get to whatever was on his mind, because I was not about to compromise myself swinging at foul balls.

"You two have gotten close over the past couple of days."

Again with the shrug. "I wouldn't say that, sir. He's a friend of my husband's. We cross paths occasionally."

"Is that right?" The pen tapped the table as he contemplated me. One corner of my mouth lifted in a noncommittal imitation of my shoulders. "So that heated discussion you had in the courtyard the other day... What was that all about?"

I kept my respiration and eyes steady, because his perusal was assessing, in search of signs of deception. If Martinez had sold me out, he was going to be sorry. And Todd wasn't going to stop me either. I doubted it would come to that though. Martinez wouldn't happen to be sitting there, looking like his life wasn't on the line, when I walked in.

A number of passersby had seen us. My social interaction with almost everyone was noteworthy these days. For God's sake, I avoided my own husband like the plague.

"Not much."

"Not much seems to get a lot of angry people in your face."

I gave him a smile that was as natural as the Styrofoam box before him. "I am still working on those interpersonal skills, sir."

"I'm going to have a talk with Martinez about this." If only he knew he didn't do menacing half as well as Uncle Richard. "Is there anything I should know before that?"

As if the consequences would be less severe. Any confession after that opening would have been naïve. Next he would monitor my interactions with Martinez to see if I tried to influence him in any way. Now that I knew O'Brien had us both on his radar, Martinez could go join Todd in a leper colony.

I maintained my silence, but shifted from one foot to the next to reassert my impatience.

"Now I distinctly remember you telling me that you and Townsend got along just fine."

My recollection and O'Brien's differed on several key points. First, there had been no conversation. O'Brien had noted our past association, then directed me to work with the colonel. Secondly, never in this lifetime would I describe my relationship with Townsend as 'fine'. 'Volatile', 'tentative', 'inappropriate' came to mind... but never 'fine'.

"I think we work well together," I said with a straight face. "Why? Has something happened? He's not happy with me?"

O'Brien's blood boiled, shooting up his neck like a volcanic eruption. His fists curled into fists. I thought he was going to explode. Then slowly, painfully, he exhaled and the tension eased. He smiled.

Oh, shit.

"Have a nice day, Koehler. I wouldn't want to hold you up any longer." As a cherry on top of his fuck-you-sundae, he dug through the plastic bag and started devouring the food I had brought him.

I left his office and went straight to my desk without looking left or right for the trap that had been sprung. I would never grow an immunity to the openness and stares. I would never be comfortable in this place. I had to leave, and sooner rather than later. I could no longer afford to anchor myself to Todd.

But first, I had to wipe my slate clean in O'Brien's eyes, and that entailed doing the analysis on Colonel Ramirez fast.

Three hours later there was still no significant activity between O'Brien and Martinez. There might have been emails crossing the floor, but I doubted it. O'Brien wouldn't employ subterfuge here; he wanted me to come clean, and for that to happen, I had to see, feel, and taste the pressure mounting. Or so he thought.

My father had kept his silence through torture. Three fingers and a kneecap later, when they finally understood he was of no use to them, they put a bullet in his head. *Let them work for it, Amy*, my father used to say, and they had. O'Brien would have to do the same.

In a brief moment of rest during which I stretched my arms and went for coffee, I noticed Martinez offloading quite a bit of work on to Byles. That he was busy was no big surprise. Christmas was weeks away, and informants liked having extra cash during the season. Selling out friends and acquaintances in the US was easy money, and the tips went to the DEA, and sometimes to the FBI. Alex Rivera Ferreiras wasn't the only Dominican living in the US against whom those at home held a grudge. Hopefully the source of the Ferreiras lead would be lost among the other tips that were being investigated.

The only thing to distinguish him from the others was my insistence on the timeline and publicity. Those were tiny details that would not come to light until arrest time. If everything ran smoothly, then O'Brien might never know I had had an interest in the case. But if he ever did, I hoped to be long gone by then. At the rate at which Colonel Ramirez was going, I would be lucky if his case was wrapped up by the New Year.

I had nothing on him. I checked and rechecked the last three months of communications: emails, text messages, Skype contacts, Instant Messenger, call records. There wasn't so much as a hint of involvement in narco-trafficking.

I was not giving up though, which had nothing to do with trying to conjure hard facts out of thin air to suit my personal sense of urgency. I did not question the intelligence that had led to Colonel Ramirez being suspect. I knew he had access to South American cocaine in its purest form. Even if Angelika had snorted her last line on her way home, cut cocaine would have only lasted a few hours. She had been high off Ramirez's score for around seven hours. It wasn't scientific, but my instincts told me Ramirez was my ticket out of Santo Domingo.

I pushed through the mounting piles of Ramirez's communications for the next hour and a half. It all came to me raw, and I had muddled through the Spanish pretty well considering there were only a handful of documents in my follow-up pile. That told me I was missing something.

The language handicap had been my father's idea as well. "*There are more than enough Latinos in America to fill the Spanish jobs,*" he had told me. "*Thirty years from now, we're still going to need Americans who can handle the Middle East.*" And so I had majored in linguistics then followed up with a Masters in the Middle East languages. The Spanish I knew I had acquired while serving in Hispanophone countries.

It wasn't nearly enough now. Martinez, the sole native hispanophone, who might shed some light on areas where I had hit a stone-wall, was a no-go. O'Brien, though my official backstop, wasn't getting a front-row invitation to examining my flaws. That left Todd.

Now that the pretense was over, there was no reason why I couldn't ask him for help with the language. Officially, my boss would have to authorize his clearance for my work file, but unofficially, I had no intention of letting my boss know that I was asking for help.

Todd's landline rang forever before he picked up. I was expecting Helen, although at the same time, I dreaded having to go through her for access to my husband. This was a pleasant surprise.

"Amy." He sounded hard and cold. "You left before I said what was on my mind."

I knew what was on his mind, and I didn't want to talk to him now if he felt the need to say it. It was late afternoon and my section was emptying out, but Scott and Martinez still lingered, shutting down their computers, clearing their desks, securing files. Even if I was now more comfortable with Todd's feelings for me, I lived a self-conscious life. I would always be painfully aware of others' views of our relationship. Scott and Martinez didn't need to witness our fight over Colonel Townsend.

"I'm sorry. I'll try again later when you're in a better mood."

"Don't hang up on me," he said tersely and, when I complied but remained silent, he sighed. It was long and ragged. I could visualize him releasing the day's tensions, only one of which was Townsend. "I didn't handle things well today."

"No, you didn't, but it's been a long day." Long enough for his anger to reach boiling point then simmer at a steady heat. I should have tended to him sooner, but I did have a lot of work and a short amount of time in which to do it.

"And you kept me up all night."

"I kept you up?" I asked incredulously. "Have you forgotten your caveman antics already? Because of you, I'll have to replace the door this weekend."

"I'm sorry, but I would not have been like that if you were where you belong."

In contrast to a few moments ago, Todd sounded calmer. As if just by being on the line with him, listening to him, his hearing my voice had soothed him. Awareness of my power over a man like him was liberating, but oddly enough it was not an advantage I wanted to exploit... only enjoy.

"You belong to me, Amy, and I will never be satisfied until you take your place beside me."

I had never been comfortable in the light. I could not see myself fulfilling the role he envisaged for me. I belonged in the shadows. Our home was where we came together, where there was no one judging.

"Come home with me tonight," he said, but I heard the silent pleading as clearly as if he had fallen onto bended knee before me.

"Yes." I told myself that his requests suited my objectives perfectly, but it wasn't the need to see and view him that had me capitulating the instant the words left his mouth. "There are a couple of things I need to do first, but I'd be glad to meet you there."

I could tell he longed for a normal life with a normal wife, but we were far from average. We dealt in secrets, manipulation and exploitation. I had a major one waiting for me in the lounge, and after last night, Todd should understand there were particular security concerns I had to face.

He assented, but he probably thought he consented, judging by the immediate shift in him. He was taking back the position of dominance. "I'll be home in about an hour. I'll see you there."

I hung up only to find Martinez shuffling folders around on his desk in a blatant attempt to attract my attention. He wasn't nearly as slick as he thought as he checked O'Brien's location before tilting his head in invitation. He wanted us to meet. I did a better job of ignoring him than he did being surreptitious. A few more minutes and he left. I went through some more of Ramirez's communications. Many more minutes later, I collected the documents from my follow-up pile and stowed them in my purse.

I didn't get to Angelika until well after 5 p.m. when the embassy had practically emptied. She was nervous, but cooperative. She understood the conditions of being at someone's mercy, but she would bend only so far before breaking, and then she would be useless to me. She proved she could perform. With a little encouragement and some reward, I could make her *want* to work with me. But it was important that she understood her boundaries before I let her go into the world.

The drive home was short and completed in silence. Angelika was exhausted from her sleepless night, her body stiff from camping out in the lounge all day. She left my blazer draped over the arm of the couch and headed for her room.

"Angelika." She came to an abrupt halt. Her spine stiffened for a split second, bracing for the hard blow she had anticipated all day. I handed her a blank envelope and waited for her to examine the contents. Her eyes were red, the only color in her pale, expressionless face as she flipped the envelope over and over. She peaked tentatively inside, as if looking for anthrax.

"It's a prepaid debit card," I explained as she unfolded the single sheet of paper. "I've deposited one thousand dollars for you. Every week from next Monday to the end of January you'll receive another one thousand dollars. Every time you work for me, I'll use that account to pay you. Don't blow it, because you will never know when the next job might be. Once you move, you will need a job to cover your living expenses."

She was silent for a long time. She stood with her fingers pressed against her temple, examining the card, running her thumb across the Visa logo. "I cannot believe it."

"Why? I promised you, Angelika."

She reared her head back so fast the pool of tears spilled over. "And I can do anything I want with it?"

"No," I told her, because carte blanche was a dangerous thing for most people. For Angelika, it could be deadly. "You have to stay out of trouble. If you end up in jail the deal is off. Don't arouse suspicion, don't attract attention, and you must maintain the identity I give you."

It was imperative that her image not be objectionable. Going to school was a good idea, because students were generally assumed to be wholesome, until proven otherwise. It also allowed her the free time for official pursuits. She could go wherever I sent her for days at a time with little or no notice.

"Do you understand?"

She nodded. There was a hint of a smile tugging at the corners of her mouth. Along with her free-flowing tears, the effect would have moved anyone prone to tender emotions. "I get a new life," she mumbled, "in a place where no one knows me and there are no expectations."

"Not quite." I adjusted the strap of my purse on my shoulder while she brushed away the tears. Why did such raw emotion not move me? Why was I thinking of all the work I had to do before I could meet Todd?

"These jobs you have for me... You want me to fuck?"

She thought that was all she was good for.

"You know you never had to sleep with him last night." I was happy she did, but not for the reasons she did it. And Townsend didn't count; he was just a proving ground. "I will never tell you how to do a job. My only concerns are the result and your safety."

"Thank you," she said and meant it, because no one in her short life had ever cared for her well-being. For a long time after I barricaded myself inside my room she stood there questioning why. She was afraid to believe me, but there was no point trying to convince her. She would see in only a few days.

I packed all my personal effects, everything I brought to the apartment, and secured them. It didn't take long. I had left my home with Todd with only one bag, which meant on any given day, I had half my belongings in my car.

How strange it was to return to the place where this began. Angelika was in my shower, after which she would retire to my bed. Only this time I was running towards Todd.

TWENTY-EIGHT

It was almost as if I had never left. I closed the front door behind me and stood in the entry hall for a moment, trying to build familiarity with my home. The house smelled of sunshine, the faint strains of tobacco, and warmth. Without looking I could tell the covered dish on the dining table contained *mofongo* with pork – Todd's favorite. The sweet aroma of *sancocho* emanated from a small pot on the stove.

Magda knew what had happened here. She had to know that I had left him, and it was only her loyalty to Todd that would spare him the humiliation. The gleaming floors and dust-free furnishings were broadcasts that she was all he needed. That was how it had been since the first day Todd brought me home from the airport.

There was nothing of me here; this was all Todd's. No wonder I felt like another nameless, faceless woman he had screwed, appearing like a blip on the radar of his life then conveniently disappearing soon thereafter. Three months of marriage was nothing compared to the relationships he maintained with Magda and the Boys' Club. There was nothing here for me … except the man himself.

I heard the shower going in the master bathroom and briefly contemplated joining him. I craved him, and it would have been so easy to give in to my urges. But there had to be more to us. Chemistry could only get us so far before the lack of trust and hopeless expectations got in the way. I wanted him… true, but I needed him more.

The door to my room was wide open. It was strange to see it like that, but as I inched closer I understood why. The smell was foreign: paint, new wood and a hint of smoke. The baseboards, moldings and doors were new. Fresh grout marked where the tiles had been replaced. A new bed with its mattress wrapped in plastic stood in the place of the old. The walls were freshly painted, as was the ceiling.

Only because I knew what to look for and where, I was able to spot the places that had been blackened by smoke. The white had not completely covered the darkness.

"Hey."

Todd stood in the doorway of the master bedroom, fresh from his shower. His hair was longer when wet despite the curls. Beads of moisture dotted his skin and smoothed the dark hair that covered his body into a south-pointing arrow. I followed it to the edge of the towel he had wrapped low around his hips. My initial reaction was to go to him, answering the call to be a drop of water trickling over his skin.

"Hey," I answered, and held onto the door frame instead

Todd was like the sun in a solar eclipse. He was as dangerous as he was compelling to gaze upon. Just when I had grown accustomed to the dark, he would reemerge and surprise me. I looked away, mapping the changes to the room that had once been mine instead of the contours and plains of his body.

"I moved your stuff back to our bedroom before the workmen started. I didn't want anyone touching them."

His voice came from the spot above my ear. He was so close, yet he didn't touch me. I felt his warmth. His breath tickled the hairs at my nape. My skin, so attuned to him, required only the knowledge of his proximity to alert all my other senses to the presence of a pleasure stimulus. Without a single touch, I was warm and wet.

It was his words that brought me back to reality… made me focus on the reasons we did not always work. Our differences gaped endlessly between us. Todd was no more welcome inside the places I kept from everyone else, and he would never be satisfied with that.

I turned to face him. Although I knew he was near, I was startled to see exactly how close. My nose might have struck his chest if I hadn't taken an instinctive step backwards.

"I was waiting for you to come home before I put a new lock on the door. I wanted you to know that I get it. I understand the extent of your needs." He reached for me, tugging me closer by the hips. My head spun from the heat and soapy clean fragrance of his body. "I'm sorry. I hope one day you will trust me enough to share this side of yourself with me."

It was a strange thing having one's mind and body at odds. One railed against the invasion, while the other pulsed with need for him. Panic and desire battled.

Todd placed a finger against my lips, followed by the slight pressure of his mouth. "I know I haven't earned that trust just yet, but I want to. I will wait as long as it takes."

And for the first time since we met, Todd's words and touch worked together to calm both my mind and body. It was like two sides of a giant jigsaw had come together. We fit and it was perfect.

We went to bed and did not make love. We lay side-by-side on top of the sheets, Todd in his underwear; me dressed in jeans and the henley from the night before. I was nestled under his arm, my fingers idly combing through the hair on his chest as he translated the documents from my Ramirez file. I had one knee planted between his legs; our feet twisted together, while Todd caressed my back. We were only ever like this for sex. I never knew it was possible for us to work together.

"This is all military administrative stuff, Amy. Who goes where, when, and for how long. If you tell me what you're looking for, maybe I can see if there is another meaning hiding in here."

Seasoned criminals usually had the time and practice needed to cover their tracks. They never spoke of their business in plain terms. Intelligence therefore was a balancing act: finding the hidden message without giving significance to the innocuous.

"He's suspected of trafficking narcotics from South America to Puerto Rico under training cooperation and equipment exchange programs."

Todd tossed the idea around his head for a while, re-examining the documents in the new light. Sound rumbled in his chest as he considered them. It warmed me, making me sigh and root deeper into him. He squeezed my butt cheek in response and I was more aware than ever of his semi-erection.

"Have you identified any keywords for database search?"

I nodded, averse to providing more details, but not for the reason that might have silenced me days ago. I didn't want to lead him on and compromise our work. It was easier, human nature in fact, to be led to believe patterns where there were none. It was more efficient for me to hold my keywords close and have Todd affirm them blindly... Or come up with his own.

"What else have you been doing?"

"Reference checks. Crossing common names, staff orders and personnel with dates of past opportunities."

"And?"

"I'm not done yet. I couldn't understand some of what he's saying. I'm not sure if these are typos, if he's using colloquial Spanish, or if it's something else entirely."

Todd sifted through the sheets of print out again and I forced myself to ignore our physical reaction to each other. "What's this?"

I tilted my head back to catch a glimpse of the sheet he held. "Oh, that," I sighed, beating back the hopeful anticipation he had caused. "It's a manifest. I have quite a few of those to go through. Based on the file properties, this is used as a master list, and names or equipment are either added or deleted accordingly. I planned on crossing the list with Colonel Townsend to verify use and need for training exercises under Ramirez's responsibility."

I tried to ignore his response to the mention of the Colonel's name. His breath, though silent, fanned the top of my head in a long gust.

"Is that going to be a problem, Todd?"

"Always," he said firmly, so tense his chest vibrated deeply. I tilted my head back so I could look into his eyes. "But as long as you're careful and don't put yourself in a position where you're at his mercy, I'll deal with it."

He kissed the top of my head and went back to translating the highlighted items on the manifest. His response made me hopeful. That he trusted me to be able to take care of myself. That he understood the futility of standing in the way of my work. That he wanted me unafraid to speak with him openly about Townsend, instead of hiding from him to spare us both the fight. That he wanted us to work.

"By the way," he added matter-of-factly, which was sufficient warning for me to brace myself, "a few friends are planning a congratulatory party for me on Friday at El Gallego." I had conveniently forgotten his appointment as Chargé since Ambassador Powell left Mission today. "I would like you to come with me. It's a couple blocks from the office and your apartment, so you won't have to go out of your way."

As if it was the distance that posed the problem.

Todd seemed to have a general awareness of my state of mind when forced into social encounters. His assumption about the cause and my means of coping were off the mark, and I had neglected to correct him. It wasn't something we talked about. In fact, he dealt with my social anxiety the same way I treated his sexual past: outwardly at least, pretending it did not exist.

Obviously he thought those days were over now. As a consequence of his coming clean last night, he expected an act of reciprocity on my part. Quid pro quo.

"I know you have concerns, Amy, and I am willing to work through them with you." One crooked finger beneath my chin opened me up to him. His eyes were serious and sad for me. Gazing into them, I felt things I didn't know I could. "These are baby steps, and I'll be there with you all the way. It's a simple fact though that we need to be seen together. I want everyone to know what I feel for you isn't going away. I also believe it would help with some of your concerns about my sexual history. I can't change my past, but I want you and everyone to know that it's behind me." His breath fanned my face moments before his lips brushed mine. "What do you say, Amy?"

Todd was asking me to step into the light with him. Two days ago it would have been inconceivable. Today, at that moment when our lips touched and our souls met in a place of hope and compromise, I knew that Todd loved me and I would try.

"As long as you are with me," I said, swallowing his taste so I could have him inside me.

"Always." Todd kissed me again and I would have been lost if not for him pulling away. "Let's finish this and then talk about Angelika."

I groaned in disappointment that it had to end, and dismay at the prospect of raising his Angel when we were in bed together.

"We seriously need to talk about her," he said, slapping the manifest against his thigh. "Mosquito."

"Did you get him?" I craned my neck to find the blood.

"Not this time." Todd would never stop, not until he was everything to me. And if he had to get me drunk on him to do that, then he would. "What are you going to do with her?"

I burrowed my head deep into his side, hiding my deception. "Cut her loose. She wants to return to Europe, and I think she deserves that much."

"You got her a passport." It wasn't a question. It wouldn't have taken much for him to find out.

"Yes. She would've been deported."

"That's not why you went for her though." Of course not. We had already established the fact that I did it to hurt him. I didn't want to say it out loud again. "Why not a visa?"

"I wanted her back here. Immigration would not have let her back in on the same day with her Ukrainian passport." I held my breath and hoped beyond reason that he would let it go.

"It was a very high price to pay, Amy." He dug my chin out of his side to stare into my soul again.

"Imagine if she had talked."

"She's one woman, Amy. It's not rocket science. In fact, I have no idea why O'Brien went along with it."

Because I misrepresented the facts… over-stated the threat to secure immediate action, then provided a solution that supported my personal agenda.

"She's earned it," I said stubbornly, although I knew he was right. I fingered the untidy stack of documents. It was also an excuse to break away from those eyes. "She will earn it."

"Okay." He said it so simply, Todd surprised me. Did that mean he would support me if it came back to bite me in the ass? I returned to his stare, trying to read an unspoken condition to his immediate acceptance.

"I want to move her this weekend. I want to establish a new past for her in the US, so when she resettles, her new identity won't be a burden." I knew I was pushing it, but I had to test the boundaries of his understanding to see how far it extended.

"Are you asking me for help, Amy?"

"You offered," I reminded him. I knew at the time it was only because he disliked the alternative, which was Townsend.

"What do you plan on giving me in exchange?" He dropped the manifest so he could draw concentric circles on my quivering middle with his fingers. He smiled at my body's immediate response – the goosebumps that spread with the heat in defiance of logic, the pebbling of my breasts that grew heavier with each breath. He trailed one finger between the heaving mounds then pressed his palm flat against me.

"What do you want?" I gasped.

"This," he said, shifting his hand over my left breast. "I want what's in here."

This time it was I who pulled him down to me so our lips could meet. There was no resistance. "You have it, Todd. My heart, my love, all of me. You never had to ask."

Todd kissed me hard then made love to me softly, his soul telling mine to never forget that promise.

TWENTY-NINE

I didn't stay with him that night. Todd didn't like it, but he understood Angelika had to be weaned. Too much freedom too soon in this environment could get her killed and place me under intense scrutiny. Todd agreed that we needed to get her out of Santo Domingo as soon as possible, and had devoted some of his resources to help achieve that end.

Angelika was booked on an afternoon flight to Miami on Saturday. Todd would arrange for her to be met at the airport by an old Marine Corps friend currently working for the US Marshall's Office who would oversee her reconditioning in Miami over the course of two weeks. As far as Todd knew she would be on her own once transferred to Europe, with the possibility of future engagement should the need arise.

He didn't know the need had arisen twelve years ago. Something held me back from sharing that with him and I didn't completely understand why.

As for Angelika, she had been moved from tears to open sobs when I explained my plans for her. She clutched the sheet of paper with her flight confirmation to her chest and stared up at me with eyes the size of saucers overflowing with a painful combination of joy, disbelief and relief.

"You do this for me?" she sobbed over and over. "You truly do this for me."

I nodded, unnerved because I wasn't sure if she was laughing or crying.

"Many have promised a lot, a little, but never has anyone given me as much as you." Finally, when sitting no longer allowed her the freedom to express herself, she crossed the small space between us and sank at my feet. "I promise you, I will never forget this. Until the day I die I promise you my loyalty."

Then she held my legs, planted her cheek on my knees and wept wracking sobs and scalding tears. I was intensely uncomfortable submitting to such an emotional outpouring, but I sensed she needed it. For as long as I had known her, Angelika had remained under control, even when entertaining, and stoic otherwise. Her shell had been cultivated over many years of exploitation. This was in fact her first honest emotion in a very long time, and she was either determined to share it with me or helpless to stem the rising tide. I sat stiffly in my armchair, unmoving for the ten minutes that Angelika cried out her heart and soul.

We sat for about an hour after, discussing our plans for her future. She nodded avidly, never questioning, except to seek clarification about the handler Todd would arrange for her.

"Do you want me to fuck him?"

I shook my head, not in the least surprised that she would expect to reciprocate with the only currency she had. Her body was all anyone had ever wanted from her. It was the sum of her worth. "You never have to do that again if you don't want to."

"What if I don't have the money to pay him? I do not know what he will ask for this."

The life we would build for her did not come cheap. Drivers license; employment, residence and credit histories; accreditation, including bogus community college records all had to be paid for. Dev, her host, would pick up the cash on Tuesday.

"Your only concern over the next two weeks should be learning about the life you had in America." I touched her arm, the first time I knew what her skin felt like. "I need you to do well, Angelika. It's two weeks to learn six years of experiences."

"I understand," she promised me, the flight confirmation still clutched to her chest and tears brimming again in her eyes.

Finally free of her grasp, I left to work in my room for another hour before it was time to get ready for work. I thought she would have been too excited to sleep, but I was wrong. She was out cold by the time I slipped through the front door.

My hours of dedication finally paid off by midmorning. All the raw data I had collected over the course of the past twenty-four hours was dumped into a database. An hour later, I pored over the results over the brim of a steaming cup of coffee. A pattern appeared and had been repeated nine times over the past twelve months. At this stage, it was more assumptions than intelligence, but I had the tools on hand to shore up the probability of those educated guesses.

The pattern in question was of simple form and design, hidden under dozens of layers of military bureaucracy. I hadn't had contact with O'Brien yet, so I couldn't judge his mood. If he was anything like yesterday, it would be a hard sell. But Townsend would go for it in a heartbeat. He had nothing to lose if my analysis proved to be inaccurate. My gut told me I was on the right track though, that the next time all four men reappeared together, trafficking would be underway.

Sergeant Ricardo Suarez was the logistics guy, organizing the movement of equipment and personnel between the Dominican Republic and Venezuela or Colombia. Captain Tommy Piño was the drop man, responsible for ensuring delivery of the contraband to Puerto Rico under the cover of counterterrorism and smuggling interdiction exercises at sea. Sergeant Arturo Machado was the export and cash courier. And Colonel Ramirez handled the permits, the contacts in South America and Puerto Rico, and the collection of payment.

A quick check revealed there were six accounts in banks in Spain belonging either to the subjects, or their children with the men acting as trustees. Now that I knew who I was looking for, it was only a matter of time before Comms could put Machado, Piño and Suarez under the microscope. Colonel Ramirez was careful to have covered his tracks with a cloak of officialdom, which was testament to his experience. The others were much younger with less wealth of knowledge or the experience required to hide even a wire transfer.

Tomorrow was Veterans Day; Christmas and Thanksgiving were just around the corner. That presented three opportunities to test my theory. I did not believe in coincidence, so it was significant that the interdiction patrols between the Dominican Republic and Puerto Rico were beefed up in the days preceding Federal holidays. With operations being combined for Christmas and the New Year in some instances, and Thanksgiving and Veterans Day in others, the number of chances Piño had had to make a drop also matched the times per year communication among all four names peaked: nine.

I set Sergeant Thomas to work digging through as much communications to and from the three new targets. I had fielded a call from Colonel Townsend earlier in the day, so I sent him a message so he didn't think I was completely avoiding him.

Me: We're onto something. Working on the supports now.

The closing ceremony for his training exercise was tomorrow. He had another social engagement with Colonel Ramirez at the Officers' Club that evening, then he would return from Baní by helicopter. It was important that we preserve the rapport between our two militaries, which meant not arousing suspicion that we were sifting through their communications, or that Colonel Townsend had acted as facilitator. I didn't want Townsend accidentally falling out of a helicopter.

I hoped earnestly that his call had nothing to do with discovery. Just this once I wished it was his personal agenda with me that had prompted the call.

I received no response from Colonel Townsend, but the frequency with which data filtered in from Comms led me to believe Sergeant Moss was no longer the sole assignee. Maybe there was something to Todd's intervention after all if it got Townsend to stick to the proper channels of communication.

I worked all through lunch. I couldn't make perfect sense of the picture fast enough, so I asked Sergeant Moss to tackle the most recent data first then progress backwards. I had not yet identified any suspicious cargo on the manifests, because Townsend had not yet responded to my predawn email. It would likely take some time for him to verify whether the contents of the list were in fact legitimately required for the type of exercises being conducted.

By early afternoon, I still had not discovered anything new to support my theory. The personnel – Piño, Suarez, Machado and Ramirez – were the only constants, coinciding on or close enough to the days our intelligence indicated a pickup or drop-off had been made.

The intel suggested a drop had been made on or around Labor Day. It matched a four-day leadership exercise, held in Venezuela in August that Machado attended, with logistic support from Suarez – hotel booking, air and ground transportation. I suspected that was the source of the narcotics shipped in September.

The next activity I could clearly establish was a tour of a decommissioned FARC camp equipped with cocaine and amphetamine laboratories in Colombia. Both Ramirez and Machado were in attendance, and logistical support was once again provided by Suarez. That was a month ago, on October 11, which meant there had been no Columbus Day drop.

With tomorrow being Veterans Day, and Thanksgiving two weeks away, I had a window of opportunity that I felt Ramirez would try to exploit. The problem was I might have already missed my chance. There was no guarantee the drops were being made specifically on the holidays; the days immediately preceding or proceeding were just as likely.

I checked the manifest for DEPROSER 24/7 patrols and found Piño on one. Sergeant Moss hadn't yet gotten to the data for earlier in the week, as per my request for current information in advance of historical. Piño might have already made the drop and had tacked on a couple more days of patrol to cover his tracks.

Still, I didn't see the harm in having a few extra eyes fixed on the waters of the Mona Passage. It was highly likely though that O'Brien and Townsend would disagree with my no harm no foul assessment. They would consider factors like the cost of scrambling air surveillance and maritime interdiction vessels on such short notice. And if we came up broke, it would be a harder sell getting them to authorize increased surveillance in the run-up to Thanksgiving. Then the new schedule probably wouldn't earn me any new friends with the personnel either. All in all, nothing new.

I kept my fingers crossed that Townsend was in town, mature enough to answer my call, and deal with the task at hand professionally.

"Townsend."

"How soon can you be available for emergency briefing?"

"Good afternoon to you too, Koehler."

I knew all the reasons why I should not have been enticed by the mere sound of his voice. Some of them had to do with Todd, but most of them were based on what I knew was best for me. Mentally I could stick to the plan, which was to stay far away from Colonel Robert Townsend. That did not mean I was physically immune to him. The deep rumble of his voice made my toes curl.

"Good afternoon, Colonel Townsend." I ignored the laser beams Jessica Byles turned my way. I would never get used to this openness. "I really need to brief you and O'Brien on something I found, and it's extremely time sensitive. I really need you here." I was desperate and I wasn't above pandering to his ego to get the job done.

"For you, Amy," he said in a quiet drawl, "I'm available."

I tried to ignore the meaning behind his comment, but I knew he would never let me. If he were a reasonable man I would have been able to sit him down and explain that my relationship status precluded any personal involvement with him, and he would have understood. But I had tried that in Jamaica and it hadn't worked at all. If anything, he had redoubled his attentions to me... And that was assuming it was me he wanted, and not the possibility of hurting Todd through me.

I sighed. "It's not going to happen."

"We should meet to discuss this, Amy."

"No, we shouldn't. There isn't anything to say."

"I deserve a chance to explain," he broke in testily. It seemed I had the uncanny ability of infuriating him at every turn. "I can imagine what he's told you."

"My husband has nothing to do with it," I told him firmly enough to attract a few extra eyes. I held my head down and pressed my fingers to my temple, using my hands as a shield against the prying eyes. It was woefully ineffective. "This is a personal decision and I believe I shared that with you before Todd and I even met."

In fact, it was moments later that Todd and I had met. Colonel Townsend had stood me up and I refused to give him another chance. Townsend didn't like my refusal to let him walk all over me, and I've been fighting off his advances ever since.

"I refuse to accept that. There were extenuating circumstances that I already explained to you." Yes, Blitzner had intervened, sending Townsend on an errand that had left him enough time for either his wife or me. He chose his wife, and I chose me. There was nothing else to it.

"We'll be in O'Brien's office waiting for you."

"I'll be there in five minutes, but I want to see you after." So, he'd been on-site after all, not in Comms but close by the Marines.

O'Brien had company. Their shirtsleeves were rolled up, figuratively speaking, while they converged over a single folder. There was no other reason for that than an itemized walk-through. They were going to be a while, time I could not afford.

O'Brien caught me looking through the glass portion of his wall. I knocked and waited for him to gesture for me to enter. He did not. He just stared right back at me. I knocked again, and even his guest turned to see who would dare. The thin, grey brows above those lichen eyes furrowed, making the nose pads of his glasses sink into the creases. I had crossed over the threshold from surprising my boss to irritating him. But at least he hooked a finger at me, granting entry.

"What is it, Koehler?" he preempted my apology. His guest turned towards me and leaned back in his seat as if to casually stretch an arm over the back of his chair. Why did that simple move give him the air of a naughty kid who had been caught in the act of committing an infraction?

There was nothing casual about the pose, because we both knew that chair was as hard as a cinderblock. Secondly, he flicked the folder closed with one finger after I caught a glimpse of a photo with the old Army Class As. The green uniforms were replaced with blue ASU last year, and as far as I could tell, there was no one currently at Mission who would have fit that uniform with the officer 'US' insignia on the lapel. Except me.

Interesting. I didn't know him. I had seen him enter half an hour earlier, escorted by O'Brien himself, which might have suggested he did not have clearance for our section. Or, O'Brien felt he deserved a personal escort. The latter seemed more likely now that I could see the document they'd had their heads bent over had TOP SECRET classification.

"I'm sorry to interrupt, sir, but this is urgent."

"So is this."

I glanced at the stranger, trying to spot any identifying characteristics, like the color or name on the ID badge that hung around his neck. He was in his fifties, dark blond hair, brown eyes, complexion too pale to have been stationed at Santo Domingo mission. So, he was visiting from cooler climes, possibly HQ, but which one? On impulse I extended my hand in greeting.

"Amy Koehler. How do you do?"

"Pleasure to meet you." He didn't offer a name, but the softly spoken words and the movement of leaning forward to shake my hand were revealing.

His teeth, index finger and thumb of his right hand were stained from tobacco. The stale aroma of too many cigarettes wafted to me as he moved closer. He had a slight twang and a slow drawl without the intonation of a born Southerner. He was most likely a Virginia transplant with more than a couple decades tucked under his belt. Added to the fact that he knew me and appeared interested in not only what I had to say but also my appearance, I concluded I was the subject of that file. In light of O'Brien's above normal hostility over the past couple of days, it would appear a decision was pending on my assignment.

If O'Brien didn't like it then neither would I. The fact that they had been at it for thirty minutes without an obvious end in sight meant the decision was open for debate. I refocused on O'Brien.

"I thought you might be interested in an opportunity to nab Ramirez in the act, especially with the window closing in about twenty-four hours."

"That was fast," O'Brien said, leaning back in his seat. I could tell from the hard set of his jaw and the harder glare he jabbed at me that it was more a question of my thoroughness than a compliment.

"I would be happy to explain if you would grant me a few moments of your time." More like an hour, and only if he listened with an open mind, which seemed a lot to ask for just then.

It was the stranger who decided for him, piping in, "I don't mind, Ted. We can pick up after if you like."

It wasn't a suggestion and O'Brien didn't take it as such. He sighed again and gestured that I take the vacant guest chair. This one was even harder than the more frequently used one and made me feel every ache and pain from last night's bout with Todd.

I was only too grateful when Colonel Townsend was admitted a minute later, on time, and breathtaking in combat utility uniform. My skin prickled in awareness, which I deftly hid by springing out of my seat and backing against O'Brien's wall. The manila folder clutched against my chest blocked any view of my hardened nipples if anyone had been curious. The beads of moisture prickling my skin mocked O'Brien's dry, nearly dead office cactus.

Townsend took the seat after shaking hands with the other men. Names were not offered, which surprisingly Townsend accepted without question. It was even more revealing that the stranger made no move to leave, nor was he invited to do so.

The colonel stretched out his legs before him, scooting his chair back, to make room for his massive frame in the shrinking office. It was remarkable how comfortable he made himself in that chair. A civilian might have thought at my expense, but that wasn't how things worked in our world. On the basis of gender, we were equals until Townsend raked the length of my body with his eyes. Then I was an object to be appreciated for what I physically added to the decor. I beat out the dying plant by a hair.

"Sometime today, Koehler." This from O'Brien, whose all-seeing eyes were suddenly blind to the colonel's frank appraisal, his intent so obvious in the way he lingered here and there, outlining, at least partly, the source of discord O'Brien had questioned the day before.

I got to the point quickly, handing out the first two copies I had made. The first was an association chart, showing my assessment of the relationship between Ramirez, Machado, Piño and Suarez. The second was a synopsis of the other circumstances that tied them together: the Spanish accounts; the official functions that were assumed by others when the full equation was not met; a frequency chart showing the spike in communications around the time of suspected pickups and drop-offs.

The data was incomplete. It did not cover the twelve-month period proposed by our intelligence. I hadn't had time for that, which Townsend knew judging by his dress and the speed with which he had arrived. He had to have been around Comms today. If that wasn't enough, then his smirk as he checked the blank back of the sheets of paper certainly was. And he was going to be an ass.

Mystery Man did not have a copy. I could have given him mine, but instead I apologized for leaving him out. Without an introduction I could not be expected to know his clearance level. I could have followed O'Brien's lead and unofficially include him, but if he were here on a human resource mission, then I was going to stick to the book. That would have been the type of bending of rules that might be hacked up to justify a decision against me later. Mystery Man did not seem to care however. He smiled amicably and waved away my apology.

"Captain Tommy Piño is scheduled to lead DEPROSER patrols of the Mona passage starting at 0200 tomorrow. It is my assessment that he will use that opportunity to shuffle narcotics to Puerto Rico."

I preempted the questions about the type and quantities of narcotics by laying out the deficiencies in the intelligence I had inherited. Neither O'Brien nor Townsend had ever shared those details with me – if they even had access themselves. What had likely started this whole case was an informant, probably on the Puerto Rico side, since all he had was the suspected drop days and Ramirez as the cash collector.

As for the type of drugs, it could have been cocaine, heroine or methamphetamines – anything that paid well enough to account for the high risk and substantial payoffs. I already knew Ramirez had access to high-quality cocaine based on Angelika's foray into undercover operations, but I deliberately kept all mention of her out of this forum. That personal tip about Ramirez's personal use could have supported my case, but it was too risky. I didn't want the passport coming up again.

I had more important matters at stake than their support in this. Angelika was needed in Europe.

I laid out the pattern I had uncovered. "As part of our cooperation with local law enforcement, the schedule of patrols of the Mona Passage is expanded to improve security of our shared borders on and around major US holidays when American interests are more vulnerable."

I went over the high volume of cruise ship and private charter traffic on the water during long weekends so these seasoned men understood the risks.

"The intelligence you provided," I nodded at O'Brien, "at first suggested that timeframe without being definitive about the occurrence."

To be frank, it had given the occurrence in terms of weeks in a month. For instance, last week of May or first week of July. But it would not hurt to let O'Brien think his premise had led to my inference.

"By cross referencing that intelligence with the communications we were able to access, thanks to Colonel Townsend, we have identified DEPROSER as the vehicle and Captain Piño as the courier.

O'Brien had his mouth and most of his chin covered by his palm. The brown spots on the back of his hand were scattered like constellations in the sky. Every now and then he would look down at the documents I had provided, as if truly interested in having the data back up my theory.

Mystery Man just stared at me. I felt his eyes as I made the tour of my audience with my own. If he could have, I thought he would have moved closer to count the beads of sweat on my upper lip and nose. I resisted the urge to smooth my hair back or deepen my breathing with the effort of settling my nerves. As if by instinct, I knew he had to leave this room with a positive outlook on my capabilities. Maintaining my composure was therefore crucial. That left Colonel Townsend to throw a wrench in the works.

"Well, Koehler, I just left your relay partners in Comms sifting through days-old documentation. So I believe the basis of your cross-reference is questionable at best." He passed the pages I had given him on to Mystery Man with obvious disdain.

"Not exactly," I jumped right back in. "I worked through the night on some of the historical data, dating as far back as twelve months ago for the principal target, Colonel Ramirez. What I found led me to request the enhanced investigation of the other three – Suarez, Piño and Machado. Once the association was corroborated, I was led to the DEPROSER schedule for Veterans Day tomorrow."

I tried to maintain my composure, neither yielding to anger or satisfaction, while defending my work. If he expected an emotional response he would be sorely disappointed.

"I can assure you, Colonel Townsend, that the premises are supported by the data. I have centered the focus of the Comms relays on the most recent information first in order to reasonably predict a timeframe for the next drop given the probable time constraints. The historical data may be used to support the investigation and/or prosecution of past occurrences. My aim is to stop any present and future attempts to undermine the security of the United States."

That last was entirely for the benefit of Mystery Man who at least was able to appreciate a well played salvo.

"That brings us to the reason for this urgent briefing." I moved away from Townsend, according him the privacy to get back on track, before launching into the heart of the matter. O'Brien seemed open, having tossed around my dismissal of Townsend's concern and determined that my methodology was sound.

"According to the pattern, another delivery is scheduled for this month, the possibilities being either Veterans Day or Thanksgiving. My recommendation would be to try to catch the targets in the act of delivery."

Colonel Townsend found his footing quickly, jumping in with the objection I had anticipated from the start. This time he was not alone. O'Brien's relaxed posture slowly became more erect as he leaned towards me.

"Are you suggesting the US openly confront its partner... an armed patrol at sea?"

Right or wrong, public opinion would stand squarely against us. "I wouldn't dream of it. My recommendation would be covert surveillance, sir." I sifted through my manila folder and distributed two more sheets, Mystery Man excluded. "I took the liberty of digging into what interdiction resources are available in Puerto Rico, and this is what I've come up with. I'll rely on your expertise here, Colonel Townsend, regarding our maritime capabilities in the area that would be suitable for recording the operation."

His face scrunched into an expression of wariness. "What time frame are we talking about, Koehler?"

"Tomorrow, sir, at 0200." I had assumed that was clear.

His breath escaped in a harsh rush. All three men checked their watches as I braced myself for the objections.

"Based on what you've given us, there is a fifty-fifty chance the delivery could be this or Thanksgiving week," O'Brien began. Both hands were flat on the table, my papers between them still open. "Hypothetically, let's say you are right about this week. There is a twenty percent chance the delivery has not already been made. That brings the probability of your being right down to ten percent."

I passed out my probability sheets, and this time, there was a copy for Mystery Man too. "I beg to differ, sir. I am one hundred percent sure these are our targets; ninety-five percent sure Piño is using DEPROSER to make the deliveries; and eighty percent certain the delivery will be made between tonight and Thanksgiving." Math never lied.

Mystery Man rocked back in his chair and chuckled, but his arms were crossed over his chest. O'Brien glanced at him briefly, then turned back to the four sheets of paper laid out before him. Townsend remained silent, but his eyes bored into me with heat. I got the feeling he was only biding his time, patiently waiting for this briefing to be over so we could meet despite my protest.

"In a few hours I will be able to say with more certainty whether or not the delivery was already made." I turned to O'Brien. "Interrogating the source of the initial intelligence may also be useful." And back to Townsend though I was undeniably more affected by his sun-kissed skin and to the way his blue eyes sparkled. "I thought you might appreciate the advance warning should we decide to respond to this threat."

Put that way – given the choice between stopping the export of illegal narcotics to the United States and allowing it to pass – neither Townsend nor O'Brien wanted to be the first to refuse, particularly in the presence of Mystery Man. Townsend looked to O'Brien while I blended into the background. O'Brien leaned back in his chair, hands linked behind his head while gazing up at the ceiling, obviously thinking. The wait seemed interminable, although it was hardly a minute. Still, it was time I could have spent shoring up the gamble that the delivery had not yet been made.

"How would you suggest conducting the operation?"

It might have been a standard follow-up question, but what made it special was the people involved. Firstly, it wasn't my job to decide how operations were run. I provided the relevant data upon which operational teams crafted their response, and if they missed something, I would let them know. Secondly, neither O'Brien nor Townsend was in a hurry to remind Mystery Man of that. Townsend, judging by the thinning of his mouth, didn't like it, but he didn't offer any protest either.

I stepped forward. "The patrol manifests place the courier on one of two 110-ft class patrol boats of US origin. She is equipped with new radar and GPS systems, and heavily armed – single cannon, an M-60, and two 50-calibers. Clearly we want to avoid open confrontation.

"If the operation were mine to run, I would deploy San Juan's MH-65 to video the drop outside radar distance, and its 87-ft Coastal Patrol Boat to pick up the cargo. Conditions are favorable to such an exercise and I'll explain why.

"There is a seventy percent chance of showers starting at 2100 this evening, which will decrease the detection range of the 87-footer. The MH-65 is an all weather aircraft with 25 km range on the HD FLIR. That should cover the covert recording of the drop, as well as GPS marking of the cargo's location for collection by the CPB.

"I would also like to add that a cruise ship will depart Charlotte Amalie at 1700 this evening, scheduled to arrive in Samaná at 0900 tomorrow. With the cooperation of its captain, we could arrange for the CPB to ghost the cruise ship. Between the noise from the pleasure boat and the rain, concealing a drifting 87-footer should not pose much of a problem. However, as a safeguard, we can run friendly interference on their radar from San Juan or Guantánamo. Our cutter picks up the cargo and we present the findings to the President and to the Minister of Armed Forces in the morning."

It was a very simplistic explanation, but not everything had to be complicated. Townsend liked the idea; there was grudging approval in the tilt of his head as he did the math. It was disingenuous of me to have asked him for details of San Juan's capabilities when I had already compared them to the locals'. The fact was I knew he would appreciate that I had yielded to his superiority in that regard.

I learned long ago that stroking an ego would catch more flies than vinegar. But O'Brien knew my game. I could tell he was not entirely convinced. I was prepared to provide details should he request it, but I would appreciate his understanding that this was not the forum for the actual planning of the exercise. Of course, demonstrating the fact that I had given more than a passing thought to the operationalization improved the palatability of my recommendation.

Although Mystery Man could not have cared less about the operation or the interdiction exercise, he seemed pleased by my thorough preparation and my ability to think on the go.

Several minutes of silent calculation and hand signals passed between the three men before O'Brien finally shrugged and nodded at Townsend. The colonel sighed and straightened his shoulders before passing the decision back to O'Brien with a single nod. I slowly released to the breath I didn't know I was holding.

"Ambassador Powell officially left office yesterday. Who do we have in the Political Office to handle this?" Mystery Man directed at O'Brien.

The air being sucked out of the room halted me in the process of mentally organizing the loose ends that needed tying up. I caught O'Brien's head tilt in my direction, which satisfied neither Townsend nor Mystery Man.

"Todd Birch," escaped my lips on a breath.

"That's your husband, Koehler?" But it wasn't really a question. I nodded, pressing hard on the lump in my throat. "Well, this shouldn't take long then with all three of you working closely together."

By the three of us, Mystery Man meant Todd Birch, Colonel Townsend and myself. I looked to O'Brien for help, hoping beyond reason that he would step up as Section Chief and backstop to replace me. But I was equally terrified that he would, only to witness the enmity between Todd and Townsend boil over.

Townsend didn't seem any more pleased at the prospect of working with me and Todd, and yet he simply sat there not saying a word against the arrangement. The last time those two were in a room together they had almost come to blows. Did he not recall? Did he not care? Was I the only one concerned by this?

"Are you going to run with this or stand there all day, Koehler?" O'Brien asked, and for the first time that day I had no idea what to say.

I wish I could have run far, far away.

THIRTY

I spent what was left of Thursday night at the apartment with Angelika. In truth she camped out in the living room watching a Law & Order: SVU marathon with homemade popcorn and diet Coke while I worked on the European front well into Friday morning. It was my last night with her. She seemed stable enough to warrant the loosening of the ties so I planned on spending Friday night at home with Todd. I kept her in the dark out of habit although I was certain she would not do anything to jeopardize her Saturday flight plans. She had not left the apartment all day, but was riding the high of her trip to America.

Her buoyancy was nothing compared to mine. I spent the rest of the day and all evening closeted in Comms with Townsend. Technically, we were not alone, and I made sure to inform Todd before Colonel Townsend got the jump on me. I did not put it past him to let it slip at the least opportune moment, giving our working together more intimacy than was truthful.

"Remember what we talked about last night?" I whispered to Todd from my mobile phone in the last cubicle of the fourth floor ladies room. It was out of my way, but afforded the most privacy because traffic was low.

"We talked about a lot of things last night. Let me see..." I felt the smile in his voice and could even hear his leather chair squeaking as he leaned all the way back. "I may have said something about how amazing it felt being so deep inside you."

My body flushed and it wasn't all from the embarrassment of knowing my communications were monitored.

"And I distinctly remember you begging me to go deeper."

"Todd." I should have been ashamed that my reprimand sounded more like a moan, but with my insides liquefying at the memory, I didn't have the inner strength to resist the pull of his seductive voice.

"Is that what you had in mind?"

"No." And to prevent him from taking a selective stroll down memory lane, I got to the point. "I meant about working with Colonel Townsend." I was met with silence and Todd's shifting gears helped me to move past my body's stirrings. "I'll be in Comms for the rest of the day. There's an exercise planned for early tomorrow morning. There should be a large team working on this and O'Brien might pop in and out, so there really isn't anything to worry about."

The silence stretched on for a while longer, and I wished I could reach through the line and touch him.

"You're going to be called in to deal with the political fallout by the way," I added, because I knew he'd be excited about that. For months I thought it was just a part of his cover – pretending to be pleased with the promotion. I was gratified knowing I was right all along.

"Call me," he said, and by his tone I knew he wasn't happy about the situation. If I was going to step into the light with him then he would just have to deal. "I'll walk you to your car when you're done."

"That may be a while, Todd."

"I don't care. I'm not leaving you there with him. Call me, Amy."

I may have overplayed the possibility of O'Brien making an appearance, as well as the size of the team. There were in fact six Marines, excluding Colonel Townsend, manning the communications for operation. They liaised with San Juan, Guantánamo, and Doral to get her assets deployed in time for the surveillance. They checked and double-checked schedules and conditions, relayed commands and waited. Then waited some more. It was almost unbearable. It was the part of my former career that I did not miss at all… get there early and wait.

I kept busy with two of the Marines skimming as much as we could as fast as we could from the targets' communications. My analysis was incomplete without the elimination of the possibility of an earlier delivery. Plus it did not hurt to confirm the pattern Ramirez had going on. There was no denying that the entire exercise would have to be repeated in a couple of weeks if Piño was spooked or decided on a Thanksgiving drop.

The eighty miles of water between the Dominican Republic and Puerto Rico were some of the most difficult in the Caribbean. The extended sandbanks, two hundred foot cliffs, and coral reefs posed real risk of grounding vessels. The variable tidal currents and easterly trade winds added a marked degree of danger to boaters. Then there was the swell – up to twelve-foot waves – which would only be made more treacherous by tonight's weather forecast, projecting winds up to twenty-one knots. If not for the scheduled patrol, Piño would have had a good excuse to delay his mission.

Tucked inside the reinforced walls of Comms, I had a relatively incident-free evening. I did not even know it had started raining until I left. I accorded zero significance to Townsend's proprietary move as he squeezed my shoulders in an unsolicited back rub. I felt the eyes of every man in the room on me, cataloging the interaction. I worked with it, relying on them as witnesses to an innocent act as opposed to spectators to a scandal, instead of giving Townsend the reaction he had truly wanted.

"Sergeant Moss, I'm interested in this text message on November 8th about thirty-five heads. Cross-reference and let's see if there is anything else about a thirty-five-man head count. The number is off for personnel on the patrol boat. And check the phone number. I want to know who is this guy." The man to my left started digging with a drag of his mouse and expert tapping of keys.

"There is no reply, but it's in his address book so it can't be a wrong number," Moss returned. I didn't have to tell them to keep digging. He switched to the mobile subscriber database and continued the search there.

I curled my shoulders into Townsend's fingers, resisting the urge to stiffen and betray my unease with his actions. Besides, there were more than a few knots and his big, thick fingers were just the thing I needed.

"You're quite tense, Amy," Townsend noted in an intimate aside.

"Hmm," I mumbled my assent, but it was Sergeant Moss who was wound so tightly he could have snapped. His fingers slowed as he watched us from the corner of his eyes, giving too much attention to the blond giant who was peering over my shoulder, working against an ever-growing lump.

"It's been a rough week," I replied then prompted Sergeant Moss with the tip of my pen against his keyboard. "The phone number," I reminded him just before a groan when Townsend hit a particularly sensitive spot.

"Let's continue this later."

The command was a rumble in his chest that vibrated through his arms and jerked my nipples to attention. There was neither the need nor opportunity to reply. Townsend strolled away to make his rounds, leaving his Marines to draw a compromising picture of things to come.

I would have been embarrassed if not for Todd's insistence on seeing me safely away. I could not deny that Todd knew his opponent well. I wondered if these were lessons learned from Mona's fall, or if Todd had known the dangers all along and left her to her own judgment. His comment about not saving her still plagued me.

In the meantime, the number from which the text message came was registered to Pablo Ortega, who was previously twice caught at sea, on migrant boats heading for Puerto Rico. He was fingerprinted and returned to the Dominican Republic without charge. The text message in question shed a new light on his situation. He was either a boat captain or coordinator, not the migrant with no hope of ever getting a visa since he'd been caught trying to cross illegally.

Why was he in contact, or coordinating, with law enforcement? Was Suarez branching off into migrant smuggling, or had he cut his tooth on people before switching to narcotics?

I put out an APB for Ortega with our Coast Guard. The next time he was caught at sea, he would be subjected to enhanced screening.

With nothing else to do but wait, I decided to do just that at home. It was after 10 p.m., and a quick call during a ladies room break alerted Todd to my impending departure. Thirty minutes later, I hit 'SEND' on my brief to O'Brien and Townsend recommending the surveillance exercise and debunking the theory of an earlier drop.

"Leaving us so soon, Koehler?"

I smiled apologetically but did not falter slinging my purse strap over my shoulder. "I wish I could stay, really, but I have an appointment with our Chargé. Goodnight." I gave a general wave to the room, avoiding Townsend's gaze as I left.

I found Todd standing outside the secure area, keeping up the pretense of not having clearance, but close enough to deter anyone who might have followed me.

It was raining steadily and although he had an umbrella in hand, his skin was moist from the spray. We huddled close together and I excused my proximity to him with the need to share shelter. The rain beat heavily against the paving stones in the courtyard, splashing my naked legs and cooling my already chilled limbs when what I needed after spending the entire day inside air-conditioned rooms was warmth. I shivered, so huddled even closer to Todd.

We took temporary shelter in a shallow alcove so he could shrug out of his jacket and wrap it around my shoulders. I thought it completely unnecessary; we were only a few meters from the parking lot and I was already wearing a blazer over my cotton shirt. But I did not protest. Todd's jacket smelled of him, so I happily stuck my nose between the lapels and breathed him in. Just that bit of him, coupled with the feel of his arms around me, warmed me from the outside in. I would never get enough of him.

"I've arranged for you to pick up a vehicle from motor pool," he said once we arrived at my rental. At some point since my first call to him that afternoon he had moved his SUV so it was parked next to mine. He really wasn't taking any chances with Townsend. "Return this rental first thing tomorrow, okay?"

At the time I got it, expediency was more important than safety. The car wasn't armored, there was no GPS, nor was it retrofitted for our particular needs: a place to hide weapons, secrets, and other tools of our trade.

I nodded. The rain fell harder around us, but neither of us made a move to leave. "Will you come into office tomorrow?" Most embassy functions were shut down for the holiday, but its intelligence functions never ceased, and neither did the political ones.

"No. I'll work on your brief from home." O'Brien must have sent it to him. "I have a couple of afternoon engagements, but I will see you at the restaurant around nine."

His eyes, so blue even in the dark, kissed my face the way I wanted his lips on me. His concern was plain to see... and his sadness too. He understood what he was asking of me, knew I would suffer through it only for him. He did not know how much he was healing me right now.

There was something fundamentally different between wanting to forget and forgetting. One was rooted in fear and the other was a manifestation of freedom. The problem – or the blessing, depending on how I looked at it – of my attachment to Todd was the fact that I forgot to be afraid. When I was with him, it became increasingly difficult to remember anything that came before. I almost believed the reason I was there was so Todd could love me.

He kissed me. I felt naked standing with him in the rain, but I didn't care. He held me tightly against his body, so close I felt the jut of his arousal pressing hard and insistent into me. I opened my mouth to let him in and Todd stroked me deeply, exploring every recess and pouring his light into me. I wanted to freeze that moment so I could feel it forever – the freedom of letting go and not being afraid to love him and accept his love in return.

From some deep, dark corner of my soul, a voice said it could not last. No one could be this happy for more than a moment in time. I pulled away, resisting against the hold Todd had on me.

"I've never wanted anyone like I want you," he whispered, licking my taste from his lips. "I can't believe the things you do to me, Amy."

I believed him. How could I not? He felt what I felt. He breathed with the same effort needed after a mad dash. And that was what this was, a race to experience and savor every moment of happiness before we were pulled apart again. His pulse throbbed at his temples. His nostrils flared to better pull my scent in. How was it possible that two people could feel the exact same thing at precisely the same time? I should have been disappointed that this exquisite feeling was not unique, but strangely enough, I didn't mind sharing it with Todd.

"Go," he said, letting his hands fall to my hips, slowly warming to the idea of allowing me to leave. I pressed closer, my fingers curling over his shoulders. Just a moment longer. "Go now. Do whatever you need to get Angelika settled tonight, because I won't let you go tomorrow."

Todd stepped away and took a piece of me with him. I turned away to open the car door. It was unlike me to show such weakness. I wasn't used to feeling so acutely vulnerable. Todd touched my arm and I forgot again.

"I'll follow you to the apartment."

The knowledge that he did not want to say goodbye either eased my fears a little more. I searched for anything that would hold us there a moment longer, so close he could smell my desire mixed with rain.

"There was a man in my Section today. He was meeting with O'Brien, but he stayed for my pitch on this operation we're working on. Dark blonde hair, brown eyes, about six feet, talks like a Virginia man but isn't really. He got a Secret access badge today... maybe yesterday. Chain smoker. Do you know him?"

The shutters came down so fast he had me reeling. "Why?"

"Because he had my file. He was talking about me today... and you."

Todd shifted and I followed. His arms dropped to his sides. "I can't say."

"So you do know him." Todd did not answer, but his stony expression was a response in itself. He looked away, searching the darkness around us for an easy way to let me down. "I won't press you if you tell me one thing. Did Richard send him?"

Todd thought about it for a long time and I gave him the space he needed. The rain continued to fall, tiny drops clinging to his face and mine. The cool night air banked the heat of past kisses.

"Richard didn't specifically send him for you. But he is here because of you. William Blitzner is moving to covert ops and made a bid for you."

It seemed Todd had not warmed me enough, because the cold seeped through my skin and froze the blood in my veins. "He set me up and almost got us killed. Why would I want to work with him?" Blitzner was the reason I was sent here. He was the reason I carried this stain.

Todd shook his head. He didn't know.

"Why would Richard allow him to come here? The last thing he wants is for me to move back into ops. And he should know I would never work for someone I cannot trust."

Todd sighed and shifted the umbrella from one hand to the next. The change in position left us momentarily exposed. Todd's free hand swiped gently at the raindrops trickling down the side of my neck.

"Because Blitzner seems to think you'll want the position as much as he wants you. Richard doesn't want to interfere. He seems to think you'll do the right thing."

My heart sank to the pit of my stomach, and it was too sudden and hard a blow for me to hide my reaction. The car keys dug into the palm of my hand as I tried to hold on to my control. *Just hold on,* I kept telling myself, *hold on.*

I had to get away from there. I couldn't let Todd see me fall apart. Nothing short of a full explanation would satisfy him, but it was too soon for us to talk about certain things. My father's career with the Counterintelligence Analysis Group of the CIA was only one of them. That was where Blitzner wanted me. I was certain of it. It was the only reason he could be certain I would take it. He knew I had not forgotten, even if everyone else had. He understood at least that I would never be satisfied until I knew who had ordered my parents' murders.

Did he know I was looking, that I'd allowed an innocent man to be killed? It was Matt Boone, the hacker, who had led me to Blerim Nesimi.

Do the right thing. Richard and Todd wanted the same thing for me – a home, safety, stability. What was right for me was not right for them. I had followed him here because they'd given me no choice. Could I leave him when circumstances changed and I did have a choice?

"Don't think about it now, Amy. These things take time. Blitzner won't be moving until after the New Year, and it will take some time for him to get settled before he can start bringing in his own people. We have time, lots of time, to think about what you want to do when we leave here."

I faced the man who was looking at me with heart-wrenching concern etched into the creases of his face and the depth of his indigo eyes. *We,* he said. Nor had he dismissed entirely the possibility that I might *want* to go.

"Will you stay with me, Todd?" I asked.

I was glad for the rain, at least I hoped it hid the truth behind my tears. Todd saw right through me. Why did I think I could fool him? He stroked my cheek with his thumb, then wiped his finger across the other where the heat of my tears stood out from the cool rain.

"Always, Amy."

I kissed him because I couldn't find the words to say how much he meant to me. I was terrified of that word, which to my lonely heart was a promise of forever, a promise he had no way of keeping. I kissed him with a hunger of twelve years and the longing of a lifetime of memories that never had the chance to be. I put everything that I was into that kiss and for the moment was not afraid that it might overwhelm us. This time was ours alone.

And Todd, he took it all and gave me everything in return. "There is no wrong or right between us, Amy. You and I are forever, come what may. I can never leave you; and you can never leave me because you are my heart and soul and I would die without you. I would die for you. Do you understand?"

"I do." Though I was terrified it might actually come to that.

"Do you promise me?"

"I promise."

"No right or wrong, Amy."

"Just us," I breathed.

He kissed me again, a ferocious pressing of lips and teeth as his fingers dug into my skull, holding me close so we could breathe the same breath and be the same being. I wrapped my arms around his neck, craning to get closer, to welcome more of him. There was the vague memory of another time when we had stood just like this, the rain falling like a curtain around us while we kissed in the feeble shelter of an umbrella. It was vague, because although I craved him even then, we had come so far since Jamaica, the memory was only a ghost of what we were now, what we could be. When there was no more to give, we broke apart.

"Go right now. I'll follow to make sure you get there safely."

I did not argue that his concern was wasted. I wanted him there as much as he wanted to be there. Even if we could not touch, and feel, and breathe each other, I wanted to know he was there.

Todd bundled me into the car. His scent on the jacket filled the small space. It got me back to the apartment. It got me through the night. He was my drug. Angelika's buoyancy was no match for mine. I was high, and Todd was my drug.

THIRTY-ONE

I was surprised to have slept so well given my euphoria. At best, I expected a restless night for want of Todd; at worst, anxiety about the operation at sea. But by the time I opened my eyes, the first light of dawn already streaked the sky, painting rainbows across the city with the last of the rain.

It was too late to run, but feeling around inside my head, I was surprised to find no need. Todd was the unicorn I'd been chasing all these years. A part of me still wanted to doubt... the part that felt unworthy of anything good, like happiness, family, a home. Perhaps I didn't deserve it, but Todd had taken the decision from me. He'd had the chance for his freedom, but he chose me instead – broken, dirty, unworthy me.

Did you hear that? He chose me. I am not alone. Not anymore.

Angelika was humming to herself, fixing eggs. Her hair was wet from a shower, the straps of a swimsuit glowing neon against her skin, peeking out from the top of the towel she was wrapped in. Either she had already packed all her clothes in anticipation of her departure tomorrow, or a swim was part of her plans for the day.

"We're out of food," she said.

I refilled the reservoir and made myself a cup of coffee. There was ice in the freezer, one chocolate bar and coffee in the cupboards, water and baking soda in the refrigerator next to the ends of a loaf of white bread. I could survive a few more days with what was in stock, but I imagined Angelika liked food with color.

I fished my last two thousand pesos out of my purse and left it on the island. "Order a pizza or have the *colmada* deliver a few things." The cash disappeared under the towel faster than I thought possible. "You leave tomorrow. Don't jeopardize that."

She smiled broadly around a mouthful of eggs. "I would not dream of it." I held her gaze. "I swear. I don't even need it," she protested, still pleasant despite her defensiveness.

I picked up my purse and headed for the door.

"You look nice today."

This type of rapport, especially with women, was unfamiliar to me. My initial reaction was that she wanted something, or was up to something, but she only picked up her plate and moved to the couch. She paused with the remote mid-click, called to attention by the weight of my suspicion.

"You do," she added with a shrug. "You look like a lady... not so cold today."

The incredulity of that remark eked a smile out of me. This snowflake thought I was cold? In retrospect, she wasn't as arctic today either. Her smile began in her eyes and her movement was easier, more comfortable. She reminded me of a sixteen-year-old detainee I had met in Iraq several years ago after he was advised of his impending release.

For days he had breathed easier, but dreading any attention he was paid. He was afraid that at any moment we would change our minds. He had dreams too of going to school, or getting a job teaching English to put to use the two years he had spent with us. Ten months after his release, he blew himself up in a crowded marketplace, trying to kill two American subcontractors.

The embassy was empty but far from deserted. There'd been no call from work during the night, no notes from Townsend, no clue as to the outcome of the early morning operation. I left my rental car for Motor Pool to return, and accepted the keys to a light-armored Ford Explorer. Just as Todd had promised, everything was taken care of, although it was barely six in the morning.

I hurried over to Comms where, as expected, the command room was abuzz with activity. A new team had relieved yesterday's, and I was happy to note Townsend's absence. There was a fresh pot of coffee and I instantly decided I liked the new guys a lot better than Moss' crew.

I helped myself to a fresh cup and checked in with Lieutenant Hall. "How did it go this morning?" He was not unattractive, with light brown hair, blue eyes, and a smile set at panty-dropping caliber. Service Charlies did a lot for him, but the firm jaw and cocky stance were all him. There was no wedding ring, which meant absolutely nothing since these guys didn't always wear them. He was around my age and, in another life, I would have given serious consideration to pursuing him.

"It was a mixed bag. You have to make sense of it to the political guys, because they always buy as much bullshit as they give."

I thought I knew something about that. Todd had spent months looking for the good in me when the bad should have sent him running in the opposite direction. But had he bought the crap I fed everyone else? Not in the least.

I held the steaming cup to my lips so Lieutenant Hall didn't think my smile was for him. "What do you mean?"

"Well," he started, scratching the back of his head with a knowing grin, "the suspects made the drop on Desecheo while pretending to look for castaways from a yola."

Yolas were small, wooden boats used for fishing and smuggling. They were unregistered and could be found on every beach throughout the Dominican Republic and Haiti.

"Coast Guard picked up the drop and preliminary tests were positive for cocaine and heroine, totaling six hundred pounds. The Dolphin got the whole thing on FLIR. Coast Guard has possession, but we're keeping things hush-hush to watch the spot to see who comes to pickup."

I waited for Lieutenant Hall to continue, but stepped away from the wall when he repositioned himself closer, whether consciously or instinctively trying to crowd me. I gave him the benefit of the doubt like the political guys he clearly had little tolerance for.

There was something about the yola that unsettled me. It could be used to add legitimacy to Piño's patrol, which struck me as too convenient.

"Tango arrived at the yola about the time a few bodies fell in the water," he continued. "They could claim no knowledge of the narcotics and blame it on the smugglers. There were only thirty-five people aboard."

By their standards that left plenty of space for other cargo. Six hundred pounds was the same as four more bodies.

That last sip of coffee tasted sour in my mouth. I pushed off the wall when Hall planted his hands on his hips and widened his stance like a bird spreading its wings, or a peacock fanning its tail. The move had him taking up all his space in the coffee corner plus some of mine.

"Do we have the video ready yet?"

"I'll send it over to you. Make yourself comfortable at console three and I'll be right over." He smiled, showing off a dimple in his left cheek. Now why did I get the impression he thought this was a movie date?

I sank into a barely cushioned chair and rolled up to the spot he had indicated. There was an empty seat positioned next to mine, so I placed my purse squarely on it, grabbed paper and a pen to mark the frames I wanted to be isolated, and planted my useless cell phone and a bottle of water on the working space above it. Headphones completed my little fort.

Although nowhere as rigid as O'Brien's guest furniture, the seat was still hard. The discomfort was meant to discourage personnel from falling asleep while poring over hours of audiovisual material. I wasn't dressed appropriately to ease the assault on my backside either. The navy, silk wrap dress was a wild-card wardrobe selection, picked up on Wednesday night during my visit with Todd.

The smooth material slicked over the seat and my skin, riding up the backs of my thighs whenever I adjusted my position. It also slipped off my knee as the natural folds of the garment did what they were meant to do, moving as I moved. Espadrilles added that softness Angelika had remarked on this morning, but propped my knees above parallel to the chair. I was going to spend all day holding the hem in place.

It was an inconvenience I didn't completely mind, because I knew Todd would appreciate the effort. The classic lines were appropriate for the wife of a man in his official position. I was prepared for the attention I would attract dressed like this – softer, lighter, warmer than everyone was accustomed to. It helped to think of my venture into the light as a role to be played. It made acceptance of the judgment of others easier to bear if all they could comment on was the lie I fed them.

Events of the early morning operation were replayed on the split screen in shades of black with intermittent bursts of light. The timestamp in the upper right-hand corner started the clock just after 2 a.m. With the counter marking the passage of time, I played the video at 8x speed until the spike in radio waves alerted me to activity.

The Coastal Patrol Boat was the first to move into position in the shadow of a hulking cruise ship. The commander of the 87 ft. cutter, with call sign Romeo, radioed the captain of the cruise ship, directing him to maintain course and speed at twenty-two knots. Romeo occasionally checked in with Central Command to relate conditions, location, personnel and environment. This was either his first nighttime interdiction, his first exercise since promotion, or he was simply very excited, because Central Command cleared the airwaves with a 10-25 prompt – unnecessary use of radio.

All was quiet for the next hour and forty-five minutes, when the screen for the Dolphin MH-65 helicopter flashed and the radio frequency spiked. Under call sign Delta, the team alerted Central Command to the approach of the suspects in a 110 ft. cutter monikered Perseus.

> **Delta**: *Central Command, this is Delta. Perseus is in sight, 38 miles west of Rincón Lighthouse, traveling due east at 40 knots. FLIR has picked up thirteen tangos on board. Delta's distance from Perseus 14 miles.*

FLIR, or Forward Looking Image Radar, was a long-range precision targeting system mounted on the helicopter that allowed us to capture and record our targets. The shortwave infrared sensor gave us day and night capability to tell what and how many we were tracking.

> **Central Command**: *Roger that, Delta. Maintain visual contact. Maintain distance.*

The HD image on screen stabilized, showing the vessel, its wake, and the glow of live bodies for another uninterrupted twenty-five minutes.

> **0425 – Delta**: *Central Command, this is Delta. We have a situation at 18.344098, -67.659302; 13.5 miles from Desecheo. Perseus is approaching a civilian conveyance, approximately 35 live humans on board.*

Just because I was prepared for what would happened next did not mean I was unaffected by it. That number, thirty-five, had plagued me all yesterday afternoon. Watching the events unfold, this was the first time it occurred to me that there might have been children onboard that piece of board floating in shark infested water, at night, in the rain and cold.

I made a note to find Pablo Ortega. From what I could remember, he was from one of the shantytowns off Calle San Antonio in Miches. If he had taken their money and put them at risk, without any real intention of taking them to Puerto Rico, he had just booked his ticket on a one-way ride to that special corner in hell that was reserved for him.

> **0430 – Delta**: *Central Command, vessel in distress. The yola is breaking apart. There are bodies overboard.*
> **Central Command**: *Romeo, have you received any transmission from Perseus?*
> **Romeo**: *10-5, Central Command. Permission to respond?*
> **Central Command**: *10-5, Romeo. All teams hold position. Delta, maintain maximum visual range.*
> **Romeo**: *Roger, Central Command.*
> **Delta**: *Roger, Central Command.*

There was a sigh, possibly of frustration from Central Command. I did not blame him. As much as the life of every smuggled migrant mattered, our mission was the surveillance of narco-traffickers.

But in all fairness to the Romeo commander with a hero complex, he did not fully understand what was happening. Some things were beyond average, human understanding. The interdiction of the yola was orchestrated; the bodies overboard planned; the search and rescue staged.

Because I liked things wrapped up neatly in tight bows, I would check the biometrics of those rescued to see if Pablo Ortega was on board or affiliated to anyone present.

> **0505 – Delta**: *Central Command, Perseus is on the go with civilian cargo, direction east at 15 knots.*

It was standard operating procedure to establish a perimeter, then search within it in concentric circles, moving outwards from the point of contact. Instead, Perseus headed directly east then stalled. With easterly winds and currents, it would be hard to explain an easterly course, unless there was information about another yola. Any castaways would have been swept west, as were the broken pieces of the wooden vessel. Additionally, 15 knots was excessive for a search and rescue mission with possible live bodies in the vicinity, particularly under current weather and light conditions.

*0520 – **Delta**: Central Command, we have an RHIB being deployed with a two-man crew riding low. Perseus is DIW.*

The rigid-hulled inflatable boat deployment was standard for marine rescue, as was the fact that Perseus had cut its engines. However, a two-man crew was inadequate manpower and should not have weighted the vessel at all. I made a note for the engineers would plot the wave heights against the depth of the boat to estimate its total load.

***Central Command**: Roger that, Delta. Shift visual to the lightweight.*
*0535 – **Delta**: Central Command, the lightweight has beached at location 18.382567, -67.485918. Tango unloading cargo, 15-piece count.*

I watched as the two mobile heat sources beached the RIB into a cove on Desecheo Island, unloaded its cargo, then covered and secured the stash with pikes.

*0545 – **Central Command**: Romeo, standby for pickup. Delta, maintain visual on the lightweight.*
*0555 – **Delta**: Central Command, RHIB has returned to Perseus. Perseus is live and changing course. Direction west at 40 knots.*
***Central Command**: Roger that, Delta. Confirm return to home base.*

There was a marked absence of audio coming on the heel of an hour of excitement. Then:

0605 – Central Command: All teams, San Juan has received radio contact from Perseus regarding a capsized yola. Perseus requests your support for search and interdiction. The commander suspects another vessel may be in the area. Perseus has set time of contact with yola at 0520. Perseus has given current time stamp at 0605.

I sighed with relief that someone in Central Command had had the foresight to get the Dominicans to verify the current time. It proved they had deliberately misrepresented the time of rescue at forty minutes later than the video record showed. It was a conscious effort to conceal the time spent traveling to and from the drop site, which would undermine whatever story was later fabricated.

0606 – Central Command: Identification and location of Perseus has been confirmed. Delta, you may proceed with search and rescue. Code 2. Please confirm or deny the presence of any other conveyance within a 30-mile radius of Perseus.
Delta: Roger that, Central Command.
Central Command: Romeo, proceed to inspect and seize contraband at 18.382567, -67. 485918.
Romeo: Roger that, Central Command.

There was more to the transmission, and I would eventually have to go through it all, but at that precise moment I had an urgent need to get the evidence of the delivery and attempted cover-up condensed.

One strategically placed finger held my hem in place as I turned in my seat to find Lieutenant Hall. It was embarrassing how quickly he appeared at my side. "I need a splice and dice at these points. Please prepare on mobile media." I handed him the list of frames in which I had an interest.

"Yes, ma'am," he drawled, one hand in his pocket as he rocked back and forth on his heels. He loomed over me, much too close for comfort. I could smell his aftershave, something lemony, or possibly bergamot. It certainly wasn't sunshine and ocean with an undertone of sweet tobacco. "Is there anything else you would like me to do for you?"

I turned back to the console and replaced the headphones, droning out any more suggestions he may have, but also hiding my guilty blush.

It was unfair that Todd had become the standard by which all men were judged. "No, thanks. That'll be all."

I spent an hour running through the rest of the surveillance video and updating the brief I had distributed last night. I added new frames to Lieutenant Hall's list, which included the arrival of Romeo on the scene of the drop.

Fifteen waterproof wrapped bales were discovered under sand-colored tarp in the cove. It wasn't the largest seizure – wasn't even in the top ten – but what made it significant was the frequency with which the conspiracy operated. If the size of the current load was typical of all their exports, then Colonel Ramirez was responsible for the export of nearly two and a half tons of narcotics to the United States in one year.

I sent my brief to O'Brien and Townsend first, then I spent an hour working the Pablo Ortega angle with Lieutenant Hall. It was a task I hoped he would have delegated, but I was not surprised when he volunteered to sift through Suarez's communications with me. He gestured for me to pull up a seat and describe point-by-point what I was looking for as he did it.

I did nothing to encourage him, but I didn't openly discourage him either. I had spent much of my life using whatever advantage I had to achieve my desired results. And here was an attractive man jumping through hoops to get me the data I needed as fast as I could request it, for no more compensation than the pleasure of my company.

I was committed, not dead. And Lieutenant Hall's pheromones wafted towards me in wave after crashing wave. Days ago, I would not have given it a second thought, but last night afforded me new perspective. My physical awareness of the man made me uncomfortable, even if my outward reaction was above-board.

O'Brien replied within the hour: "Excellent work, Koehler. Liaise with Political Affairs. Birch is aware of our desired outcome."

Based on the things Todd had told me, including those we discussed in the rain last night, I was not surprised to finally have confirmation of communication between him and my boss. Pathetic didn't begin to describe how I felt when I realized I had been suspicious of Byles and Todd's friends assigned to my Section when O'Brien could, and most likely had, provided him with everything he wanted to know. With my awareness of communication heading out to Todd, my concerns about the nature and extent of knowledge O'Brien had on our marriage and my habits redoubled.

On the one hand, O'Brien had been particularly short with me over the past few days. But on the other, he had given me everything I asked for, including an expense account for Angelika. What must he have thought as I made the case for Angelika's passport, claiming my own husband had had contact with her? Did he regard me as objective and dedicated, or plain vindictive?

I told myself it couldn't all be bad. He had just sent me unequivocal high praise. True, he had never skimped on accolades before, but at the same time, I had put him under quite a bit of stress.

Then again, he knew I was in Comms. The answer could be as simple as presenting a harmonious front to outsiders.

It did occur to me that I might be overthinking things when I had work to do. I forwarded Todd the same material I had sent my boss then dialed his mobile number from the landline.

"You're up early," Todd answered, sounding like sleep and sex all at once. His throaty voice resonated deep inside my core and warmed me like a shot of rum.

I sighed to release the breath trapped in my throat, thinking this feeling couldn't possibly last. "Some of us work for a living."

"I work," he protested without heat. "And very hard too."

"I know it hurts when you're smiling all day, but that doesn't count."

"It doesn't count that I had you limping out of here the other night? Keeping you satisfied is a full-time endeavor and I'm doing all I can now so I can afford to devote myself to that challenge twenty-four-seven in a few years."

The heat surged to my face like a geyser, pushing the breath from my lungs. I caught myself looking around guiltily to see if anyone had noticed my reaction. Lieutenant Hall gave me a smile that could have lit up Times Square. Others were beginning to take notice of his interest in me.

"Hey, listen, I just sent you a brief with the latest from Comms. O'Brien said I should liaise with your department, but neither of you mentioned who would be working it specifically." I started out a little too breathy for my own liking, but recovered well at the end. I blamed that initial failing on the pulsing heat between my legs that consumed too much of my concentration.

"Don't you want to work with me, Amy?"

I winced, although I should have expected his eagerness to handle my case personally. "I'm not sure that's a good idea."

"Why not?" It would have been a natural reaction if not for the beat that preceded it. Todd knew all the reasons why this was a bad idea.

"You do know I'm not working alone on this. It's a military case."

"Why would you think I had not considered that?" I groaned. "As much as I love you and can't get enough of you, Amy, you're not the only draw here. If Colonel Robert Townsend has proximity to my wife, you can bet your ass I'm getting involved."

I groaned again, but this time at Todd's refusal to follow the spirit of discretion and not mention names or identifying characteristics. All calls from Comms were monitored and manned by personnel whose job entailed reporting to the subject of our conversation.

"Amy," he sighed, sounding more conciliatory than a moment ago. There was nothing like the thought of Colonel Townsend to get Todd's hackles up. "Don't worry about this crap. Trust that I will have everything under control."

Except he had been decidedly out of control on Wednesday when he walked in on us. That was something Todd would have to work on, because I had a habit of bringing the worst out of the people I worked with, especially Colonel Townsend.

"I'll take a look at this and get back to you if I need anything."

I sighed, releasing some of the tension brought on by the thought of the three of us together. Unfortunately it wasn't nearly enough to ease the throbbing tension at the back of my skull. I couldn't help feeling that, although my morning had progressed well so far, it was going all downhill from here on out.

Then I heard the rustle of sheets as Todd got out of bed. I was momentarily distracted by a vision of him moving across the room in his briefs. The memory of the hills and plains of his back moving away from me was like a dream I never wanted to end.

"By the way, I spoke with Michael last night. He asked me to tell you that you are on. What's that about?"

I sucked in air. "Nothing important." I shuffled around a pile of paper. "I have more work to do and the condensed video to double check. I don't want to forget anything, and I want to anticipate whatever explanation they come up with so you're not caught unprepared. I should go."

"Okay. Do what you need to do because I'll be doing you tonight, baby," he said with an exaggerated dip in his voice. It was just a hair's breath shy of sleazy.

"Bye."

"Come on, Amy. Those guys up there are bored. Let's make their day. Say something dirty to me."

Todd got a reluctant giggle out of me. It was so out of character for me, it shocked me and egged him on.

"Okay, just make that sound you do right before you come. You know… when you catch your breath to get ready to moan." He laughed, relishing the newness of a normal life with a normal wife.

I was painfully aware of the eyes fixed on me that might not have even been there in truth. I asked myself what was the worst they could think, then compared it to the best that could come from Todd's happiness. The choice was clear; I endured.

"I love you, my beautiful wife," he said softly. It was both sober and worshipful, and anyone who cared to listen would know he meant it.

"I love you too, Todd. And I will see you later."

I didn't care who was listening, as long as Todd heard me and believed.

THIRTY-TWO

Krieger, Anne: Segafredo, Calle El Conde, Colonial Zone. 2p.m.

I discovered the message while on a bathroom break. As expected it came when I least expected it. There should have been no excuse for me to be caught off-guard. Things with Todd had progressed too far for Anne to sit idly by and observe. Still, her sudden and unprovoked appearance was revealing of a simple fact I had conveniently ignored up to present. My control over Anne extended only so far as she allowed.

The Colonial Zone was Santo Domingo's historic capital, the site of the first cathedral, the first hospital, the first sundial, and the first genocide in the New World. Anne was literally inviting me for a walk back in time but the memories she wanted to revisit were born fifteen hundred miles away.

I circumvented the pedestrian streets and was lucky to find parking five blocks away. Espadrilles were not the most suitable footwear for what turned out to be a speed walk along cobblestone streets. It didn't help that the area was crowded with tourists spilling from three tour buses and into every edifice, whether of historical importance or not. They blocked sidewalks, pulled sudden stops in the middle of narrow walkways without a thought to the hundreds of other pedestrians, some of whom had places to be. It was one of the worst possible places for a midweek lunch meeting.

The café was packed with painfully red faces – visitors unaccustomed to the constant sunshine and cheap alcohol. They ordered beer by the bucket and mooned over pizza they could have had at home. They were loud and gregarious, and I expected at least two of them would call the consulate in a panic because they had lost their passport or had been robbed.

At least half of the single men, and a quarter of the married ones, would return to their Midwest homes with a correspondence girlfriend they would eventually marry. Physically the women would be glaringly out of their league – young, beautiful and passionate. They would also be poor, which leveled the playing field.

Why would Anne want to meet in the middle of this circus?

I claimed a table outside, with Columbus Park and the Cathedral to my right at one end of Calle El Conde. To my left, was the intersection with Calle Las Damas where, during colonial rule, the ladies-in-waiting to Spanish high society enjoyed leisurely strolls. A waiter in the signature orange shirt and blue apron hanging down to his shins brought me white wine then disappeared with my lunch order.

I was almost out of wine and had finished my carpaccio when Anne appeared from nowhere, falling into her seat like a silk scarf blown off a rack. Her hair was down, cascading across her shoulders and down her back in deep chestnut disarray. It was a flattering look, and right away I decided to imitate her for my date with Todd tonight.

She looked healthy… rested, clear-headed, almost vibrant. Her eyes, those liquid pools of chocolaty sorrow, normally gave her an air of innocence that I had lost long ago. I briefly wondered about Todd's reaction to her. He had been so moved by the hint of vulnerability I had shown, even though I had not been that weak in over a decade. Would I be too much for him to save? Would he run from her…what I had once been?

It wasn't the first time I recognized I was too broken for him. I understood it was too much to ask. It was better that I keep them apart…that he never know.

"What do you think you're doing?"

She leaned back in her seat and refused to meet my stare. Her hands shook as she fingered a folded napkin, but not from anxiety or fear. Anne could hide from everyone if she wished, but not me. It was the effort of holding back her anger that had her quaking in her seat. It was heat that melted those eyes to decadent pools of rage. How strange it was to see Anne so strong.

"Look around," Anne said, as if I hadn't done enough of that while waiting for her to show herself. "There's so much history. It's like the past is still here. All these people who come and go, do you think they realize how insignificant they are?"

I didn't answer. I knew where this was going, but battling the crowds had made me hungry and I wanted to get in as much food before we got there.

She shrugged and continued, as if my answer was a formality she could live without. "They will all be gone in a few hours, only to be replaced tomorrow. But this place of living memories will always be here."

"The same could be said about everywhere," I caught the attention of the waiter and nodded that I was ready for my main course. "But I get your point. This is about Todd."

"Isn't everything about Todd now?"

I waited for the waiter to set down my lasagna and leave. He took his time, making certain I was okay, that I had everything I needed. He didn't want to have to make a second or third trip when the café was jam-packed. He finally left to once again offer a menu to a woman two tables down who was making sandwiches out of the complementary bread and cheese. She already had a neat pile going, the food carefully wrapped in paper napkins and stowed in her purse.

"You seem fixated on him. Why? I've already told you he's mine."

"I understand he is special, Amy. A rare combination of beauty, power, and protectiveness. But he isn't everything. Just like these people, Todd Birch will one day leave. And who do you think will be there to share the burden of the past?"

"He's not going anywhere. He loves me."

"He loves what he sees. Do you expect him to love what lies beneath?"

If I said yes, she would challenge me to prove it...to share with Todd the parts of me that were buried deep. If I said no, then I would have proven her point.

"He knows enough to understand." The protest was angrier than I intended, because Anne had struck too close to the core of my fears.

"Please don't be angry with me." Tears pricked at the corners of her eyes, her lips trembled. Oh, fragile Anne. "I just don't want you to forget. There are things we have to do, answers we have to find, debts to be repaid. I don't want him to distract you from what is really important. And I don't want him to come between us."

"He won't," I answered as firmly as she had her teeth clenched.

"He wants different things for you," she insisted.

I shook my head. "He wants me at his side. It's nothing I can't manage," I said, which also served as a reminder to myself. "Don't worry about Todd. I'll do what I have to do and I won't let us down."

There were so many things relying on that promise. My life would never be my own to share until I made peace with the past.

I nodded. We sat quietly for a moment watching a pigeon roost amidst broken glass bottles above a window. I finished the lasagna and the wine, then annoyed the waiter with a request for water. I made it San Pellegrino so it would be worth his while, which he seemed to appreciate. I had half a bottle of water in my purse that I had brought from home, but I would need it later when the alcohol I had consumed gave me cottonmouth.

I dug into the Nutella covered crêpes as if the two courses I'd already had were nothing but a dream. Anne did not ask to share, and I forgot to offer. Some things in life were meant for only one.

"He is ours, Amy. 'All of you', he said, which means all of me too. Don't try to hold me back anymore." She got up to leave as I swallowed the last bite of the chocolate-smeared pancake.

"Todd is not yours. He will never be yours. I will cut you out first, even if it means destroying everything we've built together. He's mine. Mine alone."

Already there were so many who claimed pieces of him. I refused to share the little I had with anyone else.

"Now you don't want to do that, Amy."

"I'm not afraid," I said and meant it. I'd been afraid for so long I'd lived only half a life. I wasn't going to be afraid anymore, as long as I could have the one thing I wanted… the only thing I needed."

"Not afraid for you, Amy. But you should be very afraid for him."

"You can't hurt him."

"No, but you can. He loves you so much, imagine what it would do to him to find you asleep at the bottom of a bathtub."

Anne did not give me a chance to respond, not that I had one ready. Todd had promised to save me even from myself. Now it seemed I would have to let him. What choice did I have?

THIRTY-THREE

I was late. It didn't happen often, because my time was usually as well organized as my wardrobe. I didn't like surprises, so the few times I was running off schedule was either the result of relying on a third party, or things were going exactly according to plan. Like Friday night.

I was exactly forty-five minutes late, and if Todd appreciated the dress as much as Lieutenant Hall had, then I didn't plan on spending more than an hour of my life at El Gallego.

Todd met me at the door. I had the feeling he had been pacing, giving only half his attention to the people who had gathered to congratulate him on his temporary appointment. His relief was palpable even if the kiss pressed to my mouth was brief. It was as if he had been afraid I might not have come. A firm arm hooked around the curve of my lower back held me in place when I would have shied away. Todd knew me so well.

"You're beautiful," he murmured, the hand at my back feeling how easily the silk smoothed over my skin. "Thank you for coming."

His eyes were appraising as they ran over me. I liked the light in them. They made me feel as if the effort I had made was appreciated. The finger slipping lower on my back promised reward. He made me smile, my cheeks heating up to color my pallor. I could do this for him.

The restaurant served Argentinian food to the large gathering of US embassy personnel. It was a welcome respite; no one in Santo Domingo could complain about a dearth of American food. They moved from table to table, sampling the fare at each, exclaiming at the sight of colleagues they had missed in the past day, and filling the space with the buzz of a healthy hive.

There was also a faithful crowd of Dominicans who didn't seem to mind that some tables had been pushed against the exposed brick walls to accommodate the milling throng. There wasn't an empty niche anywhere even if I had been of a mind to retreat into solitude... even if Todd would have let me go.

There were many faces I recognized, all of whom I would have avoided under normal circumstances. With Todd's arm permanently fused around me, there was no hope of that. It was worse than the Fourth of July cocktail in Jamaica where he had mauled me before the entire embassy. Back then there was idle speculation about our relationship. This time, they scorned our open affection with half a mind, then analyzed with the other half every nuance of our interaction, looking for discord.

Landon and Martinez showed deference to me only because of Todd. Jessica Byles made a permanent fixture of herself at a table with Lieutenant Hall and four other Marines. Helen, Todd's Secretary, stood at the ready to fulfill his every request, which apparently included engaging me every seven minutes with the type of mundane conversation that irritated me.

It wasn't all a struggle though. I no longer had to hide from the one person who mattered. Todd *knew* me but loved me just the same. It baffled everyone – his secretary, his friends, his lovers, and even myself – but it was undeniable. Anyone who saw the way he looked at me, the way he held me as if I were a part of him, the longing with which he stared after me when I moved away, knew Todd Birch loved me, faults and all.

How could I not give him what he needed? And at that moment, he needed a wife to stand with him in the light. And so I gave him everything inside me, then dug deeper and gave him more. I smiled and returned greetings, listened as they talked about people and events that marked the highlights and low points of their lives. Most of all I smiled as they talked about Todd, the things he did that made them feel special, the reasons they loved him and put up with me.

I learned things about my husband that I should have recognized before. In one crucial way, Todd was just like me. Everyone had an opinion of him, but none of them knew him like I did. None of them had ever met the man beneath the skin. They had never seen his anger; for them, his worst was cool indifference. They had never seen his need; only the physical wants. They had never seen his consummate joy either... joy as he waited for me at the end of a narrow aisle under the roses in my father's garden. How could I begrudge them the little they had of him?

I would never fully appreciate these affairs, where people's smiles belied their cruelty underneath. I wasn't quite panicked to the point where my skin grew moist and my breathing shallow. But I would never be comfortable in the hell that was their regard... their anger and confusion as they wandered 'Why her'.

That was a question I had not been able to answer in the twelve years since this life began. Why me? Why did I survive? What made me special? Why had the only man I loved sacrificed everything to save me when he knew I would be nothing, I would be lost without him?

I still felt it as a betrayal of everything my father had done for me to let Todd in. But in doing so – in letting Todd in – I began to understand why. When you love someone more than anything else in the world, you give everything to save them, even your life.

My father sent me away because he loved me more than life. And my mother gave up her life because she loved him more than anything and knew he had to save me.

By choosing me, Todd was risking his image... their adoration, without which he would never fulfill his purpose here. So I smiled and laughed and allowed him to give them little pieces of himself. And if them, then why not Anne too?

Sharing became easier as the night wore on and the faculties were numbed by wine and carbohydrates. Todd's arm dipped lower. Our backs were to the wall when his middle finger began exploring the valley between the globes of my bottom. Then the first alert came.

Angelika was on the move.

Todd felt the change in me immediately. I excused myself as evenly as possible, but I felt his eyes on me as I retreated outdoors, the phone pressed to my ear. I didn't expect her to answer but I called her anyway. I was accustomed to giving people enough rope to hang themselves, but this time it was my sincere wish to give her the benefit of the doubt.

"I am walking to the *colmada* for food. I won't be long," she answered with unusual levity. Freedom was in sight but not yet attained; it was very trusting of her to be so lighthearted. True, I had delivered everything I had promised so far, given more than I had to, much more than anyone else. In her mind, she had no reason to doubt me now.

"You didn't say I could not leave." But that was before her lapse in judgment had compromised our safety. "I promise, I will go just to the *colmada* and back. I am too nervous to sleep and there is no food in the house."

She sounded sincere, not in the least strung out. I knew she liked watching police dramas into the small hours of morning and would snack on things like popcorn, vegetables, and cheese – the latter being her only indulgence. Still, I had to give her a final warning.

"Your flight is in fifteen hours. Don't fuck it up."

"Don't worry," she said with a little laugh, trying to convince me I was over-reacting when a snowflake went trolling the streets of Naco after eleven at night. "I'm wearing my wig and I promise I'll be good. I don't need anything, just food."

"Call me as soon as you get in," I told her, to which she agreed. I would be happy when she was gone. She was like a teenager, thrilled with an inch of freedom and condescending of my concern.

I turned around to find Todd exiting the restaurant. He scanned the street, looking for the source of my angst. A garbage truck rumbled not too far away. It wasn't the latest I had seen them out.

"Everything okay?" he asked, eyes skipping between my face, the cell phone clutched in my hand, and up and down the street again.

I planted a smile on my face and tried to breathe away the anxiety. "Yes."

"What is it?" he pushed, seeing beyond my defenses again.

I considered lying, downplaying the significance of events. Old habits were hard to break. Then Todd touched me, his arm curving around me and pulling me closer. I readjusted the strap of my purse on my shoulder in an attempt to regain some distance. Todd tilted my chin and pressed his lips to mine. His tongue traced the crease between my lips. I breathed his breath.

"What is it, Amy?"

What was the point? He knew me. He knew about Angelika. He understood my concerns. He would share my burden if I let him.

"Angelika. She left the apartment on foot to go to the *colmada*. I'm waiting for her to call me back as soon as she gets home."

Todd nodded. His eyes roamed my face, gauging my sincerity, just as I would his. "We'll give her ten minutes. If she doesn't call, we'll go find her. Do you have her on GPS?" I nodded. "Good."

His approval should not have meant so much to me. I was good at what I did. Better than Todd could ever imagine. Regardless, I felt myself warming at the approbation. Or was it the growing insistence of his arousal as he pressed closer to me that had my blood heating in my veins?

"Come inside. Let everyone think I can't keep my hands off you. If we have to go find her, they'll draw their own conclusions as to why we left in a hurry. If she's fine, then we can still leave in a hurry," he said with a smile.

He kissed me again, breaching the crease he had explored moments ago. The cynic in me said it was all for show. However, the hardness of him and the depth of his moan said it was for the pure pleasure of not being able to help himself.

Todd pulled me back into place under his arm, his hand low on my spine and venturing daringly lower while a Political Analyst waxed on about the need for local election campaign funding caps and transparency – some of which we didn't even have at home. Todd praised her astuteness, and I smiled dutifully, both of us taking the reaction of least resistance so we could keep track of the time.

I was two keys short of dialing Angelika when my phone buzzed with an incoming call, followed almost immediately by an alert from the apartment. Todd stalled my escape with a firm grip on my arm. He excused us both then steered me outside, where the garbage truck had recently lumbered by, its distinctive aroma heavy in the air.

"I am home," Angelika sing-songed. She was slightly breathless, but that could have been from the walk. I heard the rustle of plastic bags. "Sorry I took so long. They had dulce de leche, so I got you some."

"Lock up," I told her and waited for her to comply.

"I had to leave two bags outside to open up and call you."

"I'll hold while you do."

She sighed, but she didn't argue. My phone pinged with the incoming alert that she was out again. She was being careless, unmindful of the risk, which could be a fatal flaw. It was the number one killer of armed services personnel at the end of their tours. They were so distracted by the lure of home, they forgot there were threats everywhere.

I wasn't surprised when it happened to Angelika.

THIRTY-FOUR

I heard her startle. I felt too the jerk of recognition. My chest ached for her as rough hands trapped the breath she had heaved for a hearty scream. I heard the blows like thunder in my ear as she struck at her assailant with the phone still clutched in her hand. I heard voices – male, Spanish, at least two – and then the slam of a door.

Todd's hands on my arms steadied me. He turned me, led me away along the deserted sidewalk, shielding me from inquisitive eyes. His fingers over mine found the speaker button. There was shuffling, mumbling, quiet voices and the crash of an open palm on skin. The phone clattered to the floor and the call ended.

"Where is she?" Todd asked, all gentleness gone now. The air of command that always surrounded him crackled with new energy. His fingers biting into my arms as he led me further into the dark lacked the consideration he'd shown all evening.

"At the apartment. I have to go." I dug in my heels against his pull. "My car is the other way."

"Mine is right here," he countered, remotely unlocking and starting the engine with the key fob.

I balked. "Todd, don't."

"Don't what?" He turned to face me in the street, the lines of his face rigid, the set of his lips uncompromising. He dropped his hands as if I had burned him. All ten fingers raked through his hair as he stepped away from me. "You don't understand, Amy." His voice was even harder, colder, angrier. "I'm not letting you go alone. This isn't just your problem anymore; it's ours. There is no mine or yours; only ours. Because I have nothing without you... Nothing worth keeping. If we can't fix it together, we will go down together."

I wanted to tell him 'no', but the look in his eyes dared me to deny what was between us. Todd could not possibly know that I had only just begun to understand what it was. It explained everything.

"Get in the car, Amy," he said, opening the door for me. How could I deny him? He had brought me into the light and I had lived it if only for a brief moment. Now, here he was, stepping into the darkness with me.

I moved. I held his face and kissed him from the depth of my soul, and Todd gave me his in return. His mouth took as hungrily as mine for a long moment before our restraint kicked in. He saw me settled and slammed the door behind me. In another second he was beside me, starting the car and pushing every speed limit and red light to get us to Naco in half the time. It was still a long five minutes.

"We need to talk," Todd said.

"This is a bad time to break up with me, Todd." My heart revved to the RPMs of the SUV as he blew through a four-way stop sign, narrowly missing a *monteconcho* with three bodies aboard.

He smiled and squeezed my hand. "Open the safe under your seat." He shrugged off the look I threw him with a 'you-learn-something-new-everyday' insouciance. " It's only big enough for one." It was a poor excuse for keeping such a secret from me.

I pushed my seat all the way back, lifted the floor mat and felt around the edges of the carpeting for a seam. It took some time during which I was tossed around like a broken up yola on the waves, but I did eventually find it. I had to work hard to remove the false door only to stumble upon a combination lock. It was an even greater challenge turning the rotary dials to numbers like 26, 43, 61.

"You said she would be worth it. Is that why we're going for her?" Todd asked, always too astute and too patient for my peace of mind. We'd had that discussion about Angelika early Wednesday night, yet he'd saved that question for when I least expected it.

"Yes."

"Why?"

I looked up at him from my place on the floor. In the glow of the passing streetlights, he looked so hard and uncompromising, I began to doubt again.

"Keep it secret," my father had said.

"Do you trust me, Amy?"

Again, it wasn't a question of whether I did or not. It was a reminder of our promise to each other. "Yes."

"Tell me why she's worth it."

I looked away even though most of his attention was focused on the road. There were still things I had to make peace with, and Todd would have to give me time to do that before I could break my father's dying wish.

"There is something I have to explain before I can tell you. You wouldn't understand what's at stake otherwise."

"Do you promise, Amy?"

I nodded although I wasn't sure he was watching me. The door to the floor safe was heavy. I had to straighten my leg and use my foot to hold it open, my back braced against the seat. Inside was a kill kit. "Yes, I promise," I answered breathlessly.

Two Glock 17s, one Sig Sauer like mine, latex gloves, a suppressor, duct tape, zip ties, one hunting knife and an EMT response knife, extra extended clips, a small hatchet, a cell phone, fifty thousand dollars in cash, giant garbage bags, and rolls of plastic sheeting. It explained the rotary dials and difficult combination. These were not tools one reached for in haste. Only by proactive decisions and thorough deliberation would Todd need these things.

"When this is over then you'll tell me." I looked up at the stranger I had married. I remembered facing three armed men alone in Jamaica because I was afraid of Todd getting hurt. No wonder he'd been so angry. He'd found me bruised, half blind from the blow to my eye, and covered in blood that gladly wasn't mine. If I knew then what I knew now, I would have done it differently. Todd was as far from helpless as I was from innocent.

"I'll tell you."

Todd nodded and took a sharp right that sent my shoulder slamming into the passenger door. I braced harder to prevent the safe from slamming on me.

"I assume you have neighbors..."

"There is one on my floor, two above and three below. I haven't met any of them, but I know of them. One woman works for a phone company. One is a bank executive. There's a pharmacist; and a guy who owns a car dealership, plus his wife. Then there's a single woman, unemployed if you don't count being someone's mistress."

I could tell where his head was. The mistress and a couple of the singles might be out on the town. At least one, possibly the couple, could be home and alarmed by the sound of gunshots. There was only so much we could do about that. I loaded one of the Glocks and affixed the suppressor then handed it to him. He didn't have any holsters, so his waistband and belt would have to do.

"The other one too," he said, indicating the twin to the firearm I had already given him. "Just in case. And the hunting knife." I got everything ready for him. "Pack a couple of gloves, the tape and some restraints." I looked at him again, harder this time. "You never know if things might get messy."

So my husband was like a crazy bag lady, overstocked with a little something for every occasion. It was either that, or he was specialized in disposal. I could separate my emotions from my body as well as the best in the field. I could kill as efficiently and clinically as the next seasoned professional. But I did not have the stomach for the type of disposal that would require an ax like Todd's. Such sang-froid was truly rare.

Finally done packing, I locked the safe and readjusted my seat. I emptied the contents of my purse onto the floor and fished my firearm and extra clip out of the debris. I checked them. Bill, my trusty knife, I slipped into the pocket of my wrap dress, and my Sig went back into my purse. From my iPad, I logged into the IP host for my surveillance system.

"We have eyes," I told Todd, as first one and then all the camera feeds appeared on-screen.

"We do?" Todd could not hide his surprise. His double-take almost had us swiping the side of an illegally parked car. He adjusted, then leveled me with open interest and possibly a bit of suspicion.

"You wired your apartment?"

"Of course. It's a new place with one way in and one way out." I did a quick headcount and tried to locate Angelika in the tiny split screens.

"Did you wire our house?"

Our eyes met across the dark space between our seats. "No. Why?"

He seemed affronted that I even asked. "Because it's an invasion of my privacy." He leaned on the horn when brake lights lit up on the car ahead of us as it approached a yellow light. Todd swerved around the vehicle, narrowly avoiding collision with oncoming traffic before running through the red at a busy intersection at fifty-five miles an hour. "Do you watch me jack off?"

I appreciated his effort at distraction, but I didn't need it. Killing was no newer to me than it was to him. His process was slightly different from mine. Like me, he would go in, do what he had to do, then walk away no more affected by the lives he had to take. But where Todd did the job *in spite of* his true nature, switching gears from one moment to the crucial next, it seemed I existed in that empty void of emotion.

"First of all, I said I don't monitor our home. Secondly, you masturbate?" He looked at me like I had two heads. He'd watched me a time or two before joining in, and yet we'd never had a discussion about his practices. "You're always ready, that's all. I just figured you were saving it all for me."

"You do crazy things to me, Amy. You could make a corpse ready." I highly doubted it, but I wasn't going to argue. I wanted to hear about his masturbation. "So yes, when I wake up in the mornings and you've left for your run. It's easy with your scent still on the pillow and the sheets still warm from your body."

Todd had said a lot of wonderful things lately that lifted my spirits. Perhaps my perspective was off, but that just counted as one of the best and most memorable. I would never get out of bed the same again.

This feeling wasn't going away. Even in the midst of calculating an assault on four men in an enclosed and relatively small space, my heart felt full to bursting.

"So is there video of the two of us making love the other night?"

"No. I turn them off when I enter the apartment." He nodded with understanding, but I sensed his hesitance... his disappointment. We were discovering new things about each other and one day, if we survived the next hours, we would have to talk. We had the element of surprise in our favor and we both knew what we were about. There was no reason why we would not have more time for discovery.

Things weren't going so great for Angelika. She was bound with her hands behind her back, gagged and made to kneel in the middle of the living room floor while one man held a gun to her head. There was one in each bedroom, tossing the place. It was a good thing I had moved my critical operational equipment to my car in the morning in anticipation of my sleepover with Todd. My laptop and paperwork were stowed in the trunk of my diplomatic plated car one block from the restaurant.

With not much in the way of furniture, they stripped my wardrobe bare. Angelika had about as much as me, enough to fill a duffel bag, including shoes and cosmetics. But we weren't even near the same size. They would ask about my stuff if they were smart and my heart thumped heavily at what she might say. It appeared we still had some time however. She was still bound and gagged.

The fourth intruder I caught in the camera from the living room that was pointed at the door. He had one of those butterfly knives – not much of an edge, so better for stabbing than slicing – and was sifting through the contents of her shopping bags. By his casual demeanor, I knew I was looking at the alpha.

He was Dominican, European in appearance, with bone straight hair pulled back into a low ponytail. He was well dressed in a button-down shirt open at the collar to display a white undershirt. That he had worn light-colored, possibly white, pants and boat shoes to a home invasion meant he didn't plan on getting his hands dirty. He didn't have to. He had brought three armed men with him to grab a girl who tilted the scales at ninety pounds.

The one rifling through my underwear drawer had a .38 stuck in the back of his pants. He was dark, his skin gleaming against the white walls and door. He could have been Dominican, but judging by his height and the matting of his hair, I decided on Haitian.

The one ripping apart Angelika's room was less fastidious about her intimate apparel. Everything she owned was tossed on the bedroom floor so he could sift through it with the toe of his shoe. He moved to the bathroom with a similar tactic, dumping everything into one heap then scanning the contents with seemingly cursory interest. Finally he returned to the bedroom to flip her mattress, which was where he found her passports, flight itinerary and the prepaid card I'd given her. Like the good worker ant he was, his loot was handed over to the man in the white pants.

I checked our location and found us on my street with my building disappearing behind us.

"Just checking the perimeter," Todd explained. "A couple of cars with no one inside."

"My bet is on the Escalade." I gestured ahead of us where the massive truck was parked. The windows were so heavily tinted they were indiscernible from the rest of the black vehicle. The rims sparkled from a healthy dose of money and elbow grease.

"My bet would be that you're right."

Todd found a parking spot almost at the end of the road, four properties from mine. I turned up the volume on the iPad while he shut down and armed up. There was a dedicated pocket in his suit for each tool – knife, restraints, gloves, clips, spare 9mm. The primary piece with the suppressor was jammed into the waistband at his back. He smoothed his jacket into place so there was nothing to distinguish him from the urbane diplomat who had once tried to dismiss my concern for our safety with the pacifist manifesto about the pen being mightier than the sword.

"What do you have?" he asked

"My Sig and Bill." I'd hardly ever needed more.

Todd looked over the contents of my purse strewn over the floor of the car. "You need a suppressor. Grab your water bottle."

"We don't have time." I tilted the iPad so he could see as well.

The fourth man, the one with the gun pressed to Angelika's head ripped the gag out of her mouth. His .357 Magnum, which wouldn't leave enough of her for identification purposes, was hanging loosely at his side. The casual hold belied his calm exterior however; he couldn't stand still, shifting from one foot to the next every few seconds. He would have to be the first to go.

With his free hand, he gripped her hair, tugging her head back so she could look up at the man in the white pants. He had what could only be her passport in hand, and casually flipped through the pages. Next was her debit card, then the itinerary. He wanted explanations, and sent the two-bedroom inspectors to look for more clues.

"¿Qué es esto, Angel? Está Americana ahora?" *What is this, Angel? You are American now?*

"We don't have time, Todd." I was urgent now that things started looking dicey.

Todd emptied my water bottle out the window, slit open the neck wide enough for the muzzle of my Sig. I handed over my firearm. It was easier to comply than to fight with Todd. He fit the plastic bottle over my piece and secured it in place with the duct tape. Meanwhile Angelika was being slapped around for answers.

"*A woman came for me at the place where they held us. I had never met her before. She worked for a man, someone who said he saw me dance at the club. I swear, Lionel, I didn't do anything. The police would've sent me back to Ukraine so I went with her. She brought me here and said I worked for him now. He paid for a passport for me. I don't know anything else. I was afraid to ask questions.*"

"*The old man you were with the other night? Is he the one?*"

She shook her head slowly, comprehension finally sinking in. Maybe she'd been too high to care then, but now the consequences were sobering. They had followed her from the club to the cabaña, and from there to the apartment. They had to know that any man with the resources to pay for an American passport would not exact payment in a room rented by the hour, especially since he'd set her up in an apartment.

"*No,*" she answered slowly. "*She sent me with the old man.*"

"*And this woman… She lives here with you?*"

I nudged Todd. "Time to go."

"Here's how this is going to happen," Todd said while I waited for Angelika's answer. It could make all the difference if they expected company.

"*No, Lionel. I think the woman was his mistress. She used to stay here before me, but not since… not anymore.*"

"We are going to walk up to the front door and ask for Angel." It wasn't much of a plan, but we had no other choice. There was one way in and one way out.

I turned the cameras off and dumped the iPad before racing to meet Todd at the front of the car. He wrapped his arm around my shoulder as we walked, assuming a cautiously hurried pace that was natural for two Americans on foot in the heart of the city late at night. My purse was clutched at my side, my finger on the trigger inside so I could adjust to the unwieldiness of the makeshift silencer. Bill was a solid, reassuring weight bouncing against my thigh as the skirt of my dress swished apace with our steps.

We made it through the pedestrian gate and into the courtyard without incident. The gate to the garbage dumpster was open in anticipation of collection. That explained how they had breached the building. I couldn't imagine Señor White Pants climbing over the wrought iron gates. It was more likely one of the others had accessed the courtyard through the open portal then admitted the others from inside.

The elevator took forever to arrive from the fourteenth floor. The trip to the sixth floor seemed even longer. At least it gave us time to come up with the rest of our plan.

"I'll knock on the door and pretend to be a neighbor inviting her out. You stand out of sight until I can get a foot in the door," I offered as we counted the floors groaning by. The elevator had never seemed so slow before.

"I'll do it. I don't want you anywhere near these lunatics." Todd shifted his 9 mm to the side for easier access.

"They're more likely to shoot you on sight." I turned to face him to stave off any further protest. "You've been right so far about everything. But you're wrong if you think I can't handle this. I've done a lot more for much longer than you can imagine."

I had never been so open with him, and the message was, if he treated me as an equal... value what I brought to our union... then I was willing to open even more to him.

"Okay," he finally agreed. He made it sound like surrender. "We'll do it together."

I accepted his compromise with a kiss – a quick one – because the elevator pinged our arrival. I shifted to Todd's left side where, tucked under his arm, my body would conceal the bulk of the Glock. His right hand gripped my elbow, but could just as easily brush the butt of the gun.

Todd knocked while I readied Bill, unfolding the blade and concealing it within the folds of my dress. Todd tugged on my hair while we waited for someone to answer the door, coaxing me to relax and play along. Appearing less of a threat as possible increased our advantage, and it was such a simple thing to accomplish. Looking into Todd's eyes was enough to warm me at my coldest – my will and the knife poised to soundlessly plunge into the heart or throat of anyone who answered the door. Todd's head was making a slow descent when we heard movement inside.

We'd been seen and judged harmless; now they would engage.

It was the man with the .357 Magnum. Luck was really on our side. He was brown skinned with black close-cropped hair and light brown eyes. He opened the door a mere crack at first then slightly wider as Todd and I beamed at him.

"Hey, man, how are you doing?" Todd asked. The other man nodded acknowledgment but otherwise gave no reply. I couldn't even tell if he spoke English. "Is Angel around? We're heading out for drinks and thought she might want to join us."

I turned to Todd. "Honey, it looks like she has company."

"No problem. He's invited too." He turned back to the man behind the door, more of him visible as he lowered our threat level even further. "You're more than welcome to join us."

"No. No Angel." He almost closed the door on us, but Todd's outstretched arm halted the dismissal.

"Where is Angel? She said she was up for something a couple hours ago when my wife saw her."

"No Angel," the man repeated slowly, as if the words alone were a threat we should heed.

"No disrespect, man, but who are you? We live at the end of the hall and we've never seen you before."

Todd was being rude, the stereotypical, brassy American, which played on the Dominican's nerves like fingernails on a chalkboard. Instead of slamming the door in our faces, the man opened it wide enough to display the silver muzzle of the gun twitching restlessly at his side.

I would have understood if his last conscious thought was 'pride goes before a fall'. One second he was posturing, and in the next all three-and-a-half inches of Bill cut through skin, slipped between bone and sank into the soft tissue of his heart. My arm braced across his body kept the hand with the Magnum at his side and propelled his fall backwards.

Before the body hit the ground, Todd had his Glock in hand and the apartment door wide open. We cleared the threshold at the same time as the corpse. I found the reassuring mass of the butt of my Sig inside my purse and easily cleared the leather opening. It may have looked like a plastic water gun, but its deadly intent was unmistakable.

The Haitian, stripped to his gray underwear, dived for his discarded pants. In his haste to administer punishment to the shivering waif bent over the arm of my couch he had been forgotten the .38 among his discarded clothes.

The Dominican who had found her passport initially had his back to the door, his knee pressed into her neck while he held her down for the other man to abuse. His .45 caliber Taurus was six feet away, resting on the single seater where I had sat two nights before as Angelika wept at my feet. He had been busy securing her gag when the now-dead man answered the door.

The one directing it all was perched on my kitchen island, a glass of the milk she had just bought halfway to his mouth. I fixed my weapon on him, and his hands went dutifully in the air. I gestured for him to put the glass down before he had any ideas about tossing it. He complied peacefully. It seemed he thought that, through cooperation, there was a chance of walking away from this alive. I shut then locked the door behind us, kicking the corpse's feet out of the way and his firearm out of reach of his twitchy fingers.

The next to go was the Haitian. His vulnerability was too glaring to ignore. A minute later and he would have been inside her. He would have stripped her back to the level of nothingness that made her think nothing good would ever come her way again... that she was undeserving... useless but for one purpose.

It struck a dangerous chord with Todd. It would have been different, ended differently for the Haitian if Monday had never happened. But Todd saw in him the brutishness of Adam Rutherford III, reducing a woman to the level of a base animal, so desperate for life that even one rife with abuse was better than none at all.

It would take a lot of effort to prove to him that I was no longer that girl, willing to endure pain and deprivation for the sake of life.

In the meantime, the Haitian fell. A short *tac*, a flash of light, and a bullet ripped through his cervical spine, paralyzing him instantly. His comrade in attempted rape wrongly assumed it was the dive for the weapon that had landed him in a growing pool of his own blood.

What was a little force among men for whom the sins of the flesh spelled profit?

His hands reached for the ceiling. "No tengo un arma," he kept saying. *I don't have a weapon.*

Angel, free once again, slipped away from him to cower out of sight behind the couch. A sob signaled she was free of her gag too.

"Ninguna arma, ninguna arma," he kept saying. *No weapon, no weapon.* He turned to stare into the barrel of the suppressor from across the room.

"No somos la policía," Todd replied. *We are not the police.* The man would never understand the lengths to which I had pushed Todd days ago. He fell with only another *tac* and a spray of pin sized drops of blood to mark the passage of a bullet through his head. He narrowly missed my white couch as he slumped to the floor.

The glass of milk shattered on the fake marble of the island.

"Do you have him?" Todd asked, firearm doing a sweep of the room.

"I do." Lionel's hands reached higher for the sky. His last sip of milk was a curdled mass in his throat that he tried several times to push past his Adam's apple.

"I'll secure the apartment."

Todd was already moving deeper into the room, slipping on latex gloves. He kicked the two firearms out of reach of the bodies and checked for signs of life. He turned the TV on for me, adjusting the volume to compensate for my makeshift suppressor. My Sig wasn't going to give a polite *tac*.

Lionel tilted his head questioningly, his eyes flicking briefly from my plastic suppressor to my face. "Me entrego. Llamar a la policía." *I give up. Call the police.*

That was the problem with hope. Even in the face of insurmountable odds, its false promise burned bright. I shot him. My suppressor was only good for one try, so I made it count. He keeled over onto the counter, falling onto the shards of glass then rolling onto the floor.

"All clear," Todd said, returning from the bedrooms with a sheet. He didn't spare a second glance for the bodies, but he scoped the place to locate my surveillance cameras.

"Are you sure this is off?"

I nodded. "I did it from the iPad." I didn't want video surfacing any more than he did. I didn't take it personally that he checked the indicator lights either before he turned to the only witness.

Angelika was still huddled on the floor, face pressed into her knees, shaking. She was a tough girl, but she was still a civilian, so the shock was understandable. It didn't help that she had been stripped from the waist down and had to pull the hem of her Puerto Rico sunset tank top down to cover herself.

Todd draped her in the sheet and picked her up. His gentleness with her was incongruous with the ease with which he stepped over the two bodies in his corner. "That one is still alive but not for long." He gestured to the fallen Haitian. "Take care of it if you want, but I wouldn't mind leaving him as is."

How well Todd fit into the dark.

With a jerk of his head, Todd left me alone with Angelika after setting her down on the flipped mattress.

"Are you going to be okay?"

She nodded and wiped angrily at her cheeks. "I am fine."

"Did they hurt you? Do you need to see a doctor?"

She shook her head. The next time she opened her eyes they were the clear chips of ice I had first encountered at the shelter. "Nothing they haven't done before," she said with a shrug.

"Did they rape you? If they did, we can see a doctor. I want to make sure that you're okay."

"No."

"Your face is bruised. There may be some swelling tomorrow when you get on your flight." I was trying to give her a bright side on which she could focus, and it was the best I could do in my search for something positive to say.

She looked at me sharply. "You will send me anyway?"

"Of course."

She bit her lip and winced when the cut there started to bleed. "Why would you send me? I fucked it up. Now the police will come."

"That won't happen," I said and held her stare so she could see me and understand. "So tomorrow you will tell anyone who asks that you were in a car accident. Do you understand?"

She nodded slowly at first, then more convincingly. Angelika sighed again and ran her fingers through her hair, rubbing the sore spots, relief finally emerging beyond the pain and fear. "How do I thank you?"

I stood. I was never comfortable in the role of support. I thought for a long time that empathy was beyond me. Yet Todd had had faith in me that I could bring Angelika around. He would have been much better at it, I was certain, but I understood his refusal to be the one so soon after she had been victimized again by men.

"Get your things together. Don't leave anything behind. It has to be as if you were never here."

She nodded and I stayed long enough to make sure she followed the instructions, and that she would be okay. I left her to find Todd. He was in the living room, assessing the contents of my cleaning closet.

"She's going to be okay."

Todd nodded his acknowledgement, but I knew if I had told him she was going to be a threat, he would have been equally okay with killing her. "She's a tough girl," he said. "She will get through it."

"They slapped her around, but they didn't rape her."

Todd sighed and turned to face me. I could see the man I had married slowly returning. I wondered what it was he saw in my face as we gazed across the room at each other, two corpses between us. Could he love this woman? I would rather send him away than hear his regrets.

"You should take her and go," I told him, suddenly cold in the presence of doubt.

Todd looked into me, removing the counter as a barrier between us. After that he didn't come any closer... didn't try to touch me.

"And do what, Amy?" His eyes, blue throughout the past half an hour grew darker now, the black of a stormy ocean at night.

"Let me fix this," I said.

"How?"

I pushed away my weakness and dug deep for the woman I was trained to be. "I have a contact with the local police. He owes me a favor."

"What kind of favor?" What was there for Todd to be angry about? I was handing him his out.

"The type that Martinez works on."

Todd nodded, a single, stern acknowledgment. Why was he making this difficult?

"Anyway, I can tell him I walked in on this."

"You'll find yourself kicked out of the country just like what happened in Jamaica." His fists were jammed into his pockets, his back so straight he might have shattered. In frustration, he stepped around me to plunge the television back into darkness and the apartment into silence. I could hear the blood racing through my veins.

"What are you afraid of?" he asked.

"I'm not afraid." Even to my ears it sounded feeble. I was terrified of being wrong, scared witless that the feeling had already run out. I should have known he would not want someone capable of the things I did.

"Why are you running? Because that's what this is. Getting yourself shipped away is the only hope you have of running from me now."

I shook my head at the truth. Even if Hernandez settled our debt, O'Brien was bound to learn about this. He would ship me off in the blink of an eye to face whatever judgment awaited me in Virginia. And Todd would be here as interim Chargé, working the Lilys of this city.

"Are you afraid of me?"

My gaze shot to his, perplexed and horrified by such an assumption. "Of course not."

"Do you think this changes anything?" His eyes didn't leave mine, but I knew by his inflection that he meant the carnage. "Do you think I could love you any less? We do what we have to, Amy. Now, do you want to be with me?"

Why was he bracing himself against my answer? He was the one with the power to break me. He was the only one who could heal me. "More than anything," I sighed. It was like saying goodbye to my father all over again.

"Then be with me," he whispered in the cold emptiness of my heart. "I've told you I won't ever leave you. Not even if you beg me to. And you promised never to leave me. I'm going to hold you to that." Todd held out a hand to me. "Come in from the cold now, Amy. You'll never be alone again."

It really was like going home. I sank into the refugee carved for me out of his own body. His arm around me locked me in place. I felt safe despite the monumental task ahead of us. His lips pressed against my face, his nose delving into my hair.

"Now listen to me. We have to hurry if we're going to make it back to the restaurant in good time," he mumbled in my hair.

"Must we?"

Todd pulled away and nodded. "Yes, to cover all your bases."

"We can't leave them here like this."

I thought about it for a moment. It was distasteful, but there was actually no reason why we could not. We could strip the apartment of her presence and leave the bodies there until the neighbors complained about the smell. There was nothing to tie Amy Koehler to the rental, and I still had two and half months left on the lease. It could work.

"No," Todd said with that uncanny ability of his to read my thoughts. "That's leaving too much to chance. The key is to continue living a normal life, as if the past half an hour never happened."

He sounded so sure of himself; it reawakened old memories. What exactly had he meant when he said he did not save Mona?

"Here is what we're going to do."

I stepped back and took note.

Todd had me retrieve the supplies from our SUV down the road. On my return, with the keys to the Escalade in hand, I moved the vehicle inside the courtyard, parking as close to the service exit as possible. It was the access through which maintenance crews cleared the garbage chute, and regulated other upkeep functions, like power, plumbing, and the cleaning of common spaces. Once the massive truck was in position, I climbed the six floors to make certain the emergency exit stairway that was intended as an alternative to the elevator was clear.

Todd wrapped the bodies in the plastic sheeting, after securing the limbs together with the zip ties. The plastic shrouds were secured with duct tape. I had rescued Bill and secured the last body by the time Angelika reemerged – showered, sedate and willing to help. She was set the task of cleaning up the blood from the floor and off the furniture. Todd carried the bodies down the steps and dumped them in the back of the Escalade while I acted as scout.

It was backbreaking labor, but we worked well together. I drove the Escalade and left it a hundred yards from the entrance to Carlito's site, then rode back to the apartment with Todd in our SUV. Angelika had things under control there, and had no misgivings about being alone in the apartment.

"It is just one more night," she said with a shrug, "and I won't sleep anyway." I gave her a couple of Xanax anyway. There was no harm in leaving her there. I would know the second she left the apartment, and her phone had been destroyed.

Todd and I removed everything I had brought into the place and stowed the duffel in the back of his car. Then we returned to El Gallego, more relaxed and disheveled then when we had left. There were stares and whispers, but none of them came close to the truth. For Todd and me, none of it mattered, for our bond was the strongest it had ever been.

EPILOGUE

Sunday afternoons at Boca Chica were my favorite. The sky was blue, the sea beneath the pier aquamarine, the thatch-covered roof of our shelter picturesque. All around us paradise stretched in varying shades of blue and white, sunbaked brown and bleached stone. The onshore wind tasted of sunshine and ocean, much like the man sitting next to me though he dragged lazily on a Cohiba.

"Don't you think there's something wrong with that?"

My head was resting against his shoulder, his arm wrapped around me keeping me where I belonged. He turned to stare at me, adoration in his eyes, and I knew I would never tire of seeing that look on his face... Even if I had to smell like a tobacco field.

"Wrong with what?"

"The senior American official openly smoking a Cuban cigar."

"I'm not breaking any laws, and I'm not a 'senior American official' right now." His smile was mocking, his teeth against his bronzed skin and blue eyes more dazzling than I had ever seen them.

"No?" I smiled because his easy manner and the ocean breeze soothed me.

"I'm just a man... having brunch... with a beautiful woman... in a beautiful place." He punctuated each break with a kiss that sent my pulse into overdrive. Todd Birch was the cure for lethargy.

Todd signaled to the waiter for another round of *Presidente*, then we settled back into silence, waiting for our paella. I had just taken the first experimental sip, assessed the possibility of getting brain freeze, when Todd folded his newspaper so one particular story stood out.

The motive behind the murder of four men whose bodies were found dumped in a luxury vehicle in Gazcue was believed to be drug-related. The police urged anyone with information to step forward.

"Have you heard from Dev recently?"

"I have." Todd drank from his own beer then pressed his cold lips against my neck. He laughed. I shivered, but didn't pull away. I would take him any way I could have him. "He's holding up."

That meant Dev was still beating Angelika off with a stick. It was a compulsion for someone in her position – receiving kindness after a lifetime of exploitation – to try to repay perceived good deeds with sex. Once, it was her only currency. Now it was her gift to give away. It would take many years, possibly the rest of her life, before she began thinking of her value in non-sexual terms.

As for the trauma of her last night at the apartment, some things were easier to forget than others. It helped that we had never spoken of it again – not Angelika, not Todd, and neither would I.

"Speaking of which…"Todd broke through my train of thought with a gentle squeeze. "You are about to tell me why she is worth everything we've done for her."

I downed a couple of generous gulps of my beer and waited for the ice to douse the butterflies inside my belly. "I was?"

Todd hummed his assent and pushed my hair over my shoulder so he could nuzzle my ear again. "Yes, you were… last week."

Todd taught me something about myself. The chances of success in getting me to open up to him increased considerably when relating side-by-side. It explained why I was more communicative in bed, if he could keep me there. Somehow my brain confused face to face with face-off. I wasn't sure if it was his training as a diplomat that first made Todd aware of it, or if it came from his library full of psychiatric literature. But all the time I'd thought he'd been tentative with me, he'd been testing his hypotheses.

He also understood the value of timing. He could sense when I needed more, and was more often than not patient enough to allow me to come around on my own. He was an expert at switching gears. "So, Ramirez has been relieved of his duties and another twenty-one officers and enlisted face disciplinary action. The President informed us on Friday that criminal proceedings are pending."

"I assume we will push for extradition of the leaders?"

It was not my decision to make, but I had recommended extradition. My efforts on this case, and Angelika sacrifice, had the potential to net more than just the four masterminds. They had information on contacts and accomplices in at least four countries. If extradited, we would have access to that font of information. Without it, all we had was an embarrassing example of corruption in the country.

"We'll push," Todd said over the mouth of his beer, "but that will take years to resolve."

I turned to catch him staring at my profile. I didn't have months to wait. Sitting next to Colonel Townsend during a briefing session, with Todd across from us, had played quite a number on my nerves on Monday morning. I never wanted to do that again, and the sooner this case was over, the less Townsend would have to look forward to.

To make matters worse, there was still no news from Blitzner, and I had not seen hide nor tail of Mystery Man. I needed something to show for the time I had spent here.

I turned to Todd. "Maybe not so long."

He narrowed his eyes at me, searching for a moment. Then Todd looked away, putting into practice the lessons learned about me. His hard work brought a smile to my lips. I kissed his cheek to bring his eyes, those mesmerizing pools of cobalt, back to me.

"Remember that favor Hernandez asked for... the one Martinez was working on?" Todd nodded. "Well, the request had political roots and next year is an election year."

"You're thinking of blackmailing them over Colonel Ramirez?"

"Barter or blackmail," I wasn't about to quibble over vocabulary. "Hernandez had specific conditions they wanted met. They want to humiliate and discredit the Opposition through their campaign financier. The governments can either work with us and we give them what they asked for; or they can refuse and we leak the story of their political agenda. There's pride at stake – the only reason to quibble over Ramirez – but he's not worth losing public opinion or the elections."

"Well, one thing's for sure," Todd said with a slight shake of his head, "you're no diplomat."

I laughed. "Look, we all know someone's going to get fucked. I'm straightforward. Some people prefer that."

Todd nodded considering me. "True, but there's no need to skimp on the lube, Amy, especially if you want more than a one night stand." That brought back memories of our own one-night stand that started all of this.

Todd leaned in to nuzzle my nose and mouth with his. "I know what you're thinking. Keep it up and we won't make it through the paella."

"If it ever gets here," I mumbled, but the complaint was weak. The food was worth the wait and I wouldn't trade the company for the world.

"Kind of like you getting to the point about Angelika."

His kiss forestalled my groan. The sensation of his tongue stroking mine sucked my resistance away like a speck of sand thrown in a gale. I was hopelessly lost when his fingers dug into my scalp and held me in place. The fire burned bright, fueled by the sound and feel of Todd becoming equally lost in me.

"Discúlpeme, Señor, Señora, your paella is ready." The waiter placed the oversized cast iron platter before us and retreated. Instead of being embarrassed, he was in a hurry to leave us to it. Here, we were nobodies... just another pair of lovers with nothing to distinguish us from all the rest.

We ate in silence for a few minutes, but I could feel the weight of his expectation heavily in the air. Todd had killed for me, not to save me, but because Angelika was important to me. Compared to my parents though she was nothing. Why wouldn't he move mountains to help me?

"Do you trust me, Amy?" He asked, his attention fixed on the mussel shell between his fingers.

"What do you know about my parents?" I asked, keeping up the pretense of interest in my food when it would have landed in my stomach like a block of cement.

"There wasn't much about your mom." No, in the files, there wasn't. Todd had searched the files. Of course, it was natural for him to want to know what he was marrying into. But he had also talked to Richard.

"Was there anything that jumped out at you?" I worked on stripping a shrimp from its shell, telling myself there was no need to fear being exposed. This was Todd.

"They never found the guys."

I nodded. "Not even Richard knows who did it."

"I'm sorry, Amy," he said, setting his fork down.

"Why? Did you do it? Do you know who did it?" It was ridiculous. Of course Todd hadn't done it, didn't know who did. It was ridiculous of him to be sorry for something that had happened that was beyond him.

"No," he said, "of course not." The wonderful paella was wasted now. It was all such a waste – my life chasing after shadows, the life of a good man and a loving wife.

"Do you know who did it, Amy?"

His eyes were serious now, full of awareness of the danger. He understood the significance of the mystery remaining unsolved even after all these years. Todd understood exactly what was at stake and the type of people who would come after me if they knew what I was doing.

"Do you really want to know the answer to that?"

"Yes." There was no hesitation on his part. His hand closing over mine was warm and heavy, but liberating at the same time.

"No, I don't know. Not yet." He squeezed my hand in reassurance that he was with me. "But I soon will."

"If you're sending Angelika away then you must already know where and who."

I nodded. "I've found someone who knows who ordered the hit. I plan on using her to get close to him."

Todd sighed and moved in close so from henceforth our words were only whispers in time, never to be heard again. "It's never as easy as you think."

"I know, but I've been watching for so long I know where he is every minute of everyday."

"You're sending her to Europe."

I nodded again. "That's why I have to go."

All was still for a time as he considered what that meant for us. Finally, he squeezed my fingers again and smiled. I melted with relief. "We'll do it together."

"That's not possible, Todd."

"Yes, it is. We haven't had a honeymoon. We deserve it and Richard will make it happen."

"You can't tell him." I pulled my hand away. I pulled myself away. The look in his eyes said he felt it. "You can't tell anyone."

Todd frowned at me. "He could help, I'm sure."

"He hasn't in a decade."

Todd assessed me for a time, watched the change come over me. "You think he's involved," he concluded.

"At least in not wanting to find the truth," I said, and it was liberating finally being able to shed that burden.

"He's like a father to you, Amy."

"My father is dead." For the first time all day I wished I had not left my sunglasses in the car. These tears were for my father and my mother. They did not belong to Todd.

"Okay," he said with a sigh. He held me and waited for it to pass. "Just us."

"Promise me."

His eyes narrowed, his jaw firmed. I had come to recognize the other man much easier in the past week, the man who carried a kill kit wherever he went. "What will you give me in return?"

"What do you want?" The real question was what could I give that he did not already own?

"A baby, Amy. I want us to have a child together."

How could I forget Todd's yearning to be a father? I had become accustomed to being alone, because the need for dependents had never struck me before. For Todd it was different. His parents were old and slowly dying; he'd spent years thinking of what it would be like to finally be alone.

It was my turn to commit wholly, unreservedly. "Yes."

"Promise me?"

"Yes, Todd."

"Right away?"

"As soon as we can. I've been on the shots for years. Even if I stopped right away, it could take months, maybe a year, before things go back to normal."

"Okay. Stop now, then we try until we get it right." He moved in to kiss me, to see our deal.

I moved away. "There is one more thing."

"What is it?"

"There's someone else… a threat. He knows too much and is about to turn."

Todd picked up his fork and dug into a pile of rice. Not for a second did I think he had forgotten about that kiss. "Who is he?"

"His name is Blerim Nesimi."

"You know where to find him?"

I nodded. "Yes."

"Then consider it done." Todd gestured to my plate, but I needed more time. The weight of what I had just done was still too fresh. "I promised to take care of you, Amy. I won't let anyone get in the way of that."

He was so determined, so hard and fast in his love for me. I looked into his eyes, where the blue was so deep and dark. The man from last Friday night was in there, waiting, ready to slay all my dragons. He loved me. How could I not trust that?

He was the perfect blend of dark in spite of the light. And he was mine.

END

Coming soon
The conclusion of Amy Koehler's story
The Wages of Sin

THREE COINS FOR CONFESSION

BOOK TWO OF THE EXILE'S BLADE

A NOVEL OF THE ENDLANDS
by
Scott Fitzgerald Gray

Cover, Design, and Typography
by (studio)Effigy

Published by Insane Angel Studios
insaneangel.com

CONTENTS